CW01500356

COLLECTION

OF

BRITISH AUTHORS.

VOL. 806.

AGNES BY MRS. OLIPHANT.

IN TWO VOLUMES.

VOL. II.

AGNES.

BY

MRS. OLIPHANT.

COPYRIGHT EDITION.

IN TWO VOLUMES.

VOL. II.

LEIPZIG

BERNHARD TAUCHNITZ

1865.

CONTENTS

OF VOLUME II.

———

A G N E S.

CHAPTER I.

The House on the Green.

Next day the Trevelyans prepared with some excitement to continue their journey to Windholm. As
for Agnes, she was the most silent of the party, feeling,
as she did by instinct, that her father, like herself,
had made, even in the joy of the meeting, a painful
discovery; and that their reunion had revealed to them
a fact, which might have been ignored so long as they
remained apart, that they never would be fully united
in heart and thoughts again. Though Agnes knew
that this was inevitable, she was too true and single-
minded not to recognise it with a pang, and it was accordingly with more sadness than joy that she set out
upon the short journey, which for the first time was to
conduct the family *home!* Roger, on the contrary,
was as pleased as a boy going home for the holidays,
with this new change. He had no *arrière pensée* to
subdue his spirits, and for a moment the novelty occupied him. Jack Charlton had already been to see
them at their hotel, and Pendarves, who had assisted
at their marriage, had also paid his respects to Mr. and
Mrs. Trevelyan; and the impression made upon that
solemn personage by the aspect of Agnes had amused

and elated her husband. And Roger was convalescent, and the sun was shining, and England, after all, bore a familiar face. "This little shaver must learn better English," he said, as he played with his boy. "By Jove! the fellow has an accent; and it's time to remember you have a stake in the country, Wat." As for Walter himself, he was in a state of intense curiosity, mingled with dissatisfaction. The grandfather whom he had seen last night through his sleepy eyelashes, somehow lacked the air which the experienced youth believed necessary to that class of the human family. Stanfield was not a grand seigneur, and the boy recognised the fact by instinct. Accordingly, he opened his eyes very wide and looked out for the château of his dreams with a jealous eagerness in which already a presentiment mingled; and to be sure Agnes, who was *clairvoyante*, divined, and was disturbed by the childish anxiety of her child. Baby had the best of it, who fell asleep placidly, and left the circumstances to arrange themselves.

As they drew near Windholm, a shade too came over Roger's face. "They might have let us have the Hall," he said, "that would have been a small boon in comparison with all your father is doing — though, after all, it's a disgusting old place, and you would have been buried alive." But after this remark, it was in silence that they arrived at the little station, and got out, themselves and their baggage, to the amazement and curiosity of the officials. "Halloo! what's the name of the place?" said Roger. "Mr. Stanfield's house on the Green, I suppose?" "Stanfield's, the blacksmith's, sir?" said the cabman promptly, and Agnes saw her husband's face redden and cloud over, and

Walter's eyes open wide. She said, "No, the new house — the house Mr. Stanfield has built," as she seated herself in the cab; and the man answered, "All right, mum," with a glance of evident recognition which disconcerted the whole party. Agnes took her baby in her arms, and leaned over it as they drove down the village street and past the house in which she had spent her youth. It was afternoon by this time, and the sun was beginning to decline behind the Cedars, throwing his full radiance, as of old, into the wide opening of the archway, and upon the parlour windows, where the blinds were down; but something which she could not define to herself — something which was not pride — a painful hesitation which made her heart sink and falter restrained Agnes from saying to her eager boy, "That is my father's house." Heaven knows it was not the meanness of being ashamed of that homely house. She bent down her head to her little daughter's sleeping face with a pang which it would be hard to describe. She said to herself — "*She* will understand," with that long, long and doubtful postponement of her hopes of sympathy, which so many mothers know; while Roger, beside her, looked out with somewhat sullen recognition, evidently relieved to see that there was nobody either at the door or window; and Walter, much bewildered, regarded everything about him with a jealous, half-frightened curiosity. In this way they drove down the street, which Agnes had left with all the sweet, absurd expectations of impossible nobleness and blessedness that come natural to a bride.

Things were better, however, when at last they arrived at the house which Stanfield had built for his only child. In the interval between the first disappoint-

1*

ment of his hopes and Agnes's actual return, the black-smith, who was no sentimentalist, had let the house, and all the obtrusive signs of novelty had disappeared. But his tenants had been sent away in time to permit him to carry out all his original ideas about the furniture and accessories. When the cab wheeled in at the open gates, and drew up before the door, Roger's countenance cleared a little. It was not a château, but at least outside it bore the aspect of a house that a gentleman might live in, Mr. Trevelyan said to himself; and even Walter, though his eyes opened wider than ever, and though he gazed with consternation at the walls and railings which enclosed it all, jumped out with eagerness, and called to his mother to look at the bright flowers on the lawn. The lime-trees were beginning to lose their leaves, and the elms were brown and rusty, but still the sunshine slanted between them with a friendly consolatory glow; and the flower-beds were gay with geraniums, and a few solitary white stars still lingered among the dark foliage of the jessamine, which concealed the wall at the point where it divided their possessions from somebody else's garden. Then there was a cheerful maid, holding wide open the door, and a pleasant gleam of firelight visible at the windows. When they went into the pretty drawing-room, Roger gave vent to his feelings in an exclamation —

"By Jove! Agnes, the old boy's a brick," said Stanfield's respectful son-in-law; and he threw himself into an easy chair, and poked the bright fire, and made himself comfortable. But after a moment, the circumstances moved Roger a little, careless though he was, and awoke his better nature. He got up again and went to his wife, who had seated herself also, silent, and not in case for conversation, with her baby in her arms, to keep her heart from running over. Roger came up to her and bent over her, and kissed her white cheek.

"You know I cannot talk sentiment," he said; "but, my darling, don't you think I don't feel his delicacy, and all that. Another man would have been here to say, 'Look, what a present I give you'" — and then Roger faltered a little, and held his wife tight, with the baby in her arms. "It is you who have brought me home, and not I you," he said, hurriedly, with a pang of humiliation and gratitude.

Agnes knew what his tone meant better than he himself did, and rose to meet it, rendered strong by this new call upon her powers.

"Roger, dear," she said, "I have brought you a great deal of trouble; that is the thing of which I am most conscious now."

But when he heard these words, Mr. Trevelyan, restored to himself, laughed and hugged his wife.

"I am very well content with all you have brought me," he said; "and as for Stanfield, he's the most generous fellow going. Put down that baby, and let us have a look over the house. Halloo, Watty! don't you think it's worth a man's while to have a grandfather? By Jove! who would have thought he could have had such good taste?"

"I will come back directly," said Agnes, whose composure was forsaking her. She was only a woman like the rest, and had to cry or die, as is the manner of women. She laid the baby down in a little bed, which was there ready for the little stranger, and fell

down beside it on her knees. No words could have
described the agony of pain and happiness, of love,
and grief, and gratitude, and disappointment, that
found their natural vent in those tears. She had come
home, and she was glad; and yet it was not to the
comforts and tranquillities of home that she had come,
and her heart was wrung with the anguish foreseen.
She owed all to her father, and she loved him, and
had a daughter's pride in his tender goodness. But,
alas! it was not to her husband she owed it; and the
pride of the wife, humiliated and mortified, ached in
her breast. But it was not many minutes that she
could spare to this little crisis of excited feeling; and
Agnes's eyes were deep, and did not always betray
when they had shed tears.

Thus the return was accomplished, and few people
were the wiser. The cabman announced to his public
that he had driven the swell as married Stanfield's
daughter to the new 'ouse on the Green; but then his
public was limited, and not composed of people who
knew Mrs. Trevelyan. And Mrs. Freke, returning
from her afternoon walk, saw the firelight shining at
the windows, and a child's face looking out, and hesitated whether she should not go and inquire whether
Agnes had arrived, feeling surely enough that her visit
at any hour could not be otherwise than an honour to
the blacksmith's daughter; and it was only a chance
meeting with little Miss Fox, from the Cedars, the
only one of the three who remained unmarried, which
hindered her from carrying out this kind intention.
The news got abroad in the evening, and created a
sensation at Windholm. Polly Thompson, who had
been bridesmaid to Agnes, and who, like Miss Fox,

was still unmarried, thrilled all over when she heard it, foreseeing social elevation to herself, to which it would be difficult to put any limit. And Agnes's old schoolfellows, most of whom had also husbands and babies of their own, betrayed all the liveliest curiosity, not unmixed with irritation, and an anxious desire to hear everything that could be told. Perhaps the most excited of all was Mrs. Stanfield, who could not, as she herself said, settle to anything, and whose determination not to have nothing to do with her stepdaughter, as had cost the master both time and money, not to speak of feelin's, had already been expressed loudly. As for the blacksmith himself, he had sedulously kept at his work all the day long, not even going to the forge door, as was his custom, to breathe the air, in case it might have happened to be that moment at which the carriage went past. He had given all his orders in the morning when he arrived at Windholm, and made a last tender inspection to see that everything was in order; and then he left his daughter, whom he loved too much to let his love come in her way, to arrive in peace, with no reminder before her that she owed her home to him. He was thinking about her all day long, though nobody knew his thoughts, and entering into her secrets by mere force of sympathy and love. He could have told, without knowing how, all about that mingled emotion in her heart that had to find utterance in tears, and knew by instinct that her pleasure in his gift must be marred by the thought that it was not her husband who had provided her a home. All this Stanfield felt with his daughter — felt it much more strongly than Roger did; to whom, by this time, it appeared the most natural thing

in the world that the blacksmith, who was rich in his
way, should build a handsome house for his only child.
When the work-day was over Stanfield changed his
dress and took his tea as usual; that is to say, the
meal was as usual, but not the Sunday suit, which he
only wore on special occasions.

Mrs. Stanfield watched him go away with a heated
and cloudy countenance.

"If it had been ere another she'd a-been civil, and
asked *me*. Them as lives upon other folks has no call
to be so high," she said; but the last words were under
her breath.

As for the blacksmith, it was not with a very
triumphant countenance that he was going to pay his
visit.

"Not to-night, Sally, not to-night," he said. "I'd
not go myself, but the child might think it unkind —
not to-night."

"Nor no night, I promise you, master, for them as
don't think me good enough to ask," said his wife; but
he was gone without hearing her. He went on his
way slowly, with a more than usually meditative look
in his eyes. His step was so leisurely, that instead of
expressing any anxiety to be there, it seemed to imply
an unexpressed, inexpressible reluctance. He could not
remain away; and yet he had a strange consciousness
that the picture he could form in his imagination would
always henceforward be more satisfactory, less disturbing than that which he saw with his eyes. Nevertheless, the new house on the Green had never looked
so cheerful. The young moon was up in the east,
looking with a little wistful curiosity over the tree-tops
into the windows; and as the curtains were not drawn

upstairs, that celestial spectator might have seen if she cared a pretty effect of light upon the flaxen hair of Madelon, who was singing the baby to sleep by the fire. Down below it was only a ruddy reflection that filled the curtained windows; but when Stanfield entered, the first thing he heard was the voice of his little grandson, filling the house with that cheerful din which only children can make. Within, Roger and Agnes were sitting in the pretty drawing-room, which was all glowing and shining with light and comfort. Agnes had learned many things in those long years. She could scarcely have believed now in the stiff and "tidy" room in which she had received Lady Charlton when she began her career. This room, which she had entered only a few hours before, looked to Stanfield as though she had been living in it all her life. It seemed already to have taken her impression by some mysterious means which he could not comprehend. He could see at a glance that there was a chair at the window, half visible between the curtains, at which she must have been sitting at work, and there was another chair near the table, which was as distinctly the throne of the mistress of the house as if she had inhabited the place for years. As for Roger, he was dozing in his easy-chair, in that moment of comfort and quiet after dinner which moves most men to that indulgence. Stanfield, who could not quite divest his mind of the idea that his daughter was still a bride, with all the sensitive feelings and instinctive claims of that crisis of life, could scarcely restrain himself from an impulse of impatience and disdain towards the man who, with such a wife opposite to him, could find no better way of enjoying her society. But as for Agnes, she was quite unmoved by Roger's slumber. Perhaps, indeed, she was glad of it for the moment, in so far as she took any notice whatever of so usual a circumstance. She rose up to meet her father, and took his two hands in hers and led him to his seat.

"At last it begins to look as if it was real," said Agnes. "Father, you have been a great deal too good to us; nobody but you would have thought of everything — would have thought so much of me."

"You are pleased," said Stanfield, with a wonderful sense of gratification — and he spoke under his breath without knowing it, and held his child's hands fast in his own.

"Pleased!" said Agnes, and made a little pause after the words; "I do not deserve that you should be half so good to me. It is like Paradise to us, who have been vagabonds and never have had a home before."

"My little one, I have nobody in the world but you," said the blacksmith. He seemed to take pleasure in giving her the name which she had said was applicable to her no longer. But this time the sound of the new voice roused Roger. Agnes might have gone on talking long enough without producing that effect, but the murmur of deeper sound disturbed Mr. Trevelyan, unused to any such interruption.

"Eh! — halloo! — why, what is it, Agnes?" he said, opening his eyes; and then awoke. "Is it you, Stanfield, come to bid us welcome?" said Roger; and he gradually lifted himself up and went forward with outstretched hands — for he was in his most genial humour — "and, upon my life, I don't know anything half good enough to say to you. I hope Agnes has

told you what we both think. By Jove! you are as
magnificent as a prince. You can't think how pleasant
it feels, after marching about so long, to find one's self
in such snug quarters. Agnes, you know how stupid
I am — I hope you've said all that you ought to
say."

It was on Stanfield's lips to say that between his
daughter and himself there was no necessity for anything to be said — for, to be sure, Roger, as was
natural, had broken the spell — but Agnes's look restrained the words.

"My father understands me, at least," she said;
"when two people know each other, it does not matter
so much about words."

"She takes it all in her own hand," said Roger.
"Look here, Stanfield. Should you think she had ever
lived anywhere else in her life? Most people, you
know, look out of sorts a little the first night; but that
is Mrs. Trevelyan's way. Where's that young shaver,
Agnes? — why don't you have them both in, as you
are longing to do, and make your little exhibition?
Halloo, Wat! — don't make such a row, you little
polyglot wretch, but come here —"

"Come and see grandpapa," said Agnes, softly;
and then she led the new little wonderful living creature
to Stanfield's knee, and put the boy's hands into his.
The fact was that the blacksmith had scarcely yet
taken this new relationship into consideration. To be
sure, Walter was seven years old, and Stanfield had
known of his existence all along; but the idea had
never taken form or shape in his mind. He could believe in the speechless, sleeping baby which, so far as
he had seen it, was only a piece of still life; but it

was hard to add on to Agnes another independent being with a will, and a mind, and a voice, and to realize that it belonged to her, and to him through her. He lifted his broad brown luminous eyes upon the boy, and held Walter fast in that look. The child's eyes were not unlike his own, and they owned the fascination; but still Walter was a little discontented and disappointed in the depths of his heart. This new grandfather lacked something the child could not tell what. He was not like Hermann's grandfather — the stately old baron with his white moustache; and it was with a momentary cloud on his little eager animated face that he stood meeting the stronger and fuller gaze with his fearless eyes.

"I don't know who he is like," said Stanfield, with his face gradually softening and lighting up.

At this moment Roger winced a little, and muttered "By Jove!" under his breath, and turned away rather hastily, while Agnes, on her part, gave a little start of surprise. It was on her lips to say "He is like you," but her husband's unconscious gesture restrained her. He had observed it, too; and though he was in his best humour and grateful to Stanfield, it was not altogether a pleasant discovery. As for Walter, he regarded steadily, with brown eyes equally luminous and deep, his grandfather's face.

"You are like mamma," said Walter; "you are like her, and yet you are not like her — I don't know how it is. Grandpapa, I suppose it is you who live at the château? When am I going to see you there?"

"The château?" said Stanfield, turning to ask Agnes what the question meant.

"Walter does not know yet that there are no châteaux here," said Agnes; but she could not conceal a little confusion. "We are coming to see you to-morrow, father. This is all so new that I cannot make sure I am back at Windholm till I see you at home."

"That is true," said Stanfield; "it will be best to get it over," and he paused and sighed. After all, this happiness of meeting again was a joy largely tinctured with bitterness, like most human joys.

CHAPTER II.

A Beginning.

"Walter," said Agnes, next morning, "you and I are going to see grandpapa, and I want to talk to you before I go."

The child did not make any answer, but he came to the table where she was sitting. Roger had not yet come downstairs. He had felt it advisable to resume his invalid habits; and accordingly Agnes and her little boy had breakfasted alone, as was almost habitual to them. Walter came and stood at the table where his mother's work was lying. He was busy himself making a whip with a branch of a shrub he had cut in the garden and a piece of string which he had possessed himself of in the carnival of unpacking which was going on upstairs. Without knowing it, the child was a little suspicious of this grandfather, whose face attracted him, and yet who had not the air of Hermann's grandfather. Accordingly, he did not make any eager response, but came and placed himself, with his eyes intent upon the manufacture he was carrying on, by his mother's side.

"What you said about the châteaux last night was silly, you know," said Agnes. "We have no châteaux here. Your other grandfather, Sir Roger, lives, I suppose, in a house a little like one, but he has not asked us to go to see him; and your kind grandpapa here, who has given us this pretty house, has not kept anything nearly so nice to himself. Do you remember what I used to tell you a true gentleman was?"

"Oh, yes!" said Walter; "the Red Cross Knight; I wonder what colour his charger was. Una had a milk-white palfrey — I remember all that. Is there a white pony, do you think, at grandpapa's? Look, mamma, what a famous whip I've made! Madelon has such lots of string upstairs."

"Well, but that is not what I meant," said the anxious mother, beginning to perceive that her teaching had been a little fanciful. "I want you to forget all about chargers and milk-white ponies for a little. I have always told you it was not the fine things a man had that made him a gentleman, but ——"

"Yes," said Walter; "I remember — it was always to take off his hat, and to open the door when anybody went out, and to pick up things for ladies — at least, that is what Giovanni used to say. But look here, mamma: here's somebody in the garden. She is looking in at the window! Why does she come and look in at the window before she knocks at the door?"

"Who is it?" said Agnes. "Is it a lady?" — for, to tell the truth, she was a little afraid of Mrs. Stan-

field, who certainly had a right to visit at her step-
daughter's house.

"I — don't know," said Walter. The boy was
confused in his ideas, what with the doubtful appearance of his grandfather, and the new visitor's investigation of the window, which went against the young
gentleman's code of manners; and Agnes turned a
rather alarmed look to the door, expecting that nobody
but her stepmother would have come so early, and
utterly at a loss how to explain such an apparition to
her clear-sighted boy. But, however, it was Mrs. Freke
who came in, with a little eagerness and the most
benevolent looks and intentions. The vicar's wife was
very plainly dressed, as vicars' wives have a right to
be (if they like) in their parish; and as the one in
question had not much dignity in her looks, a little
intellect of seven years old, much sharpened by travel,
might be pardoned for judging her summarily according to her outward appearance. Accordingly, Walter
stood by with the most vivid astonishment when he
saw this plain woman take his pretty mamma in her
arms with protecting kindness.

"My dear, I'm so glad to see you back again,"
said Mrs. Freke, "all well and safe, and so much improved. I had almost come in last night, when I saw
the light in the windows; and I declare this must be
your little boy. How do you do, my little man?
Why, Agnes, let me look at you again — I scarcely
think I should have known you. After all, it is a
great thing to be out in the world, as you have been
— you are so much improved!"

"Thank you; I am very glad you think so," said
Agnes, whose mind was much relieved by finding that

it was not Mrs. Stanfield. Though she smiled a little at this novel mode of accost, she still had too much loyalty to the past not to receive it with perfect good grace. But at present Mrs. Freke had so much to say that she left Mrs. Trevelyan very little time to speak.

"I am sure you must be pleased with this pretty house," said the vicar's wife; "I have taken almost as much interest in it as your father has. He asked my advice about the carpets long ago, when we thought you were coming home directly; but I remember he and I were not quite agreed. Upon my word, I think he has done famously, considering that he could not possibly know how such things ought to be. I suppose he consulted the upholsterers, though that is always the most expensive way. We had a long talk about you at the Cedars last night; I am sure Mrs. Fox will call when she knows you have got settled. They are all married but Milly, who used always to be called the little one, you know; but I suppose you have heard all the Windholm news? Upon my word, Agnes, I scarcely should have known you. It is such a pleasure to see you so much improved. I daresay you may feel a little awkward at first, on account of the difference; but I am quite sure all the best people in Windholm will call, if you only have a little patience to wait."

"Oh, yes! I have a great deal of patience," said Agnes, smiling a little in spite of herself; but she was rather glad, on the whole, that Roger was not downstairs to hear the amiabilities of the vicar's wife. Perhaps, however, there was something in her tone that showed her amusement, for Mrs. Freke continued, with an air of dignity —

"Oh! I daresay you have met much finer people than we are, abroad; but I always say there is nothing that a true Englishwoman prizes like recognition in her own parish. Mr. Freke, you know, has always been a great friend of yours. He says it is a shame of Sir Roger not to give you the Hall; though, for my part, I think it's a dreadful old place, and you are a great deal better off here; — and I hope you won't neglect your poor father, Agnes, now you have come home. I am sure he has been lost without you — after that strange marriage of his, too; — and what a good man he is! The vicar says he believes there never was a better man. He says he would rather talk to the blacksmith than to half the gentlemen of the county; but then, you know, Mr. Freke was always a little peculiar," said the vicar's wife.

At this point, again, Walter stole close to his mother's knee. He pulled at her dress a little with his unoccupied hand, though with the other he was cracking his whip much too near Mrs. Freke's face to be pleasant.

"Mamma, who is the blacksmith?" said little Walter; and, as one of his lessons in politeness had been not to whisper, he uttered the question audibly enough. The child was amazed, as was natural, not having met with anybody before in the course of his juvenile experience who had adopted this tone towards his mother; and, unfortunately, the demand thus made came to the visitor's ear.

"Dear me! is it possible the child does not know?" said the vicar's wife. "I must say, Agnes, I think you are very much in the wrong there. The blacksmith, my dear, is your grandfather, and a very worthy

man. It does not matter what a man's station is in
the world," Mrs. Freke added, delivering a lesson in
passing; "there are a great many gentlemen, I assure
you, my dear little boy, who are not nearly so nice or
so good as William Stanfield; and I hope you will
always be as respectful to him as if he were a duke.
He is your mamma's father, and a very good man.
Agnes, I cannot think how you could have kept your
little boy in such ignorance; it is very hard upon your
father to be despised by his own child!"

"It would be indeed, if such a thing were possible,"
said Agnes, whose patience was giving way; "but I
have never yet seen anybody who found it practicable
to do that. If my father's occupation had been a
thing that was in my mind at all, no doubt my little
boy would have heard of it. Pardon me, but I am
sure it was not of our domestic concerns that you
meant to speak when you were so kind as to come to
see me. I am not likely to forget how kind you were
to me before I went away."

At this point of the conversation it happened suddenly to Mrs. Freke to wake up out of sundry delusions with which she had entered Mrs. Trevelyan's
drawing-room. She was a woman of sense, though
she had her defects like other people; and at this moment it occurred to her all at once that it *was* Mrs.
Trevelyan, and not Agnes Stanfield, to whom she was
speaking; — perhaps the immediate cause of this discovery was that behind Agnes, and immediately in front
of Mrs. Freke, there was a mirror, which reflected with
perfect distinctness the long flowing skirt of Mrs. Trevelyan's dress, and its perfect fit, and air of simple
elegance. It was a purely feminine argument, but it

was entirely conclusive in its way. The moment that it flashed upon Mrs. Freke's mind that she was talking to a woman clothed by a Parisian milliner, the scales fell from her eyes. That she was mistaken in her idea, and that Agnes's gown had been made in Baden, under her own supervision, did not alter in the least the facts of the case. When the details of that simple toilette struck the vicar's wife, she remained speechless for the first moment; and then, all at once, it occurred to her that the kindness which Agnes thus acknowledged consisted in that serious remonstrance against the marriage which Mrs. Freke had thought it her duty to deliver. This recollection embarrassed the good woman dreadfully, and added to the force of the sudden revelation. She faltered a little in spite of herself, and could not take her eyes off the mirror in which Mrs. Trevelyan's figure, a little expanded out of its girlish delicacy, was so distinctly visible; and somehow the blacksmith's daughter, always so simple and docile, seemed to vanish out of existence as she gazed.

"I am sure I had not any intention of saying anything that was disagreeable, or taking any liberty," said Mrs. Freke. "People who don't move about forget what changes are going on;" and after this semi-apology the vicar's wife changed her tone hurriedly. "I suppose you must have met quantities of people abroad; everybody goes abroad now, I think, except the vicar and myself. Ellen Fox, who married Mr. Spencer, went to Italy for her wedding-tour; but I should have heard of it if *they* had seen you: I dare·say you must have met the Hornbys, who have such a pretty house on the Walton side; they go to Germany or somewhere every year; and then there are the Per-

2*

rins, who have been so much abroad; of course you
remember the Perrins — they live on the other side of
the Common, you know, at Elmwood. I am sure you
must have some acquaintances here."

"No," said Agnes, amused to see the same impulse
which had vexed her youth, in the case of Lady Charlton, re-appearing in the vicar's homely and kindly
wife. "I don't know anybody near Windholm but my
own people, and yourself, and Polly Thompson, if you
will pardon me for the conjunction — that is to say,
I know everybody; but that does not count, you know.
You and Lady Grandmaison," said Agnes with a smile
which she could not restrain, "you are my only friends,
apart from my own people, here."

"Lady Grandmaison!" said Mrs. Freke, aghast.

"Yes; I saw a great deal of her one year. She is
very kind, and was excessively good to me," said
Agnes, and then she was drawn by the comic character
of the situation to add another word *malice prepense*.

"You and she are the only friends I have in the
great world. I must trust my cause to you," Mrs.
Trevelyan said with a soft momentary laugh. Perhaps
the conjunction was a little piece of feminine wickedness and impertinence; but Agnes, like most other
people, had learned by this time the wonderful advantage that lay in that power of being occasionally
impertinent, which only great ladies possess in the
highest degree.

"You know very well that it is absurd to speak of
Lady Grandmaison and me together," said Mrs. Freke,
getting up with a little flush on her cheeks, "unless
you wish to affront me. But at the same time, I am
an old friend, and old friends are not to be picked up

everywhere. I hope Mr. Trevelyan is better. Give him my regards, please, and tell him Mr. Freke is going to call upon him. I am afraid I have come in upon you too early, but you know we keep such early hours in Windholm. I must go up and tell your good father how well you are looking, and how very much you are improved; I am sure he will be very glad to hear that," said Mrs. Freke; and then she shook hands with little Walter, who opened the door for her like a little gentleman, according to the principles of Giovanni of Sorrento. However, when he had closed it, and she was gone, the hardest part of the business remained; for the little questioner returned to the charge, excited by all he had heard.

"Mamma, why does she say you are improved?" said Walter, taking up his station at his mother's side with an evident determination to be at the bottom of it, and hear all that there was to hear.

"I suppose, because she thinks so," said Agnes, to whom, however, the question was not very agreeable; for, to tell the truth, that which seemed improvement to other people — a change which involved the loss of all her higher hopes and beautiful aspirations — seemed a falling off rather to the mind of the woman who, seeing nothing better was to be made of it, was conscious of having schooled herself into an endurance of her life. "She thinks me looking better, I suppose."

"Were you beautiful when you were young, mamma?" the sturdy little inquisitor went on.

"No, Walter," said Agnes, laughing; "not in the least, except perhaps to grandpapa, who did not know any better." She was more nearly beautiful at that moment than she had ever been in her tranquil youth,

but this neither she nor the child were aware of. To
be sure it is usual to say that all women are conscious
of their advantages in this respect, but then Agnes had
been brought up alone, and had never heard the question discussed, which, perhaps, may account for her
absolute want of information on the subject. Walter,
however, was in an inquisitive mood.

"Why did not grandpapa know any better?" he
said with an air of gravity almost approaching pain;
for it grieved the boy to be obliged to set down as an
inferior person this grandfather, who, after all, had
something fascinating in his face.

"Don't you know," said the mother, whose teaching
was always visionary, "when you are very fond of any
one, you like her looks whether she is pretty or not?
My father loved me better than any one else in the
world, — and he might even think me beautiful, for
anything I know — but that was because he did not
know any better. Perhaps you are too little to understand that now."

"And papa?" said Walter, without taking any
notice of this insult, "did he know better? isn't he
very fond of you too?"

"Papa is different," said Mrs. Trevelyan. "There
was once a time when papa did not know me, and did
not care anything about my looks; but now go and
get your hat, Watty, and come with me; we are going
to see grandpapa — and if you see a great many
things that surprise you, I hope my boy is a gentleman and will not say anything disagreeable about what
he sees. You will understand it better when you have
talked it over with me."

"Ye—es," said Walter; "but, mamma, I may ask what things mean, when I don't know?"

"Oh yes, as much as you please," said Agnes; and she got up and put her work away, while Walter still lingered in the excitement of his discovery, forgetting even his newly-manufactured whip.

"And is it true?" he asked, "really true? grandpapa is a —. But then I don't know exactly what that is. I suppose that there are no white ponies where he lives," the boy added, after a pause; and Walter sighed. It was the first time his ideal had been so rudely disturbed. After that he went and got his hat, and submitted to have his hair brushed with that subdued acquiescence in circumstances which is a necessary condition of existence in this unsatisfactory world. To tell the truth, it was a little hard upon Walter. If this total want of connexion between grandfathers and white ponies was true, as the evidence seemed to indicate, he did not, on the whole, see the advantage of having come home.

The child, however, had enough to distract his thoughts from this painful subject on the way to the forge — for in all his travels he had never seen anything like the English village green, with. its white palings, and all the pretty embowered houses, with their tranquil looks — and then the idea of everybody speaking English, even the babies at the cottage doors and the people in the shops, was droll to the little traveller. "It is so funny to hear them," he said; "it sounds as if they were all ladies and gentlemen," which was a view of the subject which had not occurred to Mrs. Trevelyan. As for Agnes, she seemed to be making acquaintance not with Windholm, but with a new self, whom she had never paused to look at before, as she went along the familiar street. When she caught sight of her own figure reflected in the windows of the little shops, she began to consider for the first time the change which had come upon her — even the different way in which she walked occurred to her with a strange sensation. Agnes Stanfield would have tripped along humbly, moving aside by instinct to let everybody pass who would; but Mrs. Trevelyan, though her courtesy was far more perfect and sweet than that of Agnes Stanfield, felt it to be natural that the world in general should, to some extent, make way for her, and leave her "the crown of the causeway." In this there was not the least intention or desire to be different from what she ever was: it was merely the natural action of life and circumstances which she recognised in herself with a smile.

When she saw Mr. Freke pass at a little distance, and pause with some embarrassment, not knowing whether to return to greet her or not, Agnes could not but be amused at herself, at the quiet bow with which, without thinking, she dismissed and released the vicar. In old days, his nod and smile had been an honour to the blacksmith's daughter. She felt at that moment the ease and simplicity of her own manner, as at other times she had felt its awkwardness and *gaucherie*, but with a little surprise and amusement instead of pain and confusion. Perhaps it was because, for some time past, Agnes had been so much occupied with other matters more important as to forget all about her manners. These thoughts went through her mind involuntarily as she went on to the humble house which still in her heart she called home. It was a painful thing to do in its way, if she had been a woman used to reckoning up her trials — for to Agnes, who knew so well her father's superiority, there was something at once humbling and irritating in the roused curiosity and dissatisfaction of her child. She was half angry, and yet at the same time anxious, longing to have it over, and that this little scion of the Trevelyan race should recognise and understand the character of his relationships. She took him in at once to the forge, where everything was in full movement; and Stanfield himself, in his habitual working dress and looks, was occupied, as usual, directing his workmen. The glare of the smithy fire behind threw out the grimy figures in strong relief, and showed all the details with unsparing distinctness, and even the hand with which the blacksmith took Walter's little white hand was marked with the signs of work. It was a moment of some excitement both for Agnes and her father, though neither betrayed what they were thinking; but the fact was they had both been speculating with a great deal too much gravity on the ideas of seven years old. All Walter's uncertainty disappeared from his mind at the sight of this tempting interior. He gave a little cry of delight, and swung himself off his feet, holding by Stanfield's hand.

"Oh, grandpapa, let me come in and see what they are doing," said the heir of the Trevelyans. He condoned and accepted everything with the frank and reckless generosity of a man who sees unlimited amusement and novelty before him. Mrs. Trevelyan retired with a soft laugh, which was as near crying as it could be under the circumstances.

"If Mrs. Stanfield is in, I will go upstairs and see

her," said Agnes; and so this dreaded introduction to
the house, which was not a château, and where there
were no white ponies, was got over and concluded
to the wonderful relief and satisfaction of all concerned.

Agnes, for her part, had a still more painful duty
to perform in her visit to her step-mother, who sat upstairs awaiting her in great state and grandeur. Mrs.
Stanfield was full eight years older, and had progressed
out of the remnants of youthfulness which still remained
to her overblown bloom when Agnes last saw her
into a ruder fulness — a flush which knew no softening, and from which her fiery hazel eyes shot glances
more restless and impatient than ever. It was even
whispered in Windholm that the blacksmith's wife in-
demnified herself for the lack of occasion to exercise
her temper, and keep up a current of excitement in
that wholesome and natural method, by the use of
other stimulants less innocent, perhaps, than the quarrels,
which were the only things in which Stanfield absolutely refused to indulge his wife. She got up when
Agnes came in, and made her an abrupt and sudden
curtsy, and then, without any preface, burst out into a
sudden denunciation of "them as had no manners, and
never could have no manners — them as took all they
could get, and never said thank you. It aint as *I* ever
expected any civility," Mrs. Stanfield cried, without
leaving Agnes time to utter a syllable — "though it's
my money as he's a-spending when all's done; for
what is his is mine, and if he goes a-throwing it away
on them as never shows no gratitude, I'd like to know
what's to become of his unfortunate widder when he's
dead and gone. I never expected no civility, knowing

them as I have ado with; but I did say, and I've said since ever I knew you was a-coming, as you should have a piece of my mind."

Agnes had learned a great deal since she left this room, in which it seemed so strange to find herself once more seated; but she had not learned how to reply to an excited and violent woman. She said to herself what a comfort it was that she was alone, and composed herself to support the storm to the best of her ability; and the half-hour's trial she had to go through was not a slight one. Mrs. Stanfield, when she saw that the victim did not mean to fly or call to the rescue, but disposed herself simply to endure, put forth her whole powers. She upbraided her step-daughter for being proud and for being poor-spirited — for staying away and for coming home; she reproached her for being ashamed of her origin, and then she reproached her for disgracing the Trevelyans by coming to live at Windholm, and proving to everybody that Sir Roger's son had married the blacksmith's daughter. "I'd have done a deal more for young Roger than you'd ever have done," cried the furious woman. "I told him so, for all so good as you think yourself. I give him my advice afore you was married, and he'd have took it if he hadn't a-been led away ,by them as was always designing. As for Sir Roger, I can tell you as he knows everything, and there aint nothing to be expected there. The master may be a fool with his money, but you won't do nothing with Sir Roger; but you're a deal too clever to let your poor, simple, deceived husband get sight of me, as could tell him things — you'll take good care that you don't let him come nigh *me*."

"Then you know Sir Roger?" said Agnes, with an air of carrying on the conversation which drove Mrs. Stanfield mad.

"I know him — ay, a deal better than anybody knows him," cried the passionate creature; and then she stopped short in her flood of words. Was it because the blacksmith's heavy foot was audible coming slowly up the outer stair? Anyhow, she stopped all at once in her passion, with that power of self-control which people generally have who give themselves up to the indulgence of their temper. She paused as a wild beast might have paused at the sight of its enemy, seeing that flight was the only policy, and gave a rapid look at Agnes, as if doubtful whether to dash herself at her and make an end of her, or to trust to her discretion. But there was no time to do either before the blacksmith opened the door. He came in slowly, still with his grandson's hand in his, and by this time the child was hanging about him, swinging on his hand, describing little circles round him, making little runs at him in the height of his satisfaction. Stanfield might not be like Herman's grandfather, a baron with châteaux, and hounds, and horses, but what was next best, he was a man with a workshop full of astonishing tools, red-hot iron with which a clever boy might have hopes of burning his fingers off, and all sorts of cunning inventions, which had to be fathomed; and, perhaps, even had he been a baron, and possessed the *air noble* to perfection, he would scarcely have had so ready an entrance to Walter's heart. The blacksmith lifted his great brown eyes when he went into the room. Walter was still swinging by his hand, and talking at the top of his voice without making the least account of the difficulties of locomotion, and it was on Agnes that her father turned that look, which warmed and gladdened to her heart like a broad unexpected gleam of sunshine.

"This is little Walter Trevelyan, Sally," Stanfield said, in words; but with his eyes he assured Agnes that her boy had won his heart, and that already the inevitable wounds which their meeting had caused had been softened and healed by the touch of the child's hand. He seemed to take it as natural that his wife should subside into the chair, where she sat fanning herself, and take no further part in the conversation. As for the blacksmith, his heart was full, and he could not but speak it out.

"He's well pleased on the whole," said Stanfield; "he had a moment's doubt, but it is past. The only thing he is disappointed about is the white pony, and, perhaps, for that ———"

"Not just disappointed," said Walter, "for you know I said I would lend him to mamma to go up the mountains, and there are no mountains here; and grandpapa says, I may come to the forge every day if I like, and you will let me, mamma; so that I don't see, after all, that there would be any time left for the white pony — unless, to be sure, grandpapa would let them show me how they shoe them, and then I can see that on other people's horses. But, mamma, grandpapa says ———"

Here the smile that had been growing under Stanfield's eyelashes flooded over, filling all the lines of his face with sunshine.

"My, boy," said the blacksmith, "you don't know what I said. I said I had a little box somewhere with a walnut in it, and a little nut in that, and something inside. What if it should be a white pony with a saddle and a bridle, and all ready? When I've left off work to-night I'll hunt up the little box and see."

"Ah, but that would only be a toy," said Walter; "and then besides, such boxes are only in fairy tales. It could not be a real nut or a real pony, you know. I once had a little horse of wood that was wound up with a key, and could run about on the floor. When did you say, grandpapa, you would look for the box? Haven't you time to do it just now while I am here?"

"No, not just now," said the blacksmith; "I must do my work first, and then when six o'clock has struck, and the men have left off, and I've had my tea——"

"Yes," cried Walter, with eagerness; "may *I* come and have tea with you, grandpapa; and then, you know, I could help you to look, and you would not forget?" said the politic youth.

This was how the visit terminated, of which Agnes had stood in so much fear. She had sustained a rough enough encounter in her own person, to be sure, but that, as she said to herself, "did not count." And as they went home again, her speculations as to what Mrs. Stanfield could mean, and the little stings that remained after that assault, were accompanied by such a running chorus of narrative from Walter that the wounds were more than half healed, and the wonder dissipated. It was impossible to believe that Mrs. Stanfield could have any influence, one way or other, upon Mrs. Trevelyan's fate or that of her children; and when she reached her pretty house again, Agnes recognised better than in the excitement of arrival that she had attained the security of a home at last.

CHAPTER III.

The Middle Age.

THERE is this curious difference between life itself and the story of a life, however close and faithful, that the narrative must necessarily be a narrative of certain hours and moments which do not altogether determine the complexion of that long waste of living which has to be gone through, though it is not in the least interesting to describe. To go over all the little vicissitudes of those days, in which everybody got up at the usual hour in the pretty house on Windholm-green, and went on with their usual occupations — working, walking, talking, dining, reading, receiving calls now and then, sometimes making them, occupied with expectations of the advent of Lady Grandmaison, feeling a little excitement when she came, and a little blank after that event was accomplished and over — would be as unnecessary to a clear conception of the life of Agnes Trevelyan as it would be tiresome to the hearers. Most people cry out against the tedium of such a routine, though most people, perhaps, in their hearts, if they took the trouble to think, would recognise the fact that, short of actual happiness, which comes to so few people in this world, this routine is the great support of courage and patience, and makes life practicable. It would be quite false to say that Agnes was not happy during this winter, but it would be also very false to imagine that there was anything perfect in the character of her happiness, or that she could in any sense feel herself to have entered the haven, or commenced a higher life.

Roger, as was natural, was bored to death with
those quiet days. He had nothing to do, nor had he
the habit of doing anything; and he did not possess
the placid mind which could occupy itself with garden-
ing, or take to a greenhouse, or find domestic happiness sufficient for its requirements. Even reading is
but an unsatisfactory substitute for living under the
best circumstances, and when the subject has a mind
disposed for literature — which was not Trevelyan's
case. To be sure, he might have had a day's shooting
now and then, if he had cared for that; but his illness,
and the habits it had led to, and the doctor's warnings
against exposure and fatigue, made that impracticable;
and then the visit which they paid to Lady Grandmaison, at Christmas, however pleasant in itself, made
matters rather worse when it was necessary to go back.
By degrees Roger got disgusted with everything around
and about him.

"By Jove! I think I'd better go out for a walk
with Madelon, as the children do," he said, with
a laugh, which was not pleasant to hear, when his
wife disturbed him sometimes from his idle and angry
musings.

When they were invited to the little dinners at the
Vicarage and elsewhere — which were the most digni-
fied entertainments practicable at Windholm — it was
with savage sarcasm that Roger prepared himself for
those mild pleasures; and the unrestrained yawns in
which he indulged even in Mrs. Freke's drawing-room,
made him an undesirable guest. And then, in mere
lack of anything else to amuse him, Roger's eye was
caught by the pensive air of little Milly Fox, who was
the only one unmarried, and who, in early days, had

entertained a romantic preference for the young squire. She was of opinion at present that Mr. Trevelyan would have been very different if he had married a woman who could understand him, and had a certain inflection of sympathy in her voice when she spoke to him, which infinitely tickled Roger, who was moved thereby to commence a decided flirtation. He was not sufficiently interested, it is true, to put himself to much trouble to keep it up, but when the opportunity came in his way, he devoted himself to her service with enough emphasis to scandalize the good people of Windholm, and wake a good deal of excitement in the gentle bosom of little Miss Milly, who, being the only unmarried daughter of the family, naturally felt a little aggrieved and injured, and was, besides, at the age when friendship becomes sweet, and a woman feels herself safe in assuming the office of guardian angel to a man who is not appreciated by his wife. The worst of it was, that Agnes was almost the only person who remained totally unmoved by her husband's devoted friendship; but still it was an amusement in its way.

What was worse than this, so far as Agnes was concerned, was, that Roger was seized with a certain irritation and jealousy in respect to Stanfield, which added a new bitterness, not the less bitter that it was not entirely unexpected, to Mrs. Trevelyan's life. When the blacksmith came, after his work was over, in his Sunday suit, to sit for an hour by his daughter's hearth, in the house which he had built and equipped, and, at the present moment, all but supported, the pleasure Agnes felt in her father's society was turned into sharp pain and anxiety by the doubtful words and irritable temper of her husband. The blacksmith could scarcely utter a word to which Roger did not find some exception; and the younger man disagreed, as if by instinct, with all Stanfield's opinions almost before they were expressed. Then Roger took pains to utter loudly all the scraps of club philosophy which he had picked up in his experience, touching the general meanness of human nature, and the absolute unimportance of moral distinctions; which was not because such were his own opinions, or because he himself was in the habit of reflecting at all on serious subjects, but because it was the only means in his power of thoroughly exhausting Stanfield's patience, and perhaps provoking a quarrel.

All this occurred in presence of Agnes, who had to keep her place between the two with a composed countenance, and to laugh at Roger's extravagance, as if it was meant for a joke; while she knew very well in her heart it was a covert insult, intended to irritate and provoke her father. As for Stanfield, he swallowed down his natural indignation as well as he could, with the magnanimity which was natural to him; he suffered himself to be contradicted; he supported with a smile the insolent assumption of superior knowledge with which his son-in-law waved his experience aside, and consented, though not without an effort, to be addressed as an ignorant and illiterate person; which was no inconsiderable exercise of patience for a man whose wisdom and goodness were universally acknowledged, and who had been used to have no equal in his homely sphere. But when Roger propounded his supposed "views," such as they were, Stanfield had a greater difficulty in restraining himself, especially when Walter happened to be present. The blacksmith had made a friend of the boy, as a man of a spirit so highly toned, and yet so simple, was capable of making of an open-hearted and well-conditioned child; and naturally the grandfather took for comprehension a great deal that was only sympathy, and imagined that Walter's ethics were in danger when Roger gave vent to his opinions. Thus there arose between them a strife all the more deadly that it was always covert and veiled, and that, so far as appearances went, the victory was always with the weaker side. And so it came about that Agnes sometimes almost wished that her father would give up his visits; while Stanfield, for his part, made up his mind to endure and continue them, in case of wounding her.

"She'd be grieved if I stayed away," he would say to himself, as he went slowly with that reluctant step which he had been conscious of the first evening, when he paid his first visit to his daughter's house; while, in the meantime, Agnes sat within, listening, with all her senses quickened by anxiety, for his step outside, and saying in her heart, with something like a prayer, "Perhaps to-night he will not come."

When the gate was heard to open, and Stanfield's steady, somewhat heavy foot sounded outside on the gravel, Roger would make a movement of impatience, and thrust his chair away from the table. "It is very odd that we never, by any chance, have an evening to ourselves, he would say with angry vehemence; and thus Stanfield's visits, which were far from occurring every evening, were the most painful moments of Agnes's life.

All this time, however, it was the blacksmith who principally supported the family. As for Roger, he got money somehow for his own concerns, but it did not

3*

occur to him to ask Agnes about the bills, which, no doubt, were paid somehow; and she had abandoned the idea of suggesting "something to do," as a mere aggravation, from which no good could result; but it was very hard upon her to be compelled to speak to her father about money, and she did not know what to say, nor how to express her own shame and humiliation and sense of wrong, without compromising her husband. She said, with a transparent assumption of calmness, which could deceive nobody, much less the eyes full of insight that watched her so closely —

"Father, this must all be made up when Roger comes to his kingdom, as he says. It is hard to have always such an expectation before his eyes; it keeps him from trying for himself. Don't think any worse of us than you can help," said Agnes; and she glanced at him piteously, and withdrew her eyes, afraid to trust herself to an encounter with his.

As for the blacksmith, he took her hands into his, and held them fast, with a look almost more piteous than her own; for he could not bear to see her suffer.

"I have nobody but you in the world," he cried. "What I have is all yours, Agnes; and I'm hale and strong and fit for work as ever I was. Don't you vex yourself about that. You and me," Stanfield said, with a meaning more perfect than his grammar, "have been brought up different. It's a thing your husband does not think of; and it's hard to learn, when a man has been brought up to do nothing. Don't think any more about that."

"That is just what it is," said Agnes, eagerly; "he never was brought up to it. It does not come into his head. I feel as if I could die, sometimes, rather than ask more money from you; but you see, father, it is not Roger's fault."

The blacksmith made no distinct reply, but he put a little bundle of notes into Agnes's hand. "Next quarter day will be the 10th of May," he said, with a smile; and kissed her forehead, and went away. And Roger, who, to be sure, knew no particulars of this conversation, took pains to be specially rude to Stanfield the next evening he came to the house.

Yet, even with these two resources, of flirting with Milly Fox and insulting Stanfield, the time hung heavy on Roger's hands. He took to conversation with the vicar, when nothing better was to be done, and then Agnes found herself assailed on another side. Mr. Freke was one of the men of the present generation who do not pretend to a very clear faith; and at the same time, he was not clear-sighted enough to see that Roger's speculations were the mere fruit of idleness and discontent, and had no origin whatever in real reflection. Thus Agnes, who had supported herself through all her troubles by the unquestioning certainty of her youth, that all was and must be well, however painful it might be, became suddenly aware of the objections entertained by speculative minds against the popular theory of Providence, and found the ways of God not justified but questioned by the priest, who ought to have strengthened her faith and her courage. Perhaps she was scarcely old enough to have entered for herself into that "selva oscura" out of which the soul can only find egress by the painful and roundabout road which leads through the Inferno and the Purgatory to Heaven itself, where there is rest. But it startled and

discouraged the young woman, who was so solitary
among her troubles, and who was labouring along in
the mid-career of her life, under harder burdens than
the vicar had ever known or perhaps imagined, to learn
all the difficulties that existed in the way of that simple
trust, which she had managed to maintain hitherto,
without ever losing hold upon the certainty of her
youth. Roger, to be sure, was not moved, one way or
the other, by Mr. Freke's candid statements; but that
was because Roger was not really thinking, but only
talked in the vain idea of amusing himself, and with a
charitable intention of "drawing the parson out."

"It's very easy to talk of everything being for the
best," Roger would say. "I wonder how it can possibly be for the best, for example, that a man should
be stranded here as I am? I don't mean to complain of
want of money, you know — for that is what a great
many fellows have to complain of; but it does seem an
aggravation when a man's health is attacked in addition.
I know hundreds of fellows who have taken every sort
of liberty with their constitutions, and yet are as strong
as horses; while I, that have never lived a reckless
life, and that have nothing but my health to keep me
afloat — if that's justice, it's a very queer kind of
justice. Men are bad enough, but they don't hit a
man when he's down like that. I can't say I understand what you parsons mean about Providence;
especially in face of all that one sees happening in the
world."

"My dear Trevelyan," said the vicar, "for a man
who has thought on these subjects, it is the most terrible of all mysteries. I don't pretend to fathom it, for
my part. It used to be the fashion to admire the beautiful

construction of everything, and how the human frame
was made to secure strength, and grace, and ease, and
so forth; but it's dreadful to turn to the other side of
the picture, and see how the nerves and the rest of it
are framed so as to make pain into torture; and it is
just the same often with the mind and circumstances.
Grant that there is a misfortune that a man could have
reasonably borne, there's sure to be something added on
to drive him frantic; — instead of the compensations
which it used to be the mode to talk of. I don't pretend
to understand Providence any more than you do. It is
one of the greatest difficulties for a thoughtful mind.
As for the vulgar idea, all that can be said for it, is,
that it *is* the vulgar idea; and I suppose it gives a kind
of comfort, in its way, to people who are unaccustomed
to think."

"I don't see any good in thinking, for my part,"
said Roger; "the more a man calculates the more he
is out, in a general way. It's all vanity — I suppose
that's the end of it; and I don't imagine there's half-
a-dozen men in the country, from the Archbishop of
Canterbury downwards, that really know what they
would be at."

"Oh no, that's a mistake," said Mr. Freke; "that
is one thing Low churchmen and dissenters of the
evangelical school have an advantage in. They know
what they mean in a kind of way; but, unfortunately,
the higher you ascend in the scale of intelligence, the
less one knows what one means. You may smile, Mrs.
Trevelyan, but I assure you it is true. You may fancy
now and then, I allow, that you have a vague conception of what you would yourself be at — but as for
what God means in this world, or what a single life

means, or what significance there is in the sequence of events, it is enough to drive a man crazy to attempt to understand it. Everything that is most unlikely comes to pass. When a man is struggling to make head against the world, something happens to him to take the courage out of him just at that identical moment; and another man, who is only looking on, has the happiness thrown at him when he did not want it, that would have been a cordial to the other, and set him up for his work. That is how I continually find it, when I open my study window, you know, and take a look out upon the world."

"Yes," said Agnes, who knew more about it than he did, and had that problem of life to consider, through no such tranquil medium as the study window — "I know it is true; but then what conclusion would you draw from that?"

"Heaven knows!" said the vicar, getting up from his seat — "the common conclusion is that everything is for the best. I don't draw any conclusion, for my part. I only recognise the mysterious state of affairs, and hope that perhaps we may have more light some time or other. There's the difference, you see, between a discussion which touches upon religion, and philosophy proper. Mrs. Trevelyan, who naturally takes the ethical side, desires a conclusion; but I can't stop now to enter upon that. My wife told me you were going to dine with us to-morrow — don't forget."

And the vicar shook hands, and took his leave somewhat abruptly, as was his custom. To tell the truth, he had excited himself a little by his own description of human affairs, and something in Agnes's face had moved him still more deeply. Not a word or look of complaint ever came from Mrs. Trevelyan, and yet the vicar, who had a high opinion of her, could not but bethink himself, that her life must have burdens sufficient to make his picture a little too vivid to her mind. The world generally, and especially the little world of a village, knows much more about people's affairs than they think; and Mr. Freke had a tolerably clear idea of Agnes's circumstances. He said to himself, "Good Lord! what does it mean?" as he went out. "There is a creature now," Mr. Freke reflected, "that looked as if she was made for something worth while; but, as it turns out, all that she is made for, is to take care of a discontented young fellow, that never was good for much, and that is going to fall ill, and maybe to die, for anything one knows. It would be like him to die — but yet I don't know that it would, either, for then, at least, he would be out of the way; and here are all her delicate senses wounded, and her nerves driven crazy, and her fine character wasted. Good Lord! good Lord! I would like to know what everybody means by it," said the vicar to himself. Perhaps he would have been disconcerted if he had been requested to explain what he meant by everybody — for to be sure he was a little profane in his way of thinking, as clergymen often think themselves at liberty to be.

As for Agnes, however, the effect upon her was a great deal more painful than upon Mr. Freke. It opened her eyes to that truth which most people find out sooner or later, that distress and trouble are, after all, very seldom elevating agents, and that those who are happy, are in most cases those who have the best chance of being good; and this discovery took a great part of her courage away from her, for, indeed, her soul had consoled itself often with the reflection that the sufferings she had to bear were signs of God's love, as some simple people think. But how could they be signs of God's love, when their influence was towards deterioration, and not towards improvement? If that refuge failed her, Agnes did not know where to flee; and this was what the vicar's frankness seemed to lead to. For a woman without any support in her individual difficulties and distresses, it was, perhaps, safer to recognise the misfortunes of life as blessings in disguise, meant to purify and to elevate, rather than as evils pure and simple, which were day by day undermining the health and courage of her soul. Mr. Freke gave her a great blow in her primitive belief, for thoughtful as she was, and inclined to judge for herself, yet it seemed to Agnes, if there had any longer been any certainty in the world, that the vicar would not have proclaimed his difficulties so openly; for to be sure she was only a woman, and could not have taken into account, even had she known it, the spirit of the age.

Thus it occurred that Mrs. Trevelyan, as happens so often to a soul which leaves youth behind, and begins to enter — prematurely as it happened to be — upon the painful level of the middle age, was left by herself to undergo her trial. Her father was withdrawn from her side, because, in loyalty to her husband, she could not confide in him, and a wall of separation was thus built between them, even in their tenderest moments. Her husband was withdrawn from her, because he did not comprehend, or if he comprehended, eluded and escaped from, the evils that over-

whelmed her; and even God himself — the God of her
youth, the Supreme Father — seemed to be failing the
solitary woman whom He had exposed without any
protection to all the horrors of the way. Perhaps this
was one of the reasons why Mrs. Trevelyan was so
utterly unaffected by the flirtation of her husband with
little Milly Fox. Life was pressing very hard upon
her at the moment, and things a great deal more serious
were revolving in her awakened mind.

CHAPTER IV.

Brother and Sister.

WHEN the winter had passed after this fashion,
perhaps it was not very extraordinary that Roger Trevelyan, though without any means, should avail himself of the vicinity of Windholm to London, and make
a rush up to town in May. Jack Charlton, for example,
who was still much the same Jack Charlton as he had
been at the commencement — not changed, to speak
of, in position or in occupations, though he went on
circuit — was quite content to give his old friend a
share of his chambers as often and as long as he
pleased; and if Trevelyan had lost some of the friends
of his youth, he had something to counterbalance that
loss in the multitude of people who had met him
abroad, and who were glad to greet a man whose recollection was associated with ideas of enjoyment and
freedom. Then he felt quite easy in his mind about
Agnes, who was all right with her children, and never
had shown, as he assured himself, much taste for society. It was doing her no harm to take a little

amusement for himself — amusement of which he had
such need as perhaps Agnes, on her side, could not
understand; and so affairs went on amicably and comfortably. It was at this time that he encountered Miss
Trevelyan, who certainly was eight years older, but
who had not yet changed her *rôle* in society. On the
whole, this long interval had not made the difference
in Beatrice which she had expected. Youth and bloom,
to be sure, were gone for ever; but after the first
change, to which she had already accustomed herself
before Roger's marriage, the years were merciful to
Miss Trevelyan. She seemed to have reached the
table-land upon which a woman who takes proper care
of herself may rest a long time; and though she had
given up dancing, she had not retired into the background of society, as might have happened to a person of less spirit. When she met her brother, Miss
Trevelyan was very well dressed, with that amount of
care which is suitable to her years; — the wonderful
chevelure, which had been one of her great beauties,
was as light, and feathery, and airy as ever; not so
abundant, no doubt, but then the quality of those light
locks, which had no weight, but moved with every
breath, made them capable of every kind of ingenious
torture. It was natural to them to be frizzed, and
puffed out, and elaborated, and made-up, like any detached and independent head-dress, which was an advantage that Beatrice did not despise. And then, as
she got used to it, she had ceased to turn that anxious
look into her mirror, and the pucker had softened a
little out of the forehead. Her eyes were subdued out
of their golden glow, it is true, and generally looked
like mere hazel eyes — yellow-grey. She preferred to

call them hazel, because, like most people who have a
remarkable feature, she had a vehement dislike of the
next grade to that, and despised the blue-grey with
vehemence. She had lost her early bloom altogether,
to be sure; but then, when a woman has features, she
can afford to dispense with that fleeting livery of
youth. When Roger came up to her she was seated by
a table, very well dressed, as we have said, and leaning her beautiful arm, which had never been more
beautiful, upon it. She was talking to some one who
interested her, and for whom she was putting forth all
her powers — and Beatrice was a very good talker.
She was in the middle of a sentence when she perceived Roger, and all her composure and self-command
could not keep down a start of surprise; but she finished
what she was saying, notwithstanding, before she held
out her hand to him.

"Roger! — is it possible?" she said; but though
she did not shrink from the evident duty and necessity
of speaking to him, and even though an impulse of nature prompted her towards her brother, it was not without a pang of regret on the other hand, that Miss Trevelyan postponed the business in which she was occupied to the claim of family affections; for she was
talking to a man in every way suitable and eligible,
and they were just beginning to get interested in each
other. Nobody could tell what might not have come
of it but for the apparition of the brother, at sight of
whom the stranger naturally retired; and no doubt Miss
Trevelyan felt it a little hard to purchase her re-intro-
duction to Roger at the price of such a sacrifice. Her
regretful eyes followed for a moment the departing
figure of her late companion, even while she held up her

cheek for Roger to kiss. And whatever may be thought of Beatrice, and of her anxiety to preserve her good looks and make the best of them, it may be added that her cheek was quite safe to be kissed; for she had too much good taste and knowledge of the world to carry art too far.

"Is it really you, Roger?" she said; "have you dropped from the skies? I never was more surprised. To see you at all is strange; but, of all places in the world, to see you *here!*"

"It's a very natural place to see me," said Roger. "Stanley and I spent a whole winter together. But then, I forget, you are not *au-fait* of my history of late. How is Sir Roger? I began to think you had both retired to Trevelyan for good, as I have never met you anywhere; but I suppose things have not come to that."

Roger spoke as if they had taken leave of each other a few weeks before — a tone which was not without its effect upon Beatrice.

"No, not quite," she said. "Sir Roger is very well, and I am sure would be grateful to you for your filial attentions. On the contrary, we have both been out a great deal this year."

And here there was a pause; and Miss Trevelyan's eye strayed, in spite of herself, to the person who had left her, and who at this moment was standing in the very same attitude, leaning over the chair of another lady who had pretensions to the character of a brilliant as well as a fine woman, and was a kind of rival power. They were enjoying their conversation, to all appearance; and Beatrice could not but regret more and more that she had lost her opportunity for the sake of this encounter, which was so unpromising. She gave a sigh, and then she looked up at her brother, and recommenced with a little irritation, as it was natural to expect.

"I don't suppose you came up to me now to have the 'opportunity of making such ordinary remarks. Why didn't you come and see me when you came home? Papa may be displeased, but it's an old matter now, and I don't think he would have stood out. I suppose you are not alone?" said Beatrice, looking round her. Her eyes fixed, unconsciously to herself, upon a plump young woman in white, with plenty of roses about her, from her cheeks downwards to the skirts of her dress. She was standing a little apart by herself, and contemplating the world before her with an evident mixture of excitement and uneasiness; and naturally Beatrice fixed upon this figure as that of her brother's wife.

Roger's eyes followed hers, and he laughed aloud. He was not the best husband in the world, to be sure, and was very unlikely to go into raptures about his wife; but it was pleasant to think how Beatrice was deceived, and how different was the appearance of Agnes.

"No," he said, laughing, "that is not Mrs. Trevelyan — neither she nor any one like her. After all that has happened, the only right thing for you to do would be to go down to Windholm and be introduced to my wife."

"I wondered very much you should have gone there," said Beatrice, taking no notice of this suggestion, "where everybody must know, and where it must be so awkward; but I suppose you wished the little boy to make acquaintance with his relations," she said, with malice,

and laughed a little softly and with the most perfect
grace at her own joke.

"They are the only relations he seems to have any
chance of making acquaintance with," said Roger, with
offence; and then his tone softened a little — "He's a
famous little chap, and on the whole I'd like you to
see him," he added a minute after, in his natural voice;
and either the sentiment, though expressed with perfect
moderation, or perhaps some inflection in his voice,
touched by chance the heart which always existed under
the silk and the lace which covered Beatrice Trevelyan's
breast.

"Yes," she said, with lively resentment, "it looks
like that, does it not? To be sure, you have written to
me once or twice, when you could not help it; but yet
you come to England only to go to these people, and
do not take the trouble to make the smallest overture
to us. I am not in the way of being sentimental or
saying much on such subjects; but I feel it all the
same."

"By Jove," said Roger, "you are all alike, you
women. You never have taken the trouble to say a
kind word. What sort of overtures could I make? You
may believe I have not the least inclination to be in
feud with my family. As for going there, I had no
other place to go to, when that ridiculous blockhead of
a doctor sent me home for my health."

"Home for your health!" said Beatrice. The conversation she had been watching ceased just then, and
the gentleman withdrew and disappeared into the midst
of a host of other men, when he ceased entirely to be
interesting. In these circumstances Miss Trevelyan was
left with her attention quite free and disengaged.

"Home for your health!" she repeated, lifting her eyes. "By the way, you are looking a good deal worn. I observed it the first moment I saw you, but I thought it might, perhaps, be the anxieties, and so forth. A man with what is called a young family, and not very much to live on——"

"You should say with nothing to live on," said Roger. "It is something astonishing to me how we have kept on and continued to exist from year to year. The fact is, I am very glad to have a chance of half an hour's talk with you," he continued, drawing a chair close to his sister; "for, to tell the truth, I am tired to death of this sort of life, and something must be done to bring it to an end."

"What sort of life?" said Beatrice; but her question was put coldly and without any great appearance of interest. The fact was, the rooms were getting full, and all the world had arrived, and the idea of half an hour's conversation about family matters just at that particular moment alarmed Miss Trevelyan, who, to be sure, had not made so careful a toilette with the view of sitting apart with her brother in a corner, and advising him about his future life.

"Look here," said Roger; "I am back in England because I could not help it. That fellow Farington at Baden made a fuss about my health, as these doctors do. He said quiet, &c., was necessary; and I was confoundedly ill, there is no doubt about that. We went to that beastly place the beginning of winter, you know. What was a man to do? We've got a house there, and can live quiet; there's the frightful part of it — live quiet! If ever an unfortunate fellow was bored to death it's me, Beatrice, and it's no figure of speech in my case. But at the same time we can live cheap and quiet there. You may grumble as you like, but you don't know what that sort of thing means. I wish you'd think it over, and see what can be done for us. Let's be friends! Sir Roger is horribly aggravating, but there never was anything unpleasant between you and me."

"No," said Beatrice; "but then papa is poor, if he were ever so friendly; he might set *you* right, you know, but as for your family —"

"Oh, confound my family!" said Roger; he said it without the least meaning, merely to express his impatience; but, nothwithstanding, Miss Trevelyan was sensible of a little movement of satisfaction to perceive that, after all, her unknown sister-in-law was not so disproportionately happy as she had once imagined. "My father can do something if he likes to exert himself," Trevelyan continued; "even, if there was nothing better, you know, you and he might try to get me an appointment of some kind. It's rather hard upon a man to see all the world enjoying themselves, and he alone thrust outside."

"All the world does not marry at four-and-twenty," said Beatrice; "one has always to pay for indulging one's self. At the same time, you know I have always been your friend, and I'll do what I can for you, Roger. Where are you living — with Jack Charlton? Oh, yes, I recollect, he came home with quantities of stories about — but we'll not enter on that subject," said Miss Trevelyan, with alarm, perceiving that she had almost betrayed herself into a new subject which might have protracted the conversation to any length. "I will do what I can for you, and, if papa is at all practicable, I will write to you to come to us. I must go now. There are hosts of people here I want to see. At the same time, I am very glad to have had the chance of a talk with you, Roger;" and then she hesitated a moment, not sure whether to tell him to wait for her and put her into the carriage, or not. A brother, even when he has made a foolish marriage and ruined himself thereby, is still a sufficiently respectable attendant when nobody better offers; but then if anybody better did offer, it might have been rather in Miss Trevelyan's way had she made a positive engagement with Roger, according to her first idea. Accordingly, she compromised the matter. "If you leave before I do, come and speak to me first," she said, kissing her hand to him as she moved away.

Roger, who did not know the fine people for whom his sister left him, followed her with his eyes as she made her onward progress, and acknowledged to himself, with some pride and humiliation, that Beatrice, though she was not young, looked one of the most notable people in a company which embraced many notable persons. All that she wanted to have been one of the leaders of society, was to have married some one rich enough to give her the necessary means — a duke, if that had been practicable, but failing that, anybody with a very large fortune. This condition, unfortunately, was wanting; but, at the same time, Roger acknowledged to himself that his sister had, in some sort, a right to patronize him, as she had been doing. No doubt, if she had had a mind, she, too, might have crippled and disabled herself as he had done; and it occurred to him to think with a grudge how different his own position might have been, had he, too, denied

4*

himself on that special day, nine years ago, when, had he been guided by Beatrice, he would have left summarily and for ever the dreary old Hall at Windholm. Roger did not pursue that train of thought, for at the bottom of his heart he was loyal, even without intending it, to his natural ties, and, indeed, would have found it very difficult to detach himself even in idea from Agnes, who had been his wife and companion for so many years. Still he thought of it for a moment, as he saw Beatrice, with her lofty looks and her handsome toilette, standing in the midst of a brilliant group, where she was welcomed with acclamations. It did not occur to Roger, who was not given to much thinking, that Beatrice's own estimate of the position might have been different, could he have got fairly at it. But, to be sure, that was a discovery impossible to him or to any other man in the world. Miss Trevelyan knew her position and all its necessities much too well to indulge in any confidence so indiscreet.

CHAPTER V.

A Gloomy Prospect.

MISS TREVELYAN, however, notwithstanding her good intentions, found it apparently less easy to serve her brother than she had supposed. She wrote him a note, addressed to Jack Charlton's chambers, a day or two after their meeting, and this was all she could find to say: —

"I don't know how to tell you that I have failed, my dear Roger. As for papa standing out so long, and

making a fuss over your *mésalliance*, now that it is no
longer possible to help or even to ignore it, and when
I am ready to forgive you and stand your friend, it is
ridiculous; but, notwithstanding, that is the *rôle* he
has taken up. The fact is, I suppose that he could
not receive you without doing something for you, and
we are so dreadfully poor; but he has policy enough
to play the indignant father, and to put it all down to
the score of your folly. I don't know if you will feel
so fully as I do how amusing this is; but I am afraid
I cannot do anything more for you. And besides, I
think *he* thinks that a son who is a virtuous family
man is a reproach upon his own habits. I don't in the
least excuse him, you see, but I can't do more. He is
going out of town to-morrow, and, if you like to come
and see me on Friday, I shall be at home all the
morning. He says he will take your boy and bring
him up, if you like. That is a great deal cheaper, to
be sure, than a family; and of course, let him be as
indignant as he pleases, he can't hinder the child from
succeeding. I advise you to think over this, for no
doubt it would be a great saving to you, as I suppose
he is old enough to begin his education. As for your
present circumstances, I fear you must just make the
best of them. I don't see, for my part, why you
should hesitate to let the people *where you are living*
do what they can for you. They ought to know by
this time how much you have sacrificed — if, indeed,
these kind of people ever can understand; and any
little thing they can do can never in the least make
up for what you have lost through them. I don't say
this out of any ill feeling, but only because it is true,
and from a sense of justice. As for what you said

about an appointment, you know I should be *very* glad
to be of any use; but then I don't know in the least
what you could or would do. I hope you will take
care of your health, and not mope, which is the worst
of all things for the health. As for what the doctors
say about quiet, it has always seemed to me the greatest absurdity. If, however, you are at liberty on Friday, come, and we will talk it over, and I shall be
glad to see you. It was impossible to talk the other
night before all the world.

"Affectionately,

"BEATRICE.

"P. S. — I advice you to consider seriously what
Sir Roger said about taking care of the boy."

"By Jove," said Roger, when he read the letter,
"the boy! as if he was a little dog; and I should like
to know what his mother would say."

"What is it?" said Jack Charlton, who knew all
about his friend's prospects and intentions, and that
Beatrice had promised "to stand his friend."

"She says Sir Roger will have nothing to say to
me, but he will take Walter, if I like. By Jove!"
said Roger; "and talks of him, I tell you, as if he were
a little dog."

"I should think she'd talk with a deal more interest
if he were a little dog," said Jack. "I don't think
Beatrice ever was one for children. Do you mean to
accept it, Roger? They'd do his schooling, you know,
and all that sort of thing. To be sure, there's Mrs.
Trevelyan to be consulted; but I don't know that it
would be a bad thing," he added, thinking, as was not
unnatural, of the forge, and the grandfather who was a

blacksmith. Sir Roger, to be sure, was a man without any reputation; but still his dishonour came more natural, or at least Jack Charlton thought so, than the spotless character, or, as he called it, dead respectability, of the humble ancestor, who might, without meaning it, corrupt little Walter's mind.

"Women are the very deuce," said Roger, "and when there's two of them, what is a fellow to do? I have not a doubt that was Bee's suggestion — not that she wants the boy, but it's the best way she can think of, of getting a good hit at Agnes. By Jove! she's turned out a *grande dame*, though she's not married; but, for my part, I think Mrs. Trevelyan is capable of standing up to her," Roger said, disguising his rage and disappointment under a harsh laugh. "To-morrow's Friday, ain't it? I'll go and see Beatrice, and hear what she's got to say."

"Oh, she'll have plenty to say," said Jack; "and, upon my honour, I don't think it's a bad idea; but only there's Mrs. Trevelyan to be considered; and, of course, you know better than I do what her opinion is likely to be."

"The truth is," said Roger, "that they don't in the least understand Agnes. For example, I'll tell you what Beatrice said to me the other evening. She said, 'I suppose you're not alone?' and she cast her eyes upon a country cousin of the Alvanleys, who was within sight — a creature with red cheeks and red arms, like a plump pigeon, whom she took for Mrs. Trevelyan. By Jove, that's what they think. Now, you know, Jack, a man may have his own opinion as to whether he's done a wise thing or not, in the way of marrying when he had nothing to live on; but I'd think myself a very

shabby sort of fellow indeed if I didn't stand up for
my wife."

"I should think so," said Jack, shortly. He said
it, as if that was a thing of course, without appreciating
Roger's magnanimity; for, to be sure, Jack Charlton
had eyes like other people, and had not known the
two for so many years without forming his opinion of
both. He thought, indeed, that Windholm was a mistake, and that the blacksmith grandfather was unlucky
for little Walter; but, at the same time, he could see
something in Agnes which her husband could not see,
oddly enough, though he had been sufficiently aware
of it when he was only her lover; and Jack was even
conscious of a momentary movement of indignation
when Roger declared thus apologetically the necessity
there was that he should stand by his wife.

"Yes," said Trevelyan, "*cela va sans dire;* but I'll
go to-morrow all the same, and see what Beatrice has
to say."

That interview took place when Agnes was quite
unconscious of anything that could be going on against
her peace. Her youngest child had just come into the
world, and she was tracing in its little undeveloped
countenance lines which reminded her of the others
whom she had lost, and was happy in a tranquil way,
as a woman is who has got over one of the crises of
her existence without any harm. But Roger knew
nothing of this, or, to do him justice, he would have
had very different ideas in his mind. He had a long
conversation with his sister, the only remarkable thing
in which was the cleverness with which she evaded
naming his wife, though, of course, Mrs. Trevelyan
had to be referred to by implication; and Beatrice was

perfectly candid about Walter, and made no pretence
that she herself meant to devote herself to her little
nephew. She was not "one for children," as Jack
Charlton had said. "I don't mean to say that I want
him, as maiden aunts do in novels, to be a comfort to
me," she said with a smile; "that is not my *rôle*, you
know; but of course he must succeed some day, and
he ought to have a proper education. His relations in
Windholm cannot be very good for him in that way,"
Miss Trevelyan said. Of course she meant to include
his mother among the relations who would harm little
Walter, but she was too *fine* and subtle to say it in
words.

"I wish you would recollect that he has *no* relations
in Windholm," said Roger with some vehemence; "I
have told you so a hundred times; except Stanfield,
who can't do much one way or the other. Whatever
drawbacks there may be, there are no relations — I
have always told you so."

Beatrice smiled and shrugged her shoulders the
least in the world. "It is all the same; you shall
have the benefit of my influence if you like," she
said; and the end was that Roger made up his mind
to think it all over, and reflected philosophically that
his boy must go to school one day or other, and that
Agnes must make up her mind to it. His thinking,
however, was brought to a summary end by the news
of the event which had happened in his absence, and
he gave up his engagements for the evening with a
good grace to visit his wife. When that visit had
been made, however, the mere fact of Agnes's delicate
health led her husband to return to his friends and his
pleasures. She was all right; there was nothing in the

least to be apprehended. All that she wanted was to
be quiet and take care of herself; and, on the whole,
Roger thought it was rather good of him to go and
take himself out of the way. He said to himself, with
an agreeable sense of the most benevolent intentions,
that when he was gone she could see her father at her
ease, and comfort herself among her old friends, which
could scarcely have been done while he was there to
distract the attention of the household and keep the
invalid uneasy. Perhaps he was even right, to a
certain extent, in his idea; but then it was not to be
expected that Roger could know that, present or absent, his shadow stood between Agnes and her father
— a more effectual separation still than the long years
which had changed Stanfield little, but his daughter
much.

Thus Roger returned, feeling free and at his ease,
to Jack Charlton's chambers, and enjoyed his holiday
as much as he could, and recovered several old acquaintances, and, on the whole, amused himself; while
Agnes, for her part, got better very tranquilly at home,
without the least idea of finding fault with Roger, or
imagining herself neglected. But otherwise, his absence
did not fulfil his charitable intentions; for she was
afraid to ask her father to make his visits more frequent
than usual, in case the difference should be too marked
and evident when Roger returned; and even when they
were together, the conversation languished, and the two
who had once been everything in the world to each
other, sought subjects to talk about like two strangers;
for, to be sure, the life of Agnes with her husband,
and their hopes and prospects, were all tabooed subjects
to her father. Neither of them dared to enter upon

that forbidden ground, even had it been possible; for a sudden impulse on either side might have, at an unguarded moment, led to confidences which were, of all things in the world, the most to be avoided. It was not that Agnes had wrongs to talk of, such as drive some women to frenzy, but she foresaw by instinct the danger of permitting herself to discuss her husband; and thus the talk was vague and painful, and carried on with a disagreeable consciousness on both sides. Walter was the safe subject upon which they could both express themselves freely; but then the sayings and doings of a little boy nearly eight years old, however interesting, cannot afford opportunity for many long and continued conversations. Happily, they neither of them knew that there was risk of even this resource failing them; for Roger was not bold enough to say a word about Miss Trevelyan's proposal to his wife when he found her ill. He waited until the season was over, and he was obliged to return, before making that proposal to Agnes; and that was why she never fully knew what Beatrice and Sir Roger had intended in respect to her boy.

For, unfortunately, Roger's season in town ended as Dr. Farington had predicted, and as Jack Charlton had warned his friend it would. To be sure he was very incautious, and after his horrible winter at Windholm, which was a long series of precautions, he avenged himself by taking no care whatever of his health. And the end was that he returned home very ill, just as Agnes had recovered her strength sufficiently to nurse him, which, to be sure, was a fortunate circumstance in its way. Roger was much too ill to think, much less to talk of his father's proposal to take Walter, when he came home in this forlorn condition. He was so ill, indeed, that at one time he did not seem likely to rally even temporarily, but lay exhausted, with the pallor of death in his face, unable to make any movement, or to take any nourishment, to the profound alarm of everybody around him. Mrs. Trevelyan had been anxious enough before by times, but had never been called upon to contemplate, thus close at hand, the possibilities of her position, and to realize the fact, that she might be left with her two helpless babies and little Walter, to face the world alone. To tell the truth, this was not the idea which came into her mind even then, for she had no time to think of herself; nor did the position she might occupy, or even the fate of her children, have much share in her thoughts at that moment. She had no acquaintance with death, except as she had seen it fall on the infant children whom God had withdrawn all unconscious from her arms; and though these losses had overcast her life with sad clouds, she had never yet received any blow which struck straight and deep at the roots of her happiness. The cares of life, of which she had known her share, are hard enough in their way, but they do not quench out the gladness of the light, or make life itself distasteful to a spirit still elastic and young. And so it still appeared to Agnes, that dying was the saddest of earthly occurrences, and that to lie expecting it, looking forward to it, rehearsing it, was of all things in life the most terrible.

Thus it was that she scarcely realized the anguish for herself, or the loss that began to shadow over her. Her whole mind was occupied with wonder, and horror, and dread of this trial for Roger. How was he to bear it? How was he to give up life, and compose himself to meet the terrible approach of the Unknown? She was afraid of it for him, perhaps more than he was for himself — a hundred times more than she would have been for herself — and this took away from her all those thoughts of her own future, which might have been natural to a mind differently organized. It did not seem to matter what happened *after*. All the interest collected round that terrible moment, when the companion of her life, the husband of her youth, must consent and make up his mind to be no longer. And it did not occur to Agnes to consider that Roger's mind was occupied with the details too much to be able to regard the approaching event as she did; that a little relief from suffering, or a little sense of comfort, were enough to divert a sick man from graver thoughts; or that, in fact, he was too much concerned about his little changes of sensation to have time to contemplate and rehearse, as she was doing for him, the concluding scene of all, with all its mystery and darkness. When Mr. Freke came to see the patient, Agnes was relieved and yet wounded to see how glad her husband was to take refuge in the parish gossip, and hear all the village news; and when the Vicar looked at herself with a sympathetic face, and pressed her hand, and said, "My dear Mrs. Trevelyan, you must keep up and have courage," Agnes could have found it in her heart to strike him with her trembling hand. What did it matter about her? Was not she there in horrible good health, and cruel force, unable to communicate that strength to him, with whom she would have shared everything but pain? This was how her mind was occupied in the crisis of Roger's illness. But, after all,

the trial was not so near as everybody thought. The
sufferer was respited, and everything went on again to
a certain extent as before.

This renewal of hope, however, was not very vivid
nor very consolatory. Roger got better in a poor way,
as his doctors accounted betterness. He revived so far
as to feel his miseries, and to enter a little into the
position in which Agnes's anxiety had placed him at
the height of his illness. When he began to look
forward, it dawned upon Roger that the future was
very dark and uncertain, and that nobody cared to
discuss with him the time when he should be well
again. And then he got impatient, as was natural,
with this amount of recovery, which permitted only a
voyage downstairs to the drawing-room, or a little
walk in the sunshine. He had been patient and
courageous when he was very ill, bearing what he had
to bear like a man; but as he became "better" after
this sad fashion, poor Roger began to show the smaller
side of his character, as was natural. And it was in
this state that Miss Trevelyan found him, when she
came quite unexpectedly and without any warning, in
the middle of October, to spend a few days at the
Hall.

CHAPTER VI.

Miss Trevelyan's Visit.

BEATRICE TREVELYAN had known for a long time that she had only, as her maid might have said, "herself to look to" in this world. The expression is vulgar, but the sentiment is painful. Nobody belonging to her could do much for her, or took the trouble to think of doing anything; and the world in which alone she saw any true object of ambition, and indeed, in which alone she knew how to live, was a world in which a woman in her circumstances, if she fails to keep herself in mind and to make herself agreeable and amusing, fails altogether, and comes to an end. It was as necessary for her to be seen and heard as it would be for a popular actress or prima-donna, and, indeed, perhaps her art was something of the same description. But, for all that, she was far from being without feeling. Had she married at the natural time and in the natural way, she had it in her to have been impassioned in her love; but though that had passed over, as was to be expected, she was still capable of loving, and had by no means shut her heart to the natural affections, as so many people do when they have reached the middle of life. When she heard of Roger's illness, she was concerned about him, though he had never done much to recommend himself to her. And then she had a sisterly sentiment, of the same character as that which disposed the little Miss Fox to flirt with poor Mr. Trevelyan. Without permitting herself to inquire what Roger could have been good for, she concluded

that things might have been very different with him
had he married differently — "if he had had a wife
who could understand him," Beatrice said; and when
she found that an interval of a few days intervened
between two visits which she had to pay, Miss Trevelyan came down to Windholm to the old Hall, where
the agent and the housekeeper reigned supreme. She
brought her maid, which naturally secured her a certain
amount of comfort — a bright fire in her room, for
example, lighted at the right minute, and a cup of tea
when she liked to have it; and next morning she walked
down to the village to see her brother.

Sir Roger, in the meantime, had not given up the
idea of taking Walter, and this was one of the things
which Beatrice meant to talk over with her brother.
She had made up her mind calmly enough to the
undertaking, but notwithstanding, her heart beat a
little quicker as she made her way to the house on
the Green. This time, it would be impossible not
only to avoid naming Agnes, but to do without seeing
her, and even being civil to her in some degree; and
it occurred to Miss Trevelyan, as she approached the
door, that her sister-in-law was not precisely now in
the same position as when she was twenty and the
blacksmith's daughter. She had been Roger Trevelyan's wife for nine years, and had seen, in a way,
something of the world. She had even, as Beatrice
had vaguely heard, been considered worthy of the
notice of Lady Grandmaison, who was no contemptible
chaperon; so that there was at least a possibility that
Mrs. Trevelyan knew how to defend herself. Beatrice
fortified herself by recalling Lady Charlton's pitying
mention of the young woman's ignorance and frightened

looks; but, to be sure, it was a long time since then, and a woman, especially when she is married, learns a great deal in nine years.

It was thus, with a little excitement, that Miss Trevelyan entered at the gates, which amused her by their pretension of shutting in the pretty lawn and pleasant garden. It had the air of a house in the suburbs, but notwithstanding, it was far from being a contemptible house. The visitor was conducted into the drawing-room by a maid, who declared it essential to ask whether master was able to see her before leading her to Roger's sick room, and who was not moved by hearing that she was Miss Trevelyan. "I'll ask, and let you know, ma'am, directly," said the incorruptible attendant; and Beatrice came in with a little sense of astonishment into the pretty room which Stanfield had furnished for his daughter. Already it struck her that there must be somewhere a ruler in the house, when her own air of command had so little effect. The drawing-room had something of the deserted look, which so soon betrays the presence of another domestic centre — the sick room, for which it had been abandoned. The fire was low in the grate, and the flowers on the table were beginning to droop, and the blinds were half drawn over the pleasant window where Agnes had been used to sit at work. At the first glance, Miss Trevelyan had supposed there was nobody there, but after a moment she perceived little Walter, coiled up in an easy chair, with a book in his arms. The child was altogether absorbed in his book, and felt no lack; but yet he looked a little forlorn, all by himself in the room, like a child whose father was sick, and who was suffering a momentary neglect in consequence. He did not observe the stranger till she had come in and begun to move about the room, and throw curious looks at everything, not perceiving him, for her part — for, to be sure, all the Trevelyans were a little short-sighted; and then, of a sudden, he raised upon her two broad brown luminous eyes — eyes that had no imperfection of vision, that did not belong to the Trevelyans, but were derived directly, without any question, from the blacksmith. The sight of those eyes made upon Beatrice an impression something like that of a curtain drawn aside in the partially lighted room. The silence and dimness suddenly became possessed of a soul, and looked at her and asked what she did there.

When Miss Trevelyan had got over the first effect of this look, she made an effort to recollect the child's name, and happily succeeded. "Are you Walter?" she asked, holding out her hand to him. "Come and speak to me. I am your Aunt Beatrice." Walter uncoiled himself slowly, and came down from his chair, still embracing his book in one arm. He came towards her slowly, making his investigations. Politeness required that he should respond, but the child was surprised and partly suspicious, and did not know what reply to make.

"I have come to see your papa," said Beatrice. "Come and speak to me. Have you never heard of your aunt?" She spoke a little sharply, as was natural; for besides that she never had been "one for children," it was a little irritating to observe how slowly Walter made his approach.

"Yes," said Walter, "I have heard of you; but I never knew you were coming here. Is it because papa

is so ill? When I have asked mamma if I should
ever see you, she said she did not think so. Shall I
run and tell mamma?"

"No," said Miss Trevelyan; "come here, and let
me look at you. I want to see if you are like any
one. The true Trevelyans all resemble each other."

"Are there any false Trevelyans?" said Walter.
"I know who I am like — I am like grandpapa; at
least Madelon says so, and the other servants, and all
the men at the forge."

"You are not in the least like your grandpapa; your
face is quite strange to me," said Beatrice, sharply;
and then she stopped short, and grew red. No doubt
it was the blacksmith whom he resembled; and Miss
Trevelyan felt herself shudder. The child stood looking
at her with those large brown eyes, soft and im-
penetrable, in which there seemed to lurk a certain
humour and irony, and a hundred things beside, which
she could not explain to herself. She did not know
whether he was secretly smiling at her, or looking
through and through her; and the ox-eyes had an
extraordinary effect upon her mind in spite of herself.
What if, perhaps, these were the mother's eyes? She
pushed him away from her with some energy, and
turned her face to the door instead. "Is your father
very ill?" she said; "he is not confined to bed, is he?
I wonder what preparation can be necessary before he
sees his sister. It is very bad taste to keep me here."

"Perhaps papa is having his dinner," said Walter.
"He does not have his dinner with us; or perhaps
baby is there, and has to be taken away."

These explanations were uttered so quietly that
Beatrice could not but look at him again. He was

5*

perfectly composed and abstract, regarding the facts
of the life with which he was acquainted as the natural
order of affairs; and in the meantime he held his book
fast in one arm, and gave a furtive look at it by times;
though the rules of politeness inculcated by Giovanni
of Sorrento, forbade him to read so long as the visitor
was there, and made any claims upon his attention.
He was not a picturesque child, with floating curls or
careful costume, but there was something in his eyes
which took the words out of Beatrice's lips. She felt
that he restrained her as he stood opposite looking at
her, preventing her from examining the room, and
forming her opinion of its mistress by the trifles about.
She was even glad when the maid came back again to
relieve her from the scrutiny of this open-eyed boy.
And Beatrice drew all her forces together as she went
upstairs. If the mother was like the child, the chances
were that she had here a foeman worthy of her steel;
and it was with this feeling that Miss Trevelyan
entered her brother's sick room, where he was awaiting
her alone.

It was one of Roger's bad days; for one thing, all
was cloudy and dull outside, and the damp weather
affected his breathing, and the heavy atmosphere
oppressed his mind. Nobody had come near him all
the day, not even the doctor, who was not now in
daily attendance; and he had got tired of Agnes, who
had little that was new to say, and tired of hearing
her read, as was natural. He had been amusing himself playing with the two babies, but the result had
been an unlucky little tumble on the part of baby the
elder, which made her cry, and awoke a sympathetic
scream from the other little unconscious creature; and

they had both been sent away in disgrace. Then he had been disappointed with his early invalid dinner; and his annoyance over, that brought back to his mind the still more serious and bitter discontent which was not unnatural to his circumstances — his impatience at finding himself an invalid, shut up and nursed, and obliged to take care of himself, at an age when other men were in the fulness of their strength. Poor Roger! it was hard to blame him for a petulance so natural. And then, when his sister's visit was announced to him, the name of Beatrice brought matters to a climax. What did she want here, coming spying on his privacy after she had refused to do anything for him — or, at least, had failed to do anything for him, which came to the same thing? No doubt she had come to inspect and make a study of his weak condition, and all the disadvantages of his lot. He glanced round upon the room in which he was sitting, which, in its way, was a very pretty room, but very different, as was to be expected, from the stately chambers at Trevelyan — which, indeed, was a house far too magnificent for the fallen fortunes of the family; and gave orders to admit Miss Trevelyan, with a peevish impatience.

"You need not take the trouble to go up-stairs to your mistress," he said to the maid; "she is coming down directly. Ask Miss Trevelyan to come up here."

And thus it was without Agnes's knowledge that Beatrice entered the sick room.

Miss Trevelyan was deeply touched when she saw her brother, pale and feeble, in his dressing-gown, sitting by the fire. He had the shrunken look of a man with whom affairs were very serious, and from whose wan face and weary limbs suffering had taken all the roundness of life.

"My dear Roger, I am very sorry to see you looking so poorly," she said, as she sat down by his side; and, indeed, the shock was so great that Beatrice grew a shade paler than usual, which was saying something, as she never had any complexion to speak of — and with difficulty kept from falling the tears that rose to her eyes.

"No, I am no great things," said Roger. "I suppose you've come to see the rights of it? If I stood in anybody's way, you might carry good news to them; but then the misfortune is, that I don't stand in anybody's way——"

"Don't speak like that," said Miss Trevelyan. "I know you have had a very serious illness, but now that you are able to be up, you'll make progress. Are you sure you have good advice? I would not trust to a village doctor in such a case. Wouldn't it be best for you to go to Nice, or somewhere, and shun the winter? I should think that would be the thing to do."

"On the contrary, that fellow Farington sent me home," said Roger. "I don't know what he meant by it. If there had been anyone waiting for my shoes, I might have thought it was done with a bad meaning. No, they don't say anything to me about the winter — all they recommend is quiet; and you may imagine," he added, bitterly, "I have that here."

"Yes, indeed!" said Miss Trevelyan. "I am sure I only wish I knew anything to suggest. Couldn't you be moved to town, for instance? You know we have no house now, but only hire one for the season, and, in consequence, I cannot offer——"

"No," said Roger, with a laugh; "if you could have offered, you would have taken good care not to make the suggestion. It's very mild at Trevelyan, but it does not occur to you to ask me there."

"Roger, dear, you know as well as I do," said Miss Trevelyan, with real distress, "I never go to Trevelyan myself when I can help it. You know what sort of people Sir Roger collects there."

"I don't see that matters much to me," said the invalid; "there's plenty of room. As for the society of a lot of sporting men, I don't see that it could harm me much, and it has always a chance to be amusing. But when a thing turns up that you really could do, then you begin to see the objections. That is like all my friends — they'd be glad to do for me everything I don't want; but they take precious good care not to say a word about anything that would really be of service. By-the-way, I oughtn't to say all," said Roger, with sudden compunction; "there's that good fellow, Stanfield, though I've behaved like a beast to him; and then there's Agnes's friend, Lady Grandmaison, who has done what you are sorry you can't do — offered us a house in town to be near the doctor; but then," said Roger, willingly sacrificing his own pride for the moment for the sake of aggravating his sister, "that is not for me, but for my wife's sake."

"Lady Grandmaison has offered you *her* house!" cried Beatrice, with unfeigned astonishment; and there gleamed across her mind a splendid vision of Belgrave-square which took away her breath.

"Well, it is not precisely her house," said Roger,

"it is her sister's house, who died, you know; but, all
the same, it's a charming little place. Only, unfortunately it's my wife's friends and not my own who
are willing to do something for me; and that's a
thing, you know, that rather goes against a fellow's
pride."

It went so much against Miss Trevelyan's pride
that her pale face flushed, and the puckers grew in her
forehead. "If I had anything of my own, or could do
anything!" she said. "But, at least, there are some
people in the world who will do something for me. If
you should like to go to town, I will find means to get
you a house."

Roger laughed. "Thank you," he said; "I'll go
to Lady Grandmaison's if I go anywhere. You don't
say, come to Trevelyan where it is mild, you know.
That is precisely what I say — anything I don't want,
or that is impracticable — but for something that I
should like, and which is in your power——"

In spite of herself Beatrice grew agitated, and lost
her usual composure. "Roger," she said, "to show you
how much I am willing to do, I will give up all my
engagements for the winter, and go down with you to
Trevelyan and be your nurse, if you like. I have a
great many engagements, and some of them might be
of great consequence to me," she continued, unable to
contemplate such a sacrifice even in this moment of
excitement without a movement of regret; "but I will
give them up if you say the word, and go down with
you to Trevelyan, and do all in my power to make
you comfortable."

"My dear Beatrice," said Roger, who was amused,
though not in a very amiable way, by her excitement,

"where did you learn to take care of a sick man? I
don't doubt your power, you know, to do anything you
take in hand to do; but that's unnecessary. Agnes can
make me comfortable. It's her business, and I don't
think she'd like to give it up, even to you."

Again Miss Trevelyan grew crimson to the roots of
her hair. "You know Trevelyan is not fit to receive
a — a family," she said. "You know it would be impossible to take down a whole household, nurses and
everything. You know papa could not be expected.
But for you, Roger, if you like, and even for the little
boy——"

Roger laughed, but the sound of his laugh was
displeasing to his sister's ears. "I am no great things,"
he said; "I cannot be sure, when I think it over, that
I've done my duty by Agnes, or fulfilled her expectations; but, by Jove, I'm not such a shabby beast as
you would make me out. Go off to Trevelyan with
you and accept a half reconciliation, and leave my wife
behind me as if she was not good enough to go there!
By Jove, there's nobody like a woman for meanness;
I and — the little boy; poor little Watty. If I die,
I hope that youngster will have a soul above deserting
his mother. Leave Agnes behind, who is worth the
whole set of us twice over! It's like a spiteful woman's
idea — but, by Jove, Beatrice, I thought better of
you."

Miss Trevelyan had never before heard herself
called a spiteful woman, and, indeed, had not investigated her own ideas, nor considered what sort of
proposal she was making; and even at that moment,
amid the shame and confusion with which she felt herself covered, a certain satisfaction in her brother, who,

after all, was better than herself, mixed in her humiliation. Though he was cruel in his indignation, she thought better of him as she made a struggle to reply.

"All that is very fine, Roger. I am not saying a word against Mrs. Trevelyan; but, of course, if Sir Roger made up his mind to receive her at all, it would be my duty to see that she was properly received; and if she came down with you, an invalid, and requiring all her care, how would it be possible to introduce her, and have people to see her, as would be necessary? It is all very well to think of — of your wife; but, at the same time, you ought to remember," said Beatrice, suddenly breaking down and begging the question, "that there is also — some — respect — owing to me——"

It was this moment of all others that Agnes chose for coming into the room — Agnes, pale and quiet, out of the nursery, where she had been soothing her little children, and with that look of preoccupation in her eyes which made her appear impervious to lesser troubles. She came in thus upon Miss Trevelyan, who was flushed and vexed, and almost ready to cry, convicted of meanness, and humbled from the heights of her superiority. Beatrice got up instinctively as her unknown sister-in-law came softly into the room. At the first glance, the new-comer showed no signs of beauty, and it was impossible to imagine anything more simple than her dress, which was grey, of Roger's favourite tint. She had had no warning of the visitor, and came in without any thought of finding a stranger there. Miss Trevelyan drew her short-sighted eyes together as she gazed at this woman, whose happier fate

she had been indignant at, and against whom, in her
soul, she felt such a stir of dislike and opposition.
The idea she had formed of Agnes in her own mind
was so different that she gave a little start of consternation when she saw the soft negligent grace of the
advancing figure, the small graceful head stooping under its weight of hair, the look altogether unconscious
of, and indifferent to, criticism.

"This is not Mrs. Trevelyan?" she said unawares,
under her breath, with an inquiring glance at her brother; and Roger could not deny himself the natural
triumph.

"Yes, this is Mrs. Trevelyan," he said, with a
laugh, rousing Agnes out of her abstraction. "Come
here and make acquaintance with my sister, Agnes.
It is rather late in the day, but still it is better now
than never. This is my sister Beatrice — my only
sister, whom you have heard of; she has come to see
what she can do for me now I'm ill. It is a pity she
had not thought of it a little sooner; and to make
acquaintance," said Roger, with a savage signification
incomprehensible to his wife, "with your little boy —"

Agnes was surprised, but she had the composure
of a woman who is in her own house, and is too
much absorbed in her own anxieties to be disturbed
by the entrance of any stranger. A slight colour
came to her cheek, but it was nothing to the fiery flush
which burned on that of Miss Trevelyan. There was
still in her eyes the shy, sweet appeal of her youth to
the kindness of her new acquaintance, but that did not
in the least resemble the angry embarrassment which
made Beatrice awkward for perhaps the first time in
her life. It was Agnes who held out her hand and gave

the graceful gracious greeting which at once placed the
two in their fit position — though not by any means
in the position which Beatrice considered natural.

"I am very glad to see you," Mrs. Trevelyan said;
"you are very welcome. I am sure it will do Roger
good. It was very kind of you to come."

That was all, — but it was enough to make Beatrice feel that never more could she hold her head high
in imaginary superiority over the blacksmith's daughter.
She took her seat again, no way converted or humbled,
in the amiable sense of the word; but mortified and
humiliated, which is a condition of mind not favourable to moral improvement; and Roger laughed harshly
as he sank back into his easy chair. The only one
who was unmoved was Agnes, whose sole perplexity
was as to whether or not she should order a room to
be prepared for Miss Trevelyan; — and in the meantime the October afternoon began to darken, and it was
time for Beatrice to return to the Hall.

"Roger is obliged to dine early since he has been
an invalid," said Agnes, absorbed in the cares natural
to the mistress of the house; "but, if you will pardon
me for leaving you, I will see about getting your room
ready, and about dinner. We all keep early hours
since Roger has been ill — but after to-day ———"

"Oh, pardon me; I am staying at the Hall," said
Miss Trevelyan; "indeed, I must go now to get there
before dark. I will come back again to-morrow, Roger,
and by that time I hope you will have thought over
what I have said."

"If that is all, you may save yourself the trouble,"
said Roger, somewhat rudely; "after what you have

seen, I should have thought it unnecessary for me to
say any more."

"Perhaps you may change your mind," said Miss
Trevelyan; "anyhow, I will come again to-morrow.
Good-bye for to-day."

"I am sorry you will not stay," said Agnes, who
paid no attention to this. "Could not we send for
your things to the Hall? It must be solitary there all
by yourself; and I am sure it would do Roger good to
have you with him. Don't you think you could make
up your mind to stay?"

"Thank you, no," said Beatrice; "I am very much
obliged to you, I am sure. Don't take the trouble to
come downstairs. Pray don't take the trouble; I can
find my way out quite well by myself." This was
said while going downstairs, for Agnes persisted in
following her visitor, to Miss Trevelyan's amazement
and contempt. She began to think, after all, that her
first idea was correct, and that Agnes's appearance was
a delusion. "I suppose it is considered civil in her
condition of life," she said to herself with a sense of
recovery. That was all she was thinking of on leaving
her brother's sick room; but sadder thoughts were in
the heart of his wife.

"Miss Trevelyan," said Agnes, when they had
nearly reached the door; "stop a moment, I want to
speak to you. Tell me how you think he is looking.
You saw him in town before he had this attack; and I
get so anxious that I don't know what to think. Tell
me, do you think he is very much changed?"

And then they stood facing each other — the one
anxious, the other disconcerted — while Agnes, who
was utterly incapable of concerning herself at that

moment about any one's opinion of her, stood trying eagerly to read Miss Trevelyan's judgment on Roger in her eyes. Even then it was not Roger that occupied Beatrice, but the eyes which were thus anxiously fixed upon her; they were not like Walter's. That was at least one comfort. If the boy ever came to be Sir Walter Trevelyan, nobody could say it was from his mother that he had taken his remarkable eyes.

"Indeed I can't say," she answered, coldly; "I suppose you have a good doctor; his opinion must be of a great deal more importance than mine. Thank you, good-bye! I am sorry to have given you the trouble of opening the door."

CHAPTER VII.

The Valley of the Shadow.

Roger had another attack that night; of course it was not his sister's visit that caused it; and he was indignant, even in the midst of his sufferings, when the doctor asked if he had been agitated or disturbed during the day. "Stuff!" the patient said from his bed, seeing that Agnes hesitated. "I have seen my sister; but there was nothing to agitate any one in that; not even a poor wretch with a heart like mine." But whatever it was that had caused it, the enemy was there once more assaulting the feeble frame which had not been permitted time enough to gain any strength. The house on the Green was kept in a state of terrible anxiety all night. Downstairs Stanfield sat sad and silent, overawed by the shadow of Death that hovered over the house, waiting, if perhaps he could be of any use; and in the nursery Walter woke up in the middle of the night to see the lights still burning, and Madelon crying by the fire over the baby, which wailed for the mother who could not come; and a sense of disturbance and desolation came over the child's mind, and kept him awake. All this happened while Beatrice was reposing peacefully at the Hall, encountering in her dreams this new figure of Mrs. Trevelyan, and snubbing her at leisure. Perhaps, had she accepted the invitation of Agnes, this night's watch together might have made a bond of union between the two; but, unfortunately, Beatrice this time, without any interposition of others, had taken once more the wrong turning in the doubtful and difficult path of life.

When the morning came in wintry and pale, it threw light upon a set of very wan and scared faces in the house on the Green. On Stanfield, down below, still listening intently for news from the sick room, and rousing himself, with all the colour quenched out of his cheeks, as he heard the doctor come downstairs; on little Walter above, turning a little white face to the entering light, knowing, and yet not knowing, how momentous a business was going on in the house, frightened and ready to cry, without being sure what he cried about; and on Agnes, pale also as the daylight, worn out and sick at heart, sitting by the bedside, where the patient lay in a doubtful sleep, "in no immediate danger," as the doctor said. The crisis was over, and he was not likely to die now; but Mrs. Trevelyan knew what that doubtful sentence meant, and knew that her husband's shattered frame was not able to bear another such assault which might come any day. She heard the baby wailing upstairs, but she

could not leave the bedside, where, notwithstanding the
postponement of the sentence, she seemed to see Death
slowly approaching to share her watch. That hopelessness was more terrible to bear than the certainty
itself, when it should be accomplished. When all was
over, it would be but herself who would have to bear
it; but, in the meantime, it was Roger — Roger, with
his mind all living, and young, and impatient, who
must wake up presently and face the fact that he was
going to die.

This was what Agnes was thinking of as she sat
in the absolute silence of the sick room with the pale
morning light revealing the pallor of her face and the
disorder of everything about, which gave token of the
dreadful night they had come through. As for what
was going to happen to her, the widowhood that was so
near, her mind did not touch upon that. It seemed to
her as if nothing mattered that should happen *after*.
Even in the pain of anticipation, her thoughts rushed
forward and would have embraced any expedient to
save Roger from that waiting and looking for death.
It appeared to her as if she would have been thankful
had he died then — that moment, in his sleep, and so
have been saved the hopeless weariness of the waiting;
but when that thought had passed through her mind,
nature awoke, all startled and afraid, and she got up
to lean over him and make sure that he was still
breathing. This was how the miserable morning which
brought no hope passed over Agnes. If she had been
the sufferer, she could have taken it all very bravely
and sweetly; and indeed Roger himself, though he was
of a nature different from his wife, met the darkness
like a man. What was insupportable was to sit by

and know that he must bear it, and be unable to help or to save. But then that was an anguish which one time or other befalls most women; and Mrs. Trevelyan was aware, if that had been any comfort to her, that there was nothing extraordinary or out of nature in the cross she was called upon to bear.

All these thoughts that were going through her mind, absorbed her so entirely, that almost for the moment in thinking of Roger she had forgotten him, when she was suddenly roused by a movement he made, and looking up hastily saw that he was awake and looking at her. He was so worn out, that all personal feeling seemed to have left him in his weakness; and upon her whose mind was so agitated by fear and pity for him, he looked with smiling composed eyes which she could scarcely bear.

"Well, yes, it has been a hard bout," said Roger, "and I suppose I could not stand many more; but it's always something to have a little ease. What o'clock is it? I don't suppose you have had much rest to-night, any more than I."

"It is seven o'clock," said Agnes; "you have had two hours' sleep; that will do you good, Roger; but you must not talk — everything depends upon keeping quiet, the doctor says."

"Never mind what the doctor says," said Roger. "When a man is come to this he ought to be left free to do what he likes. We are not going to be dismal for that. Sit down here and let us have a little talk."

Agnes did as she was told, with her heart disturbed between fears for him, and fears of thwarting him. It seemed hard to shut her ears to what he had to say to her — if, indeed, he had something to say; and she was longing that he should speak and say something, which, to sustain her in the long and lonely future, she could lay up in her heart.

"Poor soul, how pale she looks!" said Roger, "it is almost harder upon you than upon me; but at all events you are at home, and that is always something. What did you think of Beatrice last night?"

"Think of her?" said Agnes, vaguely. Her very understanding seemed to have failed her for everything that did not concern himself.

"She was a little put out when she saw you, I can tell you," said Roger, with a faint laugh. "She has never been able to get over the idea that you were of the Blowsibella species. By Jove! when she saw you, it gave her 'a turn,' as Mrs. Stanfield says. By the way," said Roger, whose worn and ghastly countenance looked so entirely out of accord with this ordinary conversation, "don't have anything to do, nor let the children have anything to do, with that woman. Your father's been taken in, you know — he's just the man to be taken in. But about Bee — it's a great pity she's not married. You have not told me what you think of her looks."

"Roger, dear, I can't see anybody but you," said Agnes. "I can't think of anybody. I used to be very anxious about the first meeting with Miss Trevelyan; but I don't think I had any eyes to see her with last night."

"You did just what you ought to have done, my darling," said Roger. "You made *her* open her eyes at least; and she's got fine eyes in some lights. Look at them next time you see her. Poor Bee; after all,

I believe there is some good in her, if she had been trained as she ought. She said she'd take me to Trevelyan, and nurse me, Agnes — and she such a one for society! There was kindness in that."

"Yes," said Agnes, whose heart sank within her at the idea of any one sharing her cares of love, "but you know you are used to me. I don't want any assistance. I could not be comfortable if any one was nursing you but myself."

Roger laughed faintly once more. Even at that moment it rather pleased him to make his wife jealous. "Don't be afraid," he said; "I don't look very able to go to Trevelyan, do I? and as for Bee, I daresay she has changed her mind already. Tell her the baby is Beatrice, when she comes — it's a favourite name in our family; she'll be pleased, I should think. Am I to have anything? Physic of course, and some slops after it, I suppose. By Jove! Agnes, it's a little hard upon a man at my age to be brought to this!"

"Oh, it's hard, very hard!" cried Agnes. "I dare not think of it, Roger. It must be God's will, but somehow that does not seem to make it easier to bear."

"Yes," said Roger, "some fellows are treated very differently — good health and everything in the world they can set their face to. But I suppose it's God's will, as you say. Give me the beef tea — it was atrocious stuff they sent me up yesterday; and now, if you won't talk any more, I think I shall go to sleep."

And so he did, and left Agnes watching, a prey to all those terrible thoughts that are born of suffering. Perhaps, if all this had happened a few years sooner, she could have borne it with a more Christian mind, as she had borne the death of her babies, thinking grievous sweet thoughts of the angels in heaven, who behold the face of the Father day and night. But middle age had come upon her before its time, and all the questions that rend the heart of man. She could not understand why it was that all the world was waking round her to life and hope, while Roger opened his eyes only to contemplate, drawing always nearer, the face of death; while at the same time, so many people were left in the world who would have been glad to die, and who kept alive only because they could not help it; and so many more who were a burden to the world, and whose end would be a relief to human nature. As she sat in the silence, watching her husband's sleep, she turned over all these things in her mind, in an agony which was not impious only because it was so real; for in her very doubt, demanding in her anguish an account of what her Father was doing, she was so sure of that Father, so certain that it must be right, somehow, if He would but bow down from those heavens, which were so terribly vague and distant, and explain. And then there came the other wonder, almost as great, to see Roger, so well aware of his position, and yet so perfectly like himself, and so little thoughtful, to all appearance, of that preparation for death which Agnes had been accustomed to hear of all her life as the necessary preface and accompaniment of dying. Mr. Freke came often, and read the prayers for the sick at his bedside; but then Mr. Freke, who was also so candid about his difficulties, increased the doubt rather than the faith of the anxious wife; and when the prayers had been said, she knew very well how they all relapsed into such conversation as that which Roger had been carrying on before he fell asleep. And what, then, did it all mean? She was staggered in her ideas by this first encounter with the reality; and at the same time she was no spectator, whose dismay and wonder might have passed off in words, but was so intimately and terribly concerned. She knew that Roger had thought but little in his lifetime of the serious questions of religion, and she knew it would be impossible to rouse him to think of them now, even at the risk of bringing his days to a summary conclusion by the excitement of an appeal to his conscience. And Agnes knew that the patience and gentleness with which he was regarding death, arose more from the subduing of all his faculties than from any special faith; and that Roger would die as he had lived, accepting everything without any thought or question, taking his religion as a thing outside of himself, with which his own heart and mind had next to nothing to do. She was too full of the tender prejudices of love, too full of the awe of nature, to say all this to herself in so many words; but it passed through her mind vaguely, as she sat by Roger's bedside; for up to this moment she, like all others who have never learned by experience, had been of opinion that a deathbed, of itself, must change the aspect of everything, and make a visible and conscious path between earth and heaven.

Roger had a long sleep, and woke up better; and his wife was able to leave him to see after the children, and especially the little wailing baby, which had sought its mother all through the lingering night. Agnes had gone downstairs to give her necessary orders when Beatrice arrived from the Hall, as she had promised; and it was Mrs. Trevelyan's disagreeable business to keep her sister-in-law from proceeding at once to the sick room. She stopped her in the little hall, where Miss Trevelyan would fain have passed her by with a civil salutation; but even Beatrice's stately air had no effect upon Agnes.

"Come in here," she said, opening the door of the drawing-room, where little Walter was again seated with his book, looking as if he had never moved from his position since Beatrice left him the previous day. "You cannot go upstairs at present; let me speak to you here."

"Why cannot I go upstairs?" said Beatrice, naturally defiant. She thought the poor-spirited wife was jealous of Roger's sister, and that "a due respect for herself" made it necessary for her at once to enter the lists and defend her right.

"Because Roger has been very ill all night," said Agnes; "so ill that the doctor feared the worst. The crisis is over now, and he has a little repose; but he is so weak that I dare not let you see him. Pray don't be vexed; I am as sorry to say so as you can be to hear it. Indeed I dare not let him be disturbed."

"And who imagined I would disturb him?" said Beatrice. "Do you forget that I am his sister, Mrs. Trevelyan? He was my brother before he was your husband. The rights of a wife may be paramount, even when she has brought nothing but harm; but I have yet to learn that they extend so far as to banish her husband's relations from his sick bed. I have come to see Roger, and I beg you to let me pass without any more words."

"I beg your pardon," said Agnes; "indeed, I want to banish no one from him — I asked you to stay, on the contrary; but the doctor thinks he was excited yesterday. Pardon me! — indeed I cannot help it; — he must have absolute quiet. I am not allowed to let him talk, even to me."

"Even to you!" said Beatrice, with a long-drawn panting breath of indignation and scorn. To be sure, the circumstances were a little hard, and regarding them from her point of view, it was easy enough to imagine that all this was an ingenious trick of the jealous wife. "I have business with my brother," Miss Trevelyan continued. "He expressed a desire yesterday to go to Trevelyan, and I offered to go with him, and nurse him. I must see him to arrange about the journey. I thought yesterday it might be necessary to write to Sir Roger; but as affairs are so urgent and quiet so necessary, I will take the responsibility upon myself. He will get better all the quicker in his native air, and in his father's house."

"Here he is in his own house," said Agnes — and then she was ashamed of herself for having thought of making a defence at such a moment. "He is scarcely able to move in his bed, much less to undertake a journey," she said, with tears in her eyes. "I wish you would believe that I speak with no meaning beyond my words. Roger has been very ill all night; so ill, that we thought he would die."

"And I suppose it is I that am supposed to be the cause?" said Miss Trevelyan, indignantly.

"No, I do not think so," said Agnes — "and Roger, in the midst of his pain, said 'No'; but the doctor gave me orders that he was to see no one. If you will stay with us I shall be very glad; and then,

when he is better, you can see him; or if you will wait
till the doctor comes — —"

"Yes," said Beatrice, "I will wait till the doctor
comes. Are you sure it was not your fault that my
brother was agitated yesterday? You were angry because he wanted to go to Trevelyan, and be among
his own people; and you fretted and found fault with
the poor fellow, who could not escape from you till you
brought on a crisis. I feel as sure of it as though I had
seen it; and then you prevent me from going to him.
But one cannot shut out the devoted wife from the sick
bed, even though she may be killing her husband in
the dark. Yes, Mrs. Trevelyan, I will wait till the
doctor comes."

Agnes did not make any reply to this unexpected
accusation. She bowed her head gently without speaking,
and went away, leaving her visitor in undisturbed possession of the room. What Beatrice had said was so
wild and out of reason, that it made no impression
upon the occupied mind of Mrs. Trevelyan. She went
back into her own thoughts, her many cares and
anxieties about Roger, without even recollecting, after
a little, that downstairs a hostile stranger was sitting,
waiting to get admission, and to bring an obstinate
personal will and human rivalry to disturb the tranquillity of the sick chamber, which might so soon be a
chamber of death.

———

CHAPTER VIII.

The End.

"DID you tell her what we had called the baby?" said Roger. "Poor Bee! Why would not the doctor let her come upstairs? I daresay she is furious at you and everybody. Write her a little note, Agnes, and tell her to come to-morrow, before she leaves the Hall, and bid me good-bye. She's ten years older than I am," said Roger, "yet she'll last, no doubt, ten years longer than I shall. And there's Sir Roger, you know. After all, though he's my father, he's not such a very valuable member of society; and yet it is I who have to go, and they stay."

"Dear Roger, don't say that," said Agnes, as well as she could speak in her choked voice, "it is you who will find the true life first — the greatest happiness must be for you."

"Ah! so they say," said Roger; "I'm not going against it, but only it's odd, you know. I don't see, for my part, why there should be such a difference made. I am not much good in this world, but I am more good than Sir Roger is, so far as any man can see. But indeed, after all, to go to the bottom of things, I am not so sure of that. Most likely you'll get on better without me. You'll have your father, Agnes, to give you a hand — and then there's the boy —"

"Roger, don't, if you have any pity," said the weeping wife.

"Pity, my darling? And then you are young, and

there's no telling what may happen," said Roger drearily. "I'll be happy, I suppose, and I shall not mind — I am not going against that, but only it's queer, you know. Most fellows at my age — — but it's no good thinking of that. Be sure you send for Beatrice to bid me good-bye. Have you got your writing things here? Then write now, and let me see what you say."

Agnes obeyed without any remonstrance, for even the doctor's prohibition was of less importance than Roger's wish, to which, for the brief time he had to remain in the world, everything was to bow. Though, to be sure, it was a little difficult for her to address Miss Trevelyan. She did not feel as if she could begin with the usual formula, or address as "dear" the woman who had insulted and scorned her in the time of her need; and yet there was no resentment nor bitterness in her heart; and, after all, it was very simple what she had to say: —

"Roger is anxious to see you and say good-bye, as he says. I am very sorry the doctor opposed your coming upstairs. It grieved me much to seem to stand between you and your brother, but it was not my fault. I beseech you come and see him, and bid him good-bye. He is not able to go to Trevelyan or anywhere else at present; but when he is strong enough, do not think I will oppose anything that gives my husband pleasure. I hope you will forgive me my unwilling rudeness, and come, as Roger wishes, to bid him good-bye.

"AGNES TREVELYAN."

"Let me see it," said Roger; "you write in an odd sort of way, Agnes. Did you and she have a shindy downstairs? She don't understand, that's what it is. As for going to Trevelyan, don't vex yourself. I let Beatrice talk, but I never meant it; and as for being strong enough — there, fold it up and send it away. Sir Roger wanted to have Walter, to pay for his schooling, you know, and bring him up; but I never had a chance to speak to you about it. Don't cry out. There never was anything decided, and I don't mean to do anything about it now."

"Do not let us talk of it," said Agnes, who had with difficulty restrained her cry of amazement and anguish; "we can talk about everything when you are better. Shall I read to you now?"

"Oh! yes, you may read," said Roger, "if I don't listen, perhaps I can go to sleep; that last is the best thing I can do. It saves thinking, and there's nothing very pleasant to think about. Is Freke coming to-night?"

"Yes, some time before the evening service," said Agnes; "but you must not talk any more."

"No," said Roger — "I don't know what's the good of his coming. He doesn't seem to know any more than I do. It's all very well to say a thing's odd when it comes into one's head, but I don't see the good of a clergyman, if that's all he can say to a man. He ought to know better what he's about. The doctor, you know, don't talk like that; and yet he's not a prig, like some of them. Where's that little shaver, Agnes? You can have him up, if you like; I don't think I want to hear you read."

Agnes went to ring the bell without making any
answer, and Roger went on —

"He's a queer little shaver, that; he's neither like
you nor me. I believe it is Stanfield he resembles. I
can't say I liked it when I noticed it first; but if he
lives to be Sir Walter, that will be all the better for
him. If he doesn't live, you'll have no claim upon
them, Agnes. The two little girls can never do any
good, you know. You had better take care of Watty;
he will always give you a power over them. What's
the good of crying? I see very well you're crying,
though you turn your back to me. Look here, old
boy, come and tell me what you're about."

"Nothing, papa," said Walter, coming to the bedside with wistful looks. His father's pallor, and the
wild eyes, which seemed to be set in such wide circles,
and looked so unnaturally translucent, rather frightened
the little fellow; but he did not yield to his tremor.
He came up bravely, and stood by the bedside. "Are
you very ill, papa?" he asked, forcing himself to come
nearer.

"Rather," said Roger. "I was ill all night, you
know. I'm tired, and that is the worst of it. Is there
anybody with you downstairs?"

"Nobody but Madelon, and little Agnes, and the
baby," said the boy; "they were lonely up in the
nursery. Papa, do you think it will be long before
you can come downstairs?"

"I don't know," said Roger, with a sigh; and then
he added with a little fretfulness, "It was a very odd
thing of Madelon to take the babies downstairs."

"But, papa, they were so lonely up in the nursery,"
said the child, unaware how sad a picture he was

drawing of the sorrowful household, disorganized and unsettled by the one absorbing interest which left no eyes nor thoughts for anything else; "and then they were frightened, and came down for company. It is cheerfuller downstairs."

"All the same, she had no right to go," said Roger. "Agnes, you should see to these things. Suppose Beatrice were to come, and find the room occupied so. What had she got to be frightened for, I wonder? I never could make out what you brought that thickhead with you for; it was a piece of nonsense. Because I am ill, I don't see why you should let everything go to the bad. Send her off upstairs."

"Go, Walter, and tell her to go back to the nursery," said his mother. "Roger, dear, if you talk now, you will not be able to talk to Mr. Freke."

"Oh, hang Freke!" said Roger. "I tell you, he don't know his business, Agnes. There is nothing like parsons for that. Either they pull you up short, and are sure of everything, or else they give in to you, and go further than you do. I am sick of it all. It's hard to have to do with a man that can't answer for you and take the responsibility. There, you can read a little now; but I should like to know what Madelon had to be frightened about, and why she took the liberty of going downstairs."

Agnes had to stop with a look the explanation which was on Walter's lips, in his eagerness that justice might be done — which was to the effect that Madelon was afraid, because she had heard mysterious tappings at the window, and movements about the house, such as always happened when anybody was going to die. In the heat of his desire to do Madelon

justice, Walter had forgotten that there was anything
more than a vague general prophecy of evil in the fact
that somebody might be going to die. Agnes had already learned some of Madelon's terrors, and knew
what her boy was going to say, and she sent him away
with quickened steps, and took her book and began to
read. It was a novel she was reading, strange as that
may seem to some people; and in this terrible moment,
when her heart was sinking within her under all kinds
of sorrows, it was the agonies of a young girl who had
quarrelled with her lover that the poor wife had to
read. What could she do? There are women, no
doubt, who could have been brave enough to confine
themselves at such a time to books of a character more
in accordance with a death-bed; but Agnes was a woman, humble and tender, with a sense of the impossi-
bilities and of the cravings of nature. She knew, even
if she could have done it, that it would have been no
good to read religious books to Roger, and to try at
that late period to interest him in them. She read the
Bible to him when she could, but that was only now
and then; and therefore, though she suffered horribly
as she did it, and those trivial fictitious woes seemed
to her miserable and childish beyond expression, in
face of her own, she went on reading her novel. It
amused the sufferer by times, and made him forget
himself and his pains and weakness for a moment, now
and then; and though Agnes felt in her heart that
she might have attempted something different, and had
to contend against the thought that she was yielding
to necessity, and not doing her best, she took up her
book, like a martyr, and went on. What could she
do? To have roused him a little, and made him think

tenderly and hopefully of the Father and the Son, and that new world to which he was going, was a desire stronger in her heart than anything else in the world; but in the meantime, all she found it possible to do was to amuse him, and make the precious moments, of which he had now so few, pass more gently. This was all, except praying night and day by a kind of habit, which did not abandon her mind even when she was reading. All the time, as in an undertone, she was praying God for the dying man; and meanwhile, she went on reading the novel about the lovers' quarrel with the steadiest voice. As for Roger, he gave it but a half attention, but at the same time, he was pleased to hear it. Broken thoughts about Beatrice, who was coming to see him, and about Madelon, who was a fool to be frightened, and had no right to take the babies downstairs, alternated in his mind with the story of the pretty pensive young heroine who had quarrelled with her lover; and then in the midst, like a flash of light, would come the sense that all this would come to an end suddenly, and he would be gone — who could tell where? — into the presence of God — to the judgment-throne, which it was so hard to attach his thoughts to; and then a faint sort of wonder about what he believed in would come to his mind, and his thoughts would falter into the Creed, the easiest and simplest statement, "And in Jesus Christ his Son, our Lord." After that the light would go out, as if it had been a lamp in somebody's hand, going past, and he would come back again to the story and the love-quarrel, which Agnes always continued reading with her steady voice. Heaven knows it was an unsatisfactory way to go through one's dying, and by times

the wife's heart contracted with pain, and doubt, and
self-reproach; but those who know best what death-beds
are, will, perhaps, blame Agnes Trevelyan the least.

In the morning Beatrice came, obeying the invitation she had received. Miss Trevelyan had had a
struggle with herself before she did it, but in the end
the better angel conquered. She did not say a word
to Agnes, nor acknowledge her presence except by the
coldest and briefest inclination of the head; but at
heart she did not make any attack upon her sister-in-
law, to aggravate Roger. As for Agnes, she was very
nearly unconscious, so far as she was herself concerned,
and might, indeed, have been subjected to many covert
insults without knowing it. She had forgotten, so far
as a human creature could, that she had a separate
personality at all; and, indeed, by want of nourishment
and want of rest, had attained — as perfect health and
a strong inspiring motive sometimes make possible — a
certain independence of her own bodily power and
senses, and moved about with something of the freedom
of a disembodied creature. Beatrice, who was herself
not incapable of devotion, had anything ever occurred
to her to draw it forth, perceived something of this
without being willing to perceive it, and turned her
back upon her brother's wife, that no sentiment of pity
or sympathy might move her towards the woman whom
she disliked. "If you will write to me as soon as you
are able to be moved, I will make arrangements for
receiving you at Trevelyan," she said to Roger, ignor-
ing, half by force of natural opposition and antagonism,
half because it seemed kind not to be aware how hopeless matters were, the fatal certainty that was written
in every line of her brother's face.

"I shall never go to Trevelyan," said Roger, with a sigh; "it comes too late, like most things. You can tell my father I don't bear him any malice, though he's treated me shabbily. Good-bye, Beatrice. Did Agnes tell you about the baby? I think it's like the Trevelyans, and you might take a little interest in it when it grows up. That's all I've got to say. Don't let Sir Roger bother Agnes. Good-bye! She'll write and tell you if anything happens. I hope you will have a pleasant visit; if it doesn't come to too quick an end through me —"

"I hope it will come to a very quick end through you, and that you'll call me soon to take you to Cornwall. Good-bye, Roger. Take great care, and don't let yourself be disturbed. We'll talk of everything when you get well. Good-bye!" said Beatrice. That was how she thought it best to signify her want of confidence in the wife, who had nothing to do with what they were to talk about; but though she spoke so indifferently, the kiss she gave her brother was long and sad, like a farewell, and she hurried out of the room to conceal the tears that were in her eyes. This time Mrs. Trevelyan did not follow her downstairs; on the contrary, Agnes took her place softly by the bedside. If she had any sense of relief in feeling that her husband was thus left to her tendance without fear of interruption, it was made overwhelming and terrible by the accompanying feeling, that the ties of life were thus dropping off from him, and that now nothing remained to hold him to the world but the most intimate and closest bond of all. She could not ignore, like Beatrice, the certainty that was in Roger's worn and shining eyes.

"You are tired," she said. "I am going to read the Psalms, which you said you liked yesterday, Roger. If you lie quite still, perhaps by-and-by you will get to sleep."

"Presently," said Roger. "There's Beatrice done with. She's the only one I ever cared about — not that she's much to boast of, you know; but it feels a little queer to finish off like this. It's a dismal sort of thing saying good-bye to everybody; I don't know, my darling, how I am to say it to you."

"Oh never, Roger, never!" said Agnes, putting her face down upon the thin hand which she was holding in her own.

"I suppose I shall be happy and not mind," said Roger, with a sigh. "That's what they all say, at least; but it's odd to think of it, you know. Anyhow, I'll be too far gone to know when *you* leave me; and now, if you like, you can get your book."

This was how Roger Trevelyan died — not that day, nor immediately, but before the year was ended — without very much more suffering, but also without any special intensification of feeling, or sense of awakening to the solemn things that lay before him. He made all the responses quite faithfully and humbly, and received all the consolations of the Church, without ever getting beyond the idea that he supposed he should be happy and not mind, and yet that, on the whole, it was strange and a little hard. His soul went out of the world without excitement — not complaining, certainly not afraid, but still a little surprised and at a loss what to make of it. He never made any question about his faith, nor doubted that he should be happy, as he said; but took it for granted, with a com-

posure and simplicity which would have baffled any
spectator of keen religious sensibilities. He died, and
mourning and darkness fell upon the house that all this
time had been so absorbed and preoccupied. And thus
a termination came to the second period of Agnes
Trevelyan's life.

CHAPTER IX.

Public Opinion.

Roger Trevelyan died, and darkness and silence
fell on the house on the Green — the pretty house
which Stanfield, in the first year of her marriage, before any trouble came, had built for his daughter. She
was now mistress, sole mistress of the habitation provided for her by her father's love. The grand complication of her lot had come to an end. It mattered
but little now that Sir Roger Trevelyan's son had married beneath him, that the blacksmith's daughter had
made a match out of her own sphere. Society had nothing further to do with it. Agnes was again in her
native village, supported by her father's bounty; and
those ten momentous years, which embraced all her
independent life, had passed away like a vision. Life
itself is long and weary enough in most cases: it is the
active existence — the portions of life that are worth
calling by that name — which pass away like a tale
that is told.

And, naturally, Windholm and her old friends took
possession of Agnes, who seemed thus thrown back
upon them and left at their mercy. "She never was
took no notice of in the family," Mrs. Rogers said,

7*

who took the lead in the personal discussions of the
village, "and now as *he's* gone, poor gentleman, she's
got nothing to look to. I hope it'll be a warning to
you, all you girls," the moralist continued, with that
fine faculty for improving the occasion which is common to commentators, "never to have anything ado
with *gentlemen*. A many of them's deceivers — and if
they ain't deceivers, they're no good, as is to be seen
in Agnes Stanfield. It ain't for her as I speak, for it
was allays her pride that drew it all on; but if she had
a hope as she was to be made a lady of, and lifted up
over all our heads — and I haven't no doubt in my
mind as that was what she married for — look what it
all comes to. She ain't got a penny as doesn't come
from her poor old father, and never was took no notice
of in the family; for they tell me Miss Trevelyan, as
went to see her brother at the last, warn't not to say
civil to Agnes. She's comed back on her own, with
her little 'uns, as poor Polly Abbott did, her as married the soldier. That's the end of it all. She'll never
be made a lady now-a-days, if she was to live a hundred years."

"But," said one of the younger auditors, "our
John, as works with Mr. Stanfield, says as the boy
will be Sir Walter when his grandfather dies. He says
as that bit of a child is as good as a baronet now poor
Mr. Trevelyan's dead, and he'll have the Hall, and I
don't know what he'll not have — and it stands to
reason as his mother should be my lady —"

"Nothing of the sort," said Mrs. Rogers, indignantly. "You tell him from me to talk about things
as he knows about. I tell you she'll never be my
lady if she was to live to a hundred. No, no; she's

lost her chance, Agnes has. The boy'll be put to school and brought up different, and it ain't a many young men as cares that about their mothers to make ladies of them as was never born to be ladies; even if she rares him, that's to say, and he ain't what I call a strong child; — boys is allays a trouble to rare. When they're babbies it's awful, as my poor Louisa could tell you. No, it's just an example and a warning, that's what it is. If one of mine was to take up with a gentleman, like Agnes Stanfield, I'd break my heart. He hadn't a penny, hadn't Mr. Trevelyan, for Sir Roger would have nothing to say to him, as Mrs. Stanfield herself told me; and all her grand hopes as he'd make a lady of her —"

"But ain't she a lady?" interrupted one of the daughters thus specified. "I never see nobody as looks nicer — and keeps two servants, and a nurse as is furrin'. I'd be content if it was me. If he'd give me a house like Mrs. Trevelyan's, and three servants, and to go to all the parties, and be dressed up like she is, I'd marry the first gentleman as asked me; and Mary Jane thinks the same as me."

"You're two young fools, that's what you are," said the mother. "Go off to your work and don't you answer me. There's my Louisa, as was always considered one of the Windholm beauties, and far better edicated than Agnes Stanfield — but she had too much sense, I can tell you, to have anything to say to the likes of young Trevelyan. She married a man in a comfortable way of business, as could buy them all up; and doing well and thriving, and her husband as hearty as hearty, and six as pretty children! And now you see the t'other, her as had set her heart on being

a lady, she's come back a widder, without a penny. If
she had married an honest man as could carry on old
Stanfield's business —"

The conversation was interrupted at that moment
by an apparition which sent the gossips in the back
shop into a flutter of dismay and consternation. To
be sure, there was a glass door closed between them,
and Mary Jane, who was presiding at the counter, was
innocent of any complicity in the gossip; but guilt is
never courageous. It was Mrs. Trevelyan who had
entered the shop, with Walter, to give some trifling
order. They all peeped at her from behind the little
blinds, with sensations very different from those which
the prelections of their entertainer were intended to
produce. Agnes was pale, and her profound mourning
and the close line of white round her face under her
black bonnet, increased the effect of her natural pale-
ness and of her exhausted looks. The young critics in
the back parlour were not only silenced by the sight,
but perhaps moved by a deeper touch of sympathetic
envy — a more profound admiration than if Agnes had
been "made a lady of," according to Mrs. Rogers' sense
of the words. No sort of brilliant surroundings could
have made the picture so impressive to the young imagination, even when accustomed to ruder emblems, as
the mourning of the young widow, her sadness and
quietness, and that atmosphere of profound feeling that
surrounded her. She was separated by her grief as
much as by the other peculiarities of her lot, and set
above them in a way more effectual than if Lady Trevelyan's carriage had been waiting at the door. No
doubt, Louisa Rogers, whose husband was hearty as
hearty, who was thriving in business, and had six

pretty children, was the happier woman of the two;
but if the choice between the two had been offered at
that moment to the spectators in the background, the
lot of Mrs. Trevelyan, even in her distress and widowhood, would certainly have carried the day. The young
women looked with a natural wonder and awe and
interest upon a woman who had sounded so many
depths. When she went away again with her boy's
hand in hers, there was not a word further said about
Agnes. "Who could have thought she'd come in just
at that moment!" Mrs. Rogers said, looking, experienced
woman as she was, just a little disconcerted — and it
was certain that the moral she had taken such pains to
draw failed altogether of its effect upon the minds of
her daughters and their friends, none of whom were at
all discouraged as to the results of marrying a gentleman by the sight of Agnes Trevelyan. On the whole,
if the result was to be equal, not one of these enter-
prising young women would have shrank from the necessary means.

But it was not alone in the lower regions of Windholm that Agnes and her fortunes were discussed. She
was a good deal talked of in the Cedars, where Minnie
Fox had cried over Roger's death, and had been sobered
and yet encouraged in her folly by his premature end.
She was very sorry for Agnes in her heart, which was
not a bad little heart at bottom, and a little ashamed
of herself, and yet more certain than ever that poor
Mr. Trevelyan would have been very different if his
wife had been a woman worthy of him, and who could
have made him happy. Little Miss Fox almost thought
it was her mission to devote herself to Roger's children,
and try to make up to them for the deficiencies of their

mother — but there were difficulties in the way of that
pious intention; for, to be sure, when she was in Mrs.
Trevelyan's company, Miss Minnie did not feel herself
so superior as when she looked at Agnes from a distance, and remembered that she was the blacksmith's
daughter. As for the vicar and his wife, they were
interested more seriously, yet each in a different way.
Mr. Freke, as everybody knows, was eccentric, and
had very odd ideas. It had never been his opinion,
for example, that Roger Trevelyan had had the worse
of it in the unquestionable inequality of his marriage.
No doubt there was a great difference between the
baronet's son and the blacksmith's daughter; but then
the vicar, who was always odd, took it upon him to
think that there was also a difference of another description between the woman who inherited William
Stanfield's large and tender nature, and the man who
derived to some extent the qualities of his mind from
Sir Roger Trevelyan; and, to tell the truth, Mr. Freke
was not so sorry for Agnes in her present distress, as
under all the circumstances he ought to have been.
The vicar, for his own part, was happy enough in his
way, and yet had never been particularly happy all his
life. He had nothing to complain of, and got along
very well, on the whole; and his wife was a good
woman, who, if she did not enter into his speculations,
and the special workings of his mind, still understood
him better than anybody else understood him. But
with all this moderate and temperate enjoyment, his
life had been such, that the question of happiness had
never come prominently before him, as the great question of existence; and looking at Agnes Trevelyan, not
as a wife who had lost her husband, but as a human

creature placed in better or worse circumstances for full
development, he was not, as we have said, so grieved
for her in her widowhood as would have become her
clergyman, whose duty it was to console and sympa-
thize with the wounded and sorrowful of his flock.

"So far as I can see, it was the best thing he could
do," said the vicar. "He never was good for much,
poor fellow! I don't mean to say I am not sorry for
him; — that is, I don't mean to say it is not altogether
a horrible mystery why that old sinner of a father
should be left living, and this young fellow, who was
not a bad fellow, should be hurried off so quickly; —
but it is no use talking of these things. And so far as
she is concerned, you know, I think for my own part
it was the best thing he could do."

"Mr. Freke, you are always past my comprehension," said his wife. "How can it possibly be the
best thing for her? It never was a marriage I approved
of; though I thought it my duty to stand by her, for
she was always a very good girl in her way. But nobody can deny that she has turned out very well, and
done a great deal better than anyone had a right to
expect. It is just like you to say it is the best thing
for her. I don't know anything more sad, for my part,
than to be left a young widow with little children to
bring up, and all the responsibility; and then, whatever faults Agnes may have, nobody could ever say
she was not very fond of her husband. Poor thing! I
am very, very sorry for her, for my part."

"Oh yes, to be sure," said the vicar, "that is all
right; I am sorry for her too — but on the whole, you
know, though I see very little good in philosophy, or
in anything else for that matter, one has to look at

things occasionally from the broader point of view. A big grief and to be done with it, is better than being cut into little pieces for years and years — and then a man when he dies leaves charity and peace behind him, whereas, when he lives, he is often horribly aggravating. I've seen scenes with that good Stanfield that were enough to make the poor girl hate her husband. I am sure I cannot tell why she did not. If she had been a reasonable being, with a due sense of logic, she would have conceived such a contempt for Trevelyan as is quite inconsistent with love in my way of thinking. There was Stanfield supporting them all, and yet coming in, in his modest way, as if it was they who were doing him a favour; and there was Trevelyan insulting him, sneering at him, setting him down as if he knew nothing. Agnes had a great deal too good a head not to have seen all that. Fortunately, women are inaccessible to reason, or else she would have hated him as I say."

"It is very cruel of you to call up such recollections," said Mrs. Freke. "The poor fellow is dead and gone, and it is dreadful to discuss his faults *now*."

"To be sure," said the vicar, "that is exactly what I expected you to say. Indeed, it is exactly what I have been saying. Now she forgets all that, you know. Poor Roger is restored back again to the ideal shape which I have no doubt he wore when she consented to marry him; — and these children will grow up to think their father was the best man that ever lived, and the most dreadful loss to them, instead of finding him out to be very ordinary and very useless, as they would have been sure to do had he lived. To be sure it was no virtue of his, poor fellow, to die; — but if you turn

to the other aspect of affairs, why that old reprobate
should not have been cleared off the face of the earth,
and poor Roger left to mellow in prosperity, that's what
I can't tell you. That side of the question is too terrible for me. I daresay he would have made a very
tolerable squire, and been happy enough, and given
Agnes leave to be as happy as she could. That's the
solution I should have chosen, had I had anything to
do with it. I suppose it is better as it is. At all events,"
said Mr. Freke, getting up hastily, "a man would go
mad altogether if he could not believe it *must* be
best."

"I am sure a great many people in the parish would
think you had gone mad already if they heard you,"
said his wife, with a tone of injury. "I wish you would
not talk in that dreadful way. I don't see, for my part,
why Sir Roger should be killed off to make way for
Agnes Stanfield, and make her happy. I don't suppose,
from all one hears, that the change would be much to
his benefit, poor man; and poor Roger, on the contrary, was so pious and so resigned. I am going to
call there, and ask how the baby is, Mr. Freke. It
had a little cold yesterday, when I met it out with
Madelon. There will be some change made, I should
think, when she has had time to come to herself. I
never could think how they were able to keep up three
servants and a boy for the garden, even when *he* was
living, poor fellow; and it would be quite absurd for
Agnes, who, of course, will be seeing nobody. I shall
ask her about it as soon as I have an opportunity. Mrs.
Percy would be glad to have Madelon, to speak German
in their nursery. These are things that never come into
a man's head; but it would be a great deal more sen-

sible to give a little thought to that than to say, when
the poor thing's husband dies, that it is the best thing
he could do."

"It is quite true, notwithstanding," said the vicar,
retiring a little before the practical aspect of affairs as
presented to him by his wife. He had not much to say
on that question, nor did he feel himself qualified to
advise. "For my part, I'd rather not meet her just
now, for it is hard to know what to say to her," said
Mr. Freke. "It's a little hard to tell a woman like
that, that it's all for the best. Yes, go, Harriet; you
will do her more good than I should." And with this
the vicar walked all round the room with the skirts of
his long coat flying behind him, and bolted out of the
door when he got to it the second time — which was
his general mode of retiring when he had been beaten;
as, to be sure, he generally was.

Mrs. Freke was very well aware she would do Agnes
more good than her husband; she was very sorry for
the sorrowful young woman, but her sorrow was not
of the speculative, nor even of the caressing and sentimental sort. She thought it would be a great deal
better for Mrs. Trevelyan to be roused up a little, and
recalled to her motherly anxieties about the baby, and
to the cares of economy, which were now more necessary than ever — or at least so Mrs. Freke concluded.
Perhaps, on the whole, with the kindest intentions in
the world, she was even less charitable to Agnes than
the gossips in Mrs. Rogers' back shop; for, to do them
justice, the worst they proposed was to make an example of her, as an instance of unsuccessful ambition;
whereas the vicar's wife felt a little like a benevolent
tiger, whose natural prey had been restored, and went

forth with the full intention of taking Agnes into her own hand, and making a summary end of any fine-lady affectations, or self-indulgence that was ridiculous — as Mrs. Freke concluded — in her condition of life. If Roger's widow had been a lady, then, to be sure, she might have had some right to be prostrated with grief, and unequal to any exertion; but the matter was entirely different with Agnes Stanfield. Mrs. Freke accordingly made her way to the Green, intending to "speak seriously" to Mrs. Trevelyan about her circumstances, and to tell her that it was a duty she owed her children to dismiss Madelon and diminish her household. She had even the intention of appealing to Agnes's conscience, whether it was right to go on occupying a house of that size, and whether it would not be wise, on the whole, to go back to her father's, where there was plenty of room, as Mrs. Freke knew; thus, on the whole, it was not a vague mission of consolation which led the clergy-woman of the parish to Windholm Green. Perhaps the vicar was right in thinking that to die was about the best thing Roger Trevelyan could do; but at the same time, if he was not much good to her in other ways, her husband had been a defence to Agnes. However well-disposed friends may be, they can scarcely take upon them to administer this kind of advice and admonition to a wife who has her husband to stand by her. Now all that was changed, and the natural authorities considered it not only their right, but their duty, to interfere.

"My dear, you must not fret too much," Mrs. Freke said, taking Mrs. Trevelyan's hand. "It must be for the best that things have happened as they have done. *He* is happy, and does not want you any more; and

you must bear up for the sake of your family. Poor
things! what would become of them if anything were
to happen to you? The Trevelyans might take Walter;
but think of your two dear little girls — and baby had
a very nasty cough when I met her out yesterday.
I should not have trusted her out of doors had it
been me."

Agnes was roused by this, as was natural, to sudden
anxiety — anxiety quick and sharp, that went to her
heart. In her deep depression and discouragement she
was ready to think every cloud a storm.

"Baby?" she said, faltering. "Did you think she
looked ill? I thought it was nothing. Perhaps I have
been thoughtless, and preoccupied with myself."

"My dear, I do not blame you," said Mrs. Freke.
"I am sure it is quite natural, and the cough may be
nothing, you know; but still, at this time of the year
— and then so many things come on with a cough —
and I think I have heard you say that they had never
had the measles nor anything. Speaking of that, I
should like to know what you mean to do about Madelon. I suppose you don't mean to keep her *now?* —
a foreign nurse is a kind of luxury, you know; and
then, I understand you don't have anything from the
Trevelyans, and to keep up a house like this must be
a little hard on your father, Agnes. I think I know
of a very good place for Madelon as soon as you have
made up your mind what you are going to do."

"I do not think Madelon wishes to leave us," said
Agnes, faintly. She was so quiet and composed that
Mrs. Freke had not thought a great deal of preface necessary; and Mrs. Trevelyan felt as if she had suddenly
been seized upon and dragged forth into the noise of

life out of a sorrowful dream. She woke up to answer with a painful dull surprise, and that realization of her changed circumstances which, after one of those pauses of anguish which interpret a life, always comes upon the forlorn survivor with the question, "What do you mean to do?"

"I was not talking of Madelon's wishes," said Mrs. Freke, "but of what you think best in the circumstances, my dear. I am sure you don't want so many servants now. Of course, it will be some time before you think of going into society; and being as you are with the Trevelyans, and no prospect now of coming into the property —"

"Please don't say any more," said Agnes; "I suppose I shall have to think about these things some time; but not now. It is so short a time — I am not able; don't say any more now."

"My dear, it will do you good to cry," said the vicar's wife. Don't mind me; you know that all I wish is to be a true friend to you, Agnes. I am sure there is nobody in the world more sorry than I am. I felt it as if he had been one of my own connexions," said Mrs. Freke, drying her eyes; "and so young — and so nice as he always was. I was always very fond of Mr. Trevelyan. But then he is happy, my dear! That is always the great consolation; and the longer you are of looking things in the face, the harder it will be. It is not Madelon alone, but everything. You know you have your family to think of, now that they have nobody but you. As long as they are so young, it is so much easier to save a little; and then to look after them yourself would do you good. There is nothing so good as occupation. I would advise you,

if you would be guided by me, to leave this house,
which is so expensive to keep up, and choose one of
the maids to go with you. And then you could either
go to your father's, or take a little cottage, or find
apartments, or something. That is what I would advise, if you would be guided by me."

While Mrs. Freke was making this speech, Agnes,
whose calmness was not yet so strongly established as
to be able to maintain itself in the face of mingled
condolence and attack, had broken down completely;
but even her breaking down, and the despair that came
over her, were self-restrained, and did not frighten the
spectator. The peculiarity in her grief was that it
seized upon her and struggled with her visibly, but
that she never gave herself up to it, nor abdicated her
painful sway and authority over herself. She was
scarcely able to speak when her visitor's address had
come to an end; and yet she did speak, and made an
end of the interference, which in its very kindness was
humiliating. Agnes felt all her faculties quickened
and made vivid by her grief. She was conscious of
everything that passed and everything that was said to
her as she had never been before; and even in a way
she felt the mortification which her visitor did not in-
tend her to feel. There was, perhaps, even a certain
consolation to her wounded love in this sudden proof
that things could be said to Roger's widow which never
would have been said to his wife. And thus the new
wound did the little that was possible to heal the great
wound, by giving her a new reason to mourn over
Roger — a new occasion to feel her bitter loss.

"My father will help me to arrange everything,"
said Agnes. "He is so good to me, he has not said

anything yet. Pardon me if I cannot talk about it.
God has still left me one natural counsellor — but I
know it is kind of you!" Mrs. Trevelyan added, with
a little haste. She did not say the appearance and
manner were cruel, but perhaps something in her tone
or her look conveyed that idea to the mind of Mrs.
Freke. The vicar's wife drew away her hand suddenly
and grew crimson, and had a great mind to be angry;
but then she was a good woman, and felt that Agnes
had reason for what she had said.

"Oh! I do not mean to interfere," she said; and
then there was a pause. It is not pleasant to have
good advice rejected, even when it is given unasked;
and the mortification had transferred itself to the wrong
side, and Mrs. Freke was undergoing the pain, not always disagreeable, of suffering for well-doing. And, to
be sure, she could have borne that; but then at that
moment Mrs. Trevelyan, who was one of those people
who could not be calculated upon exactly as to what
she might do or say, took back the hand that had been
withdrawn from her between her own two hands, which
were so blanched and worn, and put down her wan
face upon it.

"I have no more heart to think of anything," she
said. "It is so long that I have only planned, and
thought, and lived for *him;* and now I can do nothing
— nothing — for him," said Agnes. The words came
singly out like sobs, with a hard stifled breath between.
The vicar's wife was not a woman to resist that pathetic confidence. She put her arms round the mourn-
ful figure beside her, and burst out crying into tears
more passionate than those of Agnes. She could be
intrusive and troublesome, and even impertinent, with-

out thinking of it, but she could not fight against nature; and she was a good woman in her heart.

CHAPTER X.

Alone.

THERE are few things in this life so sad as the aspect of a house in which a long illness has come to an end, and death has taken away the object of many cares; and when it is the head of the house, the chief person in it, who is gone, the sight is yet more pathetic. The room looks so silent, so deserted, which used to be the centre of the anxious household. The white vacancy and emptiness where once so much suffering, so many cares and anxieties were, the bold sunshine entering in unabashed through the window that used to be veiled so carefully, are things that go to the heart. And then when, as in this case, there are children merry upstairs, forgetting or altogether unaware of the loss for all their lives that they have sustained; and down below, all silent, a woman by herself, pale with watching, weary of life, trying again, as far as she may, to steady herself, and set forth once more on the same road where she has been arrested, and beaten down and trampled on the ground. She has to get up again, and pick up the remnants that are left and go on; there is nothing else for it; but it is hard work; and this was what Agnes Trevelyan was making up her mind to do.

She remained alone all the afternoon after Mrs. Freke left her. She had clung to Walter when "all was over," and kept him by her; but then it came into her sad heart to think that the boy was looking pale, and she sent him away; and then she would have the baby on her lap, which being speechless was a still better comforter; but this day she continued alone. She had meant to think, but thinking is such hard work; and then it seemed so natural to ask herself what was the good of it *now;* and then, poor soul, she went searching through all her thoughts and recollections for comfort and found so little. The darkness seemed to press round her and baffle her on every side. It is not difficult to speculate upon heaven in the abstract, especially when it is only, so to speak, in one's own interest; but then Agnes had parted with her husband upon those dark and mysterious boundaries, and her heart was breaking to find some trace of him again on the other side. It was but little comfort to her to be told he was happy. The hard thing was, to be henceforward unable to form any idea of him, where he was, or what he might be doing, or even what changes his nature had sustained in the transition from one world to the other. A saintly white shade, with golden harp and glistening wings, conveyed to her no idea of Roger — no link of connexion with him; and this was why she turned back so cast down and discouraged from that search into the unknown, which is the grand occupation of the sorrowful. She read over and over all she could find in the Bible on that subject, but it gave her very little enlightenment. "In my Father's house are many mansions — I go to prepare a place for you." Enough for faith, but nothing for the avidity, and curiosity, and longing of love; not an idea where, or how, or even what he was; only that he was well; and it is so hard to content the heart with that. When she

8*

roused herself from this search in which there was so little satisfaction, the idea of new arrangements made her heart sick. And yet, to be sure, she had to think of them — to weigh with herself what it was right to do for her children's sake, and to contemplate the position in which she stood, cut off from all defence, subject to advice, and reprimand, and exhortation — not knowing what her husband's family might have to say to her, and knowing well that, except such succour as came from her father, there was nobody to take her part.

This last consideration, however, was, strangely enough, a kind of comfort to Agnes. She had a consciousness, which even his death could not quite remove, of the weakness of poor Roger's character, and the little good he had been in the world; but the more she felt his loss the greater her want of protection and defence appeared, the more she was able to exalt Roger in her thoughts. There is a sweetness even in the desolation that says to itself — "This would not have happened had he been here." She took all the consolation she could out of this, as she sat alone with the tears on her pale cheeks. If Roger had been living, the questions which she was now asking herself would have been unnecessary. If Roger had been living, nobody would have ventured to intrude on her privacy, and give her advice as to her individual affairs, which was, to a certain extent, impertinent, however well-meant it might be. Thus she seemed to herself to have the means provided to her hands of exalting and defending poor Roger's memory from any implied censure or faint approbation. And with that her mind returned to the sad freedom in which she found herself — the liberty to have her own way, which is so pleasant in some circumstances, so miserable in others. There was nobody to hinder her from doing as she pleased, or to contradict her plans, and make her efforts vain. Everything was in her own hands to establish or to destroy. But then there still remained one bond upon this desolate freedom; and that was her father, who was coming in the evening to bear her company, and comfort her as well as he could, as he had done almost every evening since Roger died.

When Stanfield arrived he found his daughter sitting by the fire, unoccupied, as Agnes had never been in the old days; and Walter standing by her side, with her arms round him, and leaning his head against her. The boy was contemplating wistfully his mother's tears, not knowing what to do or to say — keeping very quiet and looking at her, as the only practical means of being, as all the servants adjured him to be, "a comfort" to her. He had cried with her at first, but the fountain of his tears was soon exhausted, and now he could only contemplate with a little awe, and even perhaps a little weariness, the slow big tears that continued to come to her eyes. And she had talked to him a little at first, till it became apparent to Agnes that all the power of recollection and mourning that there was in her little boy's mind had been exhausted, and that it was only with a kind of mechanical melancholy that he listened to what she was saying. And then she recognised that the child could not follow her, and that she had already gone far beyond his reach without knowing it; and she became silent, but yet held him fast, with a

sense that the pain in her heart was eased a little
when Walter pressed close to her, and moved in his
childish restlessness within her arm. Stanfield thought
there could be nothing more sad than the two silent
figures by the fire — the mother gazing into it with
her eyes dilated and large with tears, and the child
regarding her with wistful wonder and sympathy.
There was still a sadder picture in store if he had
known it; but in the meantime it was near Christmas,
and all the world was making merry; and the sight of
his daughter, thus changed and broken down, went to
the blacksmith's heart.

"It is time that Walter should go upstairs," said
Agnes; "I have kept him too long, perhaps, but it was
for company. Father, if you have time, I want to
speak to you about all our affairs to-night."

"I have always time for all you have to say to
me, my darling," said Stanfield; "but don't vex yourself with affairs. If anybody comes to trouble you,
send them to me."

"Nobody has come to trouble me except Mrs.
Freke, who is very kind," said Agnes. "She offered
to get a place for Madelon, and she gave me her
advice about leaving here. I want you to tell me
what you think. You have been our support for a
long time, father. I know it very well, though I have
not said much; but now things — are different. Many
things that were necessary are — not —; that is, I
can do without them. She was quite right; I should
not put you to such expense."

"What is this about expense?" said Stanfield.
"That is my share of the business, little one. I wish
I could take your share on my shoulders too; but I

can't, for it's against nature. Never mind the easy
part of it; you have enough to bear."

"Yes," said Agnes; "but there are women that
have everything to bear — the grief, no less, and all
the cares, and perhaps to work for their children —
and you spare me everything. I am no better, no
weaker than the rest."

"God forbid!" said the blacksmith. "I've known
women that had all that to do, and I've heard them
say it was well for them; but a man is not to stand
aside and leave the burden to his only child. That
would be out of reason. You are all I have in the
world, and all that I have is yours. Don't speak of
this any more."

"But I ought to speak of it," said Agnes. "Father!
remember the change of circumstances — there were
many things necessary that are necessary no longer.
He," said Mrs. Trevelyan, gasping a little, notwithstanding her composure, "had habits, different — I
will never forget your goodness to him — but I am
your daughter, and what is good enough for you is
very good for me. Father! will you take me home?"

A passing spasm contracted Stanfield's heart — a
thrill of longing, a pang of self-restraint. To see
Agnes in her old place, and watch her children daily,
hourly growing up round him! But then the blacksmith was not used to considering himself. He took
time to think before he answered, and his broad calm
eyes shone upon Agnes with a radiance like the sunshine. It was not with any little candle of his own
that he examined what was before him, but with an
impartial daylight of observation. He shook his head
softly as he looked at her.

"You *are* at home, little one!" he said; and his
eyes went aside for a moment, to go round the room
with a certain caressing pleasure in the look; for had
he not chosen everything in it for her, down to the
minutest particular? Poor Roger, though his wife put
it all to his credit, had counted for very little in the
blacksmith's arrangements. It was even a pleasure to
him (for, to be sure, he had been only moderately
attached to Roger) to think that his daughter's comfort
was not of her husband's providing, nor in any way
dependent upon him, but that it was himself — her
father, from whom Agnes derived everything she had.
"You *are* at home," he repeated, gently; "nowhere
could you be more at home than you are here."

"Yes; but I am dependent upon you," said Agnes;
"I am to be thought of only as your daughter now;
and your daughter requires no better lodging, no
greater attendance, than you do. I am Agnes Stanfield only, so far as my requirements go."

This was a hard speech for her father; perhaps it
was harder than all that strangers had said about his
daughter's unequal match, and than all the semi-insults
and concealed ill temper of his son-in-law. Agnes
herself came in, without thinking it, to give the last
blow.

"You have always been Agnes Stanfield to me,"
he said, with something in his tone that in another
man would have been resentment; and then he made
a little pause. "There are many strange things in
this world," said the blacksmith, resuming with a painful smile, which his daughter did not understand; "but
it would be strange indeed if at this time you and me
should begin to vex each other. Such a thing might

be, my darling," said Stanfield, meeting the sudden astonished look she gave him with his calm and steady eyes, "because, you see, the chief thing in my mind is that you are my child; and the chief thing in yours, as is but natural, is that you are — that you were ——"

He stopped short, and she did not make any reply. They understood each other without any further words; and they also understood on both sides that there was something between them which prevented them from ever resuming the primitive position of father and daughter. No man could be more tender to the memory of the dead than Stanfield was, as no man could have been more tolerant and forbearing with the living — but his pride was touched in its tenderest point, and he was still fallible, even at the height of his goodness. Even her gratitude vexed her father. Why should his child be grateful, and think of him and speak of his kindness as if she was not his child, but another man's wife? This sentiment could never have been spoken in words; but Agnes knew what he meant, because she was his child, and understood him without the aid of speech.

And then there was a silence between the two, who thus discovered that they were separated without wishing it, without intending it, at the time when they had so much need of each other. Agnes felt herself roused up out of her grief by the necessity of saying something — of abridging this pause, which, in its way, was so eloquent. It was so new to her to be embarrassed and constrained with her father, and to have to search for something to say to him, that the very sense of constraint prolonged the pause; and then Stanfield perceived her hesitation, and shared it. It was he, however, who broke the silence at last.

"We'll talk no more about expenses or affairs," he said; "you are here at home, my little one. It is true you are a mother, and have little ones of your own, but still you are my child, my little Agnes. Somehow I like the name better the more it is out of reason," he went on with the gradual smile that lit up his face by degrees. "A man is of little use if he cannot stand between his daughter and the world. If I were to die — and I must die some day — you would have everything to do, my darling; and I know you would neither shrink nor fail; but just now, when anybody speaks to you of expenses or arrangements, send them to me. I was not put into this world only to hammer iron," said the blacksmith; "and now you are tired, and I am going away."

"Not tired," said Agnes. "If I could be tired with work, as some poor women are, I should be better. I have too much ease, that is all that ails me. It would be better for me, if you would only believe it, to send away my servants, and go home to you, as Mrs. Freke says."

"Mrs. Freke does not know," said Stanfield. "Don't say that any more. There are some things that are impossible. You are all I have in the world, but my house is not a place for you — *now*."

And then he said good-night to her, and went away with a heavy heart. Perhaps it was partly his own doing, that had married a woman who could never be the mistress of a house in which Mrs. Trevelyan came to live; but chiefly it was the doing of nature, who had broken the first bond to make a second more

close and intimate. To be sure, it was for Agnes
Stanfield, his daughter, that the blacksmith had done
and suffered all that was required of him; but the
worst of it was that, in her heart, she was no longer
Agnes Stanfield, but Roger Trevelyan's wife — Roger
Trevelyan's widow, a woman conscious of feelings and
thoughts which her father did not, and could not, share.
They found this out mutually just at the moment when,
according to all outward appearance, the chief cause of
their separation was removed. Before that both father
and daughter could permit themselves to think that it
was Roger — who was fond of his wife, but not of his
father-in-law — who changed the character of their
intercourse; but now that Roger was dead, and a closer
union than ever might have arisen between the sorrowful daughter and the father, who was so full of
tender sympathy, the true state of affairs became painfully clear to them both. Changed circumstances, other
experiences, long absence, and what was still more important, the character of wife, had made between Agnes
and her father a separation which had nothing to do
with external obstacles. She could not come back
over that boundary, neither could he cross it; and love
itself stood baffled and discouraged by the discovery.
To be sure it was natural; but then the only real
hardships in existence are those that come by nature
— the only ones that are inevitable and incurable, and
from which there are no means of escape.

Agnes sat long over the fire after her father left
her, till it faded and died out before her, like (as she
imagined) the fire of life, which seemed to be dying in
her heart. When she paid her usual visit to the
children's room before she went to rest, Walter woke

hastily up to see her bending over him. He was half dreaming and half awake, as children are when disturbed in their sleep. "Let me play," he said, with a little fretful toss. "I never have any time to play. I don't want to go to mamma." The child was asleep again almost before he had done speaking; and Agnes covered him up carefully, and went away without a word; but, notwithstanding, her heart bled again at this touch. Her little child was too young to understand her; and even had he been old enough, he had his own fresh life to occupy him, and was not to be diverted from that by her troubles. And her father, too, the only other living creature to whom she could go, had in a manner refused to enter into her special sorrow. She went downstairs with a sense of utter loneliness which the most solitary of human beings could not have surpassed. She was not, in actual fact, alone; she had children fair and promising, and a father who would do anything in the world for her comfort and consolation; but no one ever felt more desolate than Agnes as she went downstairs, in her own house, from the room where her boy was sleeping, to the other room, in which her baby's soft breathing made tenderest, half-audible music. There was still some one to love her, and to claim her love, but there was nobody to share the burden that was heaviest. Henceforward that closest bond was rent for ever and ever. Nobody in the world could say, "It is my sorrow as well as yours." She had to take it all upon her, by herself, and cover it up and keep it from injuring or wearying the others, who had so little to do with it. This was also a thing quite natural, and of which no one had any right to complain.

CHAPTER XI.

Jack Charlton's Commission.

THUS the days went on, and the winter came to an end; and Agnes made the discovery which everybody has to make who goes through the usual experiences of life, that Death does not rank at all so highly among the influences that affect existence as at the first glance it seems to do. The anticipation of it had not changed Roger, who descended into the dark valley without in any respect losing his identity, without gaining solemnity or even seriousness from the contact; and now, when she stood on the other side of the grave to which she had seen him go down, she also was still the same creature, though her life was changed in so many respects. And common habits and occupations had to be taken up again, and the requirements of every day were on the whole as steady, as persistent as ever. And then, even out of self-regard, she had to conquer herself — to look the world in the face, and talk in her old voice, and take an interest or pretend to do so in what was going on round her; all to defend herself from pity which she could not bear, and allusions to her "loss," which sounded like blasphemy to Agnes. So that on the whole it began to be said in the village that Mrs. Trevelyan was bearing it very well. It was thus that she presented herself to the eyes of Jack Charlton, when he came to pay her a visit in the spring.

It was the first time he had come since Roger's death. He had written to her then a few words of sympathy, and had offered, if ever he could be of any use to her — as everybody does at such times. But he meant what he said, which, perhaps, is not so general. He had always had an admiration and a kindness for Agnes since the day, long ago, when he had found her alone at Florence, sitting over her work by herself, when all the other women in his sphere were amusing themselves, or trying to amuse themselves. He had been sorry for her in her solitude, and he had seen that she was not sorry for herself; and that seemed to Jack so odd, under all the circumstances, that he had never ceased to take an interest in Agnes. But his interest was of such a kind that he would not have come to see her without a grave reason. He was a careless man enough, and not of an elevated character, but he had a kind of insight in his heart. He understood that a woman might perhaps in her weakness wonder why the father of her children should be taken out of the world, and Jack Charlton, who was not much good to anybody, left. To tell the truth, he wondered a little at it himself — not that his own life should continue, which, to be sure, seems a natural thing to every man; but that so many fellows who had nobody belonging to them should go on all sound and safe, while Roger was hurried out of the world from his wife and children. He would not have thought of presenting himself before Agnes to put such ideas into her mind, if there had not been, as we have said, a grave reason for it; and when he saw Mrs. Trevelyan, he felt a little ashamed of himself, as if the sight of her mourning was a reproach to him. He thought to himself that it was very hard upon her, as he looked at her and saw her beautiful hair covered with the symbol of her widowhood, and the black dress which set her apart from all the bright world. She was younger than himself by five or six years at least, and yet Jack felt himself at the height of life and its enjoyments; while to her, that had come to an end summarily. It was very hard on her, he said to himself; and this was why he felt almost guilty when he came, in the fulness of his strength and in perfect enjoyment of his life into the house where his schoolfellow had died, and where the woman whom he had seen a bride was sitting a widow; for Jack, though he had his faults, was in his heart a good fellow, and full of tenderness in his way. It was with this sense of compunction that he came in, sending in his name first, and waiting to know if she would receive him, with a respect as great as if he had been asking an audience of his sovereign. Perhaps Agnes felt within herself, as he had anticipated, a little thrill of contrast — a sense of the difference — when she heard his name; but she admitted him notwithstanding, after the first movement of disinclination. She was by herself, as she now began to accustom herself to being when her children were out of doors, and the lines of her face were set with a kind of rigid steadiness which Jack had not seen before. It was to keep herself from expressing too much emotion that Agnes gave this rigid look to her face — and though she did not know it, it betrayed her more than tears.

"I think I saw Watty in the garden," said Jack, with the precipitancy of a man who must plunge into conversation somehow. "He begins to grow a great fellow, fit for school, almost. Have you made up your mind at all on that subject, Mrs. Trevelyan? Do you

mean to send him to Eton? He used to be a bright
little chap when he was little; but I suppose he's not
quite such a polyglot now."

"He is only nine," said Agnes. "He is too young
for a public school."

"Yes, that is true," said Jack; "but there is
nothing like beginning there early, you know." This
was said, not that Jack Charlton had any educational
theories, but simply because he had something very
serious to say on this subject and did not know how
to begin.

Mrs. Trevelyan smiled in a faint sort of pallid way
—which went to Jack's heart all the more, because he
remembered perfectly the time when he had found out
first that Trevelyan's wife, though frightened, could
smile. She said —

"I did not know you were interested about schools;
but if you will tell me what is the best for him, it will
be very kind of you." This, which was so natural a
thing for her to say, was so far from having the effect
of opening Jack's mind and experience, that it embarrassed him more and more.

"He used to be a sharp little chap," he answered,
vaguely; and then grew crimson to his hair, and looked
out of the window with much anxiety, not to see anybody, but to hide his discomfort; and then he added,
abruptly: "I cannot conceal it from you, Mrs. Trevelyan, or open it up gradually, as I ought to do. I
ought to have been a ploughman instead of a lawyer.
I am afraid I have come to vex you, and I had rather
a great deal break my own head; however, I have un-
dertaken it, and I must give you my message."

"What is it?" said Agnes, looking at him. His

words woke a faint sensation in her, which was almost
too feeble to be called curiosity, much less fear; for
her rapid mind took a survey of the situation in that
moment, and now that the one great evil had happened,
she did not know of anything else that could alarm
her. To have suffered the worst harm that you can
conceive, is a wonderful defence against anxiety.
What he said seemed to her like a stupid pleasantry.
After what had happened, what could it matter what
any man said, or what message might have to be
delivered to her? She listened languidly, lifting her
eyes to him, and thinking how little he knew of the
state of her mind if he imagined that, at present, she
was capable of being disturbed by what any one might
say.

"I saw Beatrice Trevelyan the other day," said
Jack, speaking abruptly, in his anxiety to spare her
— "and — and, indeed, Sir Roger. Did you ever
happen to hear, Mrs. Trevelyan, that something had
been said — some arrangement contemplated — about
Walter? Forgive me," he said, growing a great deal
more agitated than she was; "I don't know how to say
it. I would not for the world hurt your feelings; but
poor Trevelyan —"

"If you will speak of him quite simply without
hesitation, and do not call him poor," said Agnes,
quickly. She did not cry, nor lose her self-possession;
she only drew a long shivering breath, and clasped her
hands tight together, as if there was some strength to
be got that way; and then she raised her eyes to her
visitor's face with a certain mute entreaty that he should
go on.

"Forgive me," Jack repeated, without knowing he

said it; "there is nothing in the world I would not
sooner do than vex you. I cannot help asking — did
he ever speak to you of any proposal about Walter?
The grandfather, you know, offered to take him to put
him to school. Nothing was settled, but they think it
was *his* wish; and then, perhaps it would be better for
the child — and save you something —"

It was only then that it became visible to Jack
that Agnes was not at first as pale as a woman could
be. She blanched visibly under this demand, so that
he seemed to see all the blood that remained rushing
back from her face.

"I heard nothing of it," she said; and then made a
pause as if something had stifled her voice. "I cannot
believe there was ever any such arrangement made,"
she went on a minute after; "it must be a mistake."

"No, it is not altogether a mistake," said Jack.
"I know the proposal was made — and, to tell the
truth, I thought it was a good proposal for my part —
I think I even advised Trevelyan to accept it. I shall
be very sorry if you think the worse of me for that;
but then, you see, there are so many things to be considered —" Here he stopped short, for it was impossible to say to Agnes that the grandfather, who was a
blacksmith, had seemed to him rather an unlucky as-
sociate for a future baronet; and he could not help
feeling that the mere suggestion of taking her boy from
her was a little cruel. "Education is very costly, and
it is only right Sir Roger should do something for his
grandson — that is why I thought it would be well to
accept."

Agnes made no direct answer, but only clasped her
hands closer on her lap. "He is too young for a public

school," she repeated, painfully, almost losing her head
in the sudden confusion and rush of ideas; and then
she forced herself to take a little time to think; and as
Jack, on his side, was silent, waiting for her answer,
recovered the thread which she had almost lost. "I
never heard anything of it," she said. "He did not
always take my advice, but he never did anything
without telling me — without consulting me. He could
not mean it; and now," said Agnes, crushing her hands
together, "everything is changed."

"Yes," said Jack. "Mrs. Trevelyan, believe me, I
feel how painful it all is. Even if Trevelyan had
made up his mind to it, it was under different circumstances. I remember even then he said it was you
that had to be thought of. It was just before you
were ill, and I suppose that was why he did not speak
of it; and then he had so little time. I thought it
would be better for me to come about it than a stranger.
The strong point is, that they think they had his consent."

Agnes remained a long time silent, revolving in
her mind many bitter thoughts, feeling more and more
distinctly that she had nobody to stand by her. As for
the child himself, the novelty of going to school would
probably prevail over all other sentiments; and it was
not certain that Stanfield might not think it a duty to
accept this offer of amity towards Walter, and help to
his mother. She kept silent, almost unconscious of
Jack Charlton's eyes, feeling the bitterness of her solitude pierce to her heart. It seemed to her even as if
Roger, in his grave, had abandoned her, which was
perhaps the hardest of all.

"He could not have consented, because he never

9*

spoke of it," she said, with a certain hoarseness in
her throat. "Have you come to make the proposal to
me?"

"I suppose I must say yes; that is the commission
I am charged with," said Jack; "but Mrs. Trevelyan,
I beg you will believe —"

"Yes," said Agnes. Her tone was not so much impatient as preoccupied. She had no time for civilities,
nor, indeed, for anything but the most urgent necessity
of the case. "I do not think it will do any good to
think it over, Mr. Charlton — I can do nothing but
refuse to accept it. It may be meant for kindness, and
I may be wrong in what I am doing. I am only a
woman like other women, though the rest have less to
bear than I have. I ought to be considered a little,
too. I cannot give up my child. There are some
things which I *must* decide for myself. He is the
greatest comfort I have in the world — and I cannot
give up my boy."

While she spoke she kept perfectly still, but a pink
flush came and went over her face, and her voice was
harsh and irregular, and by times shrill, as if in its
range there was, here and there, a broken chord. And
she stopped herself with a little effort, as if once having
begun, she could have gone on indefinitely which was,
indeed, true; but then Agnes recalled to herself that her
auditor cared nothing about what was going on in her
mind, that he wanted only an answer; and she broke
off suddenly, as she had commenced, under the domi-
nion of that idea, which was not entirely just. For, to
tell the truth, Jack Charlton felt himself in a false
position, and though he was carrying Sir Roger's
standard, had all the inclination in the world to desert

and go over to the enemy without another word being said.

"Have patience a moment," he said. "I am not going to repeat that proposal. I came to-day not for *their* sake, but because I thought I was better than a stranger. Are you able to explain to me a little? In case Sir Roger should not be content with this —"

Agnes was proud in her way, though it was not a common way of pride: she had it from her father, who was proud, too, in the height of his humility. "I am all that remains to Walter in the world," she said. "I have to be both father and mother to him. I do not see how it can go any farther. There can be no question between Sir Roger and me."

Jack Charlton was not in any way affected by this little outburst. He continued with what he was saying tranquilly, after he had paused a moment, as if to suffer the fumes to escape. "Still I have to ask you to pardon me," he said. "Did Trevelyan leave a will? — that is the great thing to know."

Once more Agnes shivered a little at her husband's name. "He had nothing to leave us," she said. "I would not have him troubled, nor did he think of it himself. Mr. Charlton, my father will tell you whatever you desire to know."

"Yes, thank you; that will be best," said Jack; but at the same time he did not conceal from himself that little Walter Trevelyan's fate would interest him much less when he discussed it with a village blacksmith, than when it was the child's pale mother, in the languor and preoccupation of her grief, who answered for him. He hesitated still after he had received that dismissal. He did not know how to make any further offer of his services without alarming Mrs. Trevelyan; and yet he could not go away without letting her know that he was not in the enemy's interests, but that his assistance, as far as it went, was at her call.

"I am to say that this is your final answer?" he asked, as he got up from his seat. "If you should change your mind at all, you will write to me? Perhaps, after you have considered it, and consulted with your friends — Once more, Mrs. Trevelyan," said Jack, "don't mistake me. If anything follows, I am not Sir Roger's adviser. Trevelyan was one of my oldest friends, and I am at your service the moment you call me. You will not forget? that is, if you hear of this any more."

"I cannot think İ will hear of it any more," said Agnes, with the decision of ignorance. "What is there that can follow? His mother now is the only authority; but thank you, Mr. Charlton, you are very kind all the same."

And she stretched out her hand to him with a smile, which was at once piteous, and in its way defiant. She wanted him to be gone, because she was nearly at the limit of her forces. A woman can bear a great deal, but in most cases there arrives a moment when she must weep out her tears, at whatever cost. This was why Agnes was so anxious to get free of her visitor. She was quite sensible that his object had been a kind one, and she believed his offer of service to be real, but then in her heart she felt sure that she could have no need for his services, and wondered a little that a man of sense should have gone out of his way to offer vaguely once more the aid which she had so little prospect of needing. It was some time before the

true sting of what she had heard had access into her
mind, disturbed as it was. When she began to think
that Roger had thus abandoned her, had thus been
willing to give up her child to the care of those who
would not receive herself, her heart sobbed as if at last
it would surely burst her straitened breast. Perhaps it
had only been his father's death which had saved
Walter to her; and the idea was very hard to bear.
Even at that moment Agnes, who, being Stanfield's
daughter, could not be altogether unreasonable recognised, in spite of herself, that there was nothing out
of nature in Sir Roger's desire to have his grandson;
but the more she perceived it, the more constantly she
repeated in her mind that she never would allow herself to be persuaded, or consent that her son should be
transferred to his grandfather's hands; and it was thus
her thoughts were occupied, with a strange disturbance
and excitement, and at the same time a sense of victory
and secure right which no one could dispute, at the
moment when Jack Charlton made his way through
Windholm to see the blacksmith — for Jack Charlton,
on his side, did not feel equally secure.

CHAPTER XII.

Sir Roger's Claim.

THE blacksmith was in the midst of his work when
Jack Charlton entered the yard, and the visitor, though
he was a man of the world, was a little embarrassed
how to address the father of Agnes, who was so mani-
festly one of the lower classes, and yet was the nearest
relation of his friend's wife — a woman who was quite

his own equal, and for whom Jack had even a chivalrous respect. He approached the forge slowly, not
quite knowing how to open his business or to introduce
himself. He was saved this trouble, however, in an
unexpected way. Something small made a rush at
him while he was looking doubtfully from a little
distance at the forge, where the fires were blazing and
the hammers ringing, and the work going on merrily.
"Is it grandpapa you want to see, Mr. Charlton?" said
Walter, who had made a bound out of the heart of it,
slightly grimed and out of breath. "He is here. He
is very busy, and I am helping him," the child added,
half ashamed, half proud, and he held out his little
black hands. "I have a little hammer all to myself,"
he continued, changing into entire exultation as he
went on; "come along, and I will show it you." And
then Walter, out of his blacksmith-furor, suddenly relapsed into a little gentleman. "Grandpapa, this is
Mr. Charlton," he said, gravely, with the air of a
master of the ceremonies. As for Stanfield, he was
always a model of courtesy. He received the visitor
as if the smithy with its roaring fires had been a
chamber of audience. "I am glad to see Mr. Charlton," he said, with a smile, and looked at Jack with
the natural scrutiny of a man who was accustomed to
be consulted, and could form an idea of what his visitor wanted, in some degree, from his face. To be sure,
Jack Charlton was not like one of Stanfield's ordinary
clientèle, who carried for the most part their perplexities
in their countenance; but still the experienced eyes of
the village philosopher could read even in the looks of
the man of the world that this was by no means a
visit of courtesy, but that he had something to say.

Perhaps Stanfield, who was not in profound grief, like his daughter, was more disposed to be anxious and take alarm about her circumstances than she was; perhaps he saw something suspicious in the look which his visitor cast upon little Walter. At all events, he put his coat on hastily, without any preliminaries, and came out to the yard, where Jack was waiting. Had he known Jack, he would have proposed the Common as the place of consultation; but he did not know him, and consequently more state and ceremony were needful. Fortunately Mrs. Stanfield was out, and they could be undisturbed upstairs.

"Walter," said the blacksmith, "go home now to your mother. Remember our bargain — I know you are a man of your word. Tell her I shall see her to-night. And now, Mr. Charlton, your pardon for keeping you waiting. Come this way." He led the way to the outer stair as he spoke, pushing Walter before him, with his large hand on his shoulder. The bargain between them was that the child should come to the forge only when his grandfather was there. Walter, for his part, was smoothing down his little sleeves, with the air of a little workman released from his occupation. To be sure, Jack Charlton was more than ever of opinion, that to have a blacksmith for a grandfather and to spend a portion of his time in a forge was not the best thing possible for a future baronet; but somehow, even at the moment he was thinking thus, the two made a pleasant picture, and he could not help feeling a little softened at his heart. Then though Walter was the heir of the Trevelyans, it could not be questioned by anyone seeing them thus together that he was Stanfield's descendant, and that all that was remarkable in his face was directly inherited from the blacksmith. Jack could not but note this in passing, as he followed up the outer stairs and watched Walter going off, dutiful and like a man of honour. The smithy had great attractions, and the workmen were entirely disposed to spoil their young visitor. It was sad to have to leave the little hammer and all the important work in which he could have lent such powerful aid; but then his word was of still greater importance, and while the two others went up to the parlour over the archway to consult over his future fate, Walter, regretful but true, put his little black hands in his pockets and marched away steadily to the house on the Green.

Stanfield gave his visitor a chair, and drew up the blinds, which were closed to exclude the sun. The sun was setting red behind the Cedars, making an end of the February day, and those last searching slanting beams revealed all the respectability of the apartment in which he was sitting to Jack Charlton, to whom it was a new experience. As for Stanfield, it never occurred to him to think what the stranger's opinion of his house might be. He sat down in his own armchair, and fixed his eyes on Jack with an attentive, expectant look. He did not ask, "What is your business?" neither was there any express demand in those broad, soft eyes, which had their effect upon Jack Charlton, as upon everybody else who saw them; but, at the same time, his whole aspect expressed a certain expectation, and that he was prepared and ready to hear.

"I have just seen Mrs. Trevelyan," said Jack, "and I was very glad when she referred me to you;

for it is hard to trouble a lady, and especially one in her position, with business. I want to make some inquiries about Trevelyan, if you will have the kindness to tell me. I have known him all my life — we were very old friends."

"Yes," said the blacksmith. "I have heard of you, Mr. Charlton; but, in the first place, is it for your own satisfaction, or is there anything else behind?"

In spite of himself Jack reddened, and grew a little embarrassed. "It is both for my own satisfaction, and there is something behind," he said hastily. "I am here, to a certain extent, to represent Sir Roger Trevelyan, and at the same time I wish you to understand that I will have nothing to do with any steps he may take to the injury of Mrs. Trevelyan. It is a stupid position, but at present I am for both sides, if you can understand what I mean."

"I can understand what you mean, but I cannot understand what are the two sides," said the blacksmith. "There is no connexion whatever between Mrs. Trevelyan and Sir Roger. She gets nothing from him, and he has nothing to do with her, so far as I can see."

"The first thing I want to know," said Jack, "if you will have the goodness to inform me, is, whether Trevelyan made a will?"

"He made no will," said Stanfield; "he had nothing to leave, poor fellow! It was better not in every way. He had borrowed money at different times, with the idea of surviving his father. I don't say it was right, but then, you know, his father would do nothing for him; and all the little he had, went to his creditors. I have arranged all that — that is to say, *they* have done it. My daughter's living is her own," said the blacksmith, with a little natural energy. "She is not indebted to Sir Roger for anything. I can't tell what there can be to raise a question between them; she is asking for nothing — there must be some mistake."

"It is about the children," said Jack. It was all he said, and his air was as subdued and uncomfortable as his words were few. As for Stanfield, he was so much surprised that he started, and made the room and the house thrill with his sudden movement.

"The children!" he repeated, aghast; and then he paused and took courage. "Sir Roger has nothing to do with the children," he said. "What do you mean?"

"I am not sure that he has nothing to do with the children," said Jack; "that is precisely the point I am in doubt upon. Little Walter is his heir, and there might be plausible reasons found to give to the Lord Chancellor, you know. But I am going too far, for they did not speak of that. Trevelyan, it appears, half consented that they should have Walter to educate, and Sir Roger has set his heart on having him; and now," said Jack, with a troubled countenance, "since Trevelyan left no will — and, to be sure, they might find plausible things to say——"

"Walter?" said Stanfield, with the air of a man suddenly knocked down. "They want Walter? — is that what you mean to tell me? And what did his mother say?"

"Mrs. Trevelyan said simply 'no,' and declined to consider the matter," said Jack; and he saw the blacksmith's face light up as he spoke; "but I don't know how far that was prudent," he went on. "I did not

like to alarm her, but I should like you to understand. They may make an application to the Lord
Chancellor; that is, Sir Roger may, and there is no
telling what the decision may be. Everything depends on how a story is told. They may make, if
they are clever about it, a very plausible case; they
may say, you know, that the child's future rank makes
it necessary——"

"Yes, I understand," said Stanfield. It was not
necessary to go further into the details. The blacksmith had experience enough to know that a story very
much opposed to the truth might be built upon the
facts that were true, and which nobody could contest.
Though he was slow in general to understand evil-
dealing, he was, in a way, used to Sir Roger, and expected no good from him. A man that thinks the
worst of human nature has, in such a case, perhaps,
the advantage of a man who thinks the best; for the
cynic recognises all the restraints of society and public
opinion, whereas the optimist, when he has consented
to recognise an evil character, is glad to concentrate
all the varieties and kinds of evil in that one exception
to the rule. Stanfield was ready to believe anything
of Sir Roger, and accordingly, though he was much
startled, he was not sceptical, as he might have been
under other circumstances. But he had to take a little
time to think it over before that mysterious threat of
an application to the Lord Chancellor took form and
shape in his mind. If there had been question of
some immediate act of despotism or cruelty, he would
have comprehended it sooner. And then the Lord
Chancellor was not to know that Agnes was too good
for Roger Trevelyan, nor which of Walter's grand-

fathers was the one who might best be trusted to watch
over his education. He paused over all this before it
entered his mind, and accordingly it was some time
before he answered Jack, who sat regarding him with
some curiosity, and a gradually increasing interest
which he could scarcely explain.

"You are right there," said Stanfield, slowly.
"Everything depends on how a story is told. But to
tell a story of this description would be to make it
public. I have read reports myself in the papers, of
applications to the Lord Chancellor, and the affairs of
a family dragged before the world. I should not like
to see the name of —— any of our names," said the
blacksmith, with that fastidious and delicate pride
which prevented him even from saying that it was for
Agnes he feared, "in vulgar print. This is a danger
so unforeseen that you find me unprepared, Mr. Charlton. I am not very strong on these points, and at
this moment, I tell you candidly, I don't know what
to say — but I will take advice and learn."

"Oh, I beg you will not take me for Sir Roger's
adviser," said Jack, hastily. "I came to-day because
I had an idea that I would be less alarming than a
stranger to Mrs. Trevelyan. If we cannot make an arrangement, I will have nothing to do with any attack
that is made upon her."

"What arrangement could we make?" said Stanfield; for though his imagination was not very powerful, the blacksmith's thoughts had gone forward in spite
of him, and he could not help realizing to himself the
romance in real life which might appear in the papers;
and how Agnes might be represented under the appearance of an ambitious young woman, who had made a

wonderfully good match, and her boy as growing up
under circumstances altogether unsuitable to his father's
rank; — a misrepresentation all the more difficult to
meet that it would be founded upon evident facts
denied by no one. This picture which gradually grew
upon him of Agnes's name "in vulgar print," as he
said, moved him more and more as he thought it over.
This was why he asked, notwithstanding Agnes's
prompt refusal which it had comforted him to hear of
— "what arrangement could we make?"

"Nothing, that I am aware of, but giving up the
child," said Jack. "It was to poor Trevelyan himself
that the proposal was made, and I think he had half
a mind to accept it. If I remember rightly, I advised
him to accept it. If Mrs. Trevelyan would consent to
think of it, we might arrange the conditions, perhaps,
on a friendly footing. He might come home to her
for part of the holidays; and then he must go to school,
you know, sooner or later," Jack continued, in an involuntarily insinuating tone. So far from desiring to
make the blacksmith-grandfather aware that his company was bad for the boy, Jack had come to feel by
this time almost as great a desire to break the shock
and make it easy to Stanfield as he had done to
Agnes, and he could not help seeing that the blacksmith's countenance fell as he went on. Walter had
grown to be the apple of his grandfather's eye, almost
without Stanfield's knowledge. He had felt his
daughter lost to him even at the moment when she had
come again to be dependent on him and have but him
in the world; and her son had filled up that intimate
and tender place from which Agnes, pre-occupied by a
closer love, had unconsciously withdrawn. To have

Walter removed, coming back for "part of his holidays," separated in mind and ideas, perhaps taught to be ashamed of his low connexions, was an idea that made Stanfield's heart fail within him. Nevertheless, he did not make any protest, or reject summarily this proposition, as Agnes had done. He looked at it in his grave way from every point of view. He recognised that Sir Roger, too, though an unworthy man, had yet a right to be considered, and that it was reasonable that he should desire to have the training of his heir. It was a terrible blow to him, but it did not change good into evil, or make him intolerant of his neighbour's rights.

"Mr. Charlton, you speak too lightly," said the blacksmith; "the child, you know, is not just a child in the abstract to us, but the light of our eyes, so to speak. What was it that his mother said?"

"Mrs. Trevelyan was a little hasty, perhaps," said Jack. "She said no, absolutely, and declined to think of it. She thought the rights of nature were supreme; but I daresay you know that, so far as women are concerned, the law is a little indifferent about natural rights. I would not say to her what I have said to you; and, then, she would not have listened to me. If Trevelyan had only had the good sense to make a will, and appoint her and you the guardians —— But it is of no use lamenting that now. To tell the truth, I think there is a little bad feeling in it," said Jack. "I think Beatrice is at the bottom of it — I mean Miss Trevelyan; and if they brought it before the Lord Chancellor, what with Trevelyan's half-consenting, and — and — other things, it seems to me they could make a very plausible case."

"And all the story would be public property!" said the blacksmith, with that tone of tender pride and delicacy which Jack Charlton did not understand, but still was conscious of. He could comprehend Stanfield's reluctance to have the romance of his daughter's life published in the papers, but he was not himself of so fine a nature as to understand why her father was too proud and too delicate to say that he feared this for her. Naturally, Jack did not think it needful to maintain the same reserve.

"No, Mrs. Trevelyan would not like it," he said, "and it would be a tempting story for the newspapers. I should not like it myself, and no doubt it would be very disagreeable to a lady. That was one of my reasons for thinking an arrangement might be made."

Stanfield's face flushed like a woman's at this speech, though nothing was farther from Jack Charlton's mind than any intention of offence. Jack had a wonderful respect for Mrs. Trevelyan, and indeed could even be chivalrous in his way in respect to her; but she was not to him a being apart, whose name must not be brought into vulgar discussion, as she was to her father. He was a little astonished, accordingly, when Stanfield, just as he thought they were about to get upon a confidential footing, broke up the conference summarily.

"I am obliged to you for letting me know our danger," said the blacksmith — "very much obliged to you, Mr. Charlton, and for the way in which you have done it. I will give it all my best consideration, though, of course, you know, it is not for me to decide; and if any other steps are taken, we shall have time to take precautions. The warning is the great thing; and if you should conduct the proceedings against us," said

Stanfield, turning upon his visitor eyes which had a momentary smile in them, though the rest of the countenance was grave, "you will do it with consideration, not sparing the truth, but sparing the aggravations. In that case — —"

"I beg your pardon," said Jack. "I have already said I will take no part against Mrs. Trevelyan. On the other hand, if she chooses to confide her interests to me — — But I trust things may not be carried to such an extremity. Perhaps you will talk it over with her, and let me know what you think?"

This was the end of their first consultation on a subject which, though they did not know it, was to have such serious results. Jack Charlton went away with a curious sense that he had been wanting, somehow, and had made but a poor second in the interview, though certainly there was nothing on the face of it, nor in what Stanfield had said, to account for this notion of his. He went away, besides, greatly shaken in various ideas which he had entertained on the subject of Roger Trevelyan and his marriage ever since that event took place. Stanfield, though he had been found at work with all the accessories of his trade around him, was no more the ideal blacksmith of Jack's imagination than Agnes was the blooming village beauty whom Beatrice Trevelyan had supposed her brother's wife to be. It was long since Jack had discovered that Roger's *mésalliance* might be contemplated under two aspects, and that it certainly was not an interested "good match" which the village girl had made; but still he had always entertained the idea that the blacksmith must have been a man "wide awake" and ambitious, who had managed the matter skilfully to secure

for her a marriage so much above her original position.
When he left Windholm he was of a different opinion.
What he began to think was, that Trevelyan had every
inducement a man could have to live and be of some
use in this world; that Heaven had favoured him beyond
any man he had ever heard of; that he had had the
gratification of making a very foolish marriage, and
withal, that this marriage had turned out better than
half the reasonable marriages which are made with the
consent of everybody concerned. Why, under all these
circumstances, Roger should have made such a shipwreck, was more than Jack Charlton could tell.

As for Stanfield, he prepared to go down to the
Green in the evening with very different feelings.
Agnes was the mistress of her own actions — of her
own children. He could be her adviser, no doubt,
but he did not even know, under the circumstances,
whether she would wish to have his advice. And then
he was not sure in his own mind, in stern equity, that
Sir Roger had not a certain right to his heir. Stanfield,
it is true, was unable to feel himself the inferior of Sir
Roger, but he was not indifferent, for all that, to the
distinctions of rank, and he would have fought as
stoutly for Walter's birthright as if he had been the
most devoted admirer of a hereditary aristocracy. The
boy was not sacred to his grandfather as Agnes was;
but nevertheless, he occupied a perfectly distinct place,
apart from all the children in the village, as much as
if he had been a little prince in disguise; and though
the blacksmith permitted him to come to the smithy
while he was himself there, he would have been probably
much more distressed than Sir Roger if the little fellow
had transgressed in word or deed what he considered

10*

the honour of a gentleman. At the same time, Stanfield was tolerant, conscious of other people's rights,
long-suffering to the bottom of his heart, and he could
not reject without a little thought the proposal of Sir
Roger. The boy was to bear his other grandfather's
name, inherit his property, carry on his race. The
present head of the Trevelyans was not a good man;
but still Stanfield found it difficult to shut him out
from his natural privileges; and he went down through
the village in the evening with a little doubt in his
mind. Perhaps he might have to differ from his
daughter in opinion, and contest her will; and yet, in
the midst of it all, it was a consolation to him to think
that she had expressed her will so decidedly, and might
reject his advice; for Walter, after all, was the desire
of his heart.

CHAPTER XIII.

Resistance.

AGNES was alone when her father went into the
room where she sat reading. Work, which is such a
resource to a woman, ceases to be of use when the
mind is distracted with grievous thoughts, which can
come to nothing. After the children were asleep, Mrs.
Trevelyan took refuge in books, where she could still
escape from herself; but this evening she was not
paying very much attention to her book. Grief has
its variations, like everything else that is human, and
by times it happens that an unreasonable demand, a
harsh word, a painful contrast, drives the sorrowful
into a kind of troubled momentary rage, which is one

of the most painful forms of the malady. Agnes was in this phase of her suffering when her father joined her. She was driven, for the moment, beyond the bounds of her modest and enduring nature. Oppression, they say, makes even a wise man mad; and for a woman, whose heart is more exposed and her sensations more acute, intense suffering by times takes the form of a temporary passion, very nearly akin to madness. She was silent; she was making no demonstration of the blind hurrying rage and intolerance that possessed her; and yet Stanfield could to some extent read it in the glitter of her abstracted eyes.

"You have seen Mr. Charlton?" she said, laying down her book; "Walter told me he had gone direct to you."

"Yes, I have seen him," said the blacksmith. "He seems very kind and friendly. What he had to say was not pleasant, but——"

"Pleasant!" said Agnes; "I do not know how you can speak so calmly. Why is it that I have all this to bear? I do not know what I am saying or doing to-night. I feel as if God was cruel, and mocked me. I am not worse than the other women, whom nobody molests. I do not say I am good, God forbid; but I am neither better nor worse than the others. How is it — oh! how is it, father? Is it not enough that I am a widow and alone, and have to go through all my life without any one to share it — but that these people — that cruel woman, that unworthy man — should take my child from me, and make me angry with my poor Roger in his grave? Father, how is it, how is it? Can you not tell me? This last is more than I can bear."

"Agnes!" said the blacksmith. He held out his
hands to her with a kind of dumb supplication not to
say any more; but he was too much startled by this
unusual outbreak to reply.

"I could count them all up to you," said Agnes,
going on with an excited steadiness, "who are my age,
and were married when I was; — and nothing has
happened to them. They are no better and no worse
than I am. If I were better or worse, I could understand it a little. They are not the wicked flourishing
like a bay-tree; and I am not the just, any more than
they are; but they are at peace, and I am tormented.
I could suffer anything — I could give up anything,
if you would only tell me why!"

Stanfield could not remain passive and see his
daughter in an agitation so terrible — an agitation that
looked all the greater because of her ordinary self-
restraint. He went to her side and took her hands in
his, and tried to soothe her.

"My darling, there is nobody who can tell you
why," he said — "no one — no one. We have to
bear it; it is the will of God!"

"Ah!" said Agnes, "it is so easy for other people
to say that; if it was the will of God for any good —
Did not He create men to live, not to die? Did not
He give children to their parents, to those that bore
them, and suffered for them? And why should all the
rules of nature be overturned to torture a poor woman?
Father, don't speak to me; I have more than I can
bear."

But he held her hands fast, though the impulse of
her passion was to snatch them away from him; and
he spoke to her, though she did not listen. Poor soul!

the madness had about run its course; her just mind
regained its balance in spite of herself. But before
that could be, as she was only a woman, it was necessary that the momentary frenzy should escape through
the medium of tears. Stanfield had never seen such
tears as those his daughter shed at this moment. It
seemed to him as if they must scald her hands as they
fell — great, bitter, burning drops — not many, but
terrible, running out of that deepest depth, which never
opens to anything less than extremity. He had lived
a calm life, and he comprehended but dimly, this standing at bay of the outraged nature which was pushed
too far. He thought the sudden brief convulsive weeping, instead of being the final relief and termination of
overstrain, was of itself a positive evil. He looked at
her with the tenderest pity, for there was no one in
the world whom he loved as he loved his only child;
but at the same time, her griefs could not be his griefs,
and he was at this moment as far off from her as if
there had been a thousand miles between them. He
did not understand it, though he would cheerfully have
undergone any personal suffering to remove hers. And
Agnes knew he did not understand it; and as she recovered, heard the voice of his bewildered exhortations
and consolations in her ears, and knew that he could
no more follow her in the sudden impulse of her passion than if he had been a stranger. Perhaps this was
as effectual as any argument could have been to bring her
back to herself.

"Father, forgive me!" she said; "go to your seat
again, and never mind me. I think I had lost my wits.
It seems so hard; but that is over now — I know very
well, however hard it is, that it must be borne."

Stanfield went back to his seat as she told him, still regarding her with his serious and pitiful eyes. It would be wrong to say that his daughter lost something of her perfection in his sight in consequence of this incomprehensible passion, for his love was of that kind of supreme love which rules in its own right, and does not go on the score of merit; but he was surprised and perplexed, as men so often are, both with the weakness and the strength of women. For that moment he could not follow her — he who was used to proceed straightforward in his plain path. He had no experience in his own life that could be put by the side of the crisis which Agnes was going through.

"Mr. Charlton was kind," said Agnes; "but all the same — he came on an errand that made it almost impossible to receive him with kindness. I know he is very friendly; I believe even he came himself, that he might 'spare my feelings,' as people say. Don't think badly of me, father. He made me feel angry — almost angry for a moment with — with; — but it could not be true."

"And you told him you would not consent?" said Stanfield. "You settled it at once — or, at least, so he said."

Agnes raised her head, which she had covered with her hands, and looked at her father, as she recovered her composure, with a certain wonder.

"What else do you suppose I could do?" she said. "It is not a thing to take into consideration; I do not require even your advice for that. I have nothing in the world that you do not give me — except my children; and there can be no parley, no consultation about anything so plain; yes, I settled it the moment he spoke."

And with that she drew towards her the basket with her work, which was on the table, and took out a little matter of her baby's dress, and began to work with a silent haste, which served her to dissipate the remaining excitement. Nothing could have shown more effectually the full certainty she had that she had settled and completed this business beyond any possibility of change. She was ready enough to listen, if necessary, to anything her father might say on the subject, but to alter her decision was impossible; this was plainly visible in her looks, and Stanfield had no difficulty in recognising it. It was even a little difficult for him to speak at all, in face of that air of silent resolution. Had she looked up, or trusted her eyes within reach of his, he would have known better what to say; but she only worked on with swift and noiseless hands, and with her head bent over her work — the very impersonation of a listener who had made up her mind to oppose an invincible disregard to all that might be addressed to her, and for whom all argument and reason were at an end.

"I am glad, in one way, that you made up your mind at once," said the blacksmith. "I don't know if my strength could have stood the test; and yet I am not so sure that you are right," he added, more slowly. "You are Walter's mother; but then, you see, the more's the pity, poor little fellow! there is but him now to be Sir Roger's heir. I think, if I was Sir Roger, I might think as he does, that I had some right to be consulted. I am not advising you, my darling, because I know you have decided — and I am glad you have decided; but then I am not perfectly sure it is the right thing to do, for my own part."

"What else was there to do?" said Agnes, looking up suddenly, and lifting upon her father her eyes, which were at that present moment so large, and worn, and over-bright. "Nobody could expect me to consent. Such a thing might have been forced from me under — other circumstances. If it is true, as they say," she went on slowly, as if every word was a pain to her, "that — Roger — had consented. But there cannot be any one so cruel as to suppose that I could give him up now."

And then there ensued a silence — a silence more eloquent a great deal than words, since it proved to Agnes in the most impressive way that her father was not satisfied, perhaps not even convinced, by what she said.

"You don't say anything?" she said, with a little return of excitement. "Why do you not speak, father? Could *you* suppose it possible? Could you wish me to give him up — Walter, who is so much older than the others, my only companion. I think, if I had the choice, I should rather die without any more ado."

"My darling!" said the blacksmith, "it happens sometimes that a worse misfortune comes. Sometimes God himself takes such a child; and even then His creatures are not permitted to despair and to die."

She lifted her eyes to him with a look aghast — her mouth a little open, her eyes shining like stars out of her pale face. Stanfield never forgot that look of terror and anguish. She did not say anything. He had told her of a thing that was possible, quite possible — such a blow as other women have sustained and

lived — and in her heart Agnes felt the strong life
beating and throbbing, and knew as by a kind of instinctive vaticination that she too could live and continue through all descriptions of anguish. It was not
from her lips but her heart, which contracted suddenly
with a physical pang, that the cry came which struck
upon Stanfield's ears; and he himself was confounded
by the effect his words had produced.

"Agnes, what I say is not to hurt the child," he
said; "he is well and strong, and God will spare him
to you and me. I mean to say, when there are women
who have to consent to give up their children altogether, that you should not reject, without thinking
it well over, what may be for his good — what may
reconcile him ——"

"Father," said Agnes, recovering herself, "you were
wrong to say that. God has a right — He has a right;
but then He is more merciful than men — more, not
less — is not that true? None of them would take my
child quite away from me, not even Sir Roger; and
God — oh! you do not mean to say God is less kind?
He would not take Abraham's son, you know, nor the
woman's — that woman that dwelt among her own
people. I can trust Him with mine," she said, with a
smile coming over her face. It was not as if she had
smiled: the light came over her pale mouth like something independent of her; and fear, deadly and terrible,
was lurking in her eyes. Perhaps it had always been
there, lying disguised; but from that day Stanfield saw
it continually, more or less distinct, but always there.

"Yes," said the blacksmith, "we will trust Him
with everything — to be according to His pleasure; but
I did not mean to bring such an idea into your mind.

They are all happy and well, and all our duty is to be thankful. It is only to think, Agnes, if it was for Walter's good that he should go partly away — if he ought to be brought up, not humbly in Windholm, but like other boys of his condition. I speak against myself," said Stanfield, with a smile; "but, my darling, I cannot forget, for my part, that Sir Roger, though I have not much opinion of him, is Walter's grandfather as well as I am. It's hard upon me to have to plead his cause; he never was to say civil either to you or me. But Walter has to succeed him, you know — to get all he has to leave, and to represent the family—"

Agnes put up her hand to beg her father to stop. She was trembling with a nervous tremor, and a sense as if the cold had suddenly gone to her heart. This talk of heirship and succession after the other suggestion was too much for her; she fell for the moment into that too natural theology of fear which is so apt to disturb a mind oppressed and imaginative. It seemed to her as if there was something impious and dangerous in speaking of Walter's succeeding, after speaking of another and darker possibility. Her instinct whispered to her that it was best not to tempt God — not to say anything to betray the hopes that were on Walter's head; and though her better spirit rose up against that pagan instinct, still it moved her, as it might have done one of the lower creatures. She was not a Christian with a great trust in God, at that instant of sudden and horrible fear — she was only a pagan, a savage, a terrified and helpless creature, shivering before the unseen Power that could do her, if it pleased, such horrible harm. It lasted but for a moment, but it left her prostrate and like a creature incapable of thought. She grasped her father's hand suddenly with hers, which was cold and trembling.

"I cannot bear any more," she said, in a low, slow voice; and then she got on her knees before the fire, not to weep or to pray, but to get a little warmth, chill and shivering as she was; the fire had burned low while they were talking, and the night was very cold. While she knelt on the hearth-rug, and shivered, and held out her hands over the dying fire, Stanfield, for his part, was struck as with a heavy and sickening presentiment. He was silent, as she had bidden him. He put his hand upon her head, or rather upon the cap, which now covered her hair. "She shall wear a veil on her head because of the angels," he thought in his heart; and he did not understand any more than other people what was meant by those mysterious words, except that they came into his head he did not know why, as he sat by and watched her, kneeling, with already the heavy marks of misfortune and grief upon her, and a future before her in which God alone knew how many sorrows might be coming. At this moment she crouched helpless and terror-stricken before the approaching fate, trying to warm her chilled frame at the faint little fire of human happiness that was dying out before her eyes.

It was at this moment that Walter, who had been enjoying a game of romps — the best he had had for a long time — with Madelon, who had recovered her spirits — came rushing in to say good-night. He threw himself upon his mother before she had any idea of his being there. He was flushed with his play, and full of unsubdued noise and commotion.

"They say I will wake baby," said the little fellow.

"It's a good thing there is not a baby here; I can make as much noise as I like down-stairs. Mamma, I have come to say good-night."

"Do you like to make a noise, Walter?" said Agnes, putting her arm round him and leaning, as she knelt, upon her child — "I don't see the pleasure in that."

"That is because you are old, mamma," said the boy, promptly. "When people are old, I suppose it is different; but I heard you say once you liked to hear me making a row in the nursery. It was you she said it to, grandpapa. Wait till I put some coals on the fire — it's nearly out. I wonder what you have been thinking of! But there's such a jolly fire upstairs. Mamma, get up, please, and let me make a good fire."

This was how the attitude, which was full of such painful suggestions to Stanfield, and yet which he did not feel able to disturb, was suddenly changed at a touch. The lively, active little figure, flushed and joyous, breathing nothing but warmth and life and commotion, heaping on new fuel on the half-extinguished fire, was as cheerful a reverse to the picture as could be conceived. And most likely it was Walter's arms thrown round her which had made an end of Agnes's shiver and brought back the light of life to her face. When he disappeared again, she drew her chair near the fire, which was beginning to blaze, and held out her hand to her father, who did not know whether he ought to renew the discussion or to let well alone — for the time, at least.

"Father, don't think me a fool," said Agnes; "it is being alone so much and staying indoors. And then what you said made my heart stop beating. God

knows best! — I don't mean to be afraid any more.
But for the other, do not press me. I know — I am
sure — it would not be for Walter's good."

And that was all the satisfaction Stanfield got before he went home, weary and sad, and doubtful of
the future; for, after all, it was not a reasonable soul
like his own, but the less steadfast spirit of a wayward
and suffering woman who was principally concerned.

CHAPTER XIV.

A Pause.

AFTER this, an interval of quiet succeeded in Mrs.
Trevelyan's affairs. She herself accepted without remark the silence of the other parties concerned, as the
simple and natural result of the decision which they
had no right to question. But as for Stanfield, his
mind was less easily satisfied. After what Jack Charlton had said to him, the quietness seemed ominous to
the blacksmith. He thought Sir Roger would have
made a greater stand for his own will, if he had been
sure that he could obtain nothing, except by Agnes's
consent; and when no further application came, and
nothing at all was heard of the matter, Stanfield grew
very uneasy, though he did not say much about it.
He took to reading law books, though he did not make
much of them, and he even went to London one day
under pretence of business, to ask the opinion of an
attorney who had managed his affairs for him for many
years — on the very few occasions, that is to say,
when Stanfield's affairs required any management. This
man was not a great authority, but he partially reas-

sured his client, and the blacksmith came home, making up his mind that his daughter had nothing to fear from any attempts that might be made against her; though, to be sure, it was the attempt itself more than the result which he feared. To be publicly proved to be a true and spotless woman, faithful to all her duties, and fit for any position to which she might be called, might have been in some people's eyes a satisfactory result enough for any trial which Mrs. Trevelyan might have to go through; but that was not her father's opinion. That her name should be called in question at all — that it should be considered necessary to prove anything about her — that the story of her youth should be revealed to vulgar eyes, even should those eyes be admiring and not disrespectful, was an idea intolerable to him. He would have suffered anything himself rather than have purchased her vindication at such a price.

But, in the meantime, Jack Charlton said nothing, and no protest nor communication of any description arrived on the part of Sir Roger Trevelyan. Perhaps the attack had been made wantonly, without any real intention; perhaps the baronet was otherwise occupied, and had forgotten all about it; perhaps — and, indeed, this was true — Walter counted for very little in Sir Roger's thoughts. At all events, everything remained quiet. Nobody molested Mrs. Trevelyan in the house which her father's bounty maintained. There Stanfield found a refuge often from the house which his wife made no home to him; and there, at the same time, such a splendid visitor as Lady Grandmaison, who had come twice in the six months to see and console the young widow, preserved for Agnes the respect and even

awe of the general community. It would have been
vain indeed for the village aristocracy to think of putting down a woman whom the great lady of the county
condescended to visit. And perhaps Agnes made more
impression in her own person on her neighbours, now
that she had lost all the imaginary advantages and
possibilities for which, in a lower circle, she was supposed to have married. The Trevelyans, it was very
well known, were now quite unlikely to "take any
notice" of Roger's widow, and she never could be Lady
Trevelyan. The sole link that remained to her, with
what was imagined in Windholm to be the great
world, was that her little boy was the heir. If Sir
Roger died, and little Walter became Sir Walter before
he was a man, no doubt his mother would reign for a
certain limited period, as queen mothers reign occasionally, and would be mistress of the dingy and dismal Hall at Windholm, as well as of the distant magni-
ficence of Trevelyan. But that was a far-off and doubtful elevation.

Notwithstanding, Agnes had never been so popular
in her native village as now, when she was seen mostly
in her father's company, and was much more visibly
the daughter of the blacksmith who lived and laboured
on the Green, than the wife of Roger Trevelyan, who
had left her, as the gossips said, without a penny.
Perhaps Lady Grandmaison had something to do with
it — perhaps her widow's dress, which looked so black
in the sunshine, and which somehow gave back to her
face the youthful look which in her great anxiety and
exhaustion it had lost. To be sure, there are a great
many people in the world who regard a young widow
with levity, as a kind of clandestine candidate for the

prizes of a second youth. But then to the good women who are themselves happy, there is something in the name that touches the heart. They, too, may all be widows, Heaven knows, one day or another. And then, perhaps, it was true that Agnes, when Roger was no longer by her side to confuse her, as he had always continued to do, with a half-conscious criticism, became more fully herself than she had ever been before. Whatever the reason might be, the result was plain enough. Living alone with her children, having nothing but what her father gave her, without any grandeur either of association or anticipation, and returning in outer respects much to her original position, Mrs. Trevelyan found, without being aware of it, the place which belonged to her by nature. She was not above the least, and she was not below the highest. She was far kinder and more tender to the poor than the prosperous shopkeepers, who kept up a kind of war with their poverty; and than the ladies, who were sorry for them without understanding their case. And as for the fine people in Windholm, there was none of them who did not confess in themselves the finer breeding of Agnes, which they all supposed to arise from the fact that she was Lady Grandmaison's *protégée*, and had seen so much of the world; whereas it was simply because she was William Stanfield's daughter, and had inherited from him that only true politeness, which is not of the surface, but of the heart. To be sure, she had been equally her father's daughter in the earlier part of her career, when she was at Florence, and Lady Charlton disapproved of her. But then, fine manners are of slow growth, and youth is generally incapable of them, except under very rare conditions. Agnes had matured since that time, had lost her timidity, had suffered a great deal, and was more than ever moved with the desire to prevent others suffering, even from the lesser pains of life. And this was how she had acquired what some people called tact, and others style, and which everybody attributed to causes entirely different from the real one. And then her little world seemed to see and find her out for the first time, now that Roger was removed from her side.

With that modification of affairs out of doors, an imperceptible change was going on within, though Agnes was no more aware of the one than the other. As the summer came on, there came a little, almost invisible, fluctuating colour to her face; and then she began to awake out of her lassitude, and to see the past in its true light, and to realise that there was a future still lying unknown before her, and that she had not yet lived through the half of her life. As the mists of grief dispersed, Agnes found her loneliness less, her consolations greater. Her father, whom she seemed to have left behind when she went into the valley of the shadow of death, came up to her again on the ordinary path, and could walk with her and know what she meant; and Walter, too, understood his mother when she was not in the bitterness of those sufferings with which no stranger and even no friend can intermeddle. Thus the sky lightened, though she scarcely knew it, gradually, slowly, by imperceptible stages.

If Mrs. Trevelyan had been aware that there was in her heart a sense of relief — a freedom from the criticisms, and exactions, and embarrassments of the past — she would have regarded herself as a monster.

11 *

And yet, in fact, there was such a sense in her inner-most mind; a feeling of freedom, though she had never desired to be free; a faint consciousness, unexpressed even to herself, that her plans would no longer be thwarted nor her wishes come to nothing. Thus she took up the broken threads of her life without knowing it, and began to make herself manifest, without any intention of doing so, in the community, as her father did in his fashion. She was a widow — a certain want, a certain incompleteness, must always remain in the existence which had entered upon this obscurer phase; but the house could not be sad where the chil-dren's voices were ringing, and the life could not be flat nor uninteresting which was beating in a breast so full of delicate strength. She could not but feel herself still young — good for many things, abounding in per-sonal faculties and energies; and it was by this means that Agnes had recovered so much of her youthful courage, and discovered to her neighbours an indi-viduality so much more important than they dreamed of, even when the autumn days returned, and the first year of her widowhood came to an end. She had by this time little fear to speak of, of anything the Tre-velyans could do to annoy her; and it did not seem to her that anything could happen that would be worth reckoning a misfortune, so long as health and safety remained in the house on the Green.

All this was because Sir Roger was intensely occu-pied with speculations and pleasures, of a character which made it expedient that they should be carried on underground, withdrawn from the observation of the clean and honest. He had been lucky in his trans-actions that year, and the Derby had brought him a little fortune, which, to be sure, he spent becomingly, without recollecting his grandson; and because Beatrice, on her side, had had a matter in hand which had not gone so successfully. Miss Trevelyan was better than her fortunes, and even now, experienced as she was, a certain shame of the part she was playing would come over her at uncomfortable moments, and interfere fatally with her success. Her bloom had long ago gone beyond recall, and yet Beatrice had still to think of marrying, urged thereto by a lively horror of the position she would have to drop into, with the very tiny income she had, when Sir Roger died; and partly by disgust for the life which Sir Roger led, and which naturally, to a certain extent, was reflected upon herself. It was still the way — the only way she had remaining, to save herself from the humiliating position of an old and poor woman of fashion, going after all manner of frivolities and amusements without the excuse of doing it for a daughter, or to please her husband, or any other plausible plea.

It was thus that "going into society" had come to be Miss Trevelyan's profession, a laborious trade from which she could not escape; but if she married, that would have changed the face of affairs; and, at forty-five, she still thought of marrying, and laid out her silken nets and made her plans accordingly. How it happened that a woman, so able and so handsome, and who had this decided aim, had not succeeded sooner, was inexplicable even to herself. She tried to account for it in various ways more or less humiliating to her self-respect; but the fact was that Beatrice did not succeed, because, after all, though she was not above many little meannesses, she was too good for the *rôle* she had taken up. She would have been content to make a marriage of *convenance*, but she would not marry a man with a damaged character, and she had her antipathies and indulged them as if she had been twenty, and had all the world before her; and then, even in the best cases, by moments, she would get disgusted with herself, and suffer her true character to appear, and lose for ever the golden fish that was almost within her net.

Miss Trevelyan had been absorbed in one of these attempts in the summer which followed her brother's death. She was in mourning, and she was not going into society, as she said; but then, what was a temporary retirement to her would have been, at any time of her life, the wildest dissipation to Agnes; and Beatrice did not lose her opportunities in consequence. The proposed victim was so *game*, and resisted with so much address, showing himself at the same time as unwilling to escape finally, as to be caught, that the fair huntress was almost interested. But then, at the trying moment, at the crisis, Beatrice as usual suffered herself to be surprised with her mask off; she suffered the object of the chase to hear some very honest and unequivocal sentences from her lips, which were, as he himself said, the reverse of what he had fondly hoped to hear from Miss Trevelyan. A woman entirely bent upon winning at any cost, would have found means to eat her words or to recant them; but Beatrice had her special code of honour, which she never transgressed, and accordingly this enterprise failed like the others. She had followed the chase so long and so far that she was a little upset by its failure, and saw the victim who had escaped herself fall all at once and without thought into a more subtile snare, with a sense of despite and disgust which was far from agreeable; for the disgust was not only with *him* and *her*, and the world in general, but with herself, which is the most uncomfortable of all sensations.

When such a crisis arrives, a woman finds it necessary to revenge herself upon something. She could not punish the man who had slighted her, nor the woman who was her successful rival, nor, except by sarcasm and bitter pleasantry, the world which was offering them its congratulations; and to punish herself was a thing which Miss Trevelyan did continually, without feeling the better for it. It was this conjunction of circumstances which made her turn her thoughts towards Agnes, and to the boy who one day would be Sir Walter Trevelyan. A human creature who has little to make her happy, who is constrained to play a mean part in the world while she feels worthy of a better one, and who finds herself baffled at every turn, has a certain tragic right to be avenged upon the world. Beatrice bethought herself of Agnes, who was not now, it is true, the blessed creature whom Providence took pains and trouble to render happy, which she had once appeared to be; but then, in the midst of her own shabby disappointment and failure, which was not of a nature to be confessed to or compassionated by any one, Miss Trevelyan was conscious of another pang of indignant envy, as she regarded her sister-in-law arrayed in the dignity of a great sorrow, which all the world respected and pitied. It seemed to her as if, even in her griefs, Agnes was somehow unjustly the favourite of Heaven. It was not mortification, humiliation, the bitterness of seeing others preferred to her, and the worse bitterness of despising herself, which were the pains that fell to the lot of the blacksmith's daughter. In place of these, what she had to bear was the hand of God, which elevated even while it wounded. And thus the very calamity which she herself had, to some extent, shared, awoke when she reflected on it a double bitterness towards her brother's wife, in Miss Trevelyan's mind.

It was just at the moment when Agnes began to recover her courage and cheerfulness that Beatrice received her last blow from an unkind fate; she was at the time on a visit in a country-house where there was a large party, and where everybody was more or less conscious of her recent failure. There was nobody there, and, perhaps, scarcely any one in the whole range of her acquaintance who would not have laughed at Beatrice's discomfiture, especially had she betrayed in any way her own consciousness of it; and so she had to be gayer than usual, and wittier and more amusing, by way of covering her defeat. But it was different with Agnes, whom Providence seemed to take a delight in setting up opposite to her as a foil. Roger's widow could retire in her weeds (which, in her heart, Miss Trevelyan had no doubt were excessively becoming to the pale woman whom she had seen only in her brother's sick-room), and close her door upon all impertinent curiosity, and carry with her the respect and sympathy of her neighbours. And then she had her children, all her own, whom nobody could interfere with. Beatrice, to be sure, was not "one for children;" but she was a woman, and she could not but feel how different her sentiments might have been had she ever had any one belonging to her, as her very own. All these ideas fermenting together, raised Miss Trevelyan's antagonism to her sister-in-law — who she could readily persuade herself had insulted her by refusing her admittance to Roger's sick-bed — to the height of a passion. She did not say to herself that she had here a means of revenging herself, if not upon the people who had injured her, at least upon a woman whom Providence (Miss Trevelyan would not say God, for she had, if not a reverence, at least a respect for religion) had visibly preferred to her, and set in a more favourable position; but she directed her thoughts upon Walter with a persistency and force which gradually convinced her that she had the greatest interest in him — that he was in danger, and that it was her duty to interfere. She began to talk of the child to her friends — at first, without any intention except to divert them from the engaging gossip about herself, which she knew to be circulating even in the house where Miss Trevelyan was such a favourite; and from that beginning she gradually allowed herself to be guided to active designs.

"A handsome boy," she said, confidentially, to a little group of listeners — "not a curled darling like *that*, you know" — and Miss Trevelyan indicated languidly with her hand a spoiled child, who was the plague of the house. "I could not see exactly whom he resembled, for, naturally, my chief attention was given to my poor brother; but it is dreadful to think he should be left to people who have so little idea how to train him. Poor Roger, you know, was so infatuated — and yet I do think, if he had lived, he would have seen how dangerous these associations were for his son; indeed, he had consented to send him to us. I think sometimes I shall be driven to kidnap him, that some justice should be done to the poor boy."

"It is dreadful to think of it," said a sympathizing friend. "Could not something be done? If I were you, I should speak to Sir Robert Blarney, who is coming on Saturday. These law people can do anything, if they try — that is to say, they can frighten people out of their lives — and then, perhaps, they would give him up. My dear, if I were you, I would never rest until I had tried something. What a thing it would be for all of us to have to receive a young man brought up like that! and, of course, I should think it was a duty to receive him, for your sake."

"Yes, I know there is something that can be done," said Miss Trevelyan. "If it had not been that I felt for her a little, you know, in her circumstances —"

"I never should think of feeling for her, for my part," said Beatrice's counsellor, who was, in reality, the most pitiful of women. "People who make those dreadful marriages, and upset a whole family, never have any feeling; and then the dear boy's interests. You will be neglecting your duty if you don't do something. I am sure I shall always say it is your fault," added the excitable confidant whom Miss Trevelyan had chosen. As for Beatrice, she softly shook her head, and set in motion the light feathery curls which waved here and there among the bands of her *coiffure*. She had taken off all her crape, but had still a black dress, which was on the whole becoming, though Miss Trevelyan felt that her complexion was not *now* quite clear enough for black; but then her beautiful shoulders and arms came out perfect out of their sombre frame, which was a consolation in its way.

"My dear, they are so dreadfully respectable," she

said in her friend's ear — "*good*, you know; but, at the same time, I think I will speak to Sir Robert when he comes; for, to be sure, there is nobody but me to do anything for him," Beatrice added, with a sigh. She was so occupied with these family considerations, that she did not hear the last *bon-mot* of the wit of the party, who, Miss Trevelyan was aware, had been making considerable fun at her expense, and upon whom she had no disinclination to retaliate. She did not hear the *bon-mot*, and she insisted on having it repeated to her, loud out, so that everybody could hear, and then she demanded that it should be explained. "I don't know what makes me so stupid," Miss Trevelyan said. "I know it must be funny, since Mr. Salter said it; but I cannot see the joke — can you, Emily? Do tell us what it means." And then the whole party found out that, after all, the joke was a very small joke indeed.

Beatrice went to her room after a while, consoled by this little victory, and set herself seriously to consider all the dangers that were awaiting Walter. A blacksmith grandfather, with a forge in the village, which naturally the little boy would haunt, getting corrupted by the company he found there; an uneducated mother, who naturally would do her best to attach her child to her own friends; a (no doubt) wide and extensive relationship — for, as Beatrice sagely reflected, these sort of people always have legions of brothers and cousins — with the shopkeepers and tradespeople of the district; and all this for a child that was the heir of an ancient family, with a baronet's title and a large entailed property. By the time her maid had done with her for the night, Beatrice had come to

feel that her sacred duty to her brother's child demanded immediate exertion; and nothing could have
been more convenient than the arrival of Sir Robert
Blarney, who was coming on Saturday; for that was
the year when Sir Robert was Attorney-General, and
there could be no doubt that he was qualified, if anybody could be qualified, to give a lady the most
thorough enlightenment possible as to the point of law.

CHAPTER XV.

The Terrors of the Law.

THIS was how Agnes was disturbed out of her calm
at the end of the first year of her widowhood. She
did not understand, at the first glance, what was the
meaning of the lawyer's letter, which intimated to her
that an application had been made to the Lord Chancellor in respect to her boy. Terror seized her, as was
natural, at the first thought. She knew very little
about the law, and she knew that by times the law
was capable of terrible cruelty to a woman, or, at least,
so she had read and heard. She did not know what
limits there might be, or whether there were any limits,
to that cruel power, and at the first glance it seemed
to her as if her child was going to be snatched away
from her without any reason. Naturally, the first thing
she did was to hasten to her father, who was much
surprised by her hurried visit. Walter was not at the
forge, and had even lost the habit of going, and was
at the present moment deep in the early mysteries of
Latin, under charge of Mr. Freke's curate, who took
pupils — so that, as far as that was concerned, the

little heir of the Trevelyans did not require the active
intervention of his aunt and the advice of the Attorney-
General so much as Miss Trevelyan hoped. The blacksmith was hard at work when he saw his daughter
come in hastily out of the sunshine under the archway,
which enshrined her like the frame of a picture. Stanfield laid down his tools instantly, and stretched out
his hand for his coat. If he was careful of Walter, he
was still more careful of Agnes, and would not have
her come to him among his workmen. He made a
little sign to her with his hand to wait for him, and
went out to join her as soon ʼs he had got his coat on
— for he had his formulas like other men, and this
was his grand signal of being ready to encounter the
world. As for Agnes, she did not wait for him, but
went hastily up into the house, leading the way, where
Mrs. Stanfield was moving about in her ordinary morning occupations. When the blacksmith followed, his
wife came into the parlour after him.

"Whatever you've got to talk about," said Mrs.
Stanfield, "I ain't a-going to be banished out o' my
own house; I don't care nothing about your secrets,
but I ain't a-going to be sent away. It's bad enough
as there's one house in Windholm where I ain't wanted
nor asked; but, thank Providence, I am at home
here."

And she sat down in Stanfield's arm-chair, and
turned her fiery eyes from the father to the daughter.
There was nothing wonderful in the fact that she
thought herself the aggrieved party, and had a firm
conviction that they plotted against her, and that it
was she who was to be the subject of the discussion;
and Agnes, for her part, was too much excited to care

particularly who was present. She said, "Never mind,"
hastily, and without any preface put the letter into
her father's hands; but she could not quite master herself sufficiently to keep silence while he read it. "What
can we do? — what do you think we can do?" she
kept saying. "They cannot have the power to do
anything so cruel?" and then she bent over the chair
Stanfield had taken, and read it once more over his
shoulder. "He is to have an education according to
his condition," she said; "you know what you fixed
upon about that. Don't you think if I were to write,
or you, and explain —"

"Yes," said the blacksmith, "to Mr. Charlton. I
have been looking for this for a long time; I don't
know if my old Mr. Ponsonby will be of much use. It
is out of his way, I am afraid. Write to Mr. Charlton
— he is the man."

"But, father, it was he who first spoke of this —
who first told me that such a thing was possible," said
Agnes, almost with a touch of resentment. "He is
kind; but, perhaps, he thinks, like the rest, that I am
incapable —, and he does not know *you*. If I were
to write to these people, and tell them exactly what
we mean to do, and that they need have no fear for
Walter —"

"To Mr. Charlton, little one," said the blacksmith,
with his tender voice; "I have been trusting they
would spare you, but there is no pity in them. This
letter is from agents — men that care nothing about
Walter; is it to them you would write?"

"I suppose Sir Roger must have consulted them,"
said Agnes, a little ashamed of her own vehemence;
"that was what I meant. You do not think they have

any power to take him? Law may not be justice, but
it cannot go in the face of justice. I am his mother,"
she said, looking with an anxious appeal into her
father's face, as if the decision rested with him. All
this Mrs. Stanfield listened to, palpitating with curiosity
and exultation as she sat in the corner in the blacksmith's chair.

"Sir Roger ain't the one to do things by halves,"
said the eager spectator. "I don't know what it is as
you're making such a fuss over — talking to the
master as if he had nothing ado but what you tell him.
It ain't the time for that, Agnes Stanfield. He's done
a deal too much for you, if the truth was known.
When you was at 'ome I never said a word; but a
daughter as is married is done with. Don't you go
a-leading of him into more expenses. If anything was
to happen to the master, I've got myself to look to,
and he ain't got no right to spend everything he has
on a married daughter. Now you've been and worried
poor Mr. Roger into his grave, you ain't a-going to begin with the master. What right have you to keep
your children more than another? What call has everybody to forget themselves for *you?*"

Mrs. Stanfield managed to utter all this notwithstanding her husband's interposition. She had risen
from her corner and come forward to the table, and
added the force of action to her eloquence. The blacksmith could not help being abashed and disconcerted
when his wife made one of these demonstrations in his
daughter's presence; for, indeed, it was only after
Agnes's marriage, when the restraint of her society
was finally removed, that Mrs. Stanfield had quite
shown herself in her true colours to the tolerant and

long-suffering man who had been content to think that
she did not understand. Stanfield felt in his heart that
it was he who was to blame for having confided his
house and his name to the keeping of such a woman,
and then he rebuked the thought, and recollected that
she was his wife, and that even in his own mind he
ought to keep loyal and indulgent to her. But this
time he had made so many efforts to stop her ineffec-
tually, that a more decided step had to be taken.

"Silence, Sally," he said; "go to your own affairs,
or be silent if you will stay here. This has nothing to
do with you. She does not understand you and me,"
he said, turning to his daughter, and trying to smile,
though he was red with mortification; "it is not her
fault. It would have been better, perhaps, if you had
sent for me; but then there is no time to be lost."
The blacksmith paused a little, for he was mortal, and
he could not quite dismiss from his mind the petty
griefs which were his own. "Leave us by ourselves,
Sally," he said. "I tell you you don't understand; and
I have told you before, you are provided for when I
die — what more would you have?" he repeated, with
a little agitation. He could not help being ashamed
of having connected this unruly and lawless creature
with the daughter who had always been to him as a
princess; and then it came over his mind that Agnes's
adversaries might make something of her stepmother,
and might even, if their attention was directed to this
weak point, make discoveries about Mrs. Stanfield,
which he himself recently had dreaded to make. If it
should turn out so, it would be his own blame, and it
would be his business to bear it, seeing he had brought
it on himself; but then it was hard to contemplate

shame in connexion with Agnes. He could endure all things for himself, but he had much less courage for his child.

"You have not answered me, father," said Agnes. She, too, was absorbed in her own affairs, as was natural. She turned her head away from Mrs. Stanfield, as from a frivolous interruption. With her, who had her mind full of Walter, her stepmother counted for so little. "But the more I think of it the more impossible it seems," she said. "What reason could they have for taking my child from me? Even law cannot go quite without reason — I am his mother. You do not think they can do anything to me?" After her confident assertion of safety, she looked wistfully into her father's eyes. To be sure she felt certain; but then however certain one is, a fact becomes always more apparent when it is repeated by another voice.

"My darling," said the blacksmith, "by all I can hear, I don't think that in this respect they can do you any harm."

"Ah, thank you, thank you for saying so!" cried Agnes. "That is all I want. You have looked so doubtful and alarmed. I have always had a feeling that you thought me in danger. If they cannot do us harm in this respect, it is impossible to touch us in any other. Now that you have said *that*, father, I will write to Mr. Charlton as soon as you like."

"Ay, that's always the best to do," said the blacksmith; but there was nothing confident or encouraging in his tone — on the contrary, he sighed and took one of those disconsolate walks round the room which people resort to when they are much perplexed, and do not know what to do. "I don't deny I've been

anxious and in a way," said Stanfield; "not that I
was frightened about Walter — my darling, it was
you."

"Me!" said Agnes, and she smiled a little. "They
can do nothing to me, father; the only person in the
world upon whom I am dependent is above being
moved by Sir Roger Trevelyan."

It was at this point that Mrs. Stanfield again broke
in. She had gone back to her seat, and established
herself in the *rôle* of listener, and had been sitting
motionless, paying the closest attention, and growing
redder and redder; but when Sir Roger's name was
spoken, she could no longer forbear: she burst in
upon the conversation with a strangled sound between
a laugh and a sob. She cried out, "Goodness gracious
me!" in the tone of a woman who could restrain herself no longer. "I should just like to know what the
likes of you knows about Sir Roger Trevelyan?" she
said. "He ain't none of your kind, nor he ain't the
man to take any notice of you, for all so grand as you
think yourself. I warned you as you was marrying
poor Roger for his ruin. Silence! I ain't one to be
silenced in my own house. Silence yourself, master,
and let her hear the truth for once, if she never hears
it again. I told you as it was for his ruin as you
married that deceived young man; and now it's for
your father's ruin as you're going against Sir Roger.
Lord bless us! if he wasn't one as could make the
master shake in his shoes — if he wasn't one as
could ——"

"I will walk home with you, Agnes," said the
blacksmith. "Don't come here any more; it is not a
place for you. Stand away from the door, Sally, or I

may do myself a mischief. I've been a deal too soft with you, I don't deny; but I am not a man that can bear other folk's meddling in his affairs. Stand aside from the door!"

He took her by the arm as he spoke, and drew her out of the way. When she felt herself within his grasp, the foolish woman had a momentary gleam of pleasure.

"You're jealous, that's what you are," she said, with a loud laugh. "Many's the time you've wanted to know how it was as I knew Sir Roger. I'm sick of you, and all your ways; and if you'll call back your lady daughter I'll let you know ——"

The blacksmith grew so pale that he was scarcely recognisable for the moment. Perhaps it was a sudden light that burst upon him — perhaps it was only extreme exasperation working upon the tolerant and tranquil nature, which, "much enforced, yielded a hasty spark;" but when Agnes was gone, that was the great point, and he could put up with the rest. He looked his wife in the face as she threw this defiance at him, and still holding her by the arm, put her back from the door by which he was about to follow his daughter.

"Take care," he said, "that you don't say something that you will repent. I can bear a deal, but there's some things no man can bear."

He had never said anything to her that was so like a menace, and the reckless creature drew back frightened in spite of herself, with an hysterical laugh. Stanfield did not wait either to hear her repentance or the fulfilment of her threat; he shut the door care-

12*

fully behind him, and followed his daughter downstairs.

As for Agnes, she was too much occupied with her
own affairs to attach any particular importance to
what her stepmother had said; and then she was like
Desdemona, and did not believe that there was any
"such woman." She waited down below till her father
joined her, with pity for him, who was bound to such
a companion, but no particular curiosity; and she put
her arm into his the moment he joined her, and returned to the subject which filled her thoughts. They
did not go back to the house on the Green, but round
by the Common, which was the blacksmith's favourite
walk when he had anything to think of. It was
morning, and all the village people were about, and
some of them thought it not a little strange to see an
elegant woman, like what Mrs. Trevelyan had come to
be, with her arm in that of the village blacksmith, in
his blue coat, which he wore on working days. As
for Agnes, she was unaware what coat her father had
on; and so far as she thought at that moment of anything but Walter and the danger that menaced her,
her sensation was one of the most entire and un-
mingled thankfulness to have such a counsellor at
hand.

"But you are still anxious," she said; "you tell
me you don't think they can take Walter from us,
and yet you look disturbed. Don't hide from me,
father, what it is. If there is anything further to be
feared, I would rather know it all at once."

"There is all to be feared that ever was to be
feared," said Stanfield. "My darling, it never was
Walter that troubled me — it was for *you.* I believe

the child is safe; but the trial — the exposure — I cannot think of it, Agnes. If it was possible to make a compromise ——"

"The exposure?" repeated Agnes — "of what? Is there anything that we can fear to have exposed? — that I am your daughter, perhaps? But then, as I am proud of that ——"

"Hush, little one," said Stanfield, sadly; "you don't know what you are saying. In some things you have more experience than I have, that am your father; but in some things you are only a child. Yes, the exposure — all your life, innocent and sweet as it has been, talked of in a public court, and printed in the papers; and your friends and everybody belonging to you; and whether you are fit, from your antecedents, to have the charge of your child; and what you have to live on; and whether your father, who is the blacksmith, will be likely to harm your boy; and a hundred things more that people will read in the papers, as if you were —— My darling, I cannot bear it; we must try to make a compromise."

Agnes, too, paused with a start, and took a little time to contemplate this unthought-of case. For a moment it had the effect her father feared, and drove the colour from her face; but at the same time Agnes was, as Stanfield had said, much more experienced than he in some things. She knew better than he did what it was to be put in the papers, how utterly evanescent the effect was, and how few people would remember next day what was the name of the person who had possessed that momentary distinction. She grasped his arm a little closer as she made her reply.

"I will write to Mr. Charlton at once," she said.

"No compromise, father. What does it matter about
the papers? If it should even be so, nobody would
remember it next day; and then I don't even think
the papers would put it in. If I had been fashionable,
it might have been different; or perhaps, if I had been
wicked," she said, with a momentary flush and smile;
"but people like us, who have never done any harm to
speak of — we are not sufficiently interesting for
that." She smiled as she said so, but Stanfield was
not reassured; for he, with the ideas of his own
humble class, did not understand that soft contempt
for the newspapers which Agnes had learned in the
bigger world. It seemed to him that a corner in the
leading journal conveyed a kind of disagreeable im-
mortality; and, notwithstanding what she said, he
hesitated still. They walked about the Common, half
the morning, discussing this matter. Agnes was as
much afraid of the very name of a compromise as he
was of the "exposure" in the papers. She would not
see that Sir Roger Trevelyan had any claim upon *her*
boy — she would not allow even that the family who
had neglected Roger and declined to acknowledge herself, had anything whatever to do with her son; and
in sight of a claim which seemed at once insulting and
injurious, the Lord Chancellor and the newspapers had
scarcely any effect upon her. To be sure, it was she
who carried the argument, for Stanfield had only the
old plea to repeat; and she, for her part, refused to
acknowledge its importance. They parted without
having, either of them, yielded or convinced the other.
The only thing they had agreed on was that Jack
Charlton was to be consulted; and this was how it
came about that her casual acquaintance of so many

years came to have for a time so large a share in
Agnes Trevelyan's life.

CHAPTER XVI.

Counsel and Client.

WITHOUT any loss of time, Jack Charlton answered
the call which Mrs. Trevelyan made upon him. He
had already refused to have anything to do with Sir
Roger's case, and it pleased him when Agnes appealed
to him. He was by no means without talent, when he
had sufficient motive to exercise it; but his indolence and
carelessness, and want of any sufficient stimulation, kept
him quite at leisure to take up at once any matter which
interested him. He answered Mrs. Trevelyan's letter in
person next day; and it would have been difficult for him
to have put his motives into words, or to have explained
why he was disposed to put himself so promptly at the
service of his friend's family. It was for Roger's sake —
and yet it is doubtful if he would have taken so much
trouble for Roger had he been living; and then the
Trevelyans were old friends "at home," and it was
awkward to embroil himself thus with a family which
was still of some importance in the county and next
neighbours to his brother. Jack declined to think what
his mother would say when she heard of it, not to
speak of the brother who was head of the house. And
he went with a certain impulse of expectation and
pleasure through the village, to Mrs. Trevelyan's house
on the Green. He had a long conversation with her,
as was natural. He told her how the application would
be made against her, and explained as well as he could
how the strength of Sir Roger's case would consist in

an attempt to prove herself and her friends unworthy
to have the charge of Walter. This was not a very
pleasant thing to do, but Jack managed it not unsuc-
cessfully. And then he found that Agnes only smiled
at this fear. Stanfield, who was sent for to be present
at the interview, looked on with a very grave and even
gloomy countenance; but as for Agnes, she smiled —
and this smile had a singular effect upon the mind of
her defender. It made him look at her again with a
new interest. Agnes was not one of the women who
know, as it is called, their own advantages, and are
aware of the best means of making their strong points
visible. Her eyes, for example, were beautiful, but she
made no use of them, so to speak. Instead of fixing
them on the individual who spoke to her, she had a
habit of occupying them with some piece of stupid
work, which was sufficiently annoying sometimes. And
then her face was not one which displayed its beauty
at the first glance. It was only when she got sufficiently interested to give up the work and give free
vent to her sentiments that a stranger found out the
grave sweetness and purity of all the lines of her face,
and the character and expression of the eyes, which
were like two windows opened into an infinite blue
heaven. But it was not her beauty, such as that was,
which struck Jack Charlton at this moment; it was the
strange discordance between her appearance, and looks
and expression, and that ideal of a blacksmith's daughter
who had made an ambitious marriage, and was bringing
up her son in debased tastes and low society, which
would have to be presented by Sir Roger's advocate
before the authorities. He smiled himself when he
thought of that, but it was an angry and indignant smile.

And as for Stanfield, he continued gloomy and melancholy. He gave his sanction to everything that Mr. Charlton judged necessary, but he was not cheerful, nor sanguine, for his part. Perhaps, being used to see her every day, it did not occur to him that Agnes's appearance of itself would have any special effect upon a lofty functionary like the Lord Chancellor; but, at the same time, his reverence for his child, who was also his ideal, made the idea of a contest about her insupportable to him. So far as he was concerned, he was almost ready to give up Walter, and decide that revolting discussion; for Agnes was above discussion, above question, to her father; and even the man who proved her superiority seemed to his eyes, which were a little fantastic in this respect, to do her wrong. Perhaps she had not the same delicacy for herself; she was no longer a girl, shy and timid. Agnes had now the nobler modesty of a woman who has had many things to do in the world, and who has found herself able to do them without exciting remark. Her humbleness was not the false humbleness which fears to be looked at, but the true humility which knows that the world has its own affairs in hand, and has wonderfully little leisure to stare at an obscure individual. For most of her married life she had been obliged to manage her affairs alone, and to go about unprotected, and she had never found any difficulty in her way. Nobody had stopped to stare at her, nor obstructed her path; and the consequence was that she was not afraid for the Lord Chancellor, nor even for the newspapers, and smiled, with a sense of something half-comic in her father's distress.

"What does it matter?" she said to him; "I am

not so important that all the world should occupy themselves with me. The people in Windholm may be
amused, perhaps, but then they know it all already,"
said Agnes. "You don't consider how little attention
people give to anything which has no connexion with
themselves."

"You are philosophical, Mrs. Trevelyan," said
Jack Charlton, who, on the whole, was more of Stanfield's way of thinking, at the present moment, than
of hers.

"No," said Agnes; "I am only a little experienced,
that is all. Polly Thompson does not like to go into
church alone," she continued, with a soft momentary
laugh; "she thinks everybody is looking at her; and
you know you are not looking at her, father, nor
thinking of her, even if by chance she should pass
before your eyes. It is more disagreeable, certainly, to
pass under people's eyes in a corner of the *Times;* but,
happily, I am just as unimportant to the world as Polly
is to you."

The blacksmith shook his head and made no answer,
for his humility in respect to Agnes was not in the
least true humility, but rather the reserve of intense
pride, which cannot believe that what is so interesting
to itself can be indifferent to others. He was even a
little irritated by her smile and her illustration. He
did not see what there could possibly be in common
between Polly Thompson and his daughter. Poor Polly
was still only Miss Thompson's niece — she was not
even married, nor had any separate standing in her
own person, and her dread of attracting observation
was amusing enough; but Stanfield, enlightened as he
was, was so far biassed by his affections that he could

not imagine even the universal British public, big and abstract as it was, to be as indifferent to his daughter as the good people in Windholm Church were to Polly Thompson and her comings and goings. And thus the consultation closed, with the principal party to it still unconvinced in his heart. Jack Charlton, who took his leave at the same time as Stanfield did, and walked with him as far as their way lay together, was as unsuccessful as Agnes had been in reconciling the blacksmith to the "exposure" that was inevitable. Stanfield went back to his work, sighing over it, in his heart. So far as he himself was concerned, the idea of shrinking from anything that might happen to be his duty, or keeping anything secret which he had ever performed, would never have occurred to him; but the matter changed completely according to his ideas, when the subject of the experience was a woman instead of a man; and changed still more when of all women in the world it was Agnes to whom this trial had come.

And, as was natural, this was far from being Jack Charlton's last visit to Windholm. He came often to consult with his clients, and to give them the particulars of the case, and the oftener he went the more inclined he felt to return. Both father and daughter exercised a certain fascination upon Jack, who was one of the *blasés* of society, too indolent to make any effort to bring himself to the notice of the world, and yet a little resentful that its notice was not bestowed upon him. To be sure, it was difficult for a man in his position not to observe the difference which people in general made between himself and his elder brother, and even which his mother, who was a good mother in her way, and loved her children, made between other

elder brothers and their juniors. If he had chosen to
go a little deeper into the matter, he would have found
out without difficulty, that, had he devoted himself to
the task of conciliating society, as some men did — or
worked hard and acquired the success which gives a
legitimate claim upon its esteem, he might altogether
have distanced the Squire. But then Jack was not
disposed to take the trouble of going deeply into anything: excepting always the case of "Trevelyan *versus*
Trevelyan," which occupied his mind to a remarkable
extent. The winter passed all the more quickly for
this interest which occupied it; and Agnes, too, became
accustomed to see Jack and to expect him, and even
to look forward somewhat eagerly to his coming. He
was her boy's champion and her own — the intermediary
between her and those omnipotent powers who could, if
they would, remove the chief charm from her life — the
society of her first-born; and accordingly it was with a
sentiment of eager interest, gratitude, and regard that
she opened her doors to Jack Charlton, whose appearance
began to be known in Windholm, and whom many people,
of whom he had no knowledge, looked at with great
curiosity as he went down the village street.

Mrs. Trevelyan's adviser had so much to tell of the
suit and its progress; of the hearings granted and the
delays interposed, and of the devices of the opposite
party and his own arrangements to meet them, that the
interviews between counsel and client generally lasted
for some time; not to say that the distance between
London and Windholm made the visit a kind of little
journey, and enforced the fulfilment on Agnes's part of
the duties of hospitality. It was true that the blacksmith was almost invariably one of the party, but that

did not stop the smiles and nods and comments of the
Windholm folks. Even Mrs. Trevelyan's servants began
to look with curious eyes upon Mr. Charlton, as speculating
what kind of a master he would be, if it came to anything; and Madelon in particular, with a more charitable
anxiety, took pains to observe his reception of the
children, who might, perhaps, some day be thrown
upon his mercy. And Jack was fond of children, like
most men of good conditions and indolent mind. Naturally, the chief person concerned was the last to know
what speculations were going on round her; Agnes, who
was occupied with her duties and her anxieties, went
and came in her ordinary way all the winter through
without finding out this conclusion made by her neighbours. There were even laughing allusions made in
her very presence, which she alone did not understand
in their true meaning. The other inhabitants of Windholm had no doubt about the matter. As for Mrs. Freke,
who naturally took a great interest in the report, she
felt a little injured and aggrieved at first, as good
women are apt to do who have put their faith in the
constancy of a widow; and then having got over that
first sense of desecration, the vicar's wife began to
make very anxious inquiries about Charlton, whom he
belonged to, and what he possessed.

Mrs. Freke, however, had not, as yet, made up
her mind that it was her duty to speak seriously to
Agnes; for she had a certain consciousness at the bottom of her heart, that on former occasions when she
had fulfilled this duty she had come off invariably
second best, and with her prestige impaired; but, at the
same time, though she kept silent, she reserved all her
rights to speak when the proper moment should arrive.

The vicar, on the contrary, was pleased with the new
idea. He was not, as we have said, a man who concluded happiness to be necessary to existence, because,
though he got on extremely well on the whole, he had
no consciousness of ever having been particularly happy
in his own person; but it appeared to his candid mind
that Providence (perhaps, being a clergyman, he did
not use that abstract word, but ventured on a still
bolder expression) owed something to Agnes in return
for the hard experiences she had gone through, and the
premature termination of that life of two, which, however either partner may fail in duty or capacity, bears
an aspect of completeness which a woman or man alone,
however excellent, cannot attain to. He thought Providence owed Mrs. Trevelyan something to make up for
her troubles; and he had a liking for Jack Charlton;
and altogether it seemed, as he said, a very reasonable
arrangement.

"When there are so many idiotic marriages," the
vicar said, "a connexion that has a little reason in it
is agreeable to see. No, I don't speak of love; I don't
understand anything about love — it is just as mad
and stupid as other things in this absurd life. I say
there's a little reason in this; and that is why I have
some doubt in my own mind whether it will ever come
to pass."

"Mr. Freke," said his wife, with restrained indignation, "one would think you were speaking of the
French way of marrying. I don't say that I approve
of Agnes Trevelyan sitting there in her widow's cap,
not eighteen months yet after poor Roger's death, and
thinking of marrying again; but I don't think so badly
of her as to believe she's going upon *reason*. I don't

know anybody but you who could entertain such an idea. It is something too shocking to think of," said the good woman, with an air of disgust. All this the vicar accepted calmly, as was his wont.

"That is the worst of it," he said; "I am not sure that I quite believe myself in her good sense, and yet in ordinary affairs she has more than good sense. We are all fools, Harriet, that is the truth. Everybody rushes at everything without thought, and a good woman like you is disgusted to think that another woman goes upon reason — that's how it is. It's easiest to put the blame upon God; but I don't feel quite sure, for my part."

"If you have not any respect for the Bible, Mr. Freke, do have a little respect for me, and don't talk in that frantic manner," said his wife, with a certain calmness of despair. The vicar did not give any distinct reply, but made his usual promenade round the room, and went away with his arms under the tails of his long coat. "It would only be just to give her a little compensation," he said to himself as he withdrew; but then Mr. Freke, as everybody knew, had curious ideas, especially on the subject of Providence, and was far from being a reassuring visitor when, as the villagers said, there was trouble in the house.

The other inhabitants of Windholm partook the sentiments thus expressed by the vicar and his wife. Some of them were shocked at Agnes's heartlessness, especially as she still wore her widow's cap; and some thought it was another effort of her ambition to get herself made a lady; and some, more charitable, imagined, with Mr. Freke, that she deserved a little consolation after having suffered so much — if, indeed, consolation was to be found in a second marriage, which most people thought unlikely; and some bewailed the poor children who were to be cast upon the tender mercies of a stepfather. And then there was a party in the village who took the supposition as a personal offence. Such was the opinion of little Miss Fox, whose feelings were so much affected that she had to retire to her own room after hearing this terrible rumour, and whose eyes were red with crying when she was summoned to dinner in the evening — so red that even her papa observed it, who was not at all, as Mrs. Fox said, a noticing man. Miss Minnie could not help crying over poor Mr. Trevelyan, who was so soon forgotten, but whom *she* had not forgotten, though his wife had done so. She could not help thinking how different it would have been had *she*, and not Agnes, been his disconsolate and inconsolable widow; and the more she cried, and the more she reflected, the more aggrieved and affronted she grew — as if it was not enough distinction for anybody to be Mrs. Trevelyan, and to possess the sad distinction of wearing those heavy robes and that widow's cap! Miss Minnie went downstairs with such red eyes that her papa, as we have said, observed it, and demanded the reason, and drove the suffering young woman to desperation. Probably it was on that evening that the report which arose in Windholm, that Miss Fox was subject to "attacks on the nerves," took its origin — for what other reason could a watchful mother give for her daughter's red eyes?

Thus it will be seen that Agnes's supposed flirtation had consequences far wider than she could have dreamt of, had she known anything about the matter;

but fortunately, or unfortunately, nobody had the courage to say to Mrs. Trevelyan that she was being talked of in the village, or that the lawsuit and the relation of counsel and client were only partially believed in by her neighbours. To be sure, the rumour came, after a time, vaguely to Stanfield's ears; but he was the last man in the world to disturb his daughter with such a piece of idle gossip. And as "Trevelyan *versus* Trevelyan" continued to hang on during the whole winter, and was not concluded even when summer returned, Jack Charlton still continued his visits, and Mrs. Trevelyan got insensibly more and more used to him and pleased to see him. Agnes had ended her youth prematurely, but yet at the bottom of her heart she was still young; and, though her children were dearer to her than anything else in the world, and her father was her chief support and prop, still there were moments when it was pleasant to talk to somebody who was near her own age, and who was not confined by those natural limits of place, and custom, and locality, which had their effect even upon the large and liberal nature with which God had endowed the blacksmith. She could talk to Jack Charlton of many things which it would not have occurred to her to discuss with Stanfield; and thus the friendship upon which the Windholm folks built such a pretty romance grew gradually to be of some importance, unconsciously to herself, in Agnes Trevelyan's life.

CHAPTER XVII.

Village Gossip.

THINGS were in this condition when Mrs. Trevelyan was called to that interview with the Lord
Chancellor in person, which was to have so much influence upon the suit of "Trevelyan *versus* Trevelyan."
No doubt this event was one which Agnes contemplated
with a certain nervousness, feeling conscious, as she
did, how much depended on it. Perhaps it was the
first time in her life that she had considered seriously
the effect that would be produced by her personal appearance, her manners, her mode of expressing herself.
She looked at herself in the glass on the morning of
that important day with a concern something analogous
to that with which Beatrice Trevelyan had so often
studied her own face; and even asked herself what
people thought of her looks with a curiosity which had
never before been fully awakened; for, to tell the truth,
it was not a subject which had occurred to the mind of
Agnes, as, according to the general verdict of the world,
it does to most women. She had had no mother to
admire her, and set off her beauty. To her father she
was not, at any time, a pretty girl, but a kind of
sacred ideal woman, not to be desecrated by such poor
praise as could be conferred by compliment. And then
Roger, after the first short rapture, had become too
critical and doubtful to flatter his wife, or inspire her
with confidence in herself; and the consequence was,
that now Agnes looked into her own face with a little
wistfulness, thinking that to be handsome for that one

day, to find somewhere the talisman of beauty, which is said to work such rare effects, was something to be wished for with all her heart, if wishes only were any good. What she saw in the glass was a middle-sized woman, of rather ordinary appearance — as she thought to herself in her anxiety — in the profound unmitigated black of her mourning. What she could not perceive was the wistful grace of her own looks — the serene and candid depths of those eyes, which nobody could disbelieve — the air of absolute purity and truth which was in her countenance. Her forehead was not the smooth, unruffled front of youth, but it had a charm perhaps more touching, for the lines on it were lines not of present pain, which go against all beauty, but of sorrow softened and subdued, and of thoughtfulness, which is always lovely in its way.

All this Agnes did not see; but she saw — what satisfied her to a certain extent, for she was only human — that her dress, though it was very black and sombre, hung as it ought to do, and was in its utter simplicity the dress of a lady, well made and seemly. Some people may think this was a poor enough consolation; and yet it did something for Mrs. Trevelyan's courage. She could not flatter herself that she was beautiful, or capable of fascinating an unimpressionable dignitary like the Lord Chancellor; but as she looked at herself in the glass, she could not help thinking that he would receive her as an equal, and understand the respect and sympathy which her appearance generally procured for her; so that, on the whole, Agnes turned away from her mirror not unsatisfied. Mrs. Freke had offered to go with her, and was waiting for her downstairs, and the vicar's wife looked

13*

but a very homely chaperone for Agnes, notwithstanding that her family was six times as important, and,
indeed, not to be named in the same breath as that of
the blacksmith, which, indeed, was no family at all.
Thus they set out on their important mission; and it
was with white lips that Mrs. Trevelyan kissed her
boy, whose fate, though he did not know it, was hanging in the balance. Perhaps, before she saw him again,
she might have been decided — if not in fact, at least
in the mind of the judge — unfit to have the care of
him; but this dread only gave dignity and gravity to
her look as she went to her trial. Mrs. Freke said
afterwards that she never saw anybody go through
anything more steadily, and that really she did not
think Agnes could have much feeling to be so uncon-
cerned at such a time. It was when they had come
back again from that momentous interview that the
vicar's wife gave her account of it to her husband, who
was showing a degree of anxiety on the subject quite
unusual to him; indeed, it was all Mr. Freke could do
to keep himself from going to the station to meet
them, as Stanfield did, to ascertain what the result had
been.

"I don't know that there is any result," Mrs. Freke
said, with a suspicion of crossness. "He was very
civil — indeed, I may say polite — and took a great
deal of notice of Agnes. To be sure, I daresay it was
a different kind of woman he expected to see; and, of
course, she gave very sensible answers; but the wonderful thing to me was, that she did not seem to feel
it a bit — not more, Mr. Freke, than if it had been
you."

"And what did he say?" asked the vicar with natural curiosity; but it was about the tenth time he had asked the question, and there seemed little hope of getting an answer.

"I am sure it would be perfectly impossible to remember all that he said," said the vicar's wife. "He asked her a great many questions; and she looked as steady all the time; — I should have been trembling like an aspen-leaf if it had been me; but somehow, I don't think Agnes has much feeling. She answered as quietly as if they had just been talking in a drawing-room; and I must say, I think she was too open — she mentioned about her father being the blacksmith, without the least hesitation. Of course, you and I know that Stanfield is a very superior man; but still, you know, in a case of this kind, I never see the good of going too much into detail. She gave him all the particulars," said Mrs. Freke, taking off her bonnet with an air of vexation and fatigue, "as plainly as she would have done to you or me."

"Of course she had to tell the truth," said the vicar. "She is a woman to tell the truth wherever she is; and — though that is an odious view of the subject, and enough to make one tell a lie if one could — still truth was the only policy in such a case."

"I am sure nobody ever said of me that I was against telling the truth," said the vicar's wife, with a little indignation, "but still there are more ways than one of doing it, you know. I don't see the use of going into every detail. His lordship was very nice all the same, and did not change to her in the least, even after she told him everything. But I must say, the thing that struck me was her coolness. She was no more put out of the way than I am, talking to you.

And then Mr. Charlton, you know," said Mrs. Freke, with a slight movement of her head, "he was there waiting for us, and paying *such* attention. I can't help saying that it makes me dreadfully impatient to see it all, and poor Roger scarcely settled in his grave, and she wearing that widow's cap."

"Poor soul! if she has a little happiness at last," said the charitable vicar, "she had not too much of that with Roger. There is something owing her after all she has gone through. I think Charlton is a good sort of fellow; and when one thinks how little comfort she has had ——"

"Mr. Freke, I wish you would not speak so," said his wife; "what you are saying strikes at the root of everything. If a woman is not happy in her married life, it is almost always her own fault; and when you think what Agnes Stanfield was, and how much poor Roger had to go through — and to see her in her widow's cap ——"

It was this that aggravated Mrs. Freke. To be sure, second marriages were not unlawful, and even took place every day; but then the costume had to be considered, and the sympathy it awakened, which was evidently procured under false pretences. It was this that upset the spectator's temper. She shook her head as she recalled it to her mind.

"I have always taken an interest in Agnes," she said; "I have always stood her friend from the first. Of course, I knew she had her faults, but I never anticipated anything like this. And to think that you can approve of it, Mr. Freke!"

Mr. Freke was not listening, but had gone off at a tangent on his own account.

"It is not the way things are managed in this world," he was saying to himself. "If she was to win her cause and marry that good fellow, and be happy ever after, it would be like a thing one had arranged one's self. It's a great deal too good to happen so; I have no faith in it, for my part."

But on the whole, it was satisfactory to know that Agnes had got safely through this momentous interview, and that Jack Charlton had been waiting for her, and had shown her a great deal of attention. Mr. Freke went away to his study with a sense that perhaps for once Providence, instead of procuring Agnes's "good" by abandoning and thwarting her — which is the usual popular explanation of the ways of Providence — might be as good to her as he himself would have been had he had the power. It was a forlorn hope; and yet, under the influence of all the favourable signs which were appearing on the horizon, the vicar tried to think that such a thing might be; but without, indeed, pausing to inquire what were the sentiments of the persons who would have to be employed as the instruments of Providence, could his benevolent intentions be carried out.

As for Agnes, she made her way home leaning on her father's arm; calm enough, as Mrs. Freke had said, and able to behave herself as usual, but with a thrill throughout all her heart and frame, and a strange haze in the atmosphere which surrounded her. She had made a supreme effort, and had succeeded. She had restrained all the little feminine impulses towards evasion or incomplete speech, and had answered fully, and largely, and clearly, the inquiries addressed to her. Nobody could doubt henceforward that the ac-

cusations brought against her by Sir Roger, of being
a person of no family and not much education, were
perfectly true; but at the same time, whatever other
people might think, Agnes came away with a certain
confidence that her judge had discovered the results
drawn from these premises to be as false as any in-
vention could be. To be sure, he had not pronounced
any decision; but yet her original confidence in the
truth of her cause was confirmed by a sense that the
supreme authority in her case had found in her a
woman whom he could treat only as an equal. A
certain excitement, long suppressed and wonderfully
concealed, made her arm thrill and tremble as it rested
on her father's, and filled the air to her with a certain
haze, as of a dream. It seemed strange to her to see
other people going about their ordinary business, as if
this was a day like any other day. She went home
and called Walter to her, and put down her head on
the boy's shoulder for a rest after she had kissed him.
He was her boy — nobody in the world could take
him from her. To be sure, it occurred to her mind at
that moment, with a dreadful shudder, that such a boy,
quite unassailed by man, had been taken by God out
of his mother's arms not very long ago, within the
very limits of the village; but it seemed to Agnes that
God was too good to send such a misery upon her.
She was a widow, and he was her first-born and her
only son. The hardest-hearted man, the sternest human
law, spares such a one — and was it for her to believe
that God was less merciful than man? She put Walter
away from her in her excitement a minute after, and
sat up and told her father everything that had happened. It seemed to her, as she spoke, as if she *must*

be safe. Men were kind in their way,[1] notwithstanding all the hard things that were said of them; and God was merciful. They could not, and surely He would not, take her child from her, and strike down to the earth all her courage and hope.

"Lord Norbury was very kind," she said; "I have confidence in him — and so has Mr. Charlton. *He* thinks we are all safe now."

Stanfield was excited, too, though he also made an effort to preserve his composure; and he had a sense that the worst was over, now that this interview had taken place. "And you were alone, and there were no newspaper people there?" he said, with a certain satisfaction in his voice.

"Why should there be newspaper people?" said Agnes, with a soft laugh. "You think our affairs are more interesting than they really are. We are safe, because nobody is thinking of us, father; and then Mr. Charlton says ——"

It was just at this moment that some visitors came to the door — Mrs. Fox and another neighbour, who took an interest in Agnes, and had come full of curiosity in the hope of hearing something. When they came in the conversation was resumed, though in a more general way; and Agnes continued what she was saying, so far as to repeat that Mr. Charlton now was of opinion that there was little to fear.

"And it must be so nice to have a man like Mr. Charlton to conduct everything," said one of the visitors, with a significant look. "A man who takes such an interest! Everybody begins to know him about Windholm. I saw him get into a cab at the station the other day, and the man never asked where he was to go to.

You know, my dear Mrs. Trevelyan, everybody connects
him with you; it is so nice to have him to manage your
affairs."

"And he seems so fond of the dear children," said
Mrs. Fox, with a sigh and a little solemnity; "that is
such a blessing!" These words, and the way in which
they both looked at her, and the sentiment in Mrs.
Fox's voice, and the laugh that was subdued in the
other, startled Agnes. She looked up first at one and
then at the other, and turned her eyes to her father,
finally, to ask what they meant. But Stanfield was
looking down on the carpet, and had a certain embarrassed and confused air, as if he himself were not quite
sure; and in that moment, excited as her own faculties
were, and suspectible with all she had just gone
through, a true perception of what they meant burst
for the first time on Agnes. For the first time it
occurred to her what an interpretation the little world
which surrounded her had been putting on her actions;
and words which had puzzled her at the moment, and
smiles for which she had been unable to account,
flashed back upon her mind like lightning with this
sudden explanation. Naturally she did the very last
thing she ought to have done, like any other innocent
woman — she blushed a sudden fiery overwhelming
blush, which being born entirely of surprise, and pain,
and innocence, and the shock she had received, looked
to the two friendly inquisitors like the fullest evidence
against her. They laughed and shook hands with her
warmly, and wished, with much meaning in their
looks, that everything might be settled comfortably,
when they went away. And Stanfield had gone before, so that Mrs. Trevelyan was left alone, with this

new question thrown like a sudden bomb into her heart, in its commotion of hope and thankfulness. It was then that she sent Walter away to play with his companions, feeling ashamed, she could not tell why, under the child's eyes. To be sure, he could not have understood the words and looks which she had found out only by chance, as it were; but still, the very suggestion in her son's presence, overwhelmed Agnes with a visionary shame. And, to tell the truth, the first feeling in her heart was that of a certain anger and bitterness, not so much against her neighbours as against Providence itself, which had made such a blunder possible. It seemed hard to her, a faithful wife and true woman, to feel herself thus thrown back again in the opinion of the little world that surrounded her, into a kind of factitious youth, as if she could begin the world again, and be moved once more by the hopes and fears which she had already had in her day, and done with like other wives. Agnes put her face into her hands to hide from herself the hot and painful blush, which was so different from the blush of youth. She asked herself what she had ever done to expose her to such a suspicion; and what was worse, she grew aware, slowly and in spite of herself, that Jack Charlton's society had been a pleasure to her; and then she came back from that thought to raise such a protest against the inequalities of life, as only suffering can wring from a dutiful heart.

Mrs. Trevelyan asked herself why was it that she should be exposed over again to those difficulties and dangers which belonged to another period of life, and not to hers? She felt not only ashamed, but wounded and sore to the depths of her heart; her woman pride, and all the prejudices of her character, and that prevailing sense of wifehood and motherhood which makes a woman sacred even to herself, had been struck at and wounded deeper than words could describe, and the wounds bled secretly and inwardly. It was this that confused her even in the moment of her apparent victory. Nobody in Windholm meant it as an accusation, not even Miss Minnie Fox, though she cried to think of the inconstancy of Roger's widow; nobody made a crime of it, nor did anything worse than laugh at the idea, that the young widow, as they said, had consoled herself. But then Mrs. Trevelyan, perhaps, was fanciful; the accusation was horrible to her, and so was the sense that she liked Jack Charlton to come, and had got used to expect him, and might miss him when he came no longer. And this, too, at the very moment when her child was in danger, and when, perhaps, he might be taken from her. At one time Agnes, with the craven impulse of nature, thought to herself that she should lose Walter as a punishment for having, even unawares and for a moment, suffered the idea of a stranger to enter into her life; and then her mood changed, and her heart swelled with a sense of the hardship of her lot.

It is hard to be left alone, with life and all its subtle influences still stirring strong in a spirit unsubdued by age — hard to be exposed to frivolous suspicions, to untimely laughter, to self-contempt, which is the worst of all. This Agnes felt bitterly and sorely — she who for so many years had never recognised herself in any other character than that of wife. From all this it will be seen that she was sadly visionary, and, indeed, fantastic in her ideas; for even Mrs. Freke had not any serious objections, though it made her impatient, as she said, to see the widow's cap under the circumstances. But the vicar's wife would have opened her eyes in utter amazement had she suspected the high-flown way in which Mrs. Trevelyan would take up a suspicion so natural; for, indeed, nobody had any intention of being hard upon Agnes, and Mr. Charlton had something of his own, though his practice was no great things, and in age and other particulars was suitable enough. If there had been supposed to be anything wrong or unseemly in it, Windholm would not have made up its mind so speedily and so cheerfully. But, to be sure, the opinions of Windholm, or even of Mrs. Freke, was not what Agnes took into consideration. And she was ashamed, and wounded, and disgusted to the bottom of her heart.

It would be vain to record all the thoughts that, under this new stimulus, passed through Mrs. Trevelyan's mind; as far as she had any egotism in her, it took this direction. She was not an admirer of herself, but still there was no point at which she could be wounded so keenly as in that delicacy and modesty of a wife, which is almost more susceptible than that of a girl. In this new light she recollected the doubtful look on her father's face, and interpreted it according to its true meaning. Stanfield, too, had been suspicious of her, and this had made his eyes shy of meeting hers, and given an embarrassed air to his face. She could not speak to him about it — which would have been the best thing to do — for her pride, which was considerable, though she did not know it, prevented her from talking to him, or any one, on such a subject. It was necessary that he and all the world should undeceive,

as they had deceived themselves, without any action on
her part. Agnes made up her mind to hear nothing
and see nothing, which was a resolution which naturally
led to her hearing and seeing far more vividly than
ever before, and getting the benefit of all the inuendoes,
the jokes, and playful observations which had been so
utterly unproductive of any effect up to this moment.
It was this, as we have said, that changed Mrs. Trevelyan so much just at this crisis; it made her a little
stiff and distant as, people said, she had never been
before; it made her reserved and unsympathetic, so far
as that was possible; and besides, it did to some extent
what Stanfield thought nothing on earth could do — it
made Agnes self-occupied, and intent upon her personal
affairs to an incredible degree.   She would even put
aside the suit of "Trevelyan *versus* Trevelyan," to at-
tend to what some gossip was saying. And the blacksmith asked himself what was the secret of his daughter's conduct, and did not like to answer. All this
mischief sprang from the looks and words of Mrs. Fox
and her neighbours, who were so kind as to take an
interest in Agnes. It was a small origin, no doubt, but
then a very little matter is enough to make a great deal
of disturbance; and it is impossible to limit the issues
of any known word or action. It confused her mind
at a moment when she ought to have had all her wits
about her; it made her impatient and distrustful of her
friends at the time when she had most need to hold by
them and their protection; and finally, it absorbed her
in what was at the best a kind of selfish anxiety, when
she ought to have been quite free to mark and observe
everything that was happening; and thus it was that
the piece of gossip which, up to this moment, had been

circulating so harmlessly in Windholm, having taken shape and form, began to help in the great designs of existence, and to prepare what turned out to be the hardest and most painful chapter of Mrs. Trevelyan's life.

CHAPTER XVIII.

A Crisis.

THE suit of "Trevelyan *versus* Trevelyan" dragged on for some time after the interview which Agnes had with the Chancellor — not that there was much to be done or said, but only that, by dint of postponements and adjournments, it is always easy to lengthen out such a process. And, naturally, in the meantime, it was impossible for her to dismiss or avoid the visits of Jack Charlton, who had more to do in Windholm than ever. When Agnes met him again after that revelation, it was difficult for her to preserve the air of unconscious friendliness and ease which had once been so natural. Perhaps Jack, who did not know of anything having happened in the meantime, might not perceive the difference, but Stanfield did vaguely, and did not know what to make of it — whether to believe that Agnes was yielding to the temptation, which, after all, it was, most probably, the best thing for her happiness that she should do, or whether she was going to preserve the ideal perfection of which he was so jealous, and keep the unity of her life unbroken. The blacksmith was not like the ordinary mass of fathers and mothers. Had his daughter married a second time, it would have been not a happiness and relief to him, but

a fresh shock, which, no doubt, his love could have got
over, but which at the same time would have been a
desecration of his idol. It was true that he had married
twice himself, not by any means to his comfort or consolation; but Agnes would have suffered in her father's
estimation could he have imagined that her happiness
could be increased by becoming the wife of Jack Charlton
or of any man; for he, too, was high-flown, and it was
from him, though nobody knew it, that Mrs. Trevelyan
took, on that, and other subjects, those fanciful ways
of thinking which this history has set forth.

As for Agnes, her curiosity was to find out whether,
when all the rest of the world had concluded upon it
as certain, such an idea had ever entered Jack's head,
or whether he was, like herself, the last to think of
such a conjunction. To be sure, she was only a
woman, after all, and perhaps a lingering remnant of
vanity in some corner of her heart would have been
gratified had Jack shown symptons of weakness in this
respect; though, so far as she was aware, all her
anxiety was to make sure that the suggestion was one
of idle gossip merely. But, however that might be, it
was impossible to make any change in her relations
with him until after the suit was over, and a natural
end should arrive to the business which drew them so
much together; so that Windholm still continued to
talk — though by times some gossiping neighbour, in
the height of a consultation on the subject, would turn
round and find Mrs. Trevelyan's eyes upon her, bright
and kindled up with an inexpressible defiance; and
that there was a certain disdain of other people's opinions in Agnes's manners at that moment which had
never, so far as any of her critics were aware, been

seen in her before. She did not say anything to anybody, but still the public became aware of a certain awakening in her eye and demeanour which put the good people on their guard. And as for Stanfield, he grew more and more confused, and did not know what to make of it. He was puzzled about Agnes, whose meaning he did not divine, and he was compunctious about Jack, to whom he could not wish a lover's reward for his trouble. It is true that, by dint of thinking about it, and accustoming himself to the idea, the report in the newspapers and the "exposure" of the trial had ceased to affect the mind of the blacksmith; but, as that passed away, something more and more painful had come in its place. Thus the time of the trial seemed to Stanfield a crisis full of pain, and discomfort, and anxiety — which, to be sure, he made all the more of, as he did not know what was to come.

But when the suit was finally decided, and the Lord Chancellor had made that little speech under which the blacksmith winced with pain, yet reddened with pleasure and pride, matters came to a crisis, as was natural. By this time it was spring, and more than two years had passed since Roger Trevelyan's death, and Windholm in general had got reconciled to Mr. Charlton, and was chiefly occupied in discussing the necessary arrangements, and where *they* were to live, and what was to be done about the children. Mrs. Freke's opinion was that Stanfield should settle what he had upon the little girls, poor little things!

"Mr. Charlton is not rich, but still he has something," said the vicar's wife, "and of course Walter must go to school. For my part, I can't see why his

mother was so bigoted against letting his father's family
have the charge of him; for, of course, if there should
be another family," said Mrs. Freke, with prudent pre-
vision — which, to be sure, was a contingency for
which nobody had thought of providing. The blacksmith, too, moved by the same sense that the crisis had
arrived, had grown very watchful and silent, divided
between fear and hope, and never quite able to deliver
himself from a certain tremor of expectation when he
saw his daughter coming to him, or approached in his
own person the house on the Green.

This complication of events, though it was Walter
who had given rise to all the difficulties of the situation, had somehow made Walter of secondary importance, as a child naturally becomes when the fate of
older people seems to hang in the balance. He was
left more to himself, though nobody was aware of it —
he was less with his grandfather, whose mind was
harassed and pre-occupied, and he was even less with
his mother, and when with her was not so much her
companion as of old; for Agnes had thoughts in her
mind at that moment which it would have been impossible for her to communicate to her child. And
perhaps it was this which made Walter take so sudden
a fancy for Mrs. Stanfield's son, who had come home
just at this time, and had stories of voyages and ship-
wrecks to tell which charmed the boy. There was not
anything to be said against Tom, so far as anybody
knew, though he had been the plague of the village
when he was a boy. Now that he had come home
from sea, with nothing particular against his character,
the just and charitable blacksmith could not refuse to
let him come to see his mother; and it was there, under

Stanfield's roof, that Walter first saw the sailor, who did all he could to attract his regard. If this had happened a little earlier, Agnes would have withdrawn her son from such equivocal society, and the blacksmith himself would have interfered to prevent so unsuitable a friendship; but at the present moment they were off their guard, and occupied with another matter — far less important, no doubt, than the interests of Walter, yet possessing a certain fascination in its way. Stanfield had nothing to say against Tom, whom he took into his house without much hesitation, though he had refused to receive the elder brother, Roger, who had turned out badly, as everybody was aware. The younger one was a little like his mother, high-coloured and hasty; but he was young and a sailor, and a certain frankness and good-humour softened down the resemblance. He was very respectful to Stanfield, and even to his mother in Stanfield's presence, which was saying a good deal; for when there was no one there to enforce a regard to observances, the sailor's filial duty was a little at fault. But then, whatever his character might be, it was under his grandfather's roof that Walter made his acquaintance; and neither Stanfield nor Mrs. Trevelyan observed, as they would have done had their minds been less absorbed, the attraction which the sailor's company began to have for the boy.

Tom had been to India, to America, to China; he had seen "natives" of every possible kind, and unknown animals, and tropical trees, and desert islands; and, what was perhaps still more attractive, storms at sea, and at least one shipwreck. Perhaps Walter did not know that something personal to herself was for the

14*

moment withdrawing from him his mother's mind; but,
without knowing what it was, the chances are that he
felt the consequences, and was vaguely conscious of
being left alone more than usual. And then Tom was
always complaisant — ready to leave anything he
might happen to be doing, and to resume the story at
the exact point where he had left it off. So that insensibly, while Agnes's thoughts were directed to another point — one which, after all, depended entirely
on her own will, and involved no external danger —
she began to encounter a risk for which she had made
no provision, and which it had not even occurred to
her to consider. Her fears were over so far as Walter
was concerned; and after having her mind directed to
her own personal interests in a manner so simple yet
so startling, perhaps it was excusable if, for the first
time, Agnes experienced in some degree the excitement
of a personal crisis. At least, excusable or not, such
at the present moment was the state of affairs in the
house on the Green.

Things were in this condition when Jack Charlton
came down one March day to announce the final
victory. The Chancellor had made a little statement,
which all the world read in the *Times*, as Stanfield had
dreaded, about Mrs. Trevelyan and her family. But,
after all, the blacksmith found that this publicity had
made wonderfully little difference in the general aspect
of the world, and that the effect upon himself, and
even upon Agnes, was not so startling as he had expected. What his lordship said was simply that he
had seen the parties to the suit on both sides, and had
carefully considered all the evidence that had been
laid before him; that so far from finding anything

against the character of Mrs. Trevelyan's relations, he found that her father had the very highest reputation in his neighbourhood, and that the family was much respected; and accordingly, that he saw no occasion to supersede the guardianship of the mother, who seemed to him perfectly qualified to have charge of her child. Circumstances might arise to alter the case, Lord Norbury added, no doubt with a recollection of the youthful looks of Walter's mother; but at present he saw no reason for interfering. All this was printed among other perfectly uninteresting particulars, in that corner of the *Times* which records the mysterious doings in Chancery; and, except the Windholm folks, few people were much the wiser. Jack Charlton came down triumphant with this news, to make Agnes aware of the utter discomfiture of her adversaries, who had all the costs to pay and all the scorn to bear. "Sir Roger lost his temper, poor man," said Jack. "It is a thing he can scarcely be said to possess at any time. But I hope he convinced the Court that he was qualified to be a child's guardian; and now I have nothing to do but congratulate you, I suppose," he added, with a sigh. He did not look at Agnes, or he might have seen the colour rising in spite of herself on her face; which was a very fortunate circumstance, since, had he but lifted his eyes and seen that consciousness, it is possible that Jack might have betrayed himself, and that at such a moment of emotion something traitorous in Agnes's heart might have responded; and there is no knowing what might have come of it; but, by good fortune, Jack Charlton did not lift his eyes. He sighed, but he only fixed his gaze upon his hat, and there was no inspiration in that. "I am very glad it is well

over, for your sake," said Jack, with a little cough,
which followed close upon the heels of the sigh; "but
I can't say I am much exhilarated on my own account.
I'm a lazy fellow, Heaven knows; but when one has
an object——— It has been very pleasant," said Mr.
Charlton, in an inconsequent way; and then again he
fell to looking at his hat, as if it had suddenly struck
him that the shape was not exactly what it ought to
be; and again gave forth from the depths of his breast
a kind of strangled sigh.

"You have been very kind," said Agnes. "I don't
know how I can ever thank you. If we had not had
so kind an advocate, things would not have gone so
well with us. To say how obliged and thankful I am
is impossible———"

"Yes," said Jack, with an uneasy movement; "I
wish you would not say it. I am an odd sort of fellow in that way — I can fancy a beggar is obliged to
me when I give him sixpence; but I hate obligation.
One never cares to have anything that another is
obliged to give."

"It was not in that sense I spoke," said Agnes,
who was a little wounded, and yet did not know what
to say, or how to say anything that might not, so
critical as the circumstances were, change the face of
affairs.

"No," said Jack, "I am sure you did not mean
anything that was not kind and good; but I seem to
have lost my temper as well as Sir Roger, I think.
By Jove, how the old fellow blasphemed! One good
thing in us is certainly, that we don't indulge in bad
language as our fathers did; not that I am one of the
people who think there is much good in us," said Jack,

giving up his hat. "On the whole, I do not know a poorer set of snobs;" and again her successful champion uttered a sigh and walked to the window, and all but turned his back on Agnes. Perhaps, when he had adopted that position, he found it more easy to speak, under guard, as it were, of the external world; for, to be sure, a man who sees nothing except the woman whom he admires greatly and feels the deepest interest in, and the four walls of an apartment altogether pervaded by the sentiment of her presence, is naturally in a position more dangerous than he whose eyes, at least, have the safeguard of the common universe out of doors, and all the things in it that run counter to the indulgence of his feelings. Standing there, Jack felt himself more able to speak.

"I am very glad for your sake," he said. "I can't say I ever had much fear after the Chancellor saw you, you know; but I thought with your father it might have been disagreeable. And then it's pleasant to win the battle; but yet I don't know; that's all on your account, and a man is selfish sometimes. It is a bore to be done with a thing one has taken an interest in. After all, there are so few things one cares about; and then, you know; I've got into the habit of coming down to Windholm. I hope you'll let me come sometimes and talk over my affairs now that yours are done with. An end is about as great a bore as a beginning," said Jack, with a certain oracular vagueness; but he was not amused to speak of even by his own absurdity, and stood at the window with his profile turned to Agnes, regarding her with a corner of his eye, and feeling a little anxious about her answer. He was a very good fellow, and his feelings were very true feelings in their way; and there was no saying what he might not have said had she wanted him to say anything, or lent him a helping hand. But then, Agnes did neither one thing nor the other, and he was not the man to take a romantic plunge regardless of consequences; but the situation was critical, perhaps more critical than either of them perceived.

"Indeed, I hope you will come to see us," said Agnes, who was almost more relieved by Jack's change of position than he was himself — "I hope you will always let Walter remember that you were his father's friend. I think," said Mrs. Trevelyan, after a pause, with a certain unconscious hypocrisy, "that I feel your kindness all the more because it is for Roger's sake."

Jack did not make any answer; he made, on the contrary, a kind of deprecating movement with his hand, and gave a slight start at this allusion — which was very sudden, and, as he thought, uncalled-for — fell upon his ear. As for Agnes, when she had found this golden vein, she fell upon it eagerly, as was to be expected, and worked her idea out.

"Perhaps you do not know — I hope you will never know," she said, with a certain mixture of superiority and humbleness — "what it is to feel that the person most dear to you in the world has left the world without showing fully what was in him; that he has, perhaps, left something behind him that might bring a shadow on his memory. Mr. Charlton, it is far more to me than anything you could have done for myself. What you have done has set my husband's name above reproach. I thank you most of all that it is for Roger's sake."

What could Jack Charlton say? He knew it was

not for Roger's sake, and so perhaps did she, even when, with tears in her eyes, she looked him in the face, and set her dead husband thus between them. It was, at the bottom, could any one have searched into it, a kind of deceit and hypocrisy which Agnes practised to put far from her the possibility of that new life which all Windholm had settled upon as a thing certain and evident. She looked him in the face, even in the eyes, with that gaze which has a purpose in it; and yet perhaps at the moment she spoke, and at the moment when her look was the most full and steady, her heart was trembling more than it had ever trembled before. Perhaps she was nearer being unfaithful to Roger, unfaithful to what she considered her trust and the occupation of her life — the guardianship of her children — at that moment than at any other point in her history. But, fortunately for them both, Jack Charlton had not eyes to see underneath the surface any more than Roger himself would have had; and he accepted her look and what she said, and the moisture which made her eyes so soft and so deep, as exponents of a heart which was not to be touched by any second affection. To be sure, he had not come with the intention of making any declaration, or committing himself in any way; but Jack, who knew no better could not help feeling a pang in his heart — a pang of mortification and disappointment, when he met the gaze of those dewy eyes.

"It is nothing," he said, confused and downcast. "I hope you will always think of me as a friend — always as a friend" — and Jack was glad and angry at the same moment to see Stanfield coming in to terminate the interview. There was a certain despair and de-

spondency in it, but yet there was a certain sweetness;
and when her father's voice was audible at the door,
and Agnes's watch upon herself relaxed a little, Jack
Charlton felt again a momentary doubt whether she,
too, was not aware in her heart of the sweetness and
the despair. But at that moment Stanfield came in,
and the ordinary world opened upon them both, and
the crisis was over. Agnes did not interrogate her own
feelings after her counsellor was gone. It was fortunately not a habit of hers, and at this moment it would
have been more than usually difficult; but somehow
she felt a strange fatigue of body and mind all the day
after. She was tired without knowing how, as if she
had been making some great physical exertion. The
strength seemed to fail out of her all at once, as if by
some treachery. She said to herself that it was the
reaction after her long anxiety, and that now, when
her mind was quite easy about Walter, it was not
wonderful that the strain should tell upon her. But, to
tell the truth, she had always had a great confidence
in her own rights, and the strain of anxiety had not
been so great as she supposed. She had very steady
and very vivid conceptions of her duty, and was not
likely to fail of carrying out what appeared to her the
right thing to do; but yet, at the bottom of her heart,
she was simply a woman like other women, subject to
the same infirmities; and perhaps that was the true reason why, on this March afternoon, though it was so
pleasant out of doors, Mrs. Trevelyan felt tired, and
was pleased when the evening set in, and she could
draw the curtains and light the lamp. She almost forgot to send for Walter at the hour when he ought to
have been at home, and had to be reminded by Ma-

delon, and felt a little vexed and annoyed with herself; but when one is very tired, one may be pardoned for a momentary forgetfulness; and on the whole there could be no doubt that she had "gone through" a good deal that day — and it was not necessary to explain to herself the nature of those experiences which she had gone through. It was enough that they were over now.

CHAPTER XIX.

Tom.

WHEN Walter came in, he was full of Tom's adventures, and all the strange sights his new friend had seen, and forgot to be penitent for forgetting to come home at the proper time — a sin which Agnes, on her part, forgot to reprove. Mrs. Trevelyan, to tell the truth, was languid and silent. She heard what her boy said, and she gave him a smile and a monosyllable now and then; but she had not yet got out of the shadow of her own thoughts, and she was not capable at the present moment of giving the large and ready sympathy which a mother can sometimes bestow. To live that vicarious life which is called living in one's children, it is necessary to avoid all personal crises, and those moments of individual existence which will arise by times, even in the mind of a woman, before age has calmed everything down. She listened and smiled upon Walter, and received a vague impression that the boy had been amused and pleased — an impression which gave her a certain feeling of benevolence towards Tom, who thus took in hand to amuse the child at a moment when she herself had, to some degree, lost the power of occupying herself with him; but, at the same time, Agnes responded but faintly, and was not sorry when Madelon appeared at the door to summon Walter to bed. But he was ten years old now — old enough to understand that something had happened; and perhaps in her heart Mrs. Trevelyan felt that there was something to be explained in her own demeanour; though Walter, for his part, was a great deal too much occupied with Tom's stories to be aware of any difference in his mother's looks.

"Walter, I want to speak to you," said Mrs. Trevelyan; "forget Tom for a moment. You have heard about the lawsuit with your grandfather, Sir Roger? It is over now; I want to tell you about it: you are to stay with me —"

"Yes," said Walter; "but then it does not matter, for I never would have left you, mamma; though I should like to have a yacht when we are rich, if you will not let me be a sailor. I should like best of all to be a sailor; but I suppose that would not please you. Tom says," the boy added, after a moment's pause, "that Trevelyan is near the sea."

"What does Tom know about Trevelyan?" said Agnes, hastily.

"Oh, only that he has been in Cornwall," said Walter. "When Sir Roger dies, and we are living there —"

"Walter," cried his mother, "you must not speak of what may happen when Sir Roger dies. I do not like you even to think of that. Sir Roger has not been very kind to me, but he is your grandfather, and I hope he will not die. He is not going to take you

from me now. The Lord Chancellor has seen him, and
settled everything" — which was Mrs. Trevelyan's
feminine interpretation of Lord Norbury's decision —
"and I am very glad he should have Trevelyan so
long as I have you."

"Yes," said Walter, with the calm confidence of his
age; "but then I never would have left you, mamma.
I am sure I don't want grandpapa to die. Tom says
he is very jolly; and then Trevelyan is near the sea."

"Does Tom know Sir Roger?" asked Agnes, more
and more surprised.

"Oh, he has seen him, he says; and Mrs. Stanfield
knows him too," said Walter. "They say we could
have a yacht there, and Tom would be captain, you
know. I'd like to sail away into the Mediterranean,
and take you to Sorrento, and Baden-Baden, and all
those places where we used to be. I wonder if Giovanni
would know me now. I'd like to have him for my
servant, if I had a servant. But, mamma, there can
be nothing so jolly as to have a yacht, and go everywhere, wherever one wants to go."

"Not to Baden exactly," said Mrs. Trevelyan.
"But, Walter, I don't like you to talk to Mrs. Stanfield
and Tom about your relations; they are a different
kind of people, you know. When you have anything
to say about Sir Roger, say it to me."

"But then, Mrs. Stanfield knows him," said Walter;
"and it is they who speak to me about him. Oh, I
forgot, they said I was not to tell you; but I would
not promise. They say a fellow should not be always
telling everything to his mamma, like a baby. But
then, about the yacht?"

"What was it they said you were not to tell me?"

said Agnes, growing a little pale. A word or two more would have roused her out of her languor, and awoke her to an anxiety graver and more painful than her former anxieties; but then Walter was only a child, and had all a child's vagueness as to particulars; the yacht was so much more interesting to him than anything about Sir Roger — and then it had never occurred to him that there was any importance in what they said.

"Oh, I don't recollect," said the boy. "Tom said grandpapa was a jolly old fellow. I did not pay so much attention to that. But there's a bay down there, where the yacht could lie quite safe, even in a storm; and then, you know, it would be such a jolly place to start from. Tom says —"

"Walter," said Agnes, "I do not like you to talk to Tom of your grandpapa, or of Trevelyan. Remember, another time; and as for yachts, you know, you must wait till you are a man, and you may change your mind before then. Now, mind you don't talk to Tom or Mrs. Stanfield about the Trevelyans; and look, Madelon is waiting for you. Good-night!"

"Yes," said Walter; "but it is they who talk to me of the Trevelyans; and then I don't care much for the Trevelyans. It is the yacht I was thinking of; no fear of my changing my mind. It is not as if I was a child, and did not know what I was talking of. I have not quite fixed the name yet — whether to call it after you and Agnes, or the Bee after baby — that would be most fun; but then, St. Agnes with the lamb, like the Madonna, on the Sorrento boats —" said the boy, upon whom the recollections of his infancy had still some visionary power; and he was still considering the subject when Madelon made her appearance, arbitrary, and not to be put off any longer. When Walter went away he left his mother all but roused into a panic. If there had been nothing in her mind to preoccupy her thoughts, she would have taken fright and made some immediate effort to secure Walter from the possible influence of her stepmother and her son; for Mrs. Stanfield had been for a long time an object of suspicion to Agnes, who felt, without asking herself how, that her father's wife was her enemy, and would injure her if she could. But then, the languor of her fatigue and her preoccupation, and sense of the crisis she had "come through," was still upon Agnes, and dimmed her energies. Instead of doing or resolving upon anything, she only considered the matter and thought it over, and ended by persuading herself that there was nothing in it — what could there be in it? Mrs. Stanfield had seized the opportunity of talking to Walter of anything that might be supposed likely to thwart and cross his mother; and Tom very likely had actually been in Cornwall and had seen Trevelyan, and, perhaps, Sir Roger; and, after all, it was not Sir Roger or Trevelyan of whom the boy was thinking, but of the yacht, which was a boyish fancy, natural enough.

With this thought, Mrs. Trevelyan let the matter glide out of her mind, with a half smile at her stepmother's spiteful endeavours to disturb Walter's imagination, and a pleased consciousness of the innocence, which remained unaware even of such an attempt The whole world might do what it pleased, but to seduce her boy's heart from her, or even introduce into his mind the idea that he could be detached from his mother, was simply impossible. And this being the case, Agnes followed her child upstairs, and kissed his fair candid face on the pillow when he was just dropping to sleep. The little fellow half opened his sleepy eyes with a drowsy smile in them, as his mother's kiss touched him. He was aware of nothing but love and security, and that sense of perfect, all-surrounding guardianship which is happiness to a child; and he was fast asleep and lost even to that felicity before she left the room. Agnes went downstairs with that lull at her heart, and sentiment of consolation and 'safety which a mother experiences when she sees her children safe and asleep; and without knowing it, fell to thinking again of her own affairs — not of Walter; he was safe and beyond the reach of any danger and though she felt herself old in some particulars, still she was not old, and life stirred in her against her will. She suffered this conversation to fall out of her mind, and went back, without intending it or wishing it, to the more exciting interview of the morning. She had no desire to begin life again on her own account. Had the question been put to her she would have answered, and answered with truth, that to live in her children was all that remained to her and all that she wished for; but then, a woman who lives only for her children must take unceasing care not to involve herself in the affairs of other people who are alive on their own account. And that is so hard to do in this world. Thus it was that Agnes was not forearmed, as she ought to have been, by the warning conveyed to her, and free of anxiety about the children, found herself left at a perilous liberty to occupy her thoughts with herself.

Nevertheless, when she thought of it next morning,

it occurred to her that it was her duty to stop this talk about the Trevelyans, if that was practicable. The only thing to be done was, if possible, to induce Mrs. Stanfield, or at least her son, to give up speaking of Sir Roger; for Agnes did not like to forbid her boy's visits to his grandfather's house. She might have taken such a step if she had been sufficiently alarmed, or she might even have made use of her father's authority; but then her fears were very trifling, and it was more a sense of unfitness in the interlocutors than any alarm for the result of the conversation that moved her. She waved her hand to her father as she passed through the archway and went on up the outer stairs, a little to his surprise; but still it was not an unprecedented step, for Mrs. Trevelyan thought it necessary to be civil to her father's wife. Mrs. Stanfield was in the parlour in the heat of a discussion with her son, which Agnes interrupted at a delicate moment. They were both redder than usual, flushed with contention and disagreement, and the red March sun which was coming in, in a flood of level light from behind the Cedars — for it was late in the afternoon, and the sun was near setting — gave a last tint of fiery colour to the scene. As for Tom, he was not only red but sullen, lowering with resistance, and repugnance to something which was being urged upon him. When Agnes entered the room the mother and son came to a sudden confused pause, and looked at her as two thieves might have looked at a man they were conspiring to waylay; and then Mrs. Stanfield got up with a civility unusual to her.

"It ain't often as I see you in this house," she said, offering her visitor a chair. "I've been a-talking to

Tom about — about his going away; I ain't one to put upon the master, and to ask him to keep a man in his house, and him not his own flesh and blood —"

Here Tom growled something inaudible to Agnes, which made his mother turn sharply round upon him. "You can't deny as I said so, you good-for-nothing!" she said. "You ain't a drop's blood to him, though I'm your mother; I don't say as I'm always the best of friends with Agnes — but she's his own child, and she's got a right to his house."

"Hush, please," said Mrs. Trevelyan; "I am sure my father has — no objection — to your son being with you; it would be unnatural if he had. I want to speak to you about my boy for a few minutes, if you will let me. I want to ask you a favour. It is not of any particular importance, but still it would be a kindness to me."

Mrs. Stanfield grew suddenly still at these words; she cast a stealthy glance at her son as if calling his attention, and then composed herself with an unnatural quietness to listen. The crisis evidently seemed to her so extraordinary, that for the moment she showed herself superior to all her ordinary rules. "It ain't what I ever expected to hear, as I was one as could do Agnes Stanfield a kindness," she said, with that pause in the midst of her excitement which showed at once how surprised and how watchful she was. As for Agnes, she looked at her stepmother with a certain sense that it was a tiger ready for a spring that was crouching before her. To be sure, the image is not a new one; but Mrs. Stanfield had placed her plump pink hands on her knees, as if they were the treacherous velvet paws upon which she was resting in her momentary quiescence.

"It is only to ask you if you would have the goodness not to speak to Walter of the Trevelyans," said Agnes, in her simplicity — "nor you," she added, turning her eyes upon Tom. "I am sure you mean no harm, and it is of very little importance; but still, if you would be so good —" She stopped, for Mrs. Stanfield's eyes were shining with a kind of savage pleasure which it was impossible to explain; and as for Tom, he stamped his foot on the floor as if to call his mother to herself.

"Oh no," said Mrs. Stanfield, "we don't mean no harm, and it ain't of no consequence, to speak of. He told you as we was talking of Sir Roger? See what it is to have a child well trained. Mine don't have no such confidence in me —"

"Hold your tongue," cried Tom, hastily — and he looked at Agnes with a significance which she could not explain to herself. What she imagined was that she had come in, in the midst of a quarrel between them, and that it was to Tom, and not herself, that her stepmother spoke.

"Oh yes, I'll hold my tongue," said Mrs. Stanfield — "I'm one as has always a desire to please when I'm took the right way. You haven't been not to say kind to me, Agnes Stanfield; but I'm one as likes to give back good for evil. I'll give you my word and promise I'll not say another word about Sir Roger to your boy. I'll never name his name no more — if I see Walter; and I keeps my word when I gives it," she said, with a look of subdued enjoyment very extraordinary to see; and then she glanced round at her

15*

son and said, "Tom, don't be a fool," with a wonderful red gleam of her fiery eyes. Agnes thought the
quarrel was recommencing, and she rose to go away.

"I am much obliged to you," she said; "I will not
interrupt your conversation any longer," and Agnes left
the room with a little courteous salutation to Tom, who
was good to Walter, and had never harmed anybody,
so far as she knew. But when Agnes had left the
forge behind her, and was walking home through the
village street speculating with a little wonder upon the
reception she had met with, and Mrs. Stanfield's ready
promise, she was profoundly astonished to see Tom a
few steps behind, evidently hastening to join her. Mrs.
Trevelyan paused till he came up, with, perhaps, a
little of the air of a superior awaiting a message. She
was quite friendly, and showed no symptoms of being
ashamed to be accosted by him in sight of all the village; but at the same time she waited with her great
lady look, which she could put on on occasion, to know
his reason for coming after her, and hear what he had
to say.

"Did you want to speak to me?" Agnes said, perhaps a little graciously, as he approached; but Tom
did not show any intention of standing still and delivering his message, and being done with it, on the
contrary, he came up with the evident intention of
going on by her side.

"Yes, but I will not keep you waiting," said Tom.
"I will walk with you a bit;" and Agnes, who was
taken by surprise, went on without knowing it. It
was a conjunction which would have wounded Stanfield
deeply had he seen it, though he admitted his wife's
son beneath his roof; but then, that Tom should con-

sider himself Agnes's equal had never entered into the blacksmith's thoughts.

"Yes, I want to speak to you," said Tom. "I've been looking for a chance, and I've never been able to get one. We're kind of relations, and I don't see why we shouldn't be friends. Look here, Mrs. Trevelyan, if I was to tell you something as would be for your good —"

Agnes did not take any notice of this concluding sentence; she only turned her eyes upon him when he spoke of being friends, and smiled a little, and said, "I am sure, if I can do anything for you —" for it never occurred to her that what he wanted was to do something for her.

"Hang it, I don't want you to do nothing for me," said Tom, abruptly, "except be friendly if you like; — that ain't what I'm a'talking of. I've always had a kind of a sneaking regard for you, Agnes; we ain't brother and sister, you know, and I suppose you'd turn up your nose at a rough fellow like me, though you're sweet enough to a snob like *that* Charlton; but you might be a little friendly all the same," said the sailor, looking at her always with the look of a man who knew something about her more than she herself knew. As for Agnes, she was stupefied with amazement and disgust. It seemed to her something incredible, which she could neither realize nor believe in; and yet there he was, with his familiar looks, walking full in the sight of all Windholm, by her side.

"You must have forgotten yourself," she said; "I am entirely at a loss as to what you mean. I can only think you must have mistaken me for some one else.

Good evening!" said Agnes, with an attempt to leave
him; but Tom was evidently prepared for that.

"By George, I ain't the fellow to make mistakes,"
said Tom. "I don't know nobody in Windholm a bit
like you; and I can just tell you it ain't to your advantage to be proud. Suppose you was Roger's
wife —"

"How dare you speak so?" cried Agnes, flaming
into sudden indignation; "how dare you name Mr.
Trevelyan so? He, at all events, was unconnected with
you."

Tom laughed.

"You'll find out as I ain't so far off as you think,"
he said. "I'm Walter's uncle, I am; — come now,
be a little bit friendly. I could tell you a deal, if I
liked — and I could stand your friend —"

"Silence, sir!" cried Agnes; "you have no right to
speak to me in such a tone — nor to claim any relationship with my son. I will speak to my father if
you say another word; he is very good, but he will
not keep any one in his house to insult his daughter.
Be silent, sir, and do not venture to follow me farther!"
This she said with a haughtiness which she could not
restrain — for naturally it seemed to her that it was
through herself, who had already suffered enough from
her father's weakness, that this low fellow claimed a
connexion with her husband and her son.

"I advise you to think it over again afore you
send me away," said Tom, insolently; and then he
lowered his voice, and his tone softened: "I'd be a
friend to you if you'd let me, Agnes," he said; "I
would, upon my honour; and I can stand your friend,

though you don't think it — if you'd only be a little friendly to me."

Agnes was so angry that the power of speech seemed to forsake her in her emergency. She went on with hurrying nervous steps, and closed her own gate upon him with hands which were perfectly steadfast in their purpose, though they trembled a little. She looked Tom in the face, and shut the gate upon him with a force of disdain under which he shrank dismayed.

"Good evening!" she said, with clear and cold distinctness, which made the words sound like two stones falling through the still air of the declining day. As for Tom, all this happened so abruptly that he stopped short on the very threshold, and had to draw back a step to avoid the sweep of the gate as it closed. He made some furious exclamation, of which Agnes took no notice, and kept standing there, watching, while, with her heart throbbing and swelling, she went into the house. Indignation and anger, and a sense of humiliation, overwhelmed all her other sentiments as she went in at the open door; and then a smile came over her face at the utter folly of the whole business. It was so absurd that it seemed to her to make her very displeasure ridiculous, as she thought it over. He would stand her friend! It was like offering her his protection — she, who was under the protection of the sacred laws of earth and guardianship of heaven! — and after awhile she began to smile at the ridiculous presumption. But as for Tom, the sailor, he went away without any smile, and with a furious determination in his heart.

CHAPTER XX.

The Trevelyans' Revenge.

THIS unexpected scene had naturally a considerable influence on Mrs. Trevelyan; but still, when she had calmed down a little, and found herself safe in the secure shelter of her home, where nobody could disturb or molest her, the effect passed away from her mind. Now that Sir Roger Trevelyan had been proved harmless, what could any one else do? And it was just at this moment that she discovered a letter lying upon her writing-table. It was a letter from Jack Charlton. She had not been in the habit of getting letters from him, and the sight of it made her heart beat a little faster in spite of herself. Perhaps even her first impulse was annoyance, as of something importunate reopening a matter which was of necessity of a disturbing and un-settling character, and which she had imagined herself to have concluded. The object of the letter was osten-sibly to convey to her some little bits of information which Jack had, as he said, forgotten; but it was in reality inspired by a very different sentiment from that of business. It was one of those letters which are inter-esting to women, even by means of the very deficien-cies which would make them aimless and foolish to a man. It was a letter which expressed everything or nothing, very much according to the inclination of the person who received it. Jack could not conceal the attraction he felt towards Windholm, the pleasure he had in Mrs. Trevelyan's society, the subtle sense of sympathy and accord which he felt to exist between them; and yet he was not a man to make a fool of himself by an unadvised "offer" to his friend's widow, or to run the risk of burdening himself with another man's family, and marrying (which was, perhaps, worst of all) a blacksmith's daughter, without even any certainty that his self abnegation would be appreciated or his offer accepted. But, at the same time, he could not give her up. He had seen a great many women in his day, but he had never happened to encounter any one quite like Agnes; and he had a sense of blossoming out and looking his very best in her presence, which was very gratifying. He took accordingly the only middle course that remained to him between the two extremes, and adopted that which perhaps awakens a more fine and subtle emotion, and certainly is the origin of more refined and charming letter-writing, than either happy love or despair. There are cases even, in which a love-letter itself has less attraction than one of those letters which skirt the borders of love, and imply everything to a mind that is open to receive the implication; without committing the writer, if his correspondent is of slow apprehension or is unwilling to understand.

To be sure, it is a kind of correspondence which, judged by a practical standard, every man must feel himself at liberty to despise. But then such letters are not addressed to men, but to women; and women are apt to find a charm in them, almost greater, as we have said, than that of the love-letter proper. Such was the epistle which Agnes received, to refresh her mind after her conversation with Mrs. Stanfield and Tom. No doubt it might have meant love, and marriage, and a new life, if Mrs. Trevelyan had been of

that way of thinking; but, at the same time, it meant
friendship, the visionary amity so dear to fanciful souls
— a tender and delicate alliance of mind and thought,
very sweet in itself, and not of necessity leading to
anything, if she were so minded. To write such letters
is a fashion of the age, in which people are so free in
correspondence; but it was the beginning of Agnes's
experience in that way, and it had a considerable effect
upon her. She was only a very little startled, and she
was a good deal moved; it brought all Jack's goodness
and kindness before her under a sudden warm light of
regard and gratitude, and, at the same time, it did not
alarm her, as his personal appearance had done. And
then there were some things in it which required an
answer; and she sat down to reply with a certain glow
of pleasure and consolation. It was pleasant to think
of having some one who understood her — some one
who could feel for her under all circumstances; and it
was with this feeling in her mind that Agnes placed
herself at her writing-table, and began her reply.

It was not a hasty note, to be replied to hastily;
on the contrary, after the first paragraph, which was a
direct response to Jack's question about a matter of
detail, Agnes insensibly fell into her correspondent's
tone. She wanted to give him delicately to understand
that, notwithstanding her regard for him, her life was
absolutely fixed, and beyond the possibility of change.
And that was so difficult a thing to say as it ought to
be said, that she took a long time to it, as was natural
— so long a time, that darkness overtook her before
she was aware; and the humble domestic appeal of "the
children's tea," which was not a thing which Mrs. Trevelyan had been in the habit of neglecting, came upon

her unawares, giving her an uncomfortable sensation.
She had forgotten the children — she who had just
been reminding herself that the sole and only life she
would now live in the world was in them and for them.
Her heart smote her as she got up hastily, and put
away her unfinished letter, and hastened to her more
urgent duties.

When the guilty mother went into the room where
little Agnes was sitting up in her high chair, a certain
sense of shame and self-disgust came upon her; for she
was aware that her thoughts were elsewhere, and that
she had but a distracted and broken attention to give
to little Agnes. Mrs. Trevelyan was highflown in these
matters, as we have said. She was as much ashamed
of herself when she sat down by the side of her little
child, and found that her mind was not there, occupied
with the legitimate cares and consolations of a mother,
but had strayed away on a new course, and interested
itself in the regard of a stranger, as if she had done
something really criminal; yet, as she sat down ab-
sently at the tea-table, she did not even remark, at
first, that Agnes was alone. It was only the little girl's
call for "Watty! Watty!" that roused the abstracted
mother. When she found out that Walter was absent,
a momentary alarm took possession of her; but then it
was not an extraordinary event. Within the last few
weeks Walter had been absent on several occasions,
detained by Tom's attractions at Stanfield's house, or
even tempted to linger with his schoolfellows; for though
he was quite unaware of it, no doubt a certain subtle
consciousness that his presence was less necessary to
his mother than of old had entered the child's mind.
Agnes gave orders that Madelon should be sent to look

for him, with an impulse of impatience which was a
relief to her own feeling of guilt. Then she sat down
by her little four-year old girl, who understood nothing
about all this, and kept on her prattle undisturbed —
trying to think that she was displeased by Walter's absence, and then relapsing into disgust with herself, and
then into a still more painful mood of self-defence.
Her early widowhood had other pangs beyond those
of grief and loneliness; humiliating dangers; to which
Agnes had never thought to be exposed. Faithful
sorrow, and solitude, and love, have their consolation
and their dignity; but to be thus thrown back against
her will without her own consent, into a second factitious and mortifying youth — and to feel again in
spite of herself the attraction of those fears and hopes,
and exhilarations and despondencies which are so sweet
the first time, when they come in due season, and so
humbling when they arrive thus after date, to disturb
the tranquillity of a life which ought to feel itself
settled and fixed for ever — was hard upon her; and
in the sense that it was hard, she tried to drown the
sense of shame with which she had found herself out.

Mrs. Trevelyan, as we have said, was highflown.
She felt a little soreness in her heart against the decrees of Providence. She thought it almost unjust that
of all the women around her, only she should be left
exposed to those betraying influences of life. None of
them all had been a truer wife, or a more faithful mother; yet it was only she whose name could be linked
with another name, and at whom the world could
smile; and it was not any fault of hers. It was against
her will — without her consent, that she had been
placed in this position, and subjected to these subtle,

unsuspected dangers. All this mist of irritation and pain which arose in her mind, may seem foolish enough to sober-minded people. Had Mrs. Freke seen into Mrs. Trevelyan's thoughts, she would have said sensibly, "If she does not like Mr. Charlton, of course she can refuse him;" which, after all, was a very succinct and true statement of affairs. But then Agnes's trouble arose from the fact that her mind was disturbed, not by the thought of marrying Mr. Charlton, but a vague sort of predilection for the presence and society of a person who did not belong to her, and never could belong to her, and whom she ought not to be thinking of.

When she went back to the drawing-room, she took out her half-written letter and put it into the fire, and began to write what she intended to be a very brief note in answer to his question. But then it was difficult to reply so shortly to a letter full of what the betraying influence in her heart called "kindness." Why should she take trouble to lose a friend? And thus Agnes began, without being aware of it, to soften again the too brief sentences, and to acknowledge again the charm and the attraction which threw sweet fitful unacknowledged lights upon her homely and dim horizon. Why should two people be hindered from being friends, by reason of a distant and impossible possibility that they might become more than friends? After all, to a woman shut out from the world, and whose existence for herself had been prematurely brought to an end, was it not an advantage to form such a pleasant link of amity with a full and living life? Thus Agnes argued with herself, persuading herself that the pain in her mind was absurd, and that nothing could

be more rational or sensible than her feelings. This
process of reasoning took up her time, and made the
evening pass so rapidly, that it was with a start she
saw Madelon's flaxen head looking in at the door.
Madelon had a scared look on her face, which alarmed
Agnes vaguely. She closed her writing-book abruptly,
without very well knowing why, and rose up to ask
what was the matter. "What is it? Has anything
happened?" she said; thinking at the same time, with
the natural rapid second-thought of a mother, that it
could not be either Agnes or the baby, as everything
was profoundly quiet in the silent house.

"It is Walter, please," said Madelon in her imperfect English. "Why comes he not? It is late, late,
too late for be out. Does Madame know where
he is?"

"Walter? has he not come in? He must be with
my father," said Agnes hastily.

"No, he is not there," said Madelon. "I have
gone there, and — everywhere. I cannot find him.
It is too late for be out. Where does Madame think
I go for find him? It is strange, and I am frightened.
He never did so before."

It was an alarming waking up out of Agnes's
dreams; but the idea of danger did not enter her mind
at first. "You must be mistaken," she said. "It is
impossible that he can be anywhere but with his grandpapa. When did he go out? I have not seen him
for some time — not since I came in. He was in the
garden when I came in," she said, recollecting herself;
and then a burning colour came over her face. It was
this letter, this foolish and shameful self-occupation,
that had turned away her attention from her child; and

it seemed now as if something must have happened to him, if only to punish her. "Bring me my shawl and my bonnet, and tell Fanny to come with me," she said, hurriedly.

As for Madelon, her fears were still more serious than those of her mistress, which, after all, had no foundation except a kind of abstract sense that she herself deserved to be punished. Madelon had a more painful knowledge at the bottom of her fears; and she, too, had something to blame herself with, and did not care to be questioned. She rushed upstairs for Mrs. Trevelyan's bonnet with a kind of desperate, silent haste, which did not strike Agnes, because she, too, felt herself so dreadfully to blame. Vague fears of accident came into her mind as she stood waiting and scarcely able to contain herself. He might have fallen into the pond, or met with some misfortune in his play. She did not think of anything else; she began to imagine what sight would meet her eyes if he was carried home lifeless, or, at the best, injured — and was it not her fault, who for a moment, for an hour, had thought of something else rather than of her children? When she was just ready to go out, on her way to the door, the sound of the bell rang through her heart, and through those of the two maids who were with her. Fanny, who was going out with Mrs. Trevelyan, made one spring through the little hall and opened the door; but it was only Stanfield who made his appearance there. He came in and shut the door after him, and took his daughter's hand and led her back into the drawing-room. This action seemed to Agnes to confirm her worst fears. She cried out, hastily, "I can bear it — tell me what has happened — tell me!"

Stanfield was almost as much agitated as she was;
but he had not the air of a bearer of tidings. He drew
her arm through his to support her, and held her fast.
"I am not come to tell, but to ask," he said. "I know
nothing. I hope nothing has happened? If you are
going anywhere, and it will be easier for you, come,
and you can tell me on the way ——"

"It is Walter," said Agnes; "he has not come
home. I thought he must be with you — oh! father,
tell me, are you sure — is he not with you? — perhaps about the forge somewhere — with Tom?" This
now remained, instead of a fear, her greatest hope.

"Tom has gone away suddenly," said Stanfield.
"Tell me, Agnes — what is it you fear? His mother
has a look that drives me distracted. There is a sort
of triumphant air; — but Walter would never go away
with him — I can't believe it. My darling, try and
compose yourself, that we may do what is best to be
done. What is it you fear?"

Agnes did not know what she feared; a vague darkness seemed to come over her. Instead of the dark
pond she seemed to see a wild country road, and her
boy lost and wandering, at the mercy of the man whom
she had repulsed and turned away from only a few
hours before. She drew her arm from her father's and
dropped into the nearest chair and hid her face in her
hands. It was only for an instant, and yet she felt
as if hours had been lost by that momentary weakness,
and as if all the world was standing still and all succour and help waiting for her, while she sat helpless
trying to realize what she feared. It is true that her
father waited by her side, and that Fanny and Madelon stood quaking at the door; but none of them were

aware that she had done anything to delay their search,
or that her silence had lasted longer than the time that
was necessary to draw a breath.

"I do not know," she said. "I thought of the
pond and of those new houses they are building. I
never thought there was any danger with Tom; no, oh
no — he would not go away. I thought of — of an
accident. Come, we are losing time. I thought of
going down to the Common to ask if anybody had seen
him — and you, father, if you would go into the village ——"

"Hush!" said Stanfield. "This is no accident;
you would have heard instantly of that. Sit down,
my darling, and let me ask Madelon. We are not
losing time. It might turn out worse than an accident;
but you shall have him back," the blacksmith said,
with a flash out of his luminous eyes, "if I should go
to the end of the world after him. My darling, my
child, keep up your heart. It is treachery only that I
fear."

It would be vain to say that these words conveyed
any information to the mind of Agnes. It was rather
a sense of meaning in what he said than any comprehension of that meaning itself which gave her
strength to keep still while he called Madelon and
questioned her. Madelon proved a reluctant and terrified witness, and in her panic she forgot, or pretended
to forget, her English, and poured forth floods of
German, which filled Stanfield with despair, and roused
Agnes a little to the reality and to the importance of
this evidence. At the end it appeared that Tom had
been doing what he could to win Madelon's confidence
for some time back; that he had joined her in her

walks with the children, and had been Walter's constant companion, as, indeed, her mistress was partially aware; and that this very afternoon she had spoken with him in the garden and given her consent that Walter should accompany him to the great gardens at Slough, where there were some Indian plants and seeds in the museum which Tom had promised to show to the boy. Madelon confessed reluctantly that Walter had wished to ask his mother, but that she had promised to make all right, under promise that they were to return by eight o'clock. And then Mrs. Trevelyan was busy, Madelon said, and she could not say anything until she grew frightened, and it was too late. Thus Agnes's sin, poor soul, though it was not a very terrible one, came back to her at every point. Slough was only three miles off across the country, a practicable walk; but at the end of the walk there was the river, with all its dangers and attractions. Heaven knew what might have happened, while the darkness was falling over the cheerful country, and while the careless mother was losing the precious moments over that letter which she thought of with horror. Agnes sat still, in a kind of stupor, looking on with a frightful callous calm at Madelon's sobs and cries, and her father's pale excitement and anxiety. It was not anxiety but despair which seemed to have taken possession of her. Had not God stretched out His hand on the moment, without leaving her a place of repentance, to launch at her head this frightful punishment? She did not recover her senses till she felt the cold night air blowing on her face, and became conscious that her father was leading her somewhere, supported on his arm, down the dark village street, where the scattered lights twinkled here and there through the soft gloom. She did not ask nor know, though he had told her, and supposed she had listened to him, where he was leading her. She was going out into the dark world, which had swallowed him up out of her sight, to find her boy.

CHAPTER XXI.

Self-betrayal.

THE village street had somehow a strange aspect that night. It was ten o'clock, and the good people had carried their lights upstairs, where they shone out of the upper windows to light the peaceable villagers to bed. There was bright light in the little tavern, flaming in a disreputable fulness in the midst of the quiet, and making visible a little circle before the door, in the centre of which stood the gig of a belated farmer, who was refreshing himself within. The light fell upon the white rail of the village green, and shed a sort of dreary gloom — what people call darkness visible — on the Green itself, as far as the lime-trees, which rose up black at the farther side. Opposite Stanfield's house, at the farther extremity of the Green, there was a flare of faint candlelight blowing about in the night air, which came from the little shop at the corner — a struggling little shop, compelled by poverty to keep open late, and to deny itself gas. All this Agnes remarked, without knowing why, as Stanfield hurried her along. She made no resistance to his will, but at the same time it was only a passive submission she yielded, as he drew her along supported on his arm towards his own house.

16*

She did not even understand what his fears were, when
he led, or, indeed, seemed to sweep her along by the
invisible influence of his great excitement, into the
house which had been her home for all the happier
part of her life. But Agnes was herself under the influence of emotion so strong, that nobody would have
suspected or believed in the stupor which enveloped all
her faculties, and prevented her from understanding
why she had been brought there. It seemed that Mrs.
Stanfield had been expecting them. She was sitting by
the fire, which was almost out, with a thick muslin
nightcap on her head, and a short, white bed-gown
replacing her dress. It appeared to Stanfield that this
costume was intended as an insult to his daughter, but
Agnes did not even observe it. She had not come here
on her own account, but on her father's, with a certain
vague trust that he knew what he was doing, and did
not mean to waste time. As for Mrs. Stanfield, she
got up in her short, full skirts, and made Agnes a
kind of defiant curtsey. She was redder than usual,
and her fiery eyes blazed with an excitement that was
partly fictitious; but besides this, there was no mistaking
the triumph in her looks.

"I ain't used to it, master, and I'm one as always
speaks my mind," she said. "She's been and paid me
two visits to-day, her as is too grand to ask her father's
wife inside her door. But there never was pride yet
but was humbled, and so she'll find — so she'll find,"
said Mrs. Stanfield. She was too much roused to await
the examination which was coming. "She'll find it
out," said the excited woman — "them as was too
fine to have aught to do with me or mine. I'll thank you,
master, to take her off home, for I'm a-going to bed."

"Sally," said Stanfield, who was trembling with a certain rage and impatience, which nobody had ever seen in him before, and yet who was intent on subduing himself, that he might get all the information possible, "I don't ask you to have any sort of feeling for her or me, for you don't understand; but I ask you for your own sake, and that's a strong reason. I'll pass over all that's come and gone, if you'll say straight out what is in your head about Walter; if you know anything — and I can't think but what you know; if there's any plot against him. His mother is here; I have brought her to ask you with her own lips. You are a mother yourself — in a kind of way. Listen to me," said Stanfield, laying his hand heavily on her shoulders, in the height of his excitement, "we are none of us all bad or all good. God made you as well as her. Tell her what you know about her boy."

The pressure of his hand on her shoulder made her turn her head in spite of herself. Agnes was standing by the table, very pale, and with her eyes enlarged to twice their usual size; and Stanfield stood by his wife's side, holding her by the shoulder with a suppressed passion, such as she had never seen before. She was so far frightened that she lost her composure and her sense of triumph for the moment, and felt herself in the grasp of an energy greater than her own; and in her state of excitement it was as easy to cry as to laugh, and to scream out loud and cry "murder," as either. Fortunately, impulse led her to do the first.

"I don't know why I should be spoke to so," she said, sinking into a whimper. "Take off your hand off of my shoulder, master, you're a-hurting of me. Am I one as goes about finding out what's happened to other people's children? I daresay as he's fallen into the pond," said Mrs. Stanfield. The blacksmith had removed the salutary pressure, and her courage rose on the moment. "He's fallen into the pond," she said, "and nothing particular either. My Tom didn't have no better luck when he was a bit of a lad. She's been and scorned my boy," cried Mrs. Stanfield, raising her voice, "and now she's the one to come and ask questions of me. If I speak, it'll be the worse for her. Master, if you'll take my advice you'll take her away. Let her go home and mind her own business, and look after her precious boy. I should just like to know what's that to me."

Agnes held out her hands to her father with a suppressed cry. "We are losing time," she said; "I think as she does, some accident has happened. Oh! come away, and do not let us lose any more time."

For the first time in his life the blacksmith did not answer his daughter's appeal. He kept his eyes fixed on his wife, out of whose face there came a certain gleam of triumph. "Ay, I'll give you my word it's that," she said; "you're in the right, Agnes — don't you lose no time. Maybe he's been took out, and they're a-bringing of him round; maybe — master, if I was you I'd send out Martha to get the drags — she ain't a-bed. I'd go myself and welcome, but, not thinking of nothing, I've been and took off my gown ——"

Stanfield grasped her again by her plump shoulder, with an excess of rage at her insolence which it was beyond his power to restrain. "Agnes, compose yourself; there is no accident. Tell her what it is," he cried, hoarsely. It was not a woman he had in his hands, but a pernicious creature taking pleasure in his daughter's pain. He seized her by her overgrown shoulders, and shook her without knowing it, exasperated and driven to the end of his patience. "You know what it is, and where her boy is — tell her!" cried the blacksmith. It was, perhaps, the first time in his life that he had encountered in a vital struggle a force inaccessible to reason, inaccessible to moral influence, and which had to be met and overawed by force like itself.

"Father," said Agnes, "let her go; she cannot know anything. Never mind if she has no sympathy. Oh, come, come — we are losing time."

The blacksmith loosed his hands with a look of despair. He came to his daughter, and took hers in his grasp with a tenderness beyond words. "My darling, have patience, have patience," he said; "what she says is a lie — nothing but treachery has happened to Walter; the pond's all a cursed delusion to turn you off the right track; I'll not touch her, but I'll have the truth. Speak as long as you have the time," he said, suddenly turning round. "I'm slow, but I'm not blind; I know what's been going on in this house; speak, and I'll pass it over. Do you hear what I am saying?" said the blacksmith, involuntarily making a step towards her. Again he said to himself she was not a woman, but some kind of fleshly devil, as she sat shrunk up in her chair glaring at him with her red eyes; and in that thought excused himself for the impulse he felt to seize her in his strong hands, and tear the secret out of her flesh. He was a good Christian, tender and kind by nature, but he faced his wife's irrational and obstinate wickedness with an impulse which felt like murder; and as for her, she crouched back further and further with a fear which came by instinct, but at the same time a confidence which was the result of experience. She was incapable of comprehending him, but yet she knew, in her miserable way, the nature which was so much above her, and felt sure that no amount of exasperation would urge him to no her any harm.

"Though you should murder me, as you're a-going to do," she cried, in her security, "I'll not say a word. Let Madame Trevelyan, as is such a fine lady, go and find it out. As for your threats, I scorns 'em, William Stanfield. I'm your lawful wife, and what's yours is mine. Go and get 'em all roused up and drag the pond, and you'll find the boy. Master, if you take hold of me like that I'll cry out, Murder! murder! Martha, he's a-going to kill me! Oh! good Lord, he's a-going to kill me! But not if I was to be hacked to pieces — not if you was to tear me in little bits — I won't, I won't say a word."

It was Agnes alone who retained her calm in this crisis; it was she who drew her father's hand from his wife's shoulder, and took him apart. The excitement which overwhelmed Stanfield had but just succeeded in awakening her in her impatience and eager anxiety to get away. As she woke up, it seemed to her that her father was right, and that there must be some cause for the determined defiance and resistance of his wife. She put herself between them, trembling as she was, and fixed her eyes on Mrs. Stanfield's face. "My father means you no harm," she said; "you know he means you no harm. I don't want to have you threatened on my account; but you once had little children yourself — boys like mine. Tell me, for God's sake, if you know anything. Suppose your child had been taken from you without warning, without preparation. Oh! have pity, have pity! and tell me if you know where is my boy."

Mrs. Stanfield roused herself at this appeal. "I told you always as pride would have a fall," she said. "It's you to come and ask me for your boy — you as never asked me to go inside of your door when all was well. What have I got to do with your boy? My Tom's gone off to sea — not to be a burden to nobody. Them as grudged him a bit of dinner, and them as was too high to speak to him when they met him, they've got their will. I wouldn't have a son o' mine stay here to be put upon, that's all as I know. I'll tell you o' my boy, but I ain't got nothing to tell you of yours. If it's my advice as you want, Agnes Stanfield," she continued, with a flash of triumph out of her fiery eyes, "my opinion is to drag the pond, and not to lose no time. If you'd not druv' my Tom back to sea, he'd have been a help — that's all as I've got to say; he'd have been a great help, if you hadn't drove him away — and don't bear no malice; but them as is scorned ain't always them as is harmless," she said, forgetting her *rôle* for the moment, and blazing out in fresh triumph. "The like of us ain't to be cast off and taken up as folks likes. He's made up his mind at last, and he's gone off, and you can find him if you can!" said Mrs. Stanfield. She had forgotten, in the sense of victory, that a minute before she had denied all knowledge of anything but her own son's departure. Now she faced her husband and stepdaughter with that sense of being able to insult them without fear of reprisals, which in its way is the testimony of the base to the noble. "Go after *him* if you like, and find him if you can!" she said, in her exultation; "if it was me, I would drag the pond, and see what's to be found there."

Mrs. Trevelyan clasped her hands tightly together, to support herself, as she stood in an agony of mingled disdain and supplication before this woman, who had it in her power to relieve her curiosity, and would not. This mention of the pond, so often repeated, sent a shiver through her, notwithstanding that her reason told her that Mrs. Stanfield made use of this horrible supposition as a snare to lead her off the true track. She stood for a moment irresolute, and knowing what to do; but recognising, what Stanfield did not recognise, the impossibility of trusting to anything that her stepmother might say. The blacksmith was not of the same opinion. It was so hard for him, notwithstanding all his experience, to believe in an utterly perverse will. He could not help thinking that it was merely because he had not found the right chord as yet that the heart had not opened and given forth the truth.

"Sally," he said, coming forward again, "I don't want to be hard on you; I've been as good to your children as they would let me be. Have pity upon *my* child! Don't urge me to recollect all your boys have done, and all you've done yourself. I will forget everything that has ever happened if you will tell me where Walter Trevelyan is."

The crimson, which was suffused over all her face, flashed into purple on Mrs. Stanfield's cheeks; her eyes stood out, glistening, out of their sockets; her very arms, which were uncovered, reddened over when these words reached her ears.

"Your child, and my boys, and Walter Trevelyan!" she cried. "I'd just like you to tell me why he's Walter Trevelyan? Because she went and married that poor bit of a lad, to his ruin, to make herself a lady. That wasn't my way. I tell you she thinks herself a fine lady and an honest woman, but she ain't done for him what I'd have done for him. Walter Trevelyan, I tell you, lies in the pond, and I'm glad of it! Him to be Sir Roger's heir! — a poor little whipper-snapper of a blacksmith's grandson! As if my boys weren't as good Trevelyans as he, and better, and born afore him!" she cried out, in her excitement. The moment after she paused and sank down into her chair, and looked with a certain fright at her hearers. They looked at each other when they heard these words — Agnes with a wondering inquiring look, but Stanfield with a bitter and burning flush, almost as purple as his wife's. He had started a little, but that was almost imperceptible; perhaps the sudden discovery, which came like a flash of light, had been so long dawning and rendering itself apparent, that the final revelation did not strike him so violently as he thought it did. He staggered slightly when this last blow was dealt him, and then went up to his daughter and drew her arm within his, to take her away.

"That is enough," he said; "my darling! this is no place for you. I've suspected a deal of things, but I don't know if I ever suspected just as clear as she has spoken. Neither you nor me has anything more to do here!" This he said sadly enough, as he had been in the habit of speaking for a long time. Not only the

joy but the honour had gone out of his life, and he
had long suspected it.   But now the blow struck him
in spite of himself.   He said "Good-bye to this house
and all that is in it!" as he led his daughter out at
the door; he did not even look again at the panic-
stricken creature who was trembling in her chair.   As
for Agnes, she was startled; but she was not sufficiently free in her thoughts to ask what it meant.
"As good Trevelyans as he" kept ringing in her ears,
but she did not feel that she had energy for anything
more than a bewildered inquiry.   Only she said it
once more under her breath as they went out into the
sharp night air, which again roused Agnes to herself.
"As good Trevelyans as he," she said, aloud; "is it
only a piece of folly, or what does it mean?"

"It is true," said the blacksmith, with a strange
thrill in his voice.   "It is all clear to me; the cause
is lost, and Sir Roger will have the boy at all risks.
He has sent some one to steal him away ——",

"But Tom?" Agnes said, wondering; and then it
all rushed upon her like a revelation.   Nobody could
be a better messenger than Tom, who was as good a
Trevelyan as little Walter, and who was Walter's
uncle, as he had dared to say, though not through her,
as she had supposed him to mean.   When the truth
flashed upon her, Agnes's first thought, even in the
midst of her trouble, was of her father, thus enlightened
and dishonoured.   She put her hands together on his
arm, and clasped it tight, with one of those bitter
caresses which people give each other when both are
in mortal pain; and then she quickened her pace without knowing it, hurrying on she could not tell where,
into the darkness and the night, where Tom, whom

she had repulsed and repelled, and yet who was doubly connected with her, had carried away her boy.

CHAPTER XXII.

The Search.

It would be pain to follow every detail of the fruitless search for Walter which the father and daughter made. The first step of all, after the first panic which led Agnes, even against her convictions and reason, to have the village, and the pond, and every dangerous spot in the neighbourhood searched and investigated, was to advertise Mr. Charlton of what had happened. Jack came down instantly full of sympathy, but it was with a kind of horror which she could not explain, and which she even knew to be unjust, that Mrs. Trevelyan looked at him. Somehow his unanswered letter, which was still lying about somewhere at the mercy of anyone who chose to read it, was identified in her mind with her boy's disappearance. No doubt the idea was foolish, because, whatever her occupations had been, it would not have occurred to her on that peaceful afternoon, when everything was precisely as usual, to put her boy under *surveillance;* and yet, perhaps, the sentiment was natural enough. But it was Jack who conducted the search, showing in it a devotion and disregard of fatigue which won Stanfield's heart entirely, though it did not move his daughter. Before Jack was appealed to they had traced Walter and his companion to Slough, to the gardens, from which they had been seen to emerge by a side gate. Some one had even remarked that the child was eager to return, and urging his companion on; while Tom, for his part, limped behind, as if he had lamed himself. There the evidence paused for a long time, and no further link could be found. It was discovered, however, that the next day Tom sailed from Gravesend in a ship bound for China, in which he had been engaged for some time, and it was proved, beyond the possibility of doubt, that he had joined his ship alone. That he should have smuggled Walter on board the vessel in some clandestine way, was no doubt possible; but there was no time for such an operation, and he had not been seen in the child's company. The opinion of the detective, who was Jack Charlton's guide and inspiring influence, was that the young gentleman had been left somewhere on the way. When the inquiry had reached this point, the cabman was discovered who had taken up a man limping, who said he had sprained his ankle, and a boy, of Walter's age and appearance, near one of the side gates of the Slough gardens, on the day of the disappearance. It even seemed to have been the child who urged his lame companion to take the cab. The driver testified that it was nearly dark, and that the man gave him his orders in an undertone to drive on to town, if his horse was fit for it. It was a good ten miles, but the horse was fresh and the fare a good one. No doubt the darkness and the rapid pace perplexed poor little Walter, and kept him from perceiving the change of route. The cabman, who suspected nothing, remembered to have heard, as he said, "some words" between his fare and the little boy, but that was nothing extraordinary; and by the time they reached their destination the child was asleep, and was lifted out

and carried, still sleeping, to the little public-house to
which Tom had requested to be driven. By this time
his ankle was a great deal better, and he paid liberally
the cabman's fare; "which was all as I had to think
of," he said, naturally, yet with a vague sense of
apology. When the trace was thus rediscovered, the
search went on rapidly and hopefully for a time. The
tavern-keeper remembered perfectly the sudden arrival
of a man who limped slightly, with a little boy, who
was fast asleep. Tom was a jovial companion, and
made a good impression upon his host. He even explained that the little shaver was going to sea, and
was a bit of a molly-coddle, and wanted to go back
to his mother; but that he, Tom, wasn't one as stood
that sort of nonsense. Finally, it appeared that Tom
had determined, apparently on the suggestion of the
landlord, to take advantage of the child's sleep, and
the night train to Gravesend.

"I said as I thought it was best to get it over at
once," the landlord said, who was like the cabman,
slightly apologetic, and yet a little defiant, in case any
one should say it was his fault. And then there
intervened another cab, and the great London Bridge
station, with a late train, no doubt, to Gravesend, but
many other trains to many other places. And then it
was proved that Tom did not arrive at Gravesend
until the afternoon of the next day, and was alone
when he arrived. Where did he go in the meantime?
Had he trusted some of his messmates to smuggle
Walter on board, or had he never been taken on
board at all, but left somewhere on the road? A man,
with a little boy asleep, at a late hour at the London
Bridge station, among travellers returning from all the

ends of the world, and travellers setting out — and
Crystal Palace trains, and Greenwich trains, and all
the flux and reflux of the immense population — how
was any eye, even that of a detective, to identify Tom
and Walter among the mass? Children asleep were
not so rare among the night travellers. Here all the
evidence, all the investigation broke down. To be
sure, Tom turned up again late next day alone, joining
his ship at Gravesend; but between the time when
he disappeared into the London Bridge station with
Walter, to that in which he reappeared alone at the
Gravesend pier, no trace whatever was to be found.
They were obliged to leave it after weeks of bootless
labour; the child had been traced to the railway, which
led everywhere — which even led in a roundabout
and troublesome way to Windholm. For anything
that could be said to the contrary, Tom, with a sailor's
ignorance of detail, might have put Walter in a carriage with the intention of sending him back to his
mother; but all that passed during that night was lost
in the darkness which gave no sign.

It was the same night which Agnes had spent in
vain searches through the village and in the neighbourhood — in frightful waiting for the daylight, in
agonized and incoherent prayers. Her heart seemed to
swell in her breast when she heard of her sleeping
boy carried from one conveyance to another in the
weariness and helplessness of his childhood. It seemed
almost impossible that such poor passive properties of
nature as time and space should be able to baffle love
and confuse humanity like this. And that was all;
the mother yearning and helpless in her ignorance,
ready to spend her very life for him if she could have

done so; the poor little fellow equally helpless, saved from pain only by unconsciousness; and between them only those few miles of space and that world of darkness; nothing but the distance and the night — and yet they were enough to vanquish the utmost efforts of love at its intensest strain. Such was the thought that went through the mind of Agnes in her despair as she heard all the evidence, and saw how it was that she had been deprived of her boy.

This extraordinary and almost incredible incident disturbed in a wonderful way the population of Windholm. There was scarcely a man in the place, when it was first known, who did not make furtive researches on his own account, with a natural English doubt of any villainous agency, and trust in the power of accident. The village, which had not always loved Agnes, began to take a kind of charge of her, with that universal sympathy which sometimes, in a case of well-known hardship or suffering, extends over a whole community, not profound, but yet vivid. Perhaps, on the whole, her neighbours were disappointed that she did not fall ill of it; for, to be sure, it was not to them to understand that of all times in the world this time of terrible uncertainty, in which there was always a kind of desperate hope that at any moment Walter might return, was the last to fall ill in, even had she had occasion; and she was strong, and had no occasion, though the people round her could see her wearing into angles, and watch the lines of pain and thought which give age to a face, appearing day by day.

Agnes did not fall sick, but Madelon did, who had so much less to do with it, and whose heart was so

lightly engaged in comparison, and was ill for some
weeks, and was nursed by Mrs. Trevelyan with a certain mixture of envy and contempt. And then there
was still another matter which remained for the Windholm world to discuss. After that night in which she
had made the extraordinary statement we have re-
corded, the blacksmith's wife had been left to dwell
alone. Stanfield never returned again to the house he
had lived in all his life. Sometimes he was seen in
the evenings, when he left off work, to turn his steps
by habit to the outer stair, but he turned back invariably. Without saying a word to any one he went
down to the house on the Green, and occupied a little
room under his daughter's roof. Nobody could tell
what was the occasion of this strange step. A vague
report first, and then the more distinct certainty, that
Tom Smith had something to do with the carrying off
of Walter, threw a very vague and partial light upon
it; but even then nobody could understand why he
could not send the woman away — the woman who
had never been a fit wife for Stanfield. He never explained himself in the least to any of the sympathizers
who surrounded him, and he bore as he best could the
frank allusions to the change he had made, with which
the good villagers, meaning no offence, addressed him.
Even Jack Charlton, who began to understand him a
little, and to whom the matter had been partly explained, could not make out why the unworthy woman
should not be sent away and provided for, somewhere
else than in the house which her very presence desecrated. Stanfield might have responded like Sir
Launcelot, when that flower of chivalry was prayed to
use a little discourtesy — "That goes against me; what

I can I will." But the blacksmith was behind in the literature of the day, and knew nothing about Sir Launcelot. He said only that it was best for Agnes not to be left alone, and gave up to his wretched wife the possession of the house.

There Mrs. Stanfield lived, at first in a vociferous, and then in a sullen triumph; and then overwhelmed by the terrible privilege of having her will, went partially mad, as the neighbours thought, and raged about the house, Martha said, like an evil spirit. Martha was the next to leave her, which she did a day or two after the disappearance of the blacksmith, and then the scenes became many and violent which took place in the house. Mrs. Stanfield hired a young girl to be her servant, and held a furious carnival of cleaning, and cooking, and raging for a day or two; and then the unhappy little maid ran away, weeping and disfigured, and told the astonished neighbours how she had been cursed and stormed at, and finally beaten. This little episode was repeated so often that the blacksmith's wife began to exhaust the poor and defenceless girls of the village. When Mrs. Stanfield had come to an end of her energies in that way, she would open the window which looked out on the court and abuse her husband from that convenient tribune; and even when the window was closed the curious and excited neighbours could hear her going about like a wild beast, as they said, moaning and crying. This was her own ideal of conduct under the unprecedented and unlooked-for circumstances of having got her own way.

All this took place while Agnes lived day after day in a kind of agony, feeling every morning that she could not bear to see another, and yet holding on

17 *

with a desperation which seemed to her to proceed from something exterior to herself. She lived without knowing how she lived — with that same sense of being out of the body which she had been conscious of during Roger's long illness, when fatigue and excitement had brought her to the end of her powers, and life and all its functions seemed to go on independent of her. All day long she was following Walter through every kind of painful scene, in which she could not get to him to shield him. Her idea was one which nobody else entertained — that he had actually gone in the ship with Tom; and to please her, letters had been sent to the agents at Singapore to make the closest examination when it should arrive. And yet, notwithstanding this notion, she had another idea, which was her great strength — that her boy might suddenly escape and find his way to her, any hour and any day. When she lay awake at night, she seemed to hear and even to feel the rush of the dark water against the side of the ship, the glide and bound of the vessel, as it made its way in silence over the silent seas. And yet she could not imagine how Walter should have gone with the sailor, and how he did not run away from him and tell his story to the first person he met with, and get home. For Mrs. Trevelyan was unaware, or at least did not realise, how easy it is to stop the complaints of a child of ten years old, and even to extinguish its scruples, and content it with a new life. She made a visit to Beatrice Trevelyan with some faint hope of being able to move her, and at least to learn something; but Miss Trevelyan received her with an air of innocent astonishment and pain which silenced Agnes.

"Pardon!" Beatrice had said. "It is for us to say that the child has not been sufficiently taken care of. Such a thing could not have happened had he been in our hands." She returned home from this fruitless errand more convinced than ever that it was the Trevelyans who had stolen her child from her, but feeling herself helpless and impotent, and in despair.

As for Jack Charlton, he had himself gone to Cornwall, and availed himself of his knowledge of the country to ascertain everything that had passed at Trevelyan since Walter's disappearance; but nothing was to be learned there. "They cannot keep him always in hiding," Jack said, when he came back. "It cannot last long; they must produce him sooner or later. It is hard to say it, but you are very brave; and if you can but have patience, dear Mrs. Trevelyan —"

Agnes heard it, and smiled as people smile when they are dying. Sooner or later! — when she did not know how to contain herself and bear her burden from one day to another. But then there are some things which it is useless to say.

CHAPTER XXIII.

The Clue.

THINGS were going on in this way, and the summer had come with that brightness which is always so painful to a heart in pain, when one day Jack Charlton arrived suddenly at Windholm. Agnes was sitting with her little girls beside her, who must be a great comfort to her, as everybody said. And so they were

a great comfort, and yet an additional pang, reminding
her in every word they spoke, and every movement
they made, continually of the other who was absent —
the firstborn, who was so much older than they, and
understood her looks and knew what she meant. They
were playing at her feet as she sat reading in the soft
May afternoon. A few months before she would have
been at work with her eyes and ears open to her
children; but it was hard to work under her present
circumstances, when thinking was nothing less than
misery. She was amusing herself and reading a novel,
as a spectator would have said; which meant that she
was making a forlorn attempt to abstract her mind a
little from the thoughts which were so fruitless, and
which made her incapable of her ordinary duties. She
kept holding by that frail thread of interest in other
people's concerns which the book gave her, as to something which kept her from falling over a precipice into
the terrible depths of her own anxiety. Perhaps it
does not require high art to fill such a function as this,
but yet it is an office which might console a writer of
fiction for a few sneers. She kept reading it, not for
the sake of the book, but for her own sake, to keep
herself at least at the book's length from herself; and
this was how she was occupied when Mr. Charlton
came in hastily upon her. The sight of him brought
a thrill to her heart and an eager glance to her eyes;
not for his sake, for all that momentary sentiment had
disappeared under the touch of this hard reality; but
because he bore in his face the look of one who has
something to tell. He was himself so eager that he
almost stepped over little Agnes in his haste. Perhaps
he had not forgotten the awaking of his heart as Agnes

had done; but still he was altogether absorbed in what he had to say.

"It is nothing," he said, hurriedly — "at least, it is not much — it is nothing certain; and yet I think it may be the clue. My dear Mrs. Trevelyan, I do not want to excite your hopes. It may be nothing. Don't give too much weight to what I am going to say——"

"No, no, no," said Agnes, overwhelmed by this exordium; "only say it; let me know what it is——"

"It may turn out to be nothing," said Jack again; "but I have found out that one of our fellows lent his yacht to Sir Roger Trevelyan — just two months ago, at the very time. The boat was lying at Southampton with crew and everything ready. He was going to take a cruise — Heaven knows where he was going! I suppose Stanhope was in with him for some turf business. Stop a moment, that is not all. The yacht sailed, he tells me, but the old boy was not in it. Sir Roger is in town at this moment, though she's still cruising about somewhere. I can't say it's anything," said Jack, growing excited. "He's an old scamp, and somebody else may be in it; but it's always a chance. I thought it best to come down and tell you before going off to Southampton. It is always a chance, and we must follow it up."

Agnes gave a little cry without being aware of it. "I knew my boy was at sea," she said. "Oh, Mr. Charlton — go, go this moment; do not lose any more time. I knew — I was sure he was at sea."

"Yes," said Jack, "I am going;" and then he stopped, perhaps with a feeling that even at such a moment the woman for whom he was taking so much pains might have thanked him for his devotion. If such a feeling existed, it exhaled in a faint sigh and troubled nobody. "I am going," said Jack, with a certain gleam of humour, which Mrs. Trevelyan was far too much preoccupied to observe; "but I can't go until the train goes, and I want to warn you ———"

"Ah! those terrible trains," said Agnes, almost unconscious that he was speaking. "I suppose they are the quickest, in the end; but it seems as if one had always to wait for them, and lose the precious hours. Mr. Charlton, don't be angry with me — he has been two months away ———"

"Angry!" said Jack — he would have liked to have taken her hand, which had grown so thin, into his, and even to kiss it, if there had been an appearance of any room for him in her thoughts; but he was clear-sighted enough to see that there was not a thought of him in Agnes's mind, and that possibly she would not have noticed his salute, had he ventured to give it. "But you must not build too much on this chance," he said, after a moment's pause. "I will go to Southampton; but the yacht is not at Southampton, but at sea — nobody knows where she is. All I can ascertain is perhaps the exact day she sailed, and if anybody remembers anything about it. Most likely he was put on board at night, if he is there; and it is two months ago. I will do all I can; but remember, it is only a chance. There may be no one there who knows anything about it, though I will do my best."

Perhaps it was this iteration which made Agnes raise her eyes. "I know you will do your best," she said, holding out her hand to him; "I know you have done everything that the kindest friend could do. If

I can't thank you, Mr. Charlton, it is not my fault; I will thank you — after ——"

As for Jack, he could not kiss the hand that was put into his with a sentiment so different from that which he felt within himself. It was Walter's mother, grateful and trusting in him for her child's sake, and not Agnes Trevelyan yielding to the mysterious attraction which draws two minds together, who placed thus her hand in his. He clasped it with a kind of despite and bitterness, notwithstanding his devotion. It was not for him but for Walter; and he knew she was grudging every moment that he spent beside her, and desiring only to speed him on his way.

It was just then that the postman came to the door, bringing a letter addressed to Agnes in a hand which she did not know, and bearing a postmark equally unrecognisable. She looked at it indifferently, for the news she had just received had turned all her thoughts in one direction, and for the moment satisfied her mind. Jack, who was always good to children, took upon his knees the little Bee who had crawled to his feet, to leave her mother at liberty to read her letter. Agnes opened it without much interest, though only a few hours ago the receipt of any letter would have made her heart beat wildly. But when she had looked at it she gave a sudden cry, and sprang from her chair to the window to devour what was in it. As for Mr. Charlton, he did not know what had happened, but he put down the child from his knees and picked up the envelope which Mrs. Trevelyan had thrown on the ground, and looked at it carefully. The postmark was Thurso, and it was directed in an unknown handwriting, but his investigations were quickly interrupted by Agnes, who came back to him with her countenance radiant and her eyes full of tears. "Mr. Charlton, he is safe, he is safe!" she cried, with sobs that checked her utterance "Oh, my boy — my darling boy! he is all safe! Oh! thank you, Mr. Charlton — thank you, thank you! He is in the yacht — he is all safe — and it is all through you ———"

This Agnes said without knowing what she was saying. She was so overwhelmed with the sudden joy, that she was incapable of thought. She threw herself into her chair again and took up little Bee, and held the astonished child against her breast, to be a kind of cover for the storm of emotion which came upon her unrestrained, now that all was over, as she thought. She had not cried much through all this dreary interval — she had been frozen and stupefied in the depth of her misery. Now it was spring that had come and loosed all the fountains. She held little Bee against her breast, and sobbed upon her baby's little shoulder, as she never could have sobbed for any sorrow. And the little one, who was frightened at first, put up her little hands to her mother's face and drew it round towards her, and searched its expression with her serious infantine eyes, which were a reproduction of Agnes's own. When little Bee read by instinct that it was not pain that caused those irrepressible sobs, she took her little part womanfully, and laughed the sweet laugh of her age, and clapped her baby hands together. Bee did not know why she was laughing any more than her mother could have explained why she sobbed. And all this scene was enacted before Jack Charlton without any explanation, while he sat looking on with an exquisite envy and despite, like a man outside a magic ring where all the joy and beauty of the world were gathered. For little Agnes, too, had climbed up to share the commotion, whatever it was, and the three clustered together in one group, like one being, belonging to each other, sharing, without even understanding them, each other's emotions. Jack Charlton sat still, and looked on and said nothing. As for him, he belonged to nobody; and the clinging arms of these little children seemed to shut out even his sympathy, although it was he who had devoted so much pains and so many efforts to set the mother's heart at rest.

"Forgive me," said Agnes, at last; "I am very foolish, but I could not help it; to see his handwriting again, and his own very words — oh, forgive me! I have suffered so much; I don't think I knew how miserable I was till now. Read it, Mr. Charlton. And, Agnes, run and tell Madelon to go for your grandpapa. No, don't tell her anything," said Agnes, brightening and smiling through her tears, without recollecting that the child knew nothing to tell; "don't tell her anything to say to him — only that she is to go instantly and tell grandpapa to come — make haste, make haste! Oh, Bee, my little Bee, we shall have our boy again," the happy mother said, dancing her baby on her knee. It was not the same Agnes that had been reading that poor novel by way of deadening a little the anguish of her thoughts. She was pale and worn still, but she was radiant with content and gladness. And this was the cause; but Jack Charlton's countenance fell a little as he read —

"MY DEAR MAMMA, — I am quite well. I have wanted to write to you a great many times, but they

would not let me;　the reason they let me write just
now is, that I have given my word not to tell you the
name of the yacht. It was not my fault that I came, and
I hope you are not angry. They carried me on board
when it was dark, and I was half asleep and thought I
was coming home; and then I was dreadfully sick and
ill.　I am quite well now, and they say I am growing
a famous sailor.　Dear mamma, I hope you are not
angry.　I will come home as soon as ever I can — as
soon as the yacht comes in again; but I must not tell
you its name, because I have given my word.　If I were
quite sure you were not angry and did not want me, it
would be very jolly here.　I like being at sea; but Tom
told me lies, and I will never have anything to do with
him any more.　Dear mamma, give my love to little
Bee, and Agnes, and grandpapa, and to Madelon, and
all the servants;　and as soon as ever I can I shall
come home.

"Your affectionate Son,
"WALTER TREVELYAN."

When Jack Charlton had read this letter he regarded with a little consternation the joyous mother,
who was still dancing little Bee on her lap, and whose
pale face was shining with a light of happiness that it
seemed cruel to disturb.　Though he did all he could,
after the first rapid glance, to conceal his amazement,
Agnes's eye was quick and caught his expression.　She
paused, and involuntarily her air grew more subdued.
"You don't think it is an imposition, Mr. Charlton?
Oh, no; I know Walter's hand; and besides, it is just
how he would write.　It is he himself.　It could be
nobody but he."

"I do not think it is an imposition," said Jack. "I think only that, after all, it does not give you much information." This he said with great hesitation, for it seemed cruel to do anything to lessen the content in her face.

"He says he is quite well," said Agnes quickly, and then she, too, made a pause, and set down her baby on the floor. "To be sure, it is true there is not the yacht's name; but then *you* know the yacht's name, Mr. Charlton. And he is to come back as soon as it gets to land. Ah!"—— said Agnes, with a faint cry. While she was speaking, the vagueness of the letter which had made her so glad came over her; the light paled out of her eyes a little, and her face lost the expansion which had smoothed out all its incipient lines. It was not that her companion undeceived her, but that she began to undeceive herself. She took up the letter again and read it over slowly; and then a long sigh came from her breast, and bitter tears filled her eyes — not the tears which had fallen a few minutes since, like a sunshiny shower, but tears burning and bitter, which did not fall. She read it over slowly line by line, with a pitiful attempt to recover her first feeling. Walter was at sea, no one could tell where. He was under strict watch and guard, as was evident; he was exposed to all the nameless dangers of a voyage. She raised her eyes to Jack Charlton's face after that, with so strange a revulsion of feeling, that it brought a stealthy tear to the corner of his eye. "At least he is well, and nothing has happened to him," she said, and then she put up her letter with a kind of despair.

Jack could not bear this change in the eyes which, through all their changes, were getting more and more dear to him; he took to walking about the room, as some men do to hide their emotion. "I will bring him back to you, if it lies within a man's power," he said, with a slightly broken voice; and then, for he was not given to large offers of service, he took refuge from his momentary *attendrissement* in the letter, or rather in the envelope and postmark. Thurso, the end of the world, the *Ultima Thule*. Jack tried to lead Mrs. Trevelyan back to the practical details; he tried to consult her as to what he should do — whether he should go there and find out whether the little prisoner had been landed, and taken to some hiding-place on shore. But it was unlikely that when they had him safe at sea they would risk the danger of a long journey through the country, where Walter might escape, if he wished to escape, or meet somebody who knew him, or make his story known somehow. Agnes, however, was no good to him in the way of counsel that day. She let him talk, and made little answer. Her practical sense seemed to have left her under the excitement and the revulsion. She sat still, with her child playing at her feet, with a look of weariness and hopelessness, that went to the heart of her companion. She had not the heart even to take up her baby, and take a little consolation from its soft caresses. The joy of the moment, overwhelming as it was, had cost Agnes dear. She was not able now even to take comfort from the assurance that Walter lived and was well, and that they were now on his track.

Hope deferred maketh the heart sick. Mrs. Trevelyan would have given everything she had in the world for that certainty a few hours ago; but from her sudden causeless seizure of security and gladness, she

fell now into the opposite extremity. She was still at
this point of profound discouragement and despondency,
when Stanfield came in hastily, in answer to her summons.
When he heard the news, the blacksmith's face lightened
with hope and confidence. "God be thanked, he's living
and well," Stanfield said, in the fulness of his heart.
And when she heard her own words thus cheerfully
echoed, Agnes's strength returned to her in a modified
degree. After this they began to consult with the trusty
counsellor and friend who was ready to spend his time
and his strength for them. As for Jack, he discussed
it all as a matter of business, as if to employ himself
in the trade of a detective was his natural occupation.
He had ceased to think of going to Southampton now
that this news had come. It occurred to him even —
instead of going to the north, to search into the movements of the yacht there, as had been his first intention
— to go to Cornwall, and engage in his service somebody at each of the little ports which were near Trevelyan, to let him know if it should arrive there.
When he went away at last, Agnes had regained her
self-command and composure, and began again to take
hope and comfort out of her letter. But in her calmness as in her excitement, Jack Charlton could not
but see that her great anxiety was to expedite his departure, and send him as soon as possible on his way.
She had no response to make to the lingering look
he cast at her when he left the house. She was not
thinking of him, though he was doing everything to
serve her — she was thinking of her boy, who had
become quite content to be away from his mother.
No doubt it was natural for Agnes, and the sentiment
most to be looked for in her position; but still, at the

same time, it must be allowed that it was a little hard
upon Jack.

CHAPTER XXIV.

'A Desecrated Home.

As the days went on, however, Mrs. Trevelyan
found greater and greater comfort in Walter's little
letter. She knew it by heart, and yet she read it
over, convincing herself ever anew by the sight of the
paper, and his handwriting, and the blots of his
childish penmanship, of its reality. There was something more consolatory than any eloquence, to the
eyes of Walter's mother, in the pencilled lines which
had been ruled to keep him straight, and in the blots
which had distressed the little writer, and which he
had mopped up so carefully with his blotting-paper.
The boy's signature was in them, much more distinctly
than in the somewhat sprawling "Walter Trevelyan"
at the bottom of the page. After a while, Agnes took
courage to tell her sympathetic neighbours that she
had news of her boy; and Windholm, though it was
not more good-natured than other villages, felt a
certain thrill of content at the intelligence. Even the
boys on the Common were glad to hear that "the
little baronet" had been heard of, and that his mother
expected him back again. But, to tell the truth,
Agnes did not like to interrogate herself too much
as to her expectations. There was as yet no word
from Jack, and there was little that was encouraging
as to his return in the child's letter, which showed
him under strict control and authority, and even docile

under it; for there was nothing in what Walter said
to lead his mother to believe that he would run away
if he had the chance, or that he would appeal to anybody's protection, or rebel against the power into
whose hands he had fallen. "If I knew you were not
angry and did not want me, it would be very jolly
here." These words went to her heart, and brought
with them a sense of distance — a sense of hopelessness — which was very hard to bear; but she preferred,
as much as she could, to avoid that part of the subject
which brought only pain to her thoughts.

On the other hand, it was no longer a vague and
mysterious darkness, like that of death itself, into
which her boy had disappeared. The unknown region,
however vague it may be, from which letters can
still come, with lines ruled and natural blots, and a
postmark, does not seem a region in which any one
can be lost beyond recall. Mrs. Trevelyan was still
very anxious, and had enough ado many times to
keep up her courage in her suspense; but yet that
suspense had changed its character. She was but
waiting now for news that, if it did not come to-day,
might come to-morrow; she was not standing before
a blank darkness which even imagination could not
penetrate. Imagination could figure now but too easily
Walter's position and circumstances. When she heard
the wind blow of nights in the lime-trees, Agnes felt
her peaceable house sway to and fro, and heard the
rushing waves in her ears, and the blackness of the
night. So far as that went, fancy was only too ser-
viceable. And then, on the other hand, she could see
her boy indulged and petted by the sailors, and made
a little prince of (as was natural, in Mrs. Trevelyan's

opinion), and getting more and more contented with
his position. Sometimes it occurred to her to consider
what might be the effect upon Walter's mind of his
grandfather's stately house at Trevelyan, and all its
advantages. He would not have chosen to leave his
mother had the alternative been proposed to him; but
perhaps, after this apprenticeship in the yacht, and
such information about his own prospects and future
rank as he would most likely have received, would it
be wonderful if Walter, just ten years old, should feel
a natural reluctance to return to the house on the
Green, and give up all the opportunities of amusement
and pleasure which might be found in his other
sphere?

Agnes pondered all this with a sinking at her
heart; and then she resolved, not without pride, to
leave him free to choose; and then turned back with a
sense of renewed desolation to read the little letter
again, and please herself with thinking of her boy's
anxiety to write to her, and of his honourable sense of
his promise; and then of the little figure bending over
the letter — of the innocent blots and ink-stained
fingers, and all the details which it was so easy to
conjure up before her. If she had been a man and
had to go out into the world, no doubt these things
would have had a less effect upon her; but then she
was only a woman, and what she had to do could
generally be done, tranquil as her existence was, without any great claim upon her mind. And, to be sure,
it is this mingled web of recollection and imagination
which fills up the most part of a woman's life.

The first interruption of these reveries came in
a sufficiently disagreeable form, through the in-

tervention of Martha, who had been the servant in Stanfield's house as long as Agnes could remember. Martha, who had grown almost as stout and red as Mrs. Stanfield, could not divest herself altogether of a certain interest in the proceedings of a woman who was to some extent a kindred soul: it was the kind of interest which impels people not to do anything themselves for a supposed sufferer, but to call the attention of other people upon whom they suppose the sufferer to have "a claim." Martha herself could not put up with such goings-on after Stanfield had left the house; but still she was of opinion that it was Mrs. Trevelyan's duty to see after her father's wife, who was going out of her mind, as all the village believed.

"The noise is like to bring the roof down," Martha said, "for all the world as if they was throwing everything in the house about — and a smell of cooking as would turn you sick; not to say nothing of the pots of beer — and worse!" added the faithful servant, lowering her voice, and with a certain watering of the mouth — for Martha, under Mrs. Stanfield's rule, had learned to love good cheer, though her respectability had proved incorruptible after the blacksmith abandoned his house. "She's got a pack of blackguards about her as robs her," said Martha; "it ain't as it's her I'm thinking of; but it's the master as has to pay, and it's all our duties to save the master. And then she's a-killing of herself, though that ain't so much matter. If I was you, Mrs. Trevelyan, as was known for a charitable lady, and her my connexion, as it were — I would go and see if I couldn't do something to stop it. That is what I would do, if it was me."

"My father would not like me to go, Martha,"

18*

said Agnes; "he would be displeased; he does not desire to have any communication at present with Mrs. Stanfield." Agnes was glad to have her father's name to support her; for, indeed, she had no inclination on her own part to carry the duties of a charitable lady to such an extent.

"I'd go without asking him, if I was you," said Martha. "I asks your pardon, Mrs. Trevelyan, but it's along of knowing you when you was but a little bit of a child. I would go without asking. He's a good man is the master, and he'd never find fault with nobody for doing their duty; and she'll do a mischief to herself — as you'd know if you knew all — if she's left all by herself like this."

When Martha had said these words she took her leave with the easy conscience of a woman who has done her duty. To be sure, it did not occur to her to see after Mrs. Stanfield in her own person; but then she had relieved her mind, and turned over the duty upon Agnes, which was in its way a great deal better, not to say easier, than doing it herself. And the seed thus sown germinated in due time, as such seeds generally do. Agnes could not cast this information out of her mind, neither could she feel herself altogether free from responsibility in respect to her father's wife. The unhappy woman was unfit to take care of herself, and she was alone, and had nobody to guide her. Agnes never took upon herself to doubt the justice of the step her father had taken, especially as it had always been a pain and horror to her to see his unfit wife by his side; but she had not been insulted beyond possibility of forgiveness, as her father had been; and she was a woman, and had pity at least for another

woman who was lost in a wretchedness all the greater
because she did not know it to be wretchedness.

Mrs. Trevelyan resisted these thoughts stoutly for
some days, and put them away from her; but she happened one evening to pass the old archway, when
sounds of festivity were coming from the open windows
above, at which she had so often sat in her innocent
days; and, before she had got out of hearing, the
sounds changed into warfare, and there was a scuffle
and struggle, and calls of murder and for the police;
which respectable body was represented in Windholm
by a very leisurely and well-disposed group of good-
natured fellows, who talked to each other at the corners
of the village street, and took care of little children
who were lost, and did sundry other friendly offices to
the community. The police came, putting on its of-
ficial coat by the way, to the admiration of the be-
holders, while Agnes still lingered to see what it was
going to come to. A little crowd collected under the
windows which were so sacred to her recollections. She
stood at a little distance until she saw a culprit led
out, followed by a crowd. Mrs. Trevelyan was moved
perhaps by shame and disgust, as much as by more
benevolent intentions. Without waiting to think or
even explaining it to herself, she turned and went
quickly back after the crowd had begun to disperse.
When it was seen that it was she who was going in
under the archway, the few spectators, who still lingered,
slunk off confused, and left Stanfield's house at peace.
Happily it was past worktime, and he was not there to
see the desecration of the home which had been so
long the most honourable house in the village, and
which, still, was called by his name.

Agnes went hastily up the familiar stair with a heavy heart, and pushed open the door, which was ajar, and went in. The house bore the air of disturbance, which was natural after a struggle; a chair in the passage had been thrown down and broken, the carpet was dragged out of its place, and everything that used to be so trim was out of order. The parlour door at the end of the passage was partially open, and out of it came a voice interrupted now and then, but never ceasing altogether — a voice which scolded, and cried, and entreated, and threatened all in a breath. It was Mrs. Stanfield who was talking, calling somebody to her assistance, who would not come, or perhaps, more likely, could not come, being absent; for not another sound was audible in the house, the door of which had been left open, no doubt to facilitate the unfaithful servant's return.

Agnes shut the door, and went quickly on to the sitting-room. When she entered the old parlour, it was a strange scene — a scene quite unparalleled in her experience — which met her eyes. Mrs. Stanfield was sitting in a corner rocking herself, crying and moaning, and calling for Lizzy. The table was covered with bottles and glasses, some of which had been upset and broken — and several of the chairs round the table had been thrown down. It was evening, and the light began to grow faint, and the aspect of the place filled Agnes, in spite of herself, with a certain instinct of horror and anger. But then these inanimate things, after all, counted for little in comparison with the living creature in the midst of them, degraded as she was. Mrs. Stanfield's cap was awry on her head, and her ruddy, unfaded locks had been pushed off her

face, and stood up round her forehead like the meta-
phorical hair, which stands on end. She was sitting
quite in the corner, embracing her knees, and calling
for Lizzy. All the restraint which Stanfield's presence
had imposed upon her was gone; she had been doing
"whatever she liked" for two months back, and naturally she talked as she liked, now that there was
nobody who could control her to hear. She called upon
Lizzy to come and be hanged, come and be d——d; and
when the girl did not answer these encouraging appeals,
she changed her tone.

"I'll forgive you if you'll only come," she cried.
"Lizzy! do you hear? I'll forgive you. It's come on
dark, and I can't stir, and there ain't a soul to do anything for me. Do you call that having one's way?
It's that devil Stanfield or his daughter as has put a
spell on me. Lizzy!" cried the unhappy woman; but
still Lizzy who, like Mrs. Stanfield, preferred her own
way, made no response. When she saw Agnes come
in, and stand silent for a moment on the threshold,
Mrs. Stanfield gave a great cry. Perhaps she thought
for the moment that it was a ghost. After that exclamation she became silent, and stared at her visitor with
a fright that it was impossible to disguise. She was
like the unclean spirits, who said, "What have I to do
with thee?" It seemed to her, certainly, as if Agnes
— if it was Agnes, and not a ghost — must have come
to torment her before her time.

"I heard you calling," said Agnes; "I don't think
there is any one in the house. I came in because the
door was open. Are you ill? Tell me what you would
like me to do for you, now that I am here."

"You look like Agnes Stanfield — come to worry

me," said Mrs. Stanfield, with a momentary gleam of her old spirit.

"I am Agnes Trevelyan, and I have come to help you, if there is anything I can do," said Agnes. She could not altogether command her looks or conceal her disgust; but her patient was not at that moment very clear-sighted. When she had got over her fright, she put up her hands by instinct to her head, and made an effort to set her cap straight and recover her faculties. To be sure, she was incapable of understanding the influence to which she yielded in spite of herself.

"I know what you want," she said, making greater and greater efforts to rouse herself, as Agnes, without saying anything, picked up the fallen chairs and put them in their places. Her very presence in the room seemed to restore an element of order of which even Mrs. Stanfield was vaguely conscious. "I know what you want," she repeated, with an attempt at her old tone of triumph; "you've took me unawares, to find out about Walter; but I ain't one to be taken in with false friends. It's just like them all," said the unhappy creature, bitterly; "they comes to you when you has anything, and when they've got everything you have, they deserts you. Lizzy! And as for *you*, it's to worry my life out about your precious boy as you've come here —"

"No," said Agnes, "you are mistaken. I know about my boy, thank God! I have got a letter from him; and I know, too, what part your son had in taking him away; but it is not for that I am here."

"You've got a letter from him! You're telling me a lie, Agnes Stanfield, or they're all fools, d—d fools!"

cried the blacksmith's wretched wife. "Good Lord, they'll take me up for mad next! You've got a letter? You'd best tell me as you're going home to Trevelyan to be made a lady of at the last. It would be just like them; oh, the fools! the d—d fools! — and it would be like you, Madame Impudence, as always was one to make yourself better than your neighbours; but I'll kill you first — I'll poison you first — afore you go there."

She got up as she spoke, and, though her limbs trembled under her weight, the aspect of the staggering fury was yet sufficiently alarming. Whatever the cause might be, the idea that her step-daughter was to be made a lady of at the last, roused the wretched woman into frenzy. She supported herself against the back of a chair, and clenched her pink hand, which even now, unwieldy as it was, had not altogether lost the dimples of its fleshly and sensual beauty. "If you tell me that, I'll kill you," she said, with her hazel eyes blazing red, sweeping the air with her heavy but nerveless fist. As for Agnes, the emergency made her heart beat a little more quickly, for she knew well enough that the woman before her was half mad with excitement, and despite, and dissipation, and owned no restraint in the world either of law or prudence. And the door was shut upon Agnes's retreat, and she would rather have died than summon help from the open windows, from which already so many disgraceful sounds had proceeded. However, she did not recede from the danger she had brought upon herself.

"I came here not to tell you about myself, but to answer your call," she said, calmly. "There is nobody in the house. If I can do anything for you, tell me.

You are abandoned, as it seems, by your friends. Shall
I send somebody to you to put all this disorder right,
and to take care of you? If you do not want anything,
I will go away."

At this moment Mrs. Stanfield dropped back into
her chair, unable to support herself. Even the presence
of Agnes, though she looked like an avenging angel,
was better than absolute solitude. The wretched creature fell to crying, as was natural enough. "Oh!
Agnes Stanfield," she sobbed out, "I'd have been a
mother to you, if you'd have let me; I'd have loved
you like my own. I've got a daughter of my own,
but I ain't set eyes on her for fifteen year. Oh, I'm
a poor creature — I'm a poor creature! There ain't
nobody in the world as minds what I say. Lizzy!
Lizzy! I've been good to that lass, I have, and give
her all as heart could desire; and look you now how
she goes and leaves me. Oh, Agnes Stanfield, I'll die
— that's what will be the end of it; and there ain't a
soul but will be glad to hear!"

Agnes could answer nothing to this maudlin fit,
and she did not attempt it. She was thinking less, indeed, of the miserable woman than of the familiar
place which was thus desecrated; and Mrs. Stanfield
went on bemoaning herself. "As for the boys, they
don't mind me; there's been years and years as they
haven't minded me," she said; "and I don't believe as
Sir Roger; — but he's gone through a deal since then."
When she said this the cunning instinct of her semi-
insanity returned to her. She gave a stealthy look at
Agnes, to see if she had remarked the name, and then,
with the rapidity of rage and dislike, rushed back into
the other branch of the subject. "If anything should

happen to Walter, you ain't got no more claim," she
said, drying her fiery eyes —"it's him as is your only
hope, my lady. No, you'll never be my lady now —
I'm glad of that; I was glad for that when poor Roger
was took, though I was sorry for him. He was no
better nor my Roger, but he was the heir; and now
there's your boy as hasn't half the right; but I don't
see as your boy'll ever come to the title. He's puny,
like all your children. I never lost one, not of mine;
they was all as hearty as hearty. He'll never be Sir
Walter, that bit of a child; and I'd like to know, if
he dies like the rest, what good it is being Mrs. Trevelyan? There ain't one of the family as will take any
notice of you."

"Mrs. Stanfield," said Agnes — who, notwithstanding all her self-possession, could not help trembling
from head to foot at this horrible prophecy—"I came
not to discuss my own prospects or my son's, but to
ask if I could help you. You know as little as I do of
what is going to happen," she said, yielding, in spite
of herself, to her natural terror. "Oh! be silent, I beg
of you; I will stay with you till your servant comes
in, if you will say no more."

"Oh yes, you're one of them as don't like to hear
the truth," said Mrs. Stanfield, with triumph. "I tell
you if Walter dies you haven't got no claim; you and
your little girls, you ain't got no expectations from the
Trevelyans no more than if you was like me; and
that's what'll be the end of it, my lady," cried the
fury — "you as set your heart on being my lady. If
he dies — and there's a deal of likelihood as he'll die
— you ain't no more than me; and you're a deal worse
than me," she continued, after a pause, "for I never

had no ambition, and knew my place, and never set
my heart on such a thing. It's a deal worse for you.
You worried the father to death, and you'll see as the
son 'll be took for a punishment; and you and your
babies, don't you think as you have got no claim; and
as for being Mrs. Trevelyan —"

Agnes had come to the end of her patience and her
strength. She could bear no longer this dreadful voice
of madness, which was mad and miserable, no doubt,
but yet in its very wickedness sounded like a prophecy of evil. She fled out of the room when the last
possibility of endurance was over, making her escape
noiselessly like a ghost; but, before she could open
the outer door, Mrs. Stanfield had changed her tone,
and was again uttering lamentable cries and en-
treaties.

"Don't leave me by myself; oh, don't leave me by
myself. Oh, Agnes Stanfield, come back and I'll not
say nothing. Oh, Lizzy, as I've been so kind to, I
can't stay in the dark — I can't be left by myself.
Oh, good Lord, they're a forsaking of me!" cried the
miserable woman.

Agnes went back without saying a word, and
lighted a candle, and placed it on the disordered table;
then she left the room and waited at the door till Mrs.
Stanfield's young maid came flying upstairs in consternation. The girl was one of those suspected girls
whom "charitable ladies" recognise by instinct in every
parish under the sun — not bad as yet, but fully in
the way of being bad, and without any particular wish
to avoid the knowledge of good and evil. When she
saw Mrs. Trevelyan, Lizzy fell back dismayed, and
began to stammer out an apology. It was almost dark

by this time, and the sight of the pale face and black
dress at the top of the stairs impressed Lizzy almost
as much as a young Catholic of her years and inclinations might have been impressed by the sudden
appearance of the Madonna or of her patron saint.
Agnes put her hand on the girl's shoulder and turned
her back.

"You are not able to take care of her in her present state, and it is not a fit place for you," she said.
"Go and call Nurse Meadows to me; I shall wait here
until you come back."

Mrs. Trevelyan sat down by herself in the dark, in
the little recess where the linen presses were, and the
window which looked into the court, and waited for
the return of her messenger.   Down below, opposite to
her, was the forge where her father did his honest work
day by day, and the court where she herself had played
when she was a child, and where her boy had played.
A momentary wonder and self-discussion whether she
herself was really the Agnes Stanfield who had once
lived here, and known no interest beyond those walls,
came into Agnes's mind. That girl, with all her beautiful hopes, was dead, Heaven knows how many
years ago; and the woman who sat there on her watch,
was so different, as she thought, from anything that
could have been prophesied of the first Agnes. Ah, if
she had but actually died then before the world began!
But when Walter's image came back to her mind a
great horror and anguish seized upon Agnes. There
was nothing, surely nothing, but a wicked woman's
fancy, which could connect death with the name of her
boy. This was how she occupied herself as she sat
and trembled, partly with a nervous panic and terror,

partly with the night-air from the open window, waiting the arrival of the nurse who alone was fit at such
a moment to have charge of the blacksmith's miserable
wife.

CHAPTER XXV.

Miss Trevelyan's Share.

DURING this time, which had produced so much
misfortune and pain to Agnes, Beatrice Trevelyan had
been pursuing her course as usual. She had put off
the last vestige of her mourning, and had even, people
said, recovered the despite and rage into which she
was thrown by the decision of the Lord Chancellor in
favour of her sister-in-law. Not that Beatrice had betrayed her rage in an unladylike way; but then the
people who knew her, knew the meaning of her looks
and ways; and there were unfortunately a great many
people who knew Miss Trevelyan. It was even said
that the lost law-suit had added one or two fine and
delicate wrinkles, which several persons in society declared themselves able to identify on her well-conserved
countenance. From which it will be seen, as has, indeed, been before said, that Beatrice retained, notwithstanding all the arts necessary to her position, a certain
truthfulness at the bottom of her character. Perhaps
the person who suffered most on the whole was, however,
the great dignitary concerned, the learned and noble
lord, the Chancellor himself, who had his weaknesses,
as even Lord Chancellors will have, and, indeed, was
known to possess some of those which are peculiar to
Lord Chancellors. Everybody knows what is the power

of an unscrupulous and acute antagonist, with a place in society, and the character of being amusing. Beatrice found out with a praiseworthy zeal, and put into lively circulation, several very pleasant anecdotes of these chancellorly weaknesses; and following the ordinary rule of vicarious punishment, it was poor Lord Norbury who suffered for the Trevelyans' humiliation and defeat.

Beatrice was more brilliant than ever in the commencement of the season, notwithstanding those signs of defeat which she was said to bear in her face. She might have been discomfited for the moment, but she was not overcome nor discouraged; and then she was a woman of resources, and now that her pride and temper, and almost everything that makes life worth having, were involved, it will be believed that Miss Trevelyan did not lose her time. It had become a necessity of existence, even, that the upstart who presumed to call herself Mrs. Trevelyan, and to claim the custody of Sir Roger's heir, should be once for all put down and made an end of. Beatrice had been galled to the heart by what she supposed Agnes's happiness, and she had been smitten with dire and miserable envy at the thought of Agnes's grief; feeling to the bottom of her heart with that perception of the truth which showed the fallen angel in her, that her own mean and paltry existence was not good enough either for the grief or the happiness. But if this had been the case, while Agnes did her no further harm than that which was implied in her capacity for a loftier, though more grievous lot, it may be imagined what Beatrice's sensations were when her sister-in-law attained the clear culpability of a victory over her. It was no longer a matter of mere feeling;

the face of affairs changed in a moment. It became a
necessity to re-arrange this fallible mortal decision, and
reverse the position of the parties. If it could have
been done by law it would have been well, but since
the law had acted so badly, nothing remained for the
Trevelyans but to act in their own right.

Sir Roger himself was more moved than he had
been by anything since his son's marriage. His mind
revolted against the idea of leaving his grandson and
heir in the hands of the woman who had, as he said,
"inveigled my poor boy into marrying her, by Jove!"
— a righteous sentiment, in which Miss Trevelyan up-
held him with all her might. It is true that Beatrice
was not acquainted with all the details by which this
just act was to be accomplished. Miss Trevelyan knew
nothing about Mrs. Stanfield or Tom Smith — or if she
had, perhaps a vague impression that such people
existed, they were beings without names for Sir Roger's
daughter. But she knew what was being done as the
miner knows about the powder, though it may be another
hand who fires it. And while this project was being
carried out, which would expose both "the family"
and their nameless assistants to certain unpleasant consequences if it should be discovered, Miss Trevelyan
occupied herself in telling pleasant anecdotes about Lord
Norbury, and lamenting that a chancellor should so often
be *low*, and unworthy of admittance into good society;
which, to be sure, was an innocent and even meritorious
way of taking her revenge. There were but two persons in the great world, so far as Miss Trevelyan was
aware, who regarded her with a doubtful eye on account
of this family affair. The one was, as was natural, Lady
Grandmaison, who was Agnes's friend, and consequently,

by the operation of the most ordinary and well-known influences, Miss Trevelyan's enemy; and who, from the first moment of Walter's abduction, had regarded Beatrice with suspicion; the other, which was much more singular (for Miss Trevelyan acknowledged the justice of the antipathy in Lady Grandmaison's case), was the lady who once made her juvenile appearance in this history under the name of Lottie Charlton. As might have been expected, she was not Lottie Charlton now, but Mrs. Oldham, the wife of a man who had covered a multitude of sins, in the way of descent and connexions, by being frightfully, almost, as Lottie herself said (but that was before her marriage), disgracefully rich. Mrs. Oldham was not specially attached to Agnes, nor had she kept up any friendship with her; but she had retained, notwithstanding the dangers and difficulties of her position, the amiable weakness of a belief in her brother, which did credit to her heart at least, if not to her discrimination. The cause which Jack defended was to a certain extent sacred to Lottie, though she was sufficiently well brought up to have known better. Had she known of that letter to which Agnes Trevelyan had never replied, the probabilities are that she might have modified her opinion. But then Lottie had no means of seeing the letter, and had no friends, neither had her maid any friends in Windholm, which was wonderful enough, so that she never knew up to the present moment how often Jack went to the house on the Green, nor how long he stayed there, nor what people were saying in the village of his inclinations and aims.

This being the case, of all persons in the world, her old friend and neighbour Lottie Charlton, whom

she had held on her knee, who had acted baby chaperon
to her early flirtations, and who had superseded her
even in the regard of the county when her day came,
developed into one of Beatrice's enemies and watchers.
It was difficult to realize the fact, but still such was
the case; and, as it happened that season, Lady Grandmaison and Mrs. Oldham were everywhere. If by chance
the one did not make her appearance, cruelly civil and
menacing, the other was there, familiar and a little fast
as of old, but equally on the watch as to all Miss Trevelyan's words. Lottie, on the whole, was the more
troublesome of the two. She said to Beatrice, in the
midst of a group of people, "Your little nephew has
been stolen, and Jack is in a terrible way about it,
after winning the cause and all. Do tell me where he
is, Beatrice. You are so clever — they will never find
him, if you don't give in to tell me." Of course this
was nonsense, which no one could take the pains to
contradict gravely; but still it had a certain effect, and
was highly disagreeable, to say the least of it; and
Lottie, though she spoke so lightly, had an air of be-
lieving, and even meaning what she said.

Under these circumstances, there sometimes arrived
a moment when the graver possibilites of her position
would flash upon Beatrice, bringing the moisture to her
forehead, and even taking the curl out of her wonderful
hair. If by any chance it should be discovered what
had been done, and her complicity in it — if even it
should be discovered in Sir Roger's lifetime, when he
would naturally throw all the blame on his daughter,
and declare it to be "the d—d spite of these women"
— the consequences might be such as even Miss Trevelyan shrunk from contemplating. She knew better

than most people how far the forbearance of society
can go; she felt even that a happy combination of circumstances — such, for example, as a low second marriage on Agnes's part — might make the abduction of
her little nephew an heroic act, entitling her to the admiration of the world. But then, on the other hand,
if nothing of that sort should occur to justify her, and
if, on the contrary, she was simply *found out* in an attempt which was certainly against the law, Miss Trevelyan
could not but feel that a woman who had a hand in
the kidnapping of an innocent child was not likely to
gain much from the act either in the estimation of men
or women. When this thought struck her, Beatrice
trembled, notwithstanding all her self-command. But
then almost everything depended on success, in that as
in most other matters in which it is necessary to take
into consideration the opinion of the world.

In this position of affairs, it may be imagined what
were the feelings of Beatrice when, one day, in the
very height of the season, Sir Roger sent for her to
make the following unparalleled proposition — namely,
that she should go, without loss of time, to a dreary
house which he possessed in Hampshire, to take charge
of the little prisoner, who was to be conveyed there at
the end of his cruise. "I'm sick of it all, by Jove!"
said Sir Roger. "If it weren't that a man can't stand
being beat, I'd be d—d sorry I ever took it in hand.
I'm not as spiteful as a woman, by Jove! and since
it's your doing, I'll thank you to take it in hand in
future. By —— —, here's that ass Bevis writing to me
for money — as if I was a man to be asked for money!
Hang him! he knows I never have enough for myself.
They can't keep cruising about for ever and ever, by

19*

Jove! all for a d—d boy. Take him and shut him up
in the cottage till it blows over. There's Jack Charlton
setting spies at Trevelyan, by —— And it's all along
of you that I'm worried to death like this. I'll give it
up, by Jove! and send him back to his d—d mother,
if you don't take it in hand yourself."

"I!" said Miss Trevelyan. She was ashamed to be
moved to this extent by any command of her father's,
but yet she could not help showing her confusion and
annoyance. "I beg your pardon, papa. If you choose
to have your heir brought up by a blacksmith, it is
nothing to me; but as for leaving town in the height
of the season ——"

"By — —," said Sir Roger, "I should think it
wasn't such a dreadful sacrifice. I should think you
were sick of it, by Jove! Never picked up a husband
yet, Bee, after twenty years' hard work and more.
By — —, I'd give in, if I were you. You're deuced
well got up, but you're ageing. You're a d—d deal
older than I am, for that matter. If you don't go, I'll
send the little wretch home, that's clear. I've got my
book to make up, which is a deal more important than
your parties; either you'll go, or ——"

"It is impossible I can go," said Miss Trevelyan —
"utterly out of the question; my engagements do not
permit me to entertain the idea for a moment. You
should have thought of the difficulties sooner. I don't
say your pursuits are not most important and instruc-
tive," continued Beatrice, in steady tones; "but you
forget this is not my business, but yours."

Upon this, Sir Roger got up and began to walk
about the room in a transport of rage and blasphemy.
"By ——, you know it's all your doing," he said;

"it ain't in my way to kidnap children. But for that d—d yacht of Stanhope's, and no other use for it, I'd never have given in to your spite; you and the rest — ha! ha! ha! — you'd be pleased, you would, if you knew who was your *collaborateur*, Miss Trevelyan. By Jove! I've half a mind to tell her. What am I to do, I'd like to know? I've sent off Bevis all this while, and put up with a d—d blockhead that has to be told everything, d—n him, and spends a lot of money — or at least gets a lot of bills, which comes to the same thing. Hang it all! what am I to do? That d—d cottage ain't let, and it's near the sea. I can't send him to Trevelyan; and it's all along of your spite against that deuced widow. By Jove, I'll have him pitched into the sea and be done with him, or I'll send him back to his d—d mother. Am I a man to be worried to death about the brat? I'll do one or the other if you don't come to your senses — by Jove, I'll do it —"

"Please to recollect," said Beatrice, coldly, interrupting her father without any ceremony, "that if you throw him into the sea you are liable for murder, and if you send him back you are liable for something else, which no doubt will be quite as bad; and you may be sure they won't let you off. And it will be pleasant to see Sir Roger Trevelyan brought to the bar by a country blacksmith, and compelled to pay damages, or costs, or something ——"

"By ——!" cried Sir Roger, with a renewed access of frenzy. When he came to himself, he changed his tone a little. "Hang it, what is a man to do?" he said. "Look you here, Bee, I don't want to be disagreeable. I'm deuced sorry I ever had anything to do with it; but now, since we're in for it — and, by

Jove, we're both in for it, for I ain't going to let you
off if it should come to that; let's stand by each other,
by ——, and get out of it the best way we can. The
country's the deuce, especially at this time of the year,
when there's nothing doing.* If you'll go and see
after the d—d little monkey and settle him, and get a
woman to look after him —; by Jove, we cannot keep
him always there — He'll have to be put to school
sooner or later, and then there's sure to be a row.
Jack Charlton is going after him like — blazes," said
the baronet; "he's after the widow, I suppose."

"Never!" cried Beatrice, roused to some excitement. "Poor Roger was enticed into it when he was
only a boy, but Jack Charlton is not the man to destroy all his prospects," she cried, with a fire and energy
which did not escape her father. Sir Roger laughed
and sneered — as men of his class sneer when a woman gets excited — thinking it much more natural to
account for the sentiment by associating it with liking
for a man than with dislike for another woman.

"So, Beatrice, it's Jack you're thinking of," said
her father, with his odious laugh. "He's a deal too
young for you, but I don't suppose that matters at
your age. Hang it, I don't want him for a son-in-law.
But he's after the boy like blazes, I tell you. Nobody
knows about the cottage; it's been a bad speculation
has that cottage. Make a run down, and visit the little
beggar and settle him. By Jove, I don't ask you to stay."

"I will tell you what to do," said Beatrice; "take
a little house in St. John's Wood or somewhere. It is
nonsense losing the rent of the cottage; and then, you

---

* It was early in June — which some people think the most beautiful
part of the year; but then that was not Sir Roger's way of thinking.

know, I could see after him without giving up everything, and you could have Bevis back. It is far more difficult to find anybody in London than in the country. If you will do that, I undertake to manage it," said Miss Trevelyan. It is true that Sir Roger did not give up his own plan without many objections and a great deal of profane language; but, then, Beatrice was used to that. She carried her point at last, notwithstanding that her father had the most urgent dislike of spending money; which as he thought, would have been unnecessary had he been able to deposit his grandson in the cottage; but then, nothing could be done without the co-operation of Beatrice, and thus it became necessary to give in.

Sir Roger went away from this interview swearing horribly at himself for having been such a fool as to have anything to do with it, and perhaps it was with a similar sentiment that Beatrice withdrew to her own section of the house — at least, she was paying rather dear for her revenge; and the idea of the danger she had escaped — the danger of being sent off to Hampshire to a semi-inhabitable cottage, made not to be lived in but to be let, just at the moment when life is most exciting and town fullest, thrilled through her when she thought of it. It was bad enough even to have to go out to the unknown suburban solitudes to look after this tiresome child; and then, Miss Trevelyan was not one for children. It was pleasant to smite Agnes at the moment of her victory, and carry away her boy, and drive her half distracted with anxiety; but still such amusements cost dear, and Beatrice began to see more clearly than at first the difficulties in the way. They could not keep a boy of Walter's age a

strict prisoner; after a while, he would have to go to
school, and if the whole matter got vent and came to
the ears of the world — which Beatrice's experience
told her was but too likely — the result would be little
to her advantage. And then Miss Trevelyan, for himself, felt wonderfully little interest in the boy; it was
not so much as her brother's son, but as Agnes's son,
that she regarded him; and Agnes had been for a long
time her type of opposition and rivalship. She wanted
to humiliate and mortify the woman who had been,
as she thought, so much better off than herself — so
much more favoured of Heaven; and to avenge the defeat Agnes had brought upon the house of Trevelyan,
and even to punish Walter for presuming to be the
heir — he who was the blacksmith's grandson. These
were the objects that Beatrice placed before her. If
any thought of love had come in — any yearning towards the child who was her own blood — the chances
are that this strange woman would have found herself
out in a moment, and seen through all her own self-
excuses; but she made no account of natural affection
so far as her little nephew was concerned, and thus
went on steadily to accomplish what some people would
call the decrees of fate.

It was indeed a moment in which Miss Trevelyan
would have felt it fatal for her interests to leave town,
and which made even her occasional absence extremely
critical; for, in fact, all this happened very shortly
after the time when Beatrice had presented to her a
Nabob of the Indian Civil Service, who had grown rich
as people never grow rich nowadays. He said he had
had the honour to know Miss Trevelyan before he
went to India, but was sadly afraid she must have for-

gotten him. It was not artifice that called up the sudden passing flush which was so becoming to Beatrice, at that startling moment; for this speech and his name together made her aware that it was her young suitor of Heaven knows how many years ago who was speaking to ·her. Of course, she did not recognise him as he seemed to have recognised her; but she knew his name, having made much use of it to herself in past years, as representing what she was pleased to call the great disappointment of her youth. And it was not Miss Trevelyan's fault if her old lover took it as a personal compliment that she was still Miss Trevelyan. He had not himself married, perhaps because he was constant to his first love, perhaps because he found it most convenient; but, at all events, he was unmarried, and things, on the whole, looked very promising.

At such a crisis it may be supposed how serious a matter it would have been had she been compelled to go to Hampshire; it was even very inconvenient to have a secret, and to be obliged to interrupt the natural course of her life in order to look after this tiresome little boy, who, very likely, would try to escape, and make himself as disagreeable as possible. But when she thought of her father's supposition about Jack Charlton, Beatrice's heart closed tight against all charitable ideas. The readers of this history will not, however, think, like Sir Roger, that this sentiment was on Jack's account. Jack was no more to Miss Trevelyan than any other Cornish man whom she was civil to when occasion required; nor was it on Roger's account, nor from that sense of inconstancy and disregard for his memory, which shocked so profoundly the feelings of little Miss Fox at Windholm; it was because Jack

Charlton, though he was not rich, was quite as good
a gentleman as Roger Trevelyan, and would vindicate
his choice, and place the blacksmith's daughter once
again in a position superior to that of her sister-in-law,
who wanted to despise her, and could not. Naturally,
this idea was quite enough to close up all the modes
of entrance into Miss Trevelyan's heart.

CHAPTER XXVI.

News.

AGNES went home, when she had established Nurse
Meadows in charge of Mrs. Stanfield, with a sense of
weight and burden on her mind, which all her efforts
could not shake off. It was a lovely summer evening,
just between the light and the dark, at the moment
when all the tints of the sky are tempered, and all the
sounds and odours most softened and sweet. Nothing
of all that she saw around her gave any warrant
to these thoughts. The night air came in her face a
little fresh, perhaps, but without giving her any excuse
to conjure up a storm at sea. On the contrary, it was
an air, soft and dewy, with the breath of the hawthorn
in it from the lanes. And yet her heart lay in her
breast like a stone — but that is a poor image; it lay
in her breast like a wounded bird, making a sudden
flutter now and then against the bars of its cage; and
she could not have given any due reason for the heavi-
ness that was in her. Perhaps it was thinking of the
miserable soul whom she had just left. But then, a
woman may be sorry for her neighbours, and yet, if
she is a mother, and all is well with her children, there

is nothing in the world that can give her such a sense of panic and trouble. It was that a sudden fear had seized her — that horror of great darkness which comes as the wind does, without any one knowing whence or how. She was saying to herself that there were other women in the world who had lost their children, and why not she? If God could have the heart to take him, the first-born — the only son of his mother! — it was not irreverence that made her frame her thoughts like this, but a dreadful reality in the position, as if God and she were standing on opposite sides, and the poor woman, who was His creature, pleading against Him. The only son of his mother, and she a widow! It was reason enough why man should not take him away from her, but was it reason enough for God? A great many people, perhaps, would blame Agnes for having such thoughts; but it is hard not to have them sometimes, as there are other people who know. All this, most likely, was brought into her mind by Mrs. Stanfield's maunderings, which were cruel enough; but even these would not have had such an effect upon Agnes's mind had she not been discouraged and cast down, and sadly worn out with her deferred hope. And then it seems so natural to a mother that something should happen to her child when she is away from him. There was only God to take care of Walter, and who could tell what God's mind was about him — to save or to slay? It is well for those to whom these heathen thoughts do not come by times, when darkness covers the earth and the sea. As she walked home alone, with all those soft influences of Nature on her way to calm her, her heart now and then started and gave a wild flutter, and then was

quiet. It is possible that this mother-passion was, as
the French say, the only passion of her life; and that
might be why these fits of panic took her without any
adequate cause.

Mrs. Stanfield was ill, as Agnes had foreseen that
she was going to be. It was an illness caused by
having her own way, and it went rather hard with her,
for perhaps she had had her will a day or two too
long; and when the fever went to her head, as her
attendants said, she talked enough to make Nurse Meadows and Lizzy — and, through them, all the village
— more fully acquainted with her past history than
even Stanfield was, who had divined it, and separated
himself from the dishonour without venturing to ask
any questions. Then it was that the truth burst upon
the Windholm folks in all its naked horror. It was
so extraordinary that some time passed before the village could habituate itself to the idea. And then they
began to remember that the eldest of Mrs. Stanfield's
two sons was named Roger, and to wonder why they
had not found it out sooner. To think that these two
lads, who had been the pest of the place, should be
Trevelyans also, in a kind of a way — and that Agnes
Stanfield should have married the young gentleman
who, without knowing it, was their brother! It was
enough to fill the village with natural consternation,
and supersede all other subjects in the ordinary talk.

All this, when he came to know of it — and he
could not but come to know of a story which was
floating about him on the very air — broke the heart
of Stanfield. He began to grow an old man — he,
who had been a model of vigour and strength up to
this last revelation. He went down to the house on

the Green in the evening, not caring to look at any
one or speak to any one. Disgrace, that dreadful
ghost, which is more terrible in his rank than in any
other, weighed upon him, and he could not stand up
against it. To be sure, nobody better than William
Stanfield could have explained to any other that a man
can be disgraced but by his own actions. But reason
is only good when people are in no need of it. He
could have borne up stoutly and cheerfully against any
sort of loss or suffering, but shame went to his heart
— though he had done nothing to bring shame upon
him, but rather was the object of everybody's pity.
Thus it was that discouragement, complete and overwhelming, fell on the house on the Green. The little
children were gay enough, but the father and daughter
would make great efforts to say a few words to each
other, and then fall silent and say nothing. There
was so little to say that it could be any comfort to
hear.

Jack Charlton, in the meantime, was rushing about
to all the corners of the island in Mrs. Trevelyan's
service. He had insisted, after all, upon going to
Thurso, though that seemed so little use; and had
heard there that the yacht had sailed for Norway, and
then that she had been reported off Cork, and then
that she had been signalled at the Channel Islands.
All this kept Agnes in a perpetual conflict of hope
and fear. And the last intelligence was that the yacht
was lying at Cowes with her passengers out of her,
and all trace of Walter was again lost. After that
Jack Charlton came back and came to see Agnes, and
sat by her, with very little to say. The only comfort
he could give was, that they could not keep Walter

long in hiding; that he would be sent to school some
time; and that he must turn up sooner or later, if
Agnes would but keep up her heart. She used to
smile when she heard this in a heart-breaking way, but
made no reply: it seemed the only consolation that
could be offered to her now.

And all this time Mrs. Stanfield's fever lasted, and
she lay and raved, and made Windholm acquainted
with all her wretched history, "like a fool as she was,"
Mr. Freke said, who did not believe very much in
delirium, but had a strong man's assured belief, that
the body never did anything without at least the tacit
permission of the mind. Her voice sometimes reached
Stanfield in the forge, and then the workmen used to
say he changed colour and faltered at his work; but
for all that, the blacksmith returned day by day to his
ordinary labour. His was not the kind of nature which
is made unfit for its work by even the heaviest cala-
mities of life. He said little on any subject, and nothing about that, but went about his daily occupations,
and daily passed through the village street, coming
and going, leaving to the woman who had shamed his
name and clouded over the end of his life, all the
tendance and care which his toil could procure for her.
If he ever spoke about his changed circumstances at
all, it was to say that his daughter had need of him
— and what he said was true; they had need of each
other at that moment, as never before in their lives,
dearly as they had loved each other, and they were of
all the more mutual comfort, because each had a special
wound, and it was not simply one grief between them.
Thus the same Providence which, in her heart, Agnes
feared and doubted so sorely, not knowing what God's

meaning might be, aided her in that moment of trial, and gave her the only support which was possible to her. She was not left alone to bear her suspense by herself.

Ten or twelve days of utter silence had interrupted the thread of Walter's history, as made out by Jack Charlton. Jack himself came as often as he could venture, always bringing with him a sickening expectation; but he had not been able to obtain the smallest clue. The child had not been taken to Trevelyan, that was certain; he had not been sent to the Hampshire cottage, which Jack knew to belong to Sir Roger, and, consequently, kept watch upon; and no information even as to his disembarkation had been procured at Cowes or Southampton. Mr. Charlton's idea was that he had been landed at some other part of the coast, but it was so hard to decide where; and, as it happened, Jack was as before, sitting by Mrs. Trevelyan, trying to console her with the old argument, that Sir Roger could not keep Walter shut up for ever, and that he must turn up, if she could but have patience, sooner or later, when the second communication from Walter arrived.

It was evening, and the blacksmith had returned from the forge, and sat in his easy chair in the Sunday suit which he always compelled himself to put on for his daughter's credit, with the newspaper in his hand. But Stanfield, who had been so strong and so upright, sat stooping forward like an old man, holding the paper before him without reading it, with that broken air which it is impossible to mistake, the look of a man exhausted and no more capable of hope. He was not taking any part in the conversation; indeed, it could scarcely be said that there was any conversation going on; Agnes was sitting near the window doing some work, which was more in a kind of deference to the presence of the stranger than any inclination on her part towards the tranquil woman's work for which her heart was now too full. Now and then Mr. Charlton said something to which she responded faintly; and the voices of the two little girls, and the sound of their play, was all that was audible in the intervals. It was just then that Walter's second letter was brought to Mrs. Trevelyan. This time it was a large letter, directed in an uneven and imperfect writing, and sealed with a great blotch of red wax, marked with a thimble. She dropped the cover out of her hands in her eagerness when she had torn it open and saw what it was. Her excitement was not so great, and yet it was greater than the first time. She no longer expected to find him at once, and come to an end of her anxiety; and yet her thirst for news of him — any news, was more intense almost than it had ever been before. She left even her father in suspense while she herself read the letter. It was impossible at the first moment, when her heart was beating so loud in her throat that she could hardly breathe, to share the first news with any one, or to read it aloud: —

"DEAR MAMMA, — I have tried ever so often to write to you, but they would not let me; I did not like to do it *secret*, because they had let me once. Oh mamma, dear, I do so want to see you, and grandpapa, and everybody! I am very unhappy here. I am quite well, but I am very unhappy. They shut me up, and then I have to go and play in the garden, and there is nobody to play with. Oh, mamma, if you would only come! It's in a village, but I don't know the name. I know it's High Street, and I think it is Hampstead, or Highgate, or Finchley, for I once got a peep of an omnibus with all three names. Why do they shut me up like this? I have seen my Aunt Beatrice twice. Oh, mamma, don't you think you could find me out? I am going to try to get out to-night when Bevis is away. If I can get out, I mean to run away and come home, and it will be no good posting this letter; but I'll post it all the same, if I can get out; it's through a window, and I think there is one of the maids that perhaps will help me. Dear mamma, good-bye! and perhaps I shall be able to get out; and if not, oh will you came and look for me? for it's just like being in prison, and I would rather die.

"Your affectionate Son,
"WALTER TREVELYAN."

When she had read this over, Agnes began, scarcely knowing what she did, to read it aloud, and then she gave it to her father, who came forward to the light to receive it, and go over it again; for such communications do not enter into the mind at one hearing.

"Have you seen this?" said Jack Charlton. He took her hand as he held up the paper before her. It was a thing which he had never ventured to do before; and besides, there was meaning in his looks. Agnes was still trembling with the shock, and with the hope. Perhaps he was on his way home even now; perhaps, for anything she could tell, he might be coming up the village street — the weary, blessed little traveller! She was terribly startled in the midst of her excitement, when Jack Charlton took her hand in this extraordinary way. He took it as a surgeon might have taken it, who wanted to see how much torture she was capable of bearing, and held up before her the paper, upon which something was scrawled in the same uneven and wretched writing in which the letter was directed. It was some time before Agnes, preoccupied as she was, could make out what the sprawling characters meant, or if they meant anything. As she looked at them, however, the devious lines grew into meaning; and this is what was written: —

"E's been and ad a fall out o' winder — if is Mamma can come its best not to lose no time."

Such was the brief and awful comment, which shone before Agnes like the writing on the wall before the Eastern king. As she deciphered it she gave a sudden cry, and looked Jack in the face, who still held her hand. Jack Charlton thought afterwards that there was in that cry a sound as if some chord had broken in her heart. That was how he explained it, not being eloquent; and, for his part, he held her hand fast, and responded to her look with all the pity and sympathy of which he was capable. The grasp of his hand, the look of his eyes, had nothing in them of selfish sentiment; they said only, "I am ready to go with you and stand by you to the end of the world." Agnes recovered her composure — or if not her composure, something, at least, which stood in its place — before her father, whose faculties were not so vivid as of old, and who was still absorbed in Walter's letter, had time to perceive that anything new had happened.

Then she loosened her hand from Jack Charlton's grasp, and got up, and turned to go away.

"Tell my father," she said; "I will go and put on my bonnet — it is time for the train."

As for Stanfield, when he saw that fatal postscript, it overpowered him so entirely that he had to sit down to keep himself from falling. His own trials had weakened him mind and body. He was an old man, and his strong vitality seemed to have been weakened at the fountain-head; a mist came over his eyes, and a faintness over his heart. "I am no good to go with her; God help my darling!" he said, with an exceeding bitter cry — a cry which forced the tears into Jack Charlton's eyes. Almost more than the despair of the mother, who was able to do everything that God might require, to the last throb of her heart, for her boy, was the despair of the old man, who, for the first time, found himself unfit for the emergency; unable to guide, and help, and sustain his child; altogether incapable of bearing her burden for her. He sat leaning his head upon his two hands before the sympathetic spectator, who, however, was ready to swear a son's service to him, and a brother's help to Agnes — silent in the bitterness of his heart. All this time the two little children were playing at the other end of the room. There was nothing extraordinary to them in the agitation about the letter, or in the grandfather's hopeless attitude, with his face bent down upon his hands; and their merry little voices ran on all the same, adding the last tragic touch of comparison to the scene. When Agnes came downstairs, ready to go out, and with a little travelling-

20*

bag in her hand, Stanfield roused himself from his torpor of incapacity and despair.

"My darling, keep up your heart," he said; "Mr. Charlton will do you more good than me. I've turned an old man in a day. But I'll come after you — I'll come after you. And if you don't find the place?" he said, turning with an anxious look to Jack.

"My sister is in town. I will take Mrs. Trevelyan there," said Jack; and as he spoke he could not restrain a sudden flush, which was partly exquisite pleasure, and partly intense pain. It was the first time he had thought of himself since he perceived the writing on the envelope; and now to feel himself the only man who could stand by Agnes in her trouble, instinctively accepted and trusted by her, and yet counting for nothing, and having no place whatever in her mind, which was filled with Walter — this mingling of sensations made itself visible in a sudden hot flush of colour; but nobody paid Jack so much attention as to remark even this; their thoughts were fixed so upon one point, that they were incapable of observing anything beside.

Agnes smiled faintly as she met her father's eye. "I shall find him," she said, though she had scarcely breath enough to make herself audible, calm as her appearance was. And then she kissed her babies and her father hurriedly, and hastened away, not to waste her strength. The evening, when they went out into it, out of the excitement and the gloom that seemed to have collected in the atmosphere indoors, was so tranquil and so sweet, that it seemed an aggravation of their trouble. And as for the Windholm folks, when they saw Mrs. Trevelyan pass, leaning on Mr.

Charlton's arm, they smiled to each other, and were
glad like good neighbours — having been softened
much in their judgment by a consciousness of "all
she had gone through" — to see that she had been
persuaded to take the air a little. "It would do her
good, poor thing!" they said, and the good people
smiled, but with a smile that was full of charity —
for, after all, as Mr. Freke said, Providence seemed to
owe her a little consolation. Such was the opinion
entertained by the village of that unusual spectacle.
It was accepted as a tacit ratification of the rumour,
and acknowledgment of Agnes's plans. And yet more
than one person remarked that it was droll they never
spoke to each other, and that Mrs. Trevelyan kept her
veil down so obstinately; though, indeed, for that
matter, the chances were that she was a little shy, or
even ashamed of herself. "For when things is at their
best, a second marriage ain't never like a first," said
one of the wise women of Windholm; which, no doubt,
was the explanation of the whole matter. And nobody
imagined that Agnes leaned upon Mr. Charlton's arm
almost without knowing whose arm it was, because her
limbs were scarcely able to support her — and did
not speak because her heart was fluttering to her very
lips, and she could not. She passed rapidly through
the village, as in a trance, seeing nothing, and was
seated in the railway carriage before it occurred to her
even to think where she was going. Then she asked
with parched lips, "What shall we do to find out?"

Jack Charlton understood what she meant, because
in his intense sympathy he had been following even
her thoughts, though she did not confide them to him
— and now he took the envelope of Walter's letter

out of his pocket. "I suppose it has been the maid whom he hoped would assist him," said Jack. "She must have got a head, or perhaps a heart, which serves the same purpose sometimes. She has put the address like a rational creature. We have nothing to do but go there."

"God bless her!" was all that Agnes could say. It did not occur to her, as it did for a moment to Jack, that the address might possibly be intended not to guide, but to mislead. She accepted it with a simplicity which gave him faith in it, and then she relapsed into silence. It was a kind of consolation to her to see the long flats of the level landscape flying past the window of the carriage, and to feel the wind of the rapid movement in her face; but her voice was stifled in her throat, and her heart in her breast, before they had made all the necessary changes, and began to ascend the hill at Hampstead. It was there that Walter had been taken, and it was necessary to slacken the pace of the horses going up the hill, and the slow progress made Agnes desperate. All this time Jack Charlton sat by her side, careful of her as a brother, and without doing or saying anything, loyal gentleman as he was, to call himself to her attention. There are people who exchange love-looks, and are comforted in their deepest trouble — but Mrs. Trevelyan was not of that fashion of women; neither was Jack Charlton a man to take advantage of his position by so much as a glance. He sat by her, close to her, her sole guardian and help, and saw that in her heart there was not a thought of him — and perhaps he felt it hard; but a woman who is a mother is different from other women; and it was thus that Agnes pursued her anxious way through the summer darkness, through the soft, odorous, dreamy gloom, now verging on midnight, to find her boy.

CHAPTER XXVII.

How it Ended.

IT was a house enclosed in a garden surrounded with walls clothed and rustling with ivy and jessamine. Some of those white flowers dropped upon Agnes's head, among the heavy folds of her veil, as she passed underneath the long sweeping branches, and lay there enclosed till the next time she put it on, which was not until sad and sore events had made the hours look like ages. The door was opened by a maid, not very clean nor particularly prepossessing, who, nevertheless, went forward eagerly at the sight of Agnes. The first words this woman said went to Mrs. Trevelyan's heart like a sentence of death. She said, "Is it you, ma'am, as is his mamma?" Agnes was not able to answer except by a hurried nod of her head. She went in, into the little square hall which looked so peaceful and pleasant; the light of the bright little lamp dazzled her eyes coming out of the darkness, and the sudden confirmation of her fears made her sick and giddy. She stumbled and tottered for the moment, so that Jack Charlton hastened forward to support her, and the maid came to her side. But Agnes was not the kind of woman that can faint on an emergency — consciousness never forsook her in these great crises of her life. The momentary blindness, and darkness, and tottering, lasted only while one could draw breath. Then, as

she stopped to recover herself, she turned to the woman
who had admitted her. "Was it you?" Mrs. Trevelyan
asked; and unconnected as the question was, it needed
no explanation to the kind soul who was to be sure a
little untidy, and did not know, as her fellow-servant
said, how to keep herself to herself.

"I hope as I didn't do no harm," she said. "There
wasn't none intended. He was took bad and he cried
for his mamma. What could I do? And I'm as thankful as I can be that you're in time."

When Mrs. Trevelyan heard this she started again
as if something had stung her. In time! It seemed
to imply everything that was most hard to think of.
She turned her face towards the stair without very
clearly seeing it, and went straight forward, stumbling
against a bench that was in her way, as in her present
state of mind she would have stumbled against anything animate or inanimate that stood between her and
her child. And what made it even more and more
terrible was that her companion made no sort of effort
to restrain her. The maid evidently felt Walter's circumstances to be too urgent for any ceremony. She
followed Agnes up the stairs with a promptitude that
said more than a long explanation. As for Jack
Charlton, after he had stood looking after them for a
minute or two, he set straight again the bench which
Agnes had stumbled against, and sat down on it with
a kind of disconsolate patience. If there are times in
life when a strong man feels the good of his strength,
there are also moments when its utter uselessness and
impotence come very clearly before him. He had been
of a great deal of service to Mrs. Trevelyan, and he
had in his heart a longing to do everything for her —

to save her from every pain; and yet at this moment
all that he could do was to sit down forlorn outside
and wait for her until she had done the work, and,
perhaps, suffered the agony with which he could not
interfere. This sense was bitter to his heart, for Agnes
had grown dearer and dearer to him, though he scarcely
knew how. He sat down against the wall in the little
vacant hall to waylay the maid if she should appear
again, and obtain some information if that was possible;
and to wait for Mrs. Trevelyan, if, perhaps, she should
want anything — support and succour, perhaps — or
even if it should only be a medicine to fetch, or some
one to go for the doctor. Jack was so honest and
thorough in his sentiments that he sat down quite
simply with his back against the wall, waiting very
sad and very anxious to know if there was anything
he could do.

And Agnes, in the blindness and dumbness of her
great suffering, went upstairs. She lingered for a
moment at the door of the room, struck at the very
height of her eagerness with that reluctance to look her
sorrow in the face, which sometimes strikes by moments
a much-suffering soul. She had not asked any questions
about Walter, what had happened to him, or how he
was. He might have only had a severe accident for
anything she could tell, or he might be dying. She
stopped for that second at the door, and her mind
naturally rushed forward to the worst, and then her
heart roused up and contradicted her mind. It seemed
to her as if it were not possible — as if God could not
have the heart to do it; and then, it occurred to her
that she was going into a sick room, where there ought
to be no unnecessary bustle or noise. She put off her

bonnet and cloak where she was standing and laid them
softly down in a corner; and all these accompanying
thoughts moved so swiftly, that the maid, who was
with her, thought she had only paused to take off her
cloak, and wondered at her self-possession. At this
moment Agnes heard a voice from the room in which
all her anxieties seemed centered. It said, "What do
I want? — I want mamma, Aunt Beatrice. You are
kind enough — oh, yes, I know you are kind; but I
want mamma — mamma! and now I can't go to her,
though she will be looking for me!" and then there
came a sound of tears.

It was at that moment that Beatrice Trevelyan
gave a strange cry and stood aghast to see a black
figure, with uncovered head and the air of a woman in
her own house, go up to the bedside. Miss Trevelyan
thought she was looking at a spirit, so extraordinary
was the apparition. She caught hold of the bedpost to
support herself, and looked on with a consternation
that drove all the blood back upon her heart. If she
could but have seen the cloak and the bonnet which
lay outside on the landing, they would have reassured
her a little. It was the sight of Agnes in her indoor
dress, as if she belonged to the house, which struck
Beatrice so strangely. Was it possible that anxiety and
grief had killed the mother, and that it was her spirit
which was coming to nurse her boy? While Miss Trevelyan stood trembling, Agnes went up to her child's
bedside. She said, "My darling, I have come to *you!*"
and bent down over him and took his two hands in
hers, and put her face down upon his. Though it
seemed to herself as if her heart was beating audibly
within her, she held Walter's hands fast to tranquillize

him, and smiled as 'if she had but parted from him yesterday. "Hush, hush!" she said; "be good and keep quiet — I am here, my own boy!" For her part, she was not conscious of Beatrice. Nothing and nobody in the world could have divided her attention with that little face on the pillow. She bent over him like a bird over her nest, with a satisfaction and an anguish inconceivable. What was it that was written in Walter's face, in the widened circles round his eyes, and the wonderful look of gravity and age that had come to him? — Something which tore with sharp violence her very heart asunder, and yet was of all sights the dearest to her in the world. Her babies at home, all safe and peaceful, passed out of Mrs. Trevelyan's mind — her father, and all the lighter ties that bound her to her life. She saw or thought of nothing in the world but her boy, her firstborn — the child who had been hers for so many long sweet years, and yet was God's first, and might soon be hers no more. She had no eyes, no ears, no capacity for anything but that he was here, and she had him now, and perhaps, God knew, might soon be without him. The bitterness was the bitterness of death, and yet the sweetness was more than that of Paradise. She took him out of the strange hands that had misused him so cruelly, without even being aware of any natural rage at such an injury; and saw no more and thought no more of her enemy, who was trembling and holding by the bed, than if she had been a woman cut out of wood or stone.

As for Walter, the child's joy was wonderful to see. His delight fought against the solemn look in his face, and for a moment got the better of it, and gleamed like wintry sunshine from the edges of that overwhelm-

ing shadow. "Is it you — is it really you?" he cried.
"I have dreamt it so often, and always woke up; oh,
mamma, I think I can feel you; I don't think I am
dreaming — is it you?"

"My darling, you must keep still," Agnes said;
and then Walter accepted the whole matter as if it
had been the most natural thing in the world. He had
no longer any strong sentiment to war against his
weakness; he yielded himself up with a child's unquestioning confidence. One thing was sure, that since
his mother was there all was well, and there was no
longer anything to desire. He held her hand against
his cheek and caressed it, and clasped his arms round
it. From that moment he was once more wrapped
round and round in natural safety and tranquillity,
such as make the profoundest happiness of a child.

"Take me home, mamma, to our own home," he
said, looking up at her with the eyes that had no doubt
in them; and Agnes said, "Yes, my darling." She
said yes, and she knew when she said it that she
should never take him home. Ah, my God! was it as
hard to be crucified? All the world receded from the
mother and the child, and left them there alone. If
matters had been less serious, Agnes would have been
eager to ask how it was, and if everything had been
done that could be done; but in the air of the sick
room, and in the solemn little face of the dying child,
there was something which hushed inquiry. When
there is no hope there is no ground for asking questions.
Yet the spectator who was looking on at this speechless junction of the living and the dying, could not,
when the first fright was over, keep silent. She drew
close to Agnes, and at length plucked at her sleeve,

seeing there was no other way of gaining her attention.
When Mrs. Trevelyan looked up she saw a face, which
she could scarcely recognise, hovering over her like an
apparition from the clouds. It was the face of Beatrice, so pallid and stricken with terror, so contracted
with care and self-reproach, so shaken out of its pride
and high estate, that for the first moment Agnes did
not recognise whose face it was.

"It was not my fault," Beatrice said in a kind of
hoarse whisper; even at that moment her heart sunk
within her with envy. Agnes was suffering as Miss ·
Trevelyan had never suffered in her life. The cross
had just been laid upon her with a heavier and more
crushing weight than Beatrice knew anything of; and
yet the woman whom God had not even taken the
pains to bestow suffering upon, looked at the other
whose heart was breaking under it, with an envy
beyond expression. She envied even the abstraction,
the momentary wonder at her apology which woke in
Agnes's eyes. *She* had never been so deeply struck
from Heaven as to be deadened to the lesser evils of
human enmity and opposition. She envied Agnes her
heart which was breaking, her anguish which was bit-
terer than death; for never, never in her paltry life,
had such shadows, which were reserved by God for his
chosen, given grandeur and dignity to *her*.

"Your fault?" said Agnes, looking in her face with
a slow apprehension of her words. "Oh no! It is
nobody's fault — except God." She did not know
what she was saying. She was angry with her Father,
poor soul; and she knew Him so well that she dared
say it. He could have saved her child from the death
that was coming — if He would; and He had not

willed it. It was His fault, and the creature He had
made upbraided Him — He who had taken to Himself
the supreme luxury of dying for the world He loved;
and yet He would not let her die for the son of her
heart. Ah me! the pulses were going so steadily in
her veins while they were failing, failing in her child's,
for whom she would have counted it joy to drain them
drop by drop. She put away with her hand the other
woman, the poor human thing that in her feeble way
was to blame. She had no heart to think of secondary
means at such a moment. She had to do with God
only, who has the issues of life and death in His hand.

As for Beatrice, though this house had been chosen
as a place in which to hide Sir Roger's heir from his
mother — though he had been brought here to satisfy
her old envy, her old rage against the woman of whom
Providence had made a favourite and treated so much
better than herself — she withdrew without a word,
and left Walter's mother in possession of the place.
Nobody said or thought that it was not Mrs. Trevelyan's own house into which she had entered. The
doctor came and he asked no questions, nor even
looked as if he thought it strange. Beatrice went
down below and lived there, unsleeping and uneating,
like Agnes herself, but possessed by a kind of despair,
and guilty horror, and miserable impotence, instead of
the dreadful anguish, and composure, and familiar
words and smiles that were above. But this change,
though it made Walter happy, did nothing for the
little bruised body which even happiness and safety
could not cure. He had fallen out of the window in
his attempt to escape; and his injuries were such, that
from the first there had been nothing to hope. He

might linger a few days, more or less, but he could not live.

All this Agnes heard, and yet had to bear it, and to know that nothing in this life was possible, except to comfort and solace him a little. Her bonnet and shawl lay outside on the landing where she had placed them, nobody having had the heart to carry them away; and the white stars from the jessamine lay all covered up in the thick folds of her crape veil. Stanfield followed her the same evening, and came into the room in the middle of the night with such a heartbroken face that the cheerful mother sent him away. "We are telling stories to make us sleepy," she said, with that smile which was all the sunshine remaining in the world for Walter; and took her place again by the bedside, and took up once more the thread of the never-ending, oft-beginning story, which beguiled the pain and tedium of the death-bed. When Stanfield went downstairs, he found Jack Charlton still sitting, forlorn, in the hall. He had not been wanted for anything, and yet he had not the heart to go away, or even to change his position. While Agnes sat telling stories by Walter's death-bed, the two men kept together downstairs, with blank, miserable faces, listening to every sound. There were many smiles in the sick room, and even little thrills of feeble laughter; but in the other parts of the house nobody could smile. It had all come so quickly, so suddenly, to all except the two chief actors in the scene. As for Walter, it seemed to him as if he had always been ill and in bed, and to his mother as if she had known this fate for years, and had never done anything but nurse him and watch him; but, on the other hand, Beatrice Trevelyan was saying to herself — Oh, if she had but yielded yester-day to the suggestion made by her own comfort, and sent back the living, longing child to the mother, from whom all her skill could not detach him! and Jack Charlton thought if he had but been a little more anxious in his search; and even the kind, untidy house-maid — if she had but divined sooner what was in the little prisoner's heart! To think that he had been well and strong only twenty-four hours ago! — this filled everybody with an additional despair down below; but in the sick room they were beyond any such thought.

Great anguish of body or mind has the effect of superseding time; it seemed to Mrs. Trevelyan as if she had been for years telling stories, smiling and caressing her dying child, and in her heart saying to God that it was He who had done it. No doubt it was He who had done it — the Father, who hateth nothing that he hath made; the Son, who alone in all the world could taste the supreme blessedness of dying for those He loved. Ah, me! they know what is best up in those tender, inexorable heavens! But do not you think it was hard upon her, who could see no farther, that the poor soul could only smile and kiss him, and tell him her woeful, cheerful story, and could not die for her first-born child?

This went on for two of those long recurrences of light and darkness, which people who have nothing particular on their mind call day and night; two days — but there was not between the mother and the child any of those conversations about death and heaven which sometimes occur in similar circumstances, and which are so heartbreaking and so sweet. Walter knew he was ill, but he did not know nor think anything about death, and it did not occur to Agnes to bring in that new thought, to thrill with wonder and apprehension the little mind which could not understand it. They said their prayers together, and by times, when he was able, Walter would tell his mother about what had happened in his absence, and how he had longed for her; and then they would return to the story-telling —

But I who write cannot give you any account of these days, oh my friends, because I know too well how such days pass. The world went and came all round and about this dim chamber, and the doctor entered from time to time, and so did Stanfield, who had a right, and even Beatrice, and the kind maid; and the summer sun shone all round, and tried hard to get in at the windows, to make his specious pretence that life is sweet; and, at the same time, the moments, which no one could arrest, swept on, and the hours ended one by one, and the will of God worked itself out. No doubt it was the will of God. It was He who was doing it, and not men and enemies, such as worked out David's afflictions in the Psalms; so that even the Psalms were not the comfort to Agnes that they are to many a mourner. It was God only, who was against her; and it seemed as if it would have been so small a thing for Him to have healed instead of killing. As for little Walter, he was troubled with no such questions. He grew confused by times in his mind, and sometimes did not know his mother, but was always capable of being roused up to recognise her, and find all the clouds clear away in the sense of her presence. And then it was all over in two days, and the little life became perfect, "rounded with a

sleep." I tell you again, my friends, I who write
Agnes Trevelyan's story, that I cannot tell you, step
by step, how this came about. Somebody at last took
the poor woman out of the room where Walter was no
longer — led her away awful in the force of her life
and self-control, unable to faint, or fall ill, or lose
anyhow for a moment the sense of what had befallen
her. Thus it all ended, God knows why. He who
had taken the trouble, by the slow processes of nature,
to bring the child into the world, and keep him there
so many sweet years; to take care of him in his childish
illnesses, and temper the wind to him, and keep the
little heart beating in his breast; and, more than that,
to put in him all manner of budding thoughts, and
comprehensions, and dear suggestions of what was to
come — of what was never to come. If anybody on
earth could tell why or what it meant, it might be a
little consolation; but then, perhaps, even that consolation would have been but of little use to Agnes
Trevelyan, as she knelt down, crushed down under
the weight of the cross which her Father had lain on
her, and which she did not know how to bear.

And thus it had all come to an end — all their
anxiety, and their search, and everything that had
been most interesting for months past in the lives of
the three people who mourned most for Walter in that
Hampstead cottage. To think it should have taken so
large a place in their minds, and occupied them with
so many labours, and yet end in a moment, like the
snapping of a thread! All the hopes that had been
centered in the boy, and all the schemes against him,
and all the anxieties — where he was, and who had
charge of him; and all the dear daily cares, ever re-

curring sweetly with every new vicissitude, which had once done so much to charm his mother's heart back again to life — oll over in one brief breathless moment! This, perhaps, was what Jack Charlton was thinking, and even to some extent Beatrice Trevelyan; and, indeed, Stanfield too a little, who had still *his* child, though *hers* was gone. But as for Agnes, I cannot tell you what she was thinking; there are so many, oh! so many, who *know;* and it would be hopeless to tell you who are outside, good, kind people as you are; you too will understand, if ever it pleases God to cut you in portions, and carry you away piecemeal, through those darkling passages which are the way to His heaven. It was a strange household that evening; and it was a lovely evening, so fresh, and tender, and sweet, breathing of nothing but peace and blessedness. Jack Charlton went and came, going about the dreadful business, which, though he could not do anything else for Agnes, he could spare her; and Stanfield went up and down stairs, into the room where she was, and into another room still more sacred, and back again to the hall, where Jack Charlton, who had grown a comfort to him in his weakness, might be expected; and in another room Beatrice Trevelyan, for the first time in her life, down upon her knees, in the abasement of a consciousness which felt like crime, was crying to God that she never would forgive herself, and crying wildly for His forgiveness in the same breath. And there enthroned in the centre of the house, as in all their hearts, was lying, all shrouded and silent, that which had been Walter Trevelyan; and all the young flowers were growing, and the soft dews falling, and the sound of

21 *

children's voices in the golden sunset air, though this
child neither heard nor saw. That was how it ended
abruptly, like a thread suddenly snapped upon the
wheel, when nobody was thinking; and no one yet
could understand the dread certainty, the blank and
final repose, which had succeeded to so much anxiety
and suspense. He was dead, and hope was dead, and
with hope fear; and yet, at the same time, the eager
throbs of the old anguish had not learned to cease con-
tending with the awful stillness of the new. They still
started at the sounds outside, as if, perhaps, it was a
dream they had been dreaming, and *he*, who now
needed no name, might still come in, all welcome and
glad, at the blessed door.

CHAPTER XXVIII.

After the End.

It has been said, in the earlier part of this history, that Agnes Trevelyan had in no way an exceptionally hard fate. The griefs of her early days were, not that her husband was cruel to her, or wittingly unkind, or that there was any want of love between them: it was only the common lot, with its drawbacks and compensations, that had fallen upon a creature only half-awakened out of the ideal, and seeking the absolute in all things, as is the manner of youth. And now, in the moment of her deepest distress, Agnes was not left utterly desolate, as some women are. She had her father by her, who loved her above everything in the world; and she had Charlton, who loved her too, and would fain have taken his place beside her, and supported her in all her afflictions. Neither of the two could enter with her into the sacred innermost chamber of sorrow. But that was no lack of love, no faintness of sympathy, but only the human disability which sentences every human creature in the supreme moments of existence to be alone. She thought the father of her child, had he been there, could have gone with her and shared all her heart; but most likely, had Roger been alive, his wife would not have been able to entertain that dear delusion. She was alone, because to be alone was inevitable to humanity, not because she was abandoned by dear love and unspeakable sympathy. She recognised this dimly in her own mind, though she got little consolation from it; for it seemed to urge upon her more and more the sense that man would have spared her in her widow-hood and weakness, but that God had not spared her; and it was so hard to see why. It was when she was trusting in Him, clinging to Him, with prayer on her lips and faith in her heart, that the Father had turned upon her and struck her all unawares. It was He who had taken the part of the cruel rich man, and taken the one lamb out of the poor man's fold; and her heart bled and sobbed out of all its wounds with the wonder of a baffled trust and the sore humiliation of disap-pointed love. She was stunned and silenced in her terrible surprise, and could not understand it, nor find any clue to the dark and dread mystery. And then God did not give her any of those softenings which He bestows upon weaker people. The spectators said to each other that it was well her health did not suffer; but, in reality, that was one of the hard circumstances of her lot. She could not get to be unconscious; none of those merciful films of bodily suffering which sometimes dim the strained sight for a moment, came over her eyes. She was unaware, indeed, of having any body, and lived without its aid, as she could have imagined, feeling every pang of the soul to the uttermost, and drinking to the last dregs the cup that had been given her to drink.

When everything was over in the melancholy house, Beatrice, who had stayed all this time in the cottage without very well knowing why, asked to see Mrs. Tre-velyan. The house had grown to be Mrs. Trevelyan's house, unconsciously to everybody; and no one had made any account of Beatrice, who kept in her own room, and felt the shame and misery of her position with a force which did not occur to any one else; for naturally she was more interested in herself and what she had done than any one else was. And then something had happened to Miss Trevelyan besides the death which had occurred in the family. The morning that Walter was laid in his grave, while she in her heart was feeling herself his murderer, a letter was brought to her which made a great change in her life. It made an end of the petty schemes for which she despised herself, without being able to abandon them, and it opened the only life which she thought worth living — the long-delayed and hoped-for existence — at last before her.

Beatrice stood aghast when she had read the letter, wondering at first, with pallid cheeks and heart that had stopped beating, whether there might not be some punishment deeper than anything she had dreamed of hid beneath this apparent happiness. She could not believe it was actually true that at last good fortune and comfort, and something worth living for, should come to her for the first time, just as the people round her were preparing to carry away the little victim of her selfish pride to his grave. After all her abasement and suffering, it seemed to her more like an exquisite revenge which somebody was taking upon her than a real and substantial good fortune. It was the man whom Beatrice within herself called her first love — though, to tell the truth, she never had been sufficiently interested in him to have given up anything for his sake— he to whom she had been re-introduced but lately, and who, if he had been like her, would have forgotten her in her absence — it was he who wrote offering to her his good heart, and honest hand, and comfortable for-

tune. He had loved her all along (or at least he said
so), as she sometimes tried to flatter herself she had
loved him; and he accepted tenderly the explanation
of her disappearance which had been current among
her friends — to wit, that Miss Trevelyan was nursing
her little nephew in an illness. "It was a dreadful
mésalliance, you know," Beatrice's friends said, "and
these sort of mothers are no good to their children."
And so it happened that Miss Trevelyan's suitor had
the most earnest and admiring belief that she had gone
to do a mother's duty to the little invalid whose own
mother was unworthy of that sacred office.

It would be saying little to say that Beatrice
trembled when she received this letter. A young girl
receiving her lover's declaration after misunderstanding,
and doubt, and delay, could not have been half so much
excited as was Miss Trevelyan. She grew pale, all the
blood went back out of her veins upon her heart, and
her whole frame shook with the violence of the shock.
If it could be believed in, it was a higher conclusion
than she had for years hoped to reach to — for the
man who thus offered to her a new life was one who
could put her in harmony with goodness, and throw a
certain tender light even over the petty struggles of her
past existence. If it could be believed in! But then
that new voice — that voice of true affection which
Miss Trevelyan was so little used to — awoke in her
a certain impulse of truthfulness which had never been
utterly dead in her mind, and yet was new to her under
the new form it took. A certain lingering fundamental
sincerity had come many a time in the way of Beatrice's
plans, hindering her from taking the last step of social
dissimulation, preventing her even occasionally from

accepting a man whom she had pursued, but whom
she could not finally make up her mind to marry, and
betraying her at unsuitable moments into a revelation
of her natural sentiments, which she herself regarded
with disgust after it was over, but could not prevent.
This, however, was different from the new impulse
which seized upon Beatrice. First of all, startled nature, seeing the prize within its grasp, thought in a
sudden horror how to conceal the truth and keep the
joy; and then truth rose up in her mind with a kind
of tragic force. The sweetness of knowing herself
loved — which was something almost inconceivable —
of imagining, too, that she had been loved all through
those lingering years — of feeling in her dry and
withered heart an impulse of gratitude, in which the
pleasant delusions of her youth found resurrection
and began to look true, — all this seemed to make it
impossible to Beatrice to leave a falsehood between herself and the man who was going to do so much for her.
If it had been a mere matter of convenience, a marriage proposed because it suited him to marry and her
to be married, any such refinement would have been
unnecessary; but Truth, though buried deep down, was
still at the bottom of the well of Miss Trevelyan's
mind; and when there came such an unhoped-for apparition as the face of Love gleaming in the unex-
pectant water, the other spirit of light, surprised, sprang
up to meet him and would not be kept down. This
was why Beatrice asked, with a humility quite unusual
to her,. to see her sister-in-law. They had not again
met since the first moment when Beatrice had said it
was not her fault, and Agnes, in her first despair, had
answered, "No."

It was now the evening of the funeral-day, and the next morning the poor mother was going home, and there was no time to lose. Miss Trevelyan questioned the maid with a closeness which was altogether unlike her usual manner with her servants. She asked how Mrs. Trevelyan was looking; whether she was able to be up, whether she was ill; and, to tell the truth, notwithstanding her new-born pity, a certain contempt for her because she was not ill, came into Beatrice's mind. She herself felt ill, or supposed she felt ill, in the excitement of the moment; and to hear that Agnes was neither in bed, nor having the doctor to see her, nor taking anything, brought her back to a little of that involuntary contempt for "that sort of person" which she had entertained so long. "These kind of people have so little feeling," she said to herself. The thought was consolatory in its way; and it was with something of this sentiment, mingling with extreme personal excitement, that she proceeded to the interview she had sought.

Agnes was in the room which she had occupied since her watch was over. She had been putting away all the little sacred things which had belonged to Walter, which were few, for it was almost a relief to Mrs. Trevelyan to find that the dresses he had been wearing were unknown to her, and unassociated with him in her mind. She was not lying down, as Beatrice would have thought right under the circumstances, but moving about with those languid, listless movements which betray the utter prostration of the heart; trying in a forlorn way to defend herself against the recollections that consumed her. She gave Beatrice a chair with the same hopeless, listless look, and herself sat

down near her, like a creature in a dream. Even in
the depths of her affliction Agnes could not go against
the tolerant nature and sweet courtesy of the heart
which she had derived from her father. She felt that
Miss Trevelyan must have some explanation to make,
something to say; and she could not refuse her the opportunity. As for the pain to herself, what did it
matter, a little more or a little less? — for, to tell the
truth, there were no such trifling words as *less* or *more*
in the vast and silent anguish which filled Agnes's
heart. Her cup was brimming over already, and another or another bitter drop could make no difference.
She sat down feeling a momentary relief in any change
of position, sinking on her seat in her languor and exhaustion; and turned the eyes that were worn with
watching and weeping, to her sister-in-law's face. But
it was for Miss Trevelyan, who had something to say,
to begin. As for Agnes, she had nothing to say to
any one in the world.

Beatrice did not find it much more easy, for her
part. The only way for a woman to speak to another
woman in such circumstances is when supporting her or
clinging to her, holding the poor hand that trembles,
or offering a charitable bosom for the support of the
fainting head. But there was no such *rapprochement*
between the two as to make that possible; and Miss
Trevelyan found it less easy, when the moment arrived,
to throw herself at the poor mother's feet than she had
imagined. She sat instead and looked at Agnes, whose
eyes seemed to have turned inwards, and whose whole
aspect betrayed a heart absorbed; and did not know
what to say to her. When she did speak she said, as

was natural, something which she did not mean, and
which came to her lips mechanically.

"Don't you think you ought to lie down? I am
sure your head aches," Beatrice said; and then the
colour came to her face when she saw something like
a faint movement of wonder in Agnes's eyes.

"No, thank you," said Mrs. Trevelyan, "my head
does not ache;" and then Agnes took pity on her old
enemy. "It is kind to come to me," she said, faintly.
"I know you are sorry;" and this was all her strength
would let her say.

"Oh, sorry is a poor word," cried Beatrice. "You
ought to hate me — it is only just that you should hate
me. I don't know what to say to you. I should like
to go down on my knees, as I have done to God —"

"No, no," said Agnes. She made a little movement with her hand, as if of fear. "If it could do
any good," she said, with a voice that was scarcely
audible. She was not upbraiding Beatrice. The
question was one that Beatrice had so little to do with;
it was between herself and God.

And then Miss Trevelyan paused, humbled more
than ever; for she had naturally expected either in hate
or in forgiveness to count for something, when she of
herself sought her brother's widow; and the fact was,
that Agnes was rapt out of her reach, and was scarcely
aware either of the part she had had in bringing about
this overwhelming misfortune, or in her repentance now
that all was over. Mrs. Trevelyan repeated softly, "I
know you are sorry." It seemed to Beatrice as if the
mother would not permit her to be anything more than

sorry, and was jealous of her child's love even when he was in his grave; but, in reality, Agnes used the word because it was the first one that came. If she could have had the heart to think of anything but her grief, she would herself have been sorry for the woman who had harmed her so profoundly, and who could do nothing to mend it. But it was not for a woman who had occupied herself only with the selfish emotions of life to understand what was in Agnes Trevelyan's eyes.

And then there was a pause, and the two sat facing each other, Agnes only half conscious and caring for nothing, but Beatrice wildly conscious, and feeling as if all the future hung upon a thread which the least accident might snap asunder. It made her shudder to bring the hopes that were beating so strong in her into the stillness that surrounded Agnes, and in which everything seemed dead; and yet she felt it necessary, even for the sake of those hopes, to get her sister-in-law's forgiveness. It did not occur to her to think that her presence and her voice, and the sight of her, were rousing Mrs. Trevelyan from the passive and exhausted condition in which she was. Beatrice thought first of herself, as was natural; a little pain, more or less, what could it matter? but to establish her own good fortune on safe grounds, and balk all possibility of further disturbance, was of unquestionable importance; so that she made an effort upon herself.

"Mrs. Trevelyan," she said, "if you and I had been friends, I could have told you all my feelings and thoughts, and how I was to blame; but you hate me, and you have reason to hate me; I am humbled to the very dust," cried Beatrice, with her better nature again breaking through; "it is my fault, and I did not

mean it; I would give my life — I would have given
my life —"

"Ah," said Agnes, with an irrepressible cry; "why
your life? God would have only his, none but his.   If
it had been a matter of life for life, God knows ———"

But here her strength gave way, and Beatrice sat
by and saw the wave of fierce anguish go over her
head, and heard the long sob in her throat that would
not be choked down.   Miss Trevelyan sat and looked
on, and then got up and walked about the room, not
daring to go and kneel down by Agnes's side and give
her the sacramental kiss, by which one woman takes
her share of another woman's sorrow.   Beatrice could
only wring her hands and look on, and wait until the
brief passion was over, and Mrs. Trevelyan had regained the control of herself.   If she had been a wise
woman she would have accepted this as enough; or if
she had been more than a wise woman — if she had
had the wisdom of a tender heart, she would have
given at that moment the magic touch of sympathy,
and won the woman whom she feared as an enemy, to
be her friend for ever and ever.   For that, all that
Beatrice had to do was to have taken courage; to have
said, "I, too, had begun to love him," and to have
wept the tears with which her eyes were hot and full.
But she had no confidence in love, not knowing it
much more than by hearsay, and she had not the
courage.   And then she was not wise enough to be
satisfied and go away, nor to see that Agnes would
never betray her.   She stayed still, agitated and
trembling as she was, and went on.

"I know you must hate me," she said; "but listen
to me a moment.   It will be better to say what I have

to say now, though it may be painful for us both. I
did not mean any harm, Mrs. Trevelyan. I meant to
do good, and not harm. No doubt I was wrong. We
thought of a better education than, perhaps, you could
have been in the way of giving him — we thought,
perhaps, that Walter ——"

Agnes had borne a great deal and said nothing;
but she could not bear her child's name — the name
that was now almost as sacred as God's name — to be
pronounced by profane lips. She started and rose up
in that sudden irritation, which is as much a part of
grief as its tears. "Oh, go away from me!" she
cried; "I cannot bear it; I am tired, tired and sick to
death. Oh! go away. I do not hate you. What
does it matter if I hated you? It is God, it is not
you. Leave me with Him; I cannot bear any more."

But still Beatrice was not content. She went up
to Agnes, holding out her hand. "Forgive me!" she
said — "Oh, forgive me! Give me your hand, and I
will leave you, as you say. I meant no harm; accidents
happen everywhere. Mrs. Trevelyan, say that you do
not bear me any malice before I go away."

Agnes was trembling all over with the torture
which was being applied to her. She caught at the
chair to support herself, and turned her head, which
she could not keep steady, away from Miss Trevelyan's
look, which moved her to a kind of sick frenzy, she
could not tell how. "I have never borne you any
malice," she said, feeling her voice flutter in her throat,
as her heart seemed to be doing; "but I am not able
to talk to any one. Have you forgotten what has
happened to-day? I will forgive you; I will say anything you like — only, for pity, do not talk to me

any more." When she had said this, Agnes sank down
wearily into her chair. It was weariness, prostration,
utter exhaustion, which were apparent in all her movements, and at the same time a sense of the intolerable,
which took away all her patience. Miss Trevelyan
took her hand and pressed it in hers, and tried yet to
say something; but there was an imperative movement
in the disengaged arm which stopped even Beatrice.
She murmured something that sounded like "God bless
you!" but which conveyed no meaning to Agnes's
tortured ears; and then at last closing the door with
studied softness behind her, Miss Trevelyan finding no
more was to be made of it, contented herself, and went
away.

When she was gone, Agnes sat still where Beatrice
had left her, in that sad inertness which does not care
to move. As the light waned out, she looked more
like a mass of black drapery, flung down anyhow upon
a chair, than a living and independent creature. What
did it matter? The heaven was brass and the earth
iron. No power could open the ear of God which had
shut fast against her prayer, and no power could open
the grave which had closed its jealous gates upon her
child. The psalms of the service that had been read
over him kept ringing in her ears — "Turn thee
again, O Lord, at the last; satisfy us with Thy mercy,
and that soon; comfort us again now after the time
that Thou hast plagued us" — and it was hard to
think what they could mean. For even God himself
could not, or at least would not, in the order of his
Providence, mend what He had done. "Take Thy
plague away from me; spare me a little!" Ah, my
God! was it not cruel to say so? when one knew that

this plague could never be taken away, and that the
suffering had not been spared. Her thoughts should
have been different; but I am not talking of what
should have been — this was what was sweeping and
surging through her mind as the evening waned. It
angered her to think of being comforted, or spared, or
recovering her strength. Such things would be just to
say if there had been no loss that could not be re-
paired; but now not even God himself could make the
world anything but a changed world. Thus the night
went on to darkness as she sat alone in her despair,
and was glad of the obscurity to cover her; and all
this time her pulse kept on beating, and her heart
throbbed steadily, and the physical frame refused to
deaden or soften the anguish of the soul. And down
below, Stanfield, who had aged ten years since that
first night, and Charlton, who had a haggard look in
his eyes, said to each other that, thank God, her
health was not affected; for, to be sure, they did not
know.

As for Beatrice, she went to her room and put her
things together to go away in the morning, for she
had not brought her maid, and it had been a great
trouble to her; and, as she pursued this occupation,
the thought of the dead boy grew fainter and fainter
in her mind, and the new event that had happened to
herself became more prominent. She was very sorry
for Walter, and blamed herself for her "foolish" conduct in the matter; and yet, by this time, perhaps,
began to be more sorry for herself than for anybody
else concerned; for, to be sure, Miss Trevelyan had
meant no harm. It was for the child's good she had
acted — and the accident was not *her* fault — and

yet it was she who would have to bear the penalty. Agnes, always the favourite of Providence, would go home pitied and mourned by everybody, while Beatrice had still before her a trial which chilled her blood in her veins — a confession which perhaps might make her suitor turn back, and overshadow again in a moment the fair prospect that was shining before her — although, certainly, it was not she who had killed Walter, or done anything except what was for his true good and ultimate advantage.

Such were the thoughts that occupied Beatrice after she had done her penance to Walter's mother. And below Jack Charlton could not but wonder in his mind whether in her grief it would be any comfort to Agnes Trevelyan to know that there was one in the world who would gladly stand by her in her trouble and console her with his love; and whether he had sufficient courage, and confidence in himself and her, to decide upon offering her that support and consolation. And thus new thoughts of life awoke again in the house he had left, while yet the first dews were still falling upon Walter's little grave.

CHAPTER XIX.

Conclusion.

NEXT morning Mrs. Trevelyan went home with her father. The Windholm folks, though they had their faults, had hearts in their bosom, and a great many of the shops were partially shut, and many a wistful face looked from the windows as the blacksmith took his daughter to her own house. But no one saw Agnes, who had sank back in a corner of the cab which conveyed her from the railway, covering her face, and not daring to look upon the world. It was bright day, the sun shining, and the birds singing, and the sweet air blowing on the Common with that breath of life and health which seems fresh enough to restore the feeblest. But these blessed circumstances of external life do nothing but make the gloom harder for those who are in the valley of the shadow of Death. Stanfield did not go in with his daughter to her changed house. He had to go up the village again in his black dress, with his worn looks, to see after the work which he had been neglecting, and the wife, who was still living and getting better, though Walter was dead.

As for Agnes, she went in alone to her house and shut the door, and seemed as she did so to turn her back upon, and leave behind her, all her actual life. When the first anguish of her return was over, and when she felt herself settled again in her old apparent tranquillity, with everything around her exactly the same as it had been a month ago, and nothing to denote the

22 *

terrible change which had taken place, this was the feeling that remained most in her mind. She had lived her life out and was done with it. Her vitality, which was so strong, had survived the first great fundamental blow, but it had not survived, and could not survive, the second. Hope could not get up again from that unlooked-for stroke. She could not grow ill or die. She could not abandon the duties which God had laid upon her in the world; but life, so far as life is a matter of personal desire, and satisfaction, and actual being, had ceased and stopped short. It would have been vain to say so to the external world which comprehends so little; but she knew it in her heart. Her neighbours gave her the profoundest pity of which the general mind is capable, and some tender women who had children of Walter's age, wept for her with a kind of anguish, feeling always that what Agnes had borne to-day, they, too, to-morrow might be called upon to bear; but no one knew the thoughts that Mrs. Trevelyan carried with her into the silent house, where the absence of Walter's voice, and of his presence, made an audible and visible solitude, which was something more than mere negation. What Agnes felt was, that she had had her day. Once there were father and son together within these walls, and she had lived her life with full measure of all its cares and complications; but now all that was over for ever.

Calm and silence had fallen upon the house. But for a certain golden gleam in the baby's eyes, that episode of living life which had made the villagers envious of the blacksmith's daughter — that marriage which had taken her, as people thought, out of her sphere, for any trace it had left behind might never have been. The Trevelyans and their distinctions, and small nobility, had disappeared from the horizon altogether. These matters had counted for little at any time in Agnes's mind; but still they had tinged her life, and now they were gone like the rest. She was now no more than the blacksmith's daughter, as she had been at first — mother of two little children, who could never take anything from the Trevelyans except their name. Perhaps this external circumstance, in its way, contributed to detach from the sombre existence that remained that fair round globe of actual life, which had been completed for ever. She sat in the silence of her house and felt that she had had her day, and it was past; and yet scarcely the half was past of that hard tale of years which sometimes God exacts to the last moment from those of His creatures to whom He has given strength to endure.

It would be false, however, to say that this thought was the hardest which came to trouble Agnes in her solitude. A woman is so much at the mercy of her thoughts. She kept looking over all the busy world, and wondering to see it so out of joint, and bewildering herself as to God's meaning — that meaning which He so seldom shows to man. Was it that by all these various ways of living it was His purpose to show the world how impossible it was to live? Sometimes she thought so as she pondered; — that as a king was accorded to Israel to prove, as nothing else could, the harm of a king, so life was also permitted to prove, by its never-ending, always-feeling experiment, how life was out of possibility. She sat sometimes all the day long with these musings in her mind, and there was little consolation to be found in them. Mrs. Stanfield

was getting better — she whose life was so doubtful
an advantage to herself, and so great a misfortune to
those who were connected with her; she who, so far as
human eye could see, had nothing to look back upon
or to look forward to, but the lowest form of existence
— mean, and selfish, and unlovely. But yet she lived,
while Walter was dead; and myriads of unfortunates
were living on, to whom death would have been the
great and only consolation. The strongest intellect in
the world might be troubled by such a thought, and
much more the mind of a solitary woman mourning
for her first-born. And then it came to her sometimes
like a gleam of light to think that, if this was indeed
God's meaning — if He meant to prove life impossible, as a father might well prove to his children the
impracticability of their desires; it was all the more
and more a proof that He had something better behind
— something to fulfil all longings and complete all
loves. Perhaps it was only a woman's reasoning,
which is not worth much, they say; but then reason is
never worth much on such subjects — and it gave a little
comfort to her.

As for Stanfield, though his daughter was in the
depths of human anguish, this was not to him the un-
happiest time of his life; for, to be sure, a man can go
even with his nearest and dearest only to a limited extent; and he had his child, though she had lost hers.
He was very sad and sorrowful, but in the midst of
his sorrow there was a kind of happiness which was
sweet. When he went down of nights to the house on
the Green, where once Walter had run to meet him
at the door and greet his arrival, his heart grew full
and was sometimes "like to break." But still it was

sweet to go in to his own child, to sit by her silently, to understand her as they both thought, and spare her the need of words. To be sure, the two had little to say; for what was the good of talking when the thoughts of the one were inexpressible, and the other understood, so far as it was possible to understand?

Stanfield, however, instead of being cast down by it, had a certain consolation in the thought that his daughter now belonged to him alone, and had nothing to look for on any side, except the cherishing, and love, and support, which he himself was so ready and anxious to give her. That disjunction from the past which marked to her what she thought the ending of her life, was to him a kind of happiness. His wife got better, thanks to the nurse Agnes had sent her, and ceased to rave for the benefit of the village, and made her appearance so subdued and humble, that it was hard for the charitable and tolerant man to carry out his resolution of sending her away. After a little time, however, when Mrs. Stanfield ceased to be frightened, she took to her old ways; and then her husband had her removed kindly and carefully out of his house, and out of the village. He said again, in the pitifulness of his tender soul, that it was not her fault if she could not understand; and though he would never see her again, he provided for her comforts, and even such luxuries as pleased her, with a liberal hand. All this made it necessary for the blacksmith to resume his work as if he had been a young man. He began to be early and late at the forge; to be more silent, less prompt to give his time and counsel to others, than he had once been. He could not abandon that position of the "worthiest," which the village folks had instinctively given him;

but perhaps he was a little less ready to listen and to be drawn aside from his work than in former days. His time was no longer his, but belonged to his daughter, and to *her* daughters — the helpless little things who had nobody but him to look to, as the Windholm folks said.

And by-and-by the two fair children clinging about his knees, became to Stanfield what Agnes herself in her baby days had been. They belonged to him, and Walter never could have belonged to him. Thus it was that the great blow which cut short the life of Agnes, was softened down and smoothed away to everybody but her. To other people, her child was only Mrs. Trevelyan's little boy who died; and sometimes it struck Agnes with surprise to see that nobody suspected it was she who had died, nor understand how her life had come to an end.

Life must end one time or another in this world. It is true that some people live until they die; but perhaps they are the minority of human creatures. Sometimes it is as Dante says, a demon who takes possession of the existing body, when the true soul goes down to Hades; sometimes, instead, it is a patient angel who enters in when the dear life is past; and years come and go, and nobody knows of the substitution, unless it be now and then some weird soul like the Ancient Mariner, who catches the glance that is from heaven or hell in the eyes of the lifeless people. The spirit that inhabited Mrs. Trevelyan's form after her life was over, was a most human spirit; it was even one that could simulate actual existence, and live a vicarious life in the little children who were growing older every day. But for all that, it was a spirit and not her very self. And her life — her individual existence — the life that it was pleasant to possess, and happiness to go on with, had broken off short, and come to an end.

When Mr. Freke came to see her — as it was his duty to do — the vicar was in great confusion of mind, and did not know what to say; and, indeed, except that it was mysterious and inscrutable, and beyond all explanation, what could any one say? He confused her more and more — or at least, did all he could to do so — with his own bewilderments and perplexities.

"I won't say it is for your good, as so many people say," the vicar exclaimed; "for I cannot see how it can be for your good; but perhaps it is for his good, poor dear child! And I cannot tell you that it is to show God's love to you, for, God knows, I cannot feel that myself. I think He will explain it, if you can but wait; and, so far as I can see, that's all. It is your fellowship in the sufferings of Christ."

"Ah!" said Agnes; "I think so sometimes. But tell me what that means."

But Mr. Freke could not tell no more than most people can tell what is the meaning of the divine words which they snatch up at random, with but a vague general sense of their powers of healing, to staunch the wounds, for which human art has no remedy; but he did better than try any explanations. He said, "Tell me what it is you think sometimes," knowing — because he had a tender affection for Agnes, which gave sight to his eyes — that the best help for her would come out of her own multitude of thoughts.

"I think sometimes that there is a kind of mass being always said in the world," said Agnes — "a kind of repetition every day of His sacrifice; not because of any priest's saying, but because of God's appointing. Perhaps it is only fancy; and some of us are always being chosen to carry it on. We ought to be glad; but at the end even He was not willing, except because it was God's will — any more than we are willing. It is hard to be put up on the cross to show the other people how blessed they are; but that is not what I wanted to say. Sometimes I think it is to keep up and carry on the spectacle of loss, and pain, and anguish; and I have my mass to say, though I am not willing. Sometimes it comforts me a little; I think He would have raised them all like Lazarus, if it had been possible; and it was not possible; and and now we have all to put on our priest's garments, and hold up the host, that all the world may see. We were a long time in Italy," she said, with a faint smile, breaking off; and as she gave this last apology and explanation of what she had been saying, there came before Agnes's eyes, as if by a gleam of sunshine, the lovely Sorrento sea, and the terrace, and the orange gardens, and the procession winding up the steep streets, with the priest under his canopy, and the faint candles flaring in the daylight. The offering she had to make, which was not made willingly, was perhaps as far from a perfect one as was the poor wafer in the Sacramentary; but yet there was in it a fellowship with His offering which was divine.

This we quote, not because there is much satisfaction in it, but because it explains a little the kind
of thoughts that were coming and going in Mrs. Trevelyan's mind; and how now and then she fell upon
some fancy — for, to be sure, it was little better than
a fancy — which was a momentary balm to her wound.
And then she would take her children in her arms,
and clasp them close to her, close against her breast,
as if the pressure could, perhaps, deaden a little the
pain in her heart; and thus got through the heavy
days, and chanted her sad mass like the nightingale,
that "leaned its breast up till a thorn —"

As for the other people, Beatrice Trevelyan told
her story very frankly and honestly to her old lover;
but yet in the telling, either because she herself, being
acquainted with it, could explain the intention as it
existed in her own mind, and not the mere bungling
performance which people could judge for themselves;
or because of some involuntary softening in the narrative; the result was that he admired and trusted her
more than ever, and thought her penitence and candour
noble; and they were married, and Miss Trevelyan,
though so late, entered into the life which she had so
long longed for, and was a very good wife, and made
her husband happy. She would have kept up a kind
of friendship with her sister-in-law, had Agnes been
disposed to it, and did not hesitate to say, that though
it was a dreadful trial to the family, Roger's marriage
had turned out a great deal better than could have
been expected, and that Mrs. Trevelyan was an estim-
able person in her way.

As for Jack Charlton, he kept always loitering

vaguely about Windholm; and though it was hard to say whether he was most afraid to risk a rejection or an acceptance, his good sense kept him from doing or saying anything to commit himself. And Mrs. Stanfield lived on and was very comfortable in the place where the blacksmith had placed her. And Stanfield himself worked harder than ever, and was more patient than ever, though more difficult to be persuaded to give counsel; and every night he put on his coat and came slowly down the Green, until from the open door little Agnes and little Bee, the youngest tottering on her baby feet, came out with a rush to meet him. For his own house was shut up, and he could not leave Agnes, who had need of him; and the blacksmith, as we have said, was not unhappy.

It is thus once more apparent that Agnes Trevelyan's was no tragic exceptional case, but that she had only the common lot, darkened by great sorrows, but not without consolations. Yet her epic was over, and her individual life ended. The vicarious life in which most women spend the latter part of their days might still remain for her; but her own life was over and done, and the Amen said. Life must come to an end somehow, and she was not one of those who live till they die. So that I have told you all her story, as well as if I had put a gravestone over her and written the last date on it, which may not be ascertained for many years.

But when you say your prayers, oh, good people, good friends! — when you come to that which names the little children, pause and take a charitable thought, if not for Agnes Trevelyan, yet for many another woman who has no other heritage — that the good God may grant to them to find again, at the end of many days, a sweet life by proxy to heal their bitter wounds.

THE END.

PRINTING OFFICE OF THE PUBLISHER.

802742

Printed in Great Britain by
Amazon.co.uk, Ltd.,
Marston Gate.